GOLDEN LEGACY
PART ONE

BY
CRAZYCAE

I dedicate this to my fellow freaks, weirdos, outcasts and losers. Rise up and let your imagination run free and never let anyone or anything hold you back.

Be yourself.
Tell your story.
Live your legacy.

Thank you to everyone who has been a part of this journey, without you, this story would not be told. I hope you enjoy the story of us.
With love,

Aladora

This story begins like any other. Since the beginning of my reign, the Kingdom of Vassuren has thrived peacefully. Children play in the green grass fields that stretch beyond Palavon's village limits. Everyone wakes to the sound of doves cooing and little lambs bleating. The scent of flowers and fresh bread fills the air. And the one thing that beats it all is watching my little girls frolic among the roses outside the castle gates.

My name is Aladora, Queen of Vassuren and I rule alongside my husband, Cassius. Together we have two daughters, Vivalda and Riverlynn who are our pride and joy and headstrong heirs to the throne. When we found out I was pregnant with our first child, Cassius was adamant we were going to have a prince but instead we were gifted with two mischievous princesses. They never cease to bring us much happiness as the days pass.

Our lives began unfolding beautifully as we started growing the family we always wished for. The joy of welcoming our children to the world is a feeling I'll never forget. Each day brought new adventures and challenges, but we faced them together.

Before I thought my life could get any better, we welcomed Riverlynn into the world and since then, our children have been loved from beyond the castle gates.

As our family grew, so did our bond, creating a tapestry of love, laughter, and cherished memories that would forever bind us together and over the years,

Vivalda and Riverlynn grew very close, refusing to be separated.

Riverlynn has always been Vivalda's little shadow. Wherever Vivalda went, Riverlynn followed closely behind. It always makes my heart happy to see them get along so well. Growing up, they hardly stayed within the castle gates and were always exploring their kingdom. Some people are surprised that the princesses are often seen being active outside rather than staying at home and learning how to fulfill traditional expectations associated with their title.

Don't get me wrong, they do tend to their studies with me, but I refused to keep them tied down at such a young age. I want them to grow to be strong, independent and full of life, while being free to have fun when they please. Especially when there's more to life than their responsibilities.

Unfortunately, one day, our happiness began to dim. When Vivalda was a young teen, her health randomly declined. She lost weight, she couldn't hold down food, she'd wake drenched in sweat, and she struggled with many other bodily challenges.

Cassius and I called for healers across the kingdom and thankfully, we had many trustworthy men and women ready to help our little girl.

It was heartbreaking to see Vivalda go from being an adventurous young girl to then being bedridden for days on end. It was never in her character to be held back from doing what she loves and being sick kept her from many things she enjoyed.

The healers did everything they could to try to figure out what was wrong with her, but they said she was a case they had never seen before. They did everything they could with every healthy herb known to man, hoping something would help, all to no avail. Eventually I felt hopeless, I'm always supposed to protect my children, and I felt like at that moment I failed because I felt hopeless.

I wished with all my power I could take away everything from Vivalda and bare it upon myself, but not even gods could make that possible. All I could do was stay by her side and pray for a miracle.

This cycle went on for many moons and nothing helped Vivalda out of her situation. But no matter what challenges there were to face, she remained strong and stayed in the best mood she could.

"I'll be okay mama." Vivalda would always tell me, no matter how much it hurt for her to speak.

It was hard to look at her without tears filling my eyes. She'd lie curled up in her bed. Her skin, pale with a slight green tint. I wanted to believe her words every time she said she'd be okay, but I always feared one day I'd wake up, and she wouldn't.

I prayed to the gods every day, wondering why she had to go through such turmoil and not me. What did she do to deserve it all?

Back then, there was always so much going on. From taking care of my people, royal duties, Vivalda being sick and trying to keep my family together, it was a battle to face every day.

I quickly noticed how everything affected Riverlynn. My poor girl. She'd wait by her big sister's side every day. I'd often hear her read a story to her big sister or simply lay next to her and hold her hand.

One morning, I went to get Vivalda some water from the castle well. Before I walked back into her room, I heard Riverlynn whisper something.

I peeked through the door that was open by an inch, and I could see her lying in front of her big sister. With one hand, she glided her little finger up and down the bridge of Vivalda's nose while she slept and with the other hand she moved the red pieces of hair out of her face.

"You've got to fight this Viv. You're the strongest warrior I know. And when you're better, we have a lot of adventures to go on. I would go by myself, but they're not fun without you." Her high-pitched voice whispered.

It was at that moment I felt my legs grow weak and I slid my back against the door frame to bury my face in my hands with my knees to my chest. As I did, I heard tiny footsteps running towards me. The door swung open, and I felt a tiny hand touch my shoulder.

"Why are you crying momma?"

At the time, I didn't know whether to be honest or hide the tears. With Riverlynn being so young at the time, I didn't know how much she would understand.

"I'm just sad, sweetheart."

She turned and sat on my lap.

"Don't be sad, Viv will be fine!" Riverlynn told me happily.

"You think so?" I asked as she peered into the room and then turned back to me with the most precious gaze with her light blue eyes full of hope.

"I know so. Viv and I always play a game where I am the princess and she is a mighty warrior, she never loses the game."

I hugged her and held on to her for as long as she'd allow. That day, her words gave me a spark of hope that everything would go back to the way it used to be.

"What's this momma?"

She picked up my gold necklace dangling a metal sword pendant.

"It's my symbol of hope."

Many moons passed and I held onto whatever hope I had left as Vivalda remained in bed, sleeping. Even with the continued help from our healers, nothing helped and eventually, Vivalda wouldn't move or speak.

Occasionally she'd open her eyes but even then, when she looked at us, I don't think she was genuinely looking at us. The look on her face showed nothing but an empty void. I thought I had lost her.

One morning, Cassius woke me after I fell asleep on the white wool chair that's next to Vivalda's bed.

"Darling, wake up. I need to speak to you" I peeled my eyes open and saw him looking at me with sunken eyes due to the lack of sleep.

Cassius took my hand and led me out of the room and into the throne room. All the windows surrounding our family chairs are covered by purple curtains.

"What is it you need to speak about?" I ask as he leads me to my chair and kneels with distraught in his eyes, trying not to cry.

"I'm lost, I'm very lost. I know you feel the same but what more can we do before her days come to an end?" He asks while stumbling through his words.

This was a conversation I saw coming but didn't prepare myself for.

"I- I don't know what you mean." He lowers his head; his breath becomes shaky and his fists clench.

"You know what I'm trying to say. Tell me truly, do you have faith Vivalda will wake? She's eating and drinking less and less. Our people are counting on us, and we've stayed away for so long due to our situation. The season is coming to an end, and soon the leaves will turn red. We don't know if she's in pain and it kills me to NOT know. So please tell me...do you truly think she will wake?" My eyes widened and filled with tears.

"We can't give up, I know she's there somewhere. I know she's fighting just as hard as we are trying to remain hopeful. We can't let her go."

I fell off my throne and onto my knees, gliding into Cassius' arms, sobbing and screaming.

I leaned into him, and it felt as if all my emotions were stripped from my soul and I was left standing in a pitch black abyss. Cassius gently pushed me forward and put both hands against my cheeks, wiping my tears away.

"We will get through this one way or another. I promise. I just don't want her to suffer more than she already is." He reassured me.

One day while standing on the castle balcony, strange dark clouds began to form in this distance, but I was quickly distracted by the sight of the knights walking in formation.

I observed one of my esteemed knights, Atticus, mentoring his adolescent son Orion in their duties. Teaching him what it's like to be a knight. Eventually as time passed, I knighted young Orion after he showed much potential to serve the kingdom.

I watched Atticus and Orion enjoy their time together as their lessons continued and it reminded me of joyful memories I share with my daughters.

I slowly drifted away into my own thoughts, and I heard the doors open behind me. Cassius walked onto the balcony with me.

"Good morning my love." He greeted me with a warm smile.

"Where's Riverlynn?" I asked since I didn't wake up to her jumping on our bed.

"She's out in the pasture tending to the ponies with Lyla. She was very eager to do chores this morning, or so I heard."

Lyla is one of our maids who's been helping our family for many years. Vivalda and Riverlynn love helping her with chores. But since Vivalda got sick, it was rare to see Riverlynn do much around the castle.

I looked out to the distance and kept my eyes set on the mysterious clouds that began to set over Vassuren. Dark clouds grew ever closer.

"Do you think a storm is brewing?" Cassius asked.

"I'm not sure. The clouds have been there for many days, bringing nothing but a slight breeze. Maybe it's because of the changing seasons."

Before Cassius could let a word out, we both heard footsteps running. We jolted around and saw one of our healers, Amir.

"Your majesties- there's something you must see now! Please come to the princess' room immediately."

The urgency in his tone made my heart drop. We acted hastily and darted down the castle halls to get to Vivalda's room.

When Amir opened the door, we saw something we never thought would come. Vivalda was speaking softly and moving around very slowly.

Without hesitation, Cassius and I ran to her side, crashing to our knees.

"Oh, my baby!" I screamed as I held both her and her father very tightly without hurting Vivalda.

"Please bring Riverlynn here at once." Cassius demanded.

My heart was full of many wonderful emotions. I couldn't help but cry, laugh and smile all at the same time. I swear, it sounded like I was going mad, and I knew everyone else felt the same way.

I held her face with both hands and looked into her beautiful brown eyes and I finally saw my little girl.

"Hi mommy." Her voice was hoarse and dry but the smile on her face told me she had come back to us as she was before.

"Hello darling." I say while continuing to hold her.

Riverlynn came running into the room at full speed while almost crashing into everything.

"Viv! Hiiiiii!" She screamed as she ran around the bed and jumped into her sister's arms.

We all held onto each other for a very long time, and I didn't want to let go. I feared that moment would never come.

Our miracle came in time and Vivalda was returned to us.

Vivalda

(Years later, current time)

Mother often asks me if I recall falling asleep or waking up and she asks if I ever heard anything while being asleep, but the answers always remain the same. I don't remember falling asleep, nor do I know what happened between then and when I woke up. I do, however, remember everything afterwards. Even as an adult, I still think about it to this day.

When Riverlynn and I were young, my family and I would visit the Palavon village when there was time. We'd go to spend time and play various games with the village children. Riverlynn and I always had a good time while mother and father regularly checked on our people.

Despite our royal status, everyone always treated us as if we were family. We never ask for free items, food or anything of the sort. They treat us as we are...human. No one asks about "riches" and "wealth". No one questioned our "fancy" way of living. No one has ever tried to steal from us. And no one purposely tried to get close to us in hopes of getting something out of it. And we, the royal family, never treat anyone as if they're lower than us. That would tarnish what my family stands for.

A few days after I woke up, my family and I went to Palavon to visit our people. Everyone met in the village hall and at the time, I found it very hard to focus and be there in the moment. I suddenly began to feel that something about myself was different than before. My head constantly spun and throbbed and a sharp pain constantly shot through my knees, making it difficult to walk and do the activities I used to love.

Eventually my family and the royal helpers noticed this change in my health, and it caused mother to worry the most.

No herbs or natural remedies would help the constant pain that follows me to this day. No matter what, I push through.

One of the scariest incidents I experienced with my health was when Riverlynn and I were spending time with our friends in the village. I had what the healers call a dizzy spell that caused me to fall to the ground and cut my brow on the sharp edge of a metal table. When episodes like that happen, it feels as if my body gets stabbed by a billion tiny needles, causing my legs to shake and in most cases, go numb momentarily. Sometimes I can't control my stance or balance, and my vision gets blurry, causing me to fall and wake up on the floor, disoriented. When that happens, all I can do is recuperate by resting and drinking plenty of water.

As I've physically matured, I've learned to control them better, so I don't hurt myself. They don't happen as often, thank goodness, but they're still scary to experience. I think what bothers me most is when they happen in front of other people because I don't want anyone to worry.

It was embarrassing considering the first dizzy spell happened in front of a lot of people and no one knew what was going on. A few people looked at me like I was putting on some kind of concerning show. I had no way to ask for help, but thankfully, my family was always there to help me however they could.

After the incident, people started speaking badly about me and the challenges I must face. I'm not sure why they changed when the day prior, they spoke of me kindly. It was mainly kids who spoke rudely but occasionally, I'd hear adults making certain remarks. To hear grown adults speak poorly about a teen boggled my mind, but at the same time, I didn't fully grasp the concept of bullying.

Some people would say I'm a "curse" or a "weak link" to the kingdom since things went downhill in the time, I was asleep.

Kids would call me "weak", "fragile" and some would even call me a "coward" for not participating in activities that may result in me getting easily hurt. They'd even go as far to say I'm faking my struggles and that our kingdom is doomed if I ever take the throne. Now, as an adult, a part of me doesn't want to step foot near it.

Riverlynn would pick fights with those who bullied me and I love her for that, even though she'd take it too far sometimes, but who was I to stop her when I was afraid to do it myself?

One day, I heard someone say I'd be the reason if the kingdom ever falls and Riverlynn didn't hesitate to punch him right in the temple, causing him to have two black eyes the next day.

Our parents never endorse violence, but when it comes down to us standing up for each other, they let it pass occasionally.

Those who spoke poorly of me didn't understand that it wasn't anyone's fault, it was a natural occurrence.

As much as I try to ignore any negativity, their words still run through my mind daily, causing me to fall into a very dark trap. I know to never let their words get to me but what can I say?

I'm only human.

Everyone who has ever tried to bring me down will realize I'm so much more than the challenges that hold me back.

In case it may not be obvious, I never made many friends. I didn't fit in with others. I wasn't a social butterfly, unlike my sister. Riverlynn was always doing what she could to be close to Orion when he was a young knight in training.

The only friend I had next to my sister was a boy named Kyson, the son of our kingdom's blacksmith. I met Kyson a few days after I woke up when I saw him sitting alone on a bench while playing with a small piece of metal. His father practically started teaching him how to craft with metal as soon as he was born, so it was easy to tell he easily picked up the craft. When I sat with him, the metal he fiddled with was a very tiny flower that he made by hand, and he gave it to me. After that, we grew to be very close friends.

After my first dizzy spell, mother wouldn't allow me to leave the castle due to the fear my health would decline without her nearby. So, she and my father decided it was best for me to remain at home.

During the years I remained home, I was constantly resting, regaining my strength and tending to my royal lessons that I thoroughly enjoyed.

My sister, on the other hand, never enjoyed her lessons, she found them to be very boring. But for me, it was all very fascinating to learn the ropes from our own mother who is one of the greatest queens to ever rule Vassuren. It doesn't sound like something a young adult would enjoy but it was what I looked forward to everyday. Mainly because I have always been afraid of failure and learning helps me steer away from that.

Surely, I'd miss going on adventures and exploring the kingdom but due to being tired often, I ended up preferring to focus on my lessons more than anything else. And no matter how I'd feel, Kyson lingered on my mind, and I questioned if he'd forget about me.

After my eighteenth birthday came around, lessons became more intense. It was the age of becoming a "proper princess" and my royal duties weighed heavier and heavier on my shoulders.

On my birthdays, I spend most of the day in the lesson room reading old books about the royal codes and the obligations of a queen and king. Diving into older doctrines made me realize how much my parents took into their own hands and presented a new way of ruling over the land compared to past generations. Kings and queens of our past were once so rude and cruel to our land and people, but my parents changed it and because of them, the land flourishes beautifully.

I truly hope to do something just as amazing once I take my mother's throne. I want to make my family proud. That's all I ever wanted.

Anyways, back to my birthday.

I slept in late that day and my sister woke me by jumping on my bed, causing it to rattle and shake. She'd always wake us up in the most dramatic way possible. But no matter how excited she was, her joy and enthusiasm always brought the family a smile. We both thought it'd be a great idea to ask for our parents' permission to go to Palavon for the day, even though a part of me wished to stay home and write. But I couldn't deny how much I missed the days when we'd spent time outside of the castle and I never wanted to deny my sister that chance to spend time with me. She was alone without me for a long time when I slept, and I'd try my best to make up for it.

It took a while to convince our parents to allow us to leave but they ultimately agreed as long as our knights Atticus and Orion would accompany us. Of course we both agreed and we left after celebrating with our parents and the castle staff.

Going to Palavon for the first time made me nervous and excited at the same time. I was so paranoid about what others would say about me. But when we arrived at the village, I don't think anyone recognized me. I found that to be a good thing since it made things less awkward for me.

Riverlynn went off to spend time with her friends and I went into Tricky's Tavern since I was of age to go inside. I didn't go for the booze, instead I wanted to listen to the live performers who played beautiful music.

After spending some time by myself, I saw a young man sit at a table adjacent to mine. I recognized his face and jet-black hair, and I knew it was the boy I knew when I was a child. Kyson.

14

Seeing him after being absent for a long time made my stomach erupt in butterflies. I couldn't contain my excitement despite being nervous at the same time.

That's when my social skills were tested. It took me a long time to say something and when I finally struck a conversation with him, he didn't recognize me. And when he asked my name, I told him it was Elaine. Now thinking about it, I realize how ridiculous it was of me to give myself a random name just because I was shy.

I'm embarrassed to look back at that memory, but in that current state, I wanted to play around and see how long I could get away with it.

Kyson and I spent the day dancing to the music, archery and trying new things I've never done before. We ended the day hanging out at a table, getting to know each other as if I had no idea who he was.

At the end of the day, the tavern doors opened, and Atticus walked through to find me. I remember burying my head in my hands.

Eventually the knights revealed who I was and the look on Kyson's face when he realized it was so sweet. He immediately knelt to bow, and he caught everyone's attention.

Seeing that smile on his face after he heard my name made my heart explode.

From that day on, I promised Kyson I'd see him again and again. And from there, Riverlynn teased me on and on and my mother was happy to hear we had rekindled our relationship. It was a day I'll never forget.

Once mother and father heard about our day at the village, we were able to convince them to let us leave during the day when we pleased, as long as Atticus and Orion joined us.

Our safety and protection have always been their priority.

Aladora

(Current time)

Over the years, the princesses grew into incredible young women. It took some time for me to be fully comfortable with the girls leaving the castle whenever they please. But as Vivalda and Riverlynn became more persistent, they convinced us to allow them to go outside the castle gates when they please. During their adventures and village visits, they diligently maintained their royal responsibilities and duties simultaneously.

Every time they visit the village; the girls usually stop by our blacksmith's shop "Flame Forge" to hang out with Kyson and Rowan. Rowan has been making weapons, armor and gear for our kings since he was a young adult. His craft is exceptionally incredible and he's a very good family friend. As our families grew closer, we'd often invite the gentlemen to the castle when they're free from work to give them some company.

Despite Vivalda occasionally struggling with her physical health, she has always remained strong, and she pushes through the best she can. And Riverlynn has always remained by her side, never to be separated. I know one day in the future they will make amazing leaders.

If that's the path they choose.

On this beautiful morning, I wake to the sun beaming brightly through a small opening in my silky red curtains.

I roll over on my left side to see Cassius facing me, still sleeping. His curly dark brown hair falls over his eyes. I gently move it with my hand, making sure not to wake him and I lightly caress the side of his cheek. I look down and notice his frizzy beard needs some maintenance and I lean over to kiss his forehead as he lets out a quiet snore.

I listen to the sweet sound of birds singing while I get out of bed, making sure to make as little noise as possible so I don't wake my husband, and I close the curtain, so the light doesn't wake him.

I go to my mahogany wardrobe to retrieve my red overdress, slide it over my black night dress and lace it from my stomach to my chest.

Once washed up and dressed, I leave the bedroom and walk out into the main hall where I'm immediately greeted by our elder maid Lyla who carries a cleaning cloth and bucket in her hand.

"Good morning your majesty!" She looks up and smiles before greeting me with a bow.

"Good morning my dear, how are you?" The smile on her face is so warm and wholesome, it's always a joy to see her at the beginning of my day.

"Oh, I'm doing just wonderfully! The princesses are on the balcony enjoying the morning sun." She gestures down the hall towards where the balcony is.

"Wonderful, thank you. Don't worry about our room until Cassius wakes up. I'd like him to get as much sleep as possible. And as always, don't work too hard, okay?"

My family and I treat our maids, servants and healers like they're a part of the family. I'd never treat them like their only purpose for existing is to tend to us until the end of time. They're all lovely people and we're lucky to have all of them.

I walk down the long hall that curves to the balcony that's at the front of the castle. It overlooks a big chunk of Vassuren, giving us a gorgeous view of thick trees and bright blue skies.

I peer through the glass windows before walking through the double doors and I see the girls sitting on the stone bench. Riverlynn is braiding Vivalda's long brown and red hair while she lays on her lap with her eyes closed.

Even at adult age, seeing them be so close to each other brings me much joy.

I open the doors, catching Riverlynn's attention.

"Good morning mother!" She shouts and waves at me while continuing to play with her sister's hair.

"Good morning little ones." I walk up to them slowly and Riverlynn ties Vivalda's half braid with a piece of scrap fabric. Riverlynn jumps up from her seat and lungs to hug me.

"Thank you, River." Vivalda says as she slowly sits up.

"You'rrrrreeee welcomeeeeeee!" Riverlynn sings loudly and her voice echoes around us.
"Goodness, are you trying to wake the entire kingdom?" I tease and laugh.

Riverlynn is the family wild child. She's always full of energy and she keeps everyone on their feet with her positive energy.

"I wouldn't question it, mother. For all we know, her happy screams could start an entire war." Vivalda smirks and arches her brows.

Riverlynn glares at us mischievously, gets up from the bench, walks over to the stone ledge and leans back dramatically to take a deep breath.

"Well, now you've done it." Vivalda says before covering her ears.

"GOOD MORNING VASSUREN!" Riverlynn screams to the top of her lungs. Out of the corner of my eye, I see a small flock of birds flying off into the distance.

Her scream echoes over the balcony and once she's done, she turns back to us, panting with her face red as a tomato.

"How's that for waking up the entire kingdom?" She says proudly, lifting her chin while catching her breath.

I lean over the balcony and see all the knights on duty looking up, laughing.

They're used to my daughters being silly at all hours of the day. I wave to them, and they return the gesture with smiles on their faces.

"Ha ha, very funny Riverlynn. Hopefully you didn't wake up your father." I say as I proceed to sit next to Vivalda.

Riverlynn's eyes widen as if a giant light bulb went off in her little mind.

"Don't you do it." I arch my brows down and point my finger at her because I know exactly what she planned to do.

"I'm gonna do it!" Riverlynn squeals and runs back into the castle, down the hall towards my room, indicating she's on her way to wake up her father.

"You both should be used to it by now. You practically ask for it by egging her on. It's about time you start *Riverlynn-proofing* the whole castle." Vivalda leans her head on my shoulder.

I gently lift her head and cradle her face with both hands to examine her condition, noting that her brown eyes are closing heavily.

"You look tired. Did you not sleep well again?" She rubs her eyes with her hands and yawns.

"Mmm, I woke up drenched in sweat and extremely dehydrated. My body can't keep up that well today. I feel like a sloppy slug." She laughs while rubbing the sides of her head.

"Did you drink your herbal tea when you woke up?" I run my hand on her back.

"Yes, and I promise I'm alright. I think once I'm fully awake I'll feel better and more energized. River and I were thinking about going to Palavon today if that's okay with you and father." Vivalda quickly perks up, sitting up straight. I can't tell if it's because she's genuinely excited to spend the day out or if she's covering up the fact that she doesn't feel good.

She often hides how she's truly feeling because she doesn't want anyone to worry about her. For me, it's nearly impossible not to worry due to the frights we've experienced in the past. I know it scares her to think about it too.

"You know my rule for leaving the castle grounds. You MUST-"

"Take at least one knight with us for safety. I know, mother. I'm an adult now. I'm more than capable of taking care of my rambunctious little sister and myself. Must we always have someone supervise us? Still?" She interrupts, mumbling, annoyed.

"I know you're of age, even if you hadn't gotten sick, I'd still have a guard go with you. And besides that, your father and I can't risk something happening to you both. If you were to go out on your own, you'd have no way of defending yourself if something were to go wrong." Vivalda sighs heavily and lays on her side to rests on my lap.

"If I had never gotten sick, you'd be more lenient with me, wouldn't you?" The sadness in her voice causes my attention to shift to her golden brown and red hair.

"Listen to me." I say softly, and she rolls over, turning her face to the sky. I run my fingers through the red part of her hair that frames around her face.

"Sick or not sick. In pain or none. I will always worry. Not because I am queen, but because I'm a mother. You girls are also my world. I never want anything to happen to you two. I will always be protective of my treasure. We almost lost you once, I'm never risking that again as long as I'm here. Do you understand that?" My heart is heavy, full of sorrowful joy. I hate to hear her feel so down, especially when it comes to her self-doubt.

Vivalda grabs my hand and holds it to her chest.

"With how much you worry for my safety, does that mean you also worry I won't be fit to lead the kingdom?" Her question strikes me like a stake to the heart. She and I both stand up and I face her while holding her hands in mine.

"Oh, my child, you are stubborn. The state of your health has never once made me question your ability to lead. If anything, you have only proved that you can do that and so much more. You show nothing but endless strength, potential and loyalty. And what you show me;

you show the entire kingdom. I know they see it just as much as I do." I watch a sweet smile form on her face and her honey brown eyes gleam in the sunlight.

A beautiful warm smile forms on her face and her brown eyes sparkle in the sunlight.

"I needed that. Thank you." She speaks softly and leans in for a hug.

"I'm glad, now, go wash up and get dressed for the day. Don't let River rush you with her excitement." We both laugh. "I'll meet you two downstairs for breakfast shortly." We both stand and I hug her before she goes back inside.

After Riverlynn loudly wakes her father, everyone meets downstairs to have breakfast before the girls leave the castle.

While enjoying our food and engaging in different conversations alongside our cook and staff, one of our maids Lyla walks in with a scroll in her hand.

"This was dropped off for you, your majesty." Lyla bows and hands it to me. Cassius leans closer, trying to peek at the rolled-up paper, but I keep it closed.

"Was it handed in urgency?" I ask Lyla while everyone else stares at us, curiously. "No, it wasn't." She responds with a smile. Since I'd prefer to spend the morning with my family, I decide I'll get to reading the message when I have free time to tend to royal matters.

"Wonderful, well in that case, could you please put it in my study room? I'll get to it once we're finished." I hand the scroll back to Lyla and she happily walks away to do what I asked.

Cassius rests his hand on my lap, trying to get my attention. I nod and smile, assuring him all is well, and we continue enjoying our time at the table.

"Father? Can Vivalda and I go to Palavon after we've finished?" Riverlynn asks and Cassius looks at me, expecting me to answer for him.

"Well, um- are you both caught up on your studies?" Cassius waits for me to reply since I'm responsible for teaches the girls.

"Yes, they're both doing well. So well, in fact, that I say they deserve a day out." Cassius smiles warmly at his children.

"In that case, I don't see why not. I'll have Orion and Atticus prepare the horses for when you're ready." He says as both girls finish their plates and put them in the wash.

"Thank youuuuuuuuu!" Riverlynn sings with joy, gets up from the table and runs to hug her father.

I put my plates and utensils in the wash bucket and prepare to go to my study room.

"Girls, go get ready and I'll see you before you leave." Riverlynn takes off like a bullet into the hall and Vivalda follows steadily behind.

Cassius stays back to help clean the table and wash dishes since he enjoys helping the castle servants with their tasks when he's allotted the time.

I go to my study room, just one room away from Vivalda's, and when I walk in, I see the scroll laying on my table, still rolled up.

Vivalda

While going through my wardrobe, I find my favorite dark blue dress with a silver belt that ties around my waist. I slip on my black flat shoes and in the mirror reflection, something sparkles brightly in the light.

Next to my mirror is a small table and on it is the small metal flower Kyson made me when we were kids. I pick it up and reach behind to twist it into my hair.

I neatly braid the top half of my hair and secure it with the flower accessory positioned in the back. A section of hair on each side of my head that's a beautiful shade of red and the red strands twist around the brown sections in such a beautiful way that it forms a brown and red candy cane design.

Some days I enjoy putting effort into my appearance and I like dressing nice and fancy. Other days, I'll wear a simple overcoat over a plane dress and call it a day.

A moment later, Riverlynn finally comes into my room, wearing a baby pink dress with white flats and her hair tied in a pink ribbon.

"Did you dress like a doll to show off to Orion...again?" I tilt my head and tease, and my bashful sister rolls her eyes and scoffs. She's used to being teased about Orion. I know how she feels about him.

"Oh, just like how you're dressed ever so elegantly for Kyson?" She teases back, giggling.

I saw that coming.

"If you must know, I'm dressed up because as the future queen, it's good for me to look presentable for our people. You, however, didn't answer my question so I'll take that as a yes." We both laugh at each other's nonsense and finish getting ready.

Riverlynn stands in front of my mirror, struggling to retie her pink hair bow, and I approach her to help.

"Let me do that for you." I untie the bow from her dark brown hair and comb it down with my fingers so it's not fizzy.

From the corner of my eye, I see her looking in the mirror smiling.

"What?" I ask while letting out a laugh and she continues to look at me thought the mirror.

Her bright blue eyes glimmer from the sunlight that peeks out from the window.

"Oh nothing. This reminds me of the days when we were kids. You dressing like a proper queen, tying my hair up because I can't do it myself. I guess I'm glad to see that some things never change."

I finish tying the silk bow in her hair and I continue to stand behind her, looking at us both in the mirror.

I wrap my arm around behind her and hug her tightly, making the smile on her face widen even more.

"I never want this to change." I say quickly and after a moment she giggles and hops away.

"Come on! Let's go!" She tries to drag with her, but I retract my hand from her grip.

"I probably shouldn't run right now, but I'll meet you in the throne room okay?" Riverlynn proceeds to the door.

"Okay, I'll see you in a bit, slow poke!" She giggles before darting out of the room and down the hall.

I take my time and steadily make my way down the hall, but I quickly stop dead in my tracks when I hear a faint whisper coming from mother's study room where she told Lyla to leave the new message. Once I approach closer, I notice the door is partially open. Mother must not have closed it all the way and not realized.

I walk up to close it for her, but before I do, I can hear her talking to herself while pacing back and forth. I peek through the opening of the door, avoiding making any noise while constantly looking back to ensure no one is walking down the hall. Once comfortable, I look in and see mother reading the scroll quietly to herself to the point where I can't make out what she's saying.

I suddenly felt a massive surge of pain shoot through my entire body, causing me to take a slight tumble backwards. I try to do everything I can to keep silent and gain my composure so she can't hear me. Thankfully she's so concentrated on reading the message that she doesn't notice or hear anything.

I feel waves of pain like this often, but this time, it's different. It feels like thousands of swords stabbing my stomach, chest and legs simultaneously. I may have a high pain tolerance now, but that doesn't mean I'm invincible.

The pain slowly fades away and I go back to the door and see my mother continuing to read the scroll. When she turns to the side, she looks concerned and worried. She holds her thumbnail to her lips while she talks quietly, but I can't make out what she says.

I've never seen her so tense before.

Once she's done reading the message, she rolls it back up before quickly tossing it on her desk and she walks quickly to the washroom that's on the left side of the room.

After the door closes, I lightly skip on my toes and go inside the room to read the scroll. I pick it up with both hands but when I unravel the paper, there was not a single word written on it. I start to think I'm imagining things, but I know consciously that I'm not. I tilt the page toward the window so the light cascades across it and still, not a single word is written on the entire roll of paper.

I hear my mother's footsteps approaching. Quickly, I put the scroll back down where she left it and I run out of the room. I keep the door open by an inch so I can continue to peek inside. I watch her walk out in different clothing. She's now wearing a deep red long-sleeved dress with white fabric that treads down the center.

Not seeing words on the scroll continues to confuse me, but I assume I was just seeing things and maybe my curiosity got the best of me.

Mother rolls up the scroll and proceeds to the wooden cabinet in the far corner of the room, next to the single-colored glass window. She opens the cabinet's double doors and reveals a hidden compartment that blends into the shelf. When she pushes down on the wood, it reveals a lifted platform in the shape of a cylinder. And inside of the platform, she takes out a key. She uses the key to unlock another secret compartment along the back wall of the cabinet. And when she opens the secret door, I see many other scrolls stacked inside.

She gently piles the newest scroll on top of the others and locks the door before returning the key where she got it.

Once she begins to walk towards the door, I quickly dart across the hall to hide behind the curtains that spread across a large window, and I move it in front of me so it fully covers my body. I hear the clacking of mother's shoes as she walks out of the room and closes the door behind her before vigilantly walking down the hall.

Once she's out of sight, I move out from behind the curtains and I look at the dark wooden door, debating if I should go back inside to investigate. But before I can rest my hand on the doorknob, a small voice at the back of my mind says I'm just paranoid and overthinking. I assure myself it was a message from the neighboring kingdom and mother needs to go over for another meeting. And as I've said to myself before, if something was wrong, she'd tell us.

I ultimately decide to leave it be and try to ignore my raging paranoia.

I proceed down the hall and back into the dining room where our staff continues to clean and organize the table. Across the room is another door that leads to the throne room.

Upon opening the door, the royal throne chairs are lined against the far-left wall. There, I see my father and Riverlynn sitting in their chairs telling jokes and laughing. It takes me a moment to walk to them since the throne room is so large. On the opposite side of the throne chairs, there's a huge window that covers most of the stone wall. Resting to the side are long dark purple curtains that sway from a gentle draft.

"Took you long enough!" Riverlynn shouts in a sassy tone. I smile at her and make my way to my chair that sits between her and our mothers. "Sorry, I had to take care of something." I say while getting comfortable in my seat.

Riverlynn leans forward, looking at me suspiciously.

"Are you okay?" She asked as she fiddled with my long, golden-brown hair. "Yes, I was feeling a bit sick earlier, but I'm okay now." I responded quietly, barely focusing on my words because I'm distracted, stuck on what I witnessed in the lesson room.

I want to tell Riverlynn and our father about it to get their thoughts, but since I don't know the full context of the situation, I keep it to myself.

"That's been happening a bit more frequently than usual. Maybe we should stay home today just in case." Riverlynn says quietly and I quickly turn to face her.

"I promise I'm fine. Besides, I don't want to be the last-minute reason why you miss another day of fun," I reassure her while knowing my limits and how much I can handle when it comes to sickness and pain.

My sister looks at me, worriedly while cracking a gentle smile

"I trust you. Maybe we should let mother know?" Riverlynn pauses and her attention is turned to the door, and we see our mother make her way into the room.

"Now, where have you been? We've been waitingggg!" Riverlynn's squeal startles me and causes my ears to ring with a high-pitched frequency. I uncover my ears and glare at her.

"Must you keep yelling like that?" Riverlynn leans back in her chair, giggling and mother approaches to sit on her throne while adjusting the gold crown that rests on her head.

"I apologize for making you wait. The message I received earlier was informing me I must go to Astryn to discuss financial circumstances between our kingdoms. I'm going to make sure the peace is kept and that everything else is in order." Mother's explanation takes a big weight off my shoulders and lessens my paranoia. But I still don't understand how there was nothing written on the scroll.

"That sounds serious. Do I need to come along this time?" Father asks as he reaches over to hold her hand.

Mother goes to the kingdom of Astryn often, I guess their king *Lael* is calling another emergency meeting.

"No, my love. I promise it's nothing I haven't handled before. It's not too far, so I'll be back before nightfall." She responds while rubbing her thumb over father's hand.

"Well in that case, we'll head out now, that way we can be back before you." Riverlynn and I get up from our chairs, but father halts us by holding up his left hand.

"Just a moment, young ones. We need to make sure your mother approves." I stand frozen in my track with my shoulders hunched up.

"What do you mean? You already gave them permission." Mother asks, confused.

"Yes, but that was before I heard Viv was feeling sick a moment ago. Your judgment is better than mine when it comes to her health." I slowly twist myself around and relax my shoulders.

"Yes, I was feeling a bit woozy earlier, but there's no need to fret because I'm perfectly fine, I promise. If I didn't have the energy to go out today, I simply wouldn't go. You know this, mother." Mother gets up from her chair and analyzes me, looking me up and down.

"Please stay on the trails and return home if you start to feel unwell, do you both understand me?" Her tone is deep and serious.

"Yes, we understand, mother." Riverlynn responds for both of us, cheerfully.

"Good. We love you both. Have a wonderful time." Mother smiled and we turn around to make our way to the castle entrance. We walk into the corridor and two guards open the tall wooden doors and escort us out.

"Princesses, the horses are ready." One guard says and they both bow as we walk by and proceed down the stairs. There are several knights lining up on each side of the staircase and each of them bow as we walk down the white steps.

At the bottom, Orion and Atticus wait for us with our horses. I notice Orion is smiling at Riverlynn and I look over to see her blushing intensely, trying hard not to squeal.

Riverlynn has had a crush on Orion since we were kids but even now, I don't think she'll ever admit it. Even when it's painfully obvious to everyone in the castle that she has feelings for him.

Once we reach the bottom of the stairs, the knights bow with pleasant smiles on their faces.

I walk up to my horse and run my hand through his long black mane.

"Good morning, young troublemakers. What adventures are we going on today?" Atticus asks with a warm welcoming smile.

My horse turns his head and rests it against my chest as if he's hugging me and I wrap my hands around his large muzzle.

"I think it's a beautiful day to spend Palavon, it's been a while since we've visited."

The men help us hop on our horses and we follow each other to the castle gates that's opened by two other knights.

Riverlynn and I ride side by side as we're guided by Atticus and followed by Orion. As we walk through the woods we pass by enormous trees and beautiful blooming flowers. Birds sing elegantly in the trees and young animals are emerging from their homes. When I look up, I can see the sun peeking through the thick treetops that stretch over our path.

I slowly close my eyes and take a deep breath, trying to ignore my stress and focus on nature's lullaby.

"What's wrong?" Riverlynn walks her horse closer to mine, my eyes widen, and I turn my attention to her, nearly releasing the reins.

"Uh, nothing. I'm fine. Why do you ask?" I quickly compose myself and sit up straight, trying to hide my lie.

Riverlynn's eyes squint and she tilts her head to the side. "You can't hide anything from me, you know that. Tell me what's on your mind." She says gently, walking steadily by my side.

I think to myself for a moment, trying to figure out the proper words to say. But before I can speak, Atticus slows down and walks on the opposite side of Riverlynn.

"You know, we're all practically family here, you don't need to act so secretive around us. If either of you need to talk, we're here to listen. And anything said, stays between us." Atticus says with a warm smile, looking at both my sister and me.

"I promise I'm listening from back here too!" Orion shouts behind us, which causes us to laugh.

I'd try to move over so he could walk next to us, but if I did, he'd get whacked in the face by long tree branches.

"What's troubling you, princess?" Atticus asks as we walk in a horizontal line. I take a deep breath before responding.

"When you were chosen to be a royal knight, did you ever fear you wouldn't do a good job at keeping the family safe?" Atticus chuckles to himself and shrugs his shoulders.

"Oh yes, all the time." I find it hard to believe him since he's one of the bravest and most confident knights in the kingdom.

"How did you get over that fear?" I ask quietly, not completely sure how to properly ask my questions.

"I simply faced it. Now, I know that sounds easier said than done. But, when the time came to be brave, I didn't hesitate to face my calling." His words send chills down my spine.

"Why do you ask?" Atticus asks while I fiddle with the reins in my hands.

"Lately, I've been feeling doubtful about my ability to lead an entire kingdom. I spend countless days learning and yet, I feel less and less prepared for when the day comes." Out of the corner of my eye, I see Riverlynn shake her head sympathetically.

"Ah the responsibilities of wearing fancy crowns and dresses...who knew such weightless items could be so heavy?" Atticus teases before continuing. "Crowns, books, creeds, lessons- they all weigh the same in the end. No matter what your mind makes you see or feel, others around you see and hear all truth. I bet you probably fear you'll let the queen down, don't you?" I quickly turned my head to face him, shocked he's able to assume something that's true.

"How do you figure that?" I look at Riverlynn who sits silently, smiling, keeping her eyes focused on the dirt road. Atticus scoffs and turns around to look at his son.

"I went through the same thing when Orion was training to be a knight. He worried day and night that he wasn't good enough to stand next to the general of the royal army. He feared he'd embarrass me." I twist around and see Orion smiling bashfully.

"It's true." He says, nodding with a gleaming smile.

"I see the way the queen looks at both of you and it's always with pride. Never disappointment. There's no rush to move forward. You're perfectly fine right where you are. We still have many adventures to go on, not even time can take that from us. You both will be just fine. For now, try not to worry about what's to come tomorrow or years from now, let's focus on the fun we'll have TODAY." Atticus reaches over to pat Riverlynn on the shoulder.

"Thank you." I say cheerfully.

"Yeah! Like he said, it's going to be a good day!" Orion shouts and Riverlynn looks back at him and laughs.

"You didn't pay attention to any of that, did you?" She asks, smirking at him.

"Well, I may have gotten distracted for a second but I was I fact listening...until you all stared at me." Orion laughs and encourages his horse to trot closer to us.

"What distracted you this time?" I ask, expecting a ridiculous answer.

"There was a mother deer, and she had a baby with her! It was so cute; I couldn't help but watch!" Orion says in a high-pitched tone.

"That's my son for you. A strong, brave knight whose duty is to serve and protect." I can tell Atticus is trying everything he can to not burst out laughing.

"Shall we go on a run?" Atticus asks. Riverlynn and I look at each other, smile and gather our reins before taking off, zooming down the path.

Atticus' horse takes off quicker than ours and Orion runs alongside us.

While running through the forest, I feel free. All my worries and stress disappear. I listen to the horses' hooves hitting the dirt and the wind howls past my ears. I can't help but smile and I feel my stress slowly float off my shoulders, allowing me to let loose and enjoy the moment.

Riverlynn darts past me, catching me off guard. She looks back at me as her curly brown hair flies in front of her face.

"Slow poke!" she yells and runs off even faster.

I grip the reins tighter in my hands and right before encouraging my companion to go faster, I feel a sudden throb in my head that travels down to my chest and into my stomach, causing me to slowly pull back on the reins. Once I come to a full stop, I rest my head in my hands, trying to rub the pain away.

Orion speeds past me before noticing and quickly turns around. I hear Atticus and Riverlynn slow down from ahead.

While rubbing the sides of my temple, out of the corner of my eye, I see something moving around in the forest. I turn my head to the side and while squinting, I see a dark shadow rush behind a thick tree that appears to be slowly dying.

"Is everything alright your highness?" Orion asks urgently as he trots up beside me.

"Yeah, I'm okay. I got a headache is all. I just need a moment for it to pass." Atticus and Riverlynn approach, running side by side.

"What happened Viv?" Riverlynn asked, concerned. I let out a laugh to cover the pain I feel.

"Yes, I'm fine. It's just a little headache." I moan, annoyed because all their attention is on me when I don't want it to be.

"You can dismount and sit if you need to. We're in no rush to get to Palavon." Atticus says gently.

"Yes, I'll take a moment, but you both should continue on. Orion and I will meet you at Flame Forge. I don't want to keep you waiting. Orion will keep me company until we catch up! We're not too far anyways" Atticus looks at Orion and then back to me.

"I'm perfectly fine with that." Orion looks at his father, insisting he and my sister keep going down the trail.

"Aright. Reach the forge as soon as you feel better and don't go wandering off into uncharted lands, do you both understand?" I nod with my head still resting in my hand. "Remember the code and your training." After Atticus and Riverlynn take off down the trail, I dismount my horse and sit on a thick patch of green grass. Orion follows and sits next to me.

"Are you sure we shouldn't return to the castle? I'm sure the queen will bite my head off if-" I cut him off with a hiss.

"She won't hear about anything. My mother doesn't need to be made aware of the smallest things that I can handle on my own. I'm not this fragile doll everyone thinks I am. Pain-" I pause, realizing I'm raising my voice, and I take a deep breath before continuing.

"Pain is nothing I can't handle. I'm used to it and refuse to let it stop me from simply enjoying what I can." I remove my hands from my head and see Orion's head lowered to the ground. My vision is slightly blurry, and the sun rays cause my head to pulsate in pain.

"I'm sorry. I didn't mean to snap." My word is true, I do feel bad for snapping at him. But it's also true that I've been treated like I'm fragile since I was a little girl.

"No, I apologize. I never knew how you felt, and I never thought to question it." Orion speaks softly, looking at me sympathetically.

"You've only ever done what you've been asked or told. Sometimes I forget all that my mother asks of you because she worries for my safety."

I feel the pain begin to fade and I slowly stand up to get back on my horse. But before I can lift my foot up into the stirrup, I hear a voice coming from behind me. I quickly turn around, looking for where the voice came from, but ultimately, I don't see anything out of the ordinary. Orion looks at me confused, trying to see what I'm looking for.

"Does something else ail you? Do you need more time to relax?"

I peer deeply into the trees, but see nothing but soft green grass, and birds flying overhead. But as I focus, I see a giant tree with a gaping hole in the middle of its trunk.

I ask Orion to stay back with the horses so I can take a quick walk. As I walk closer, I hear a strange whistling whisper that floats with the wind. And once I approach the tree, I see a perfectly charred hole that has been caused by fire.

I look closer to seeing brown stems stretching out from all sides of the hole, indicating it's beginning to heal itself.

It's beautiful to see mother nature do what it must to regrow and heal. But as beautiful as it is, I don't know if a blaze of fire could burn a perfectly symmetrical circle through the tree. I bend down and I choke on my breath when a dark shadow shoots past my gaze, causing me to shriek and jump back.

I hear Orion rushing towards me, but I quickly halt him. "I'm fine, stay with the horses, I'll be right back!" I don't bother to look back and instead, I walk deeper into the forest to see if I'm imagining things or not.

I walk past the tree, searching for a strange shadow. I feel the wind shift directions, pushing me back. I see scuffed up dirt and grass that leads to an uneven dirt path and I decide to follow it so I don't get lost.

I run deeper into the woods and the nature around me grows louder and louder. The wind howls and shakes the trees violently and the animals around me screech, sing and bellow. After a moment, I feel my knees begin to hurt and I start to feel a bit dizzy, so I slow down to catch my breath.

Out of the blue, the smell of smoke and fire catches my attention. And once I look up, I'm stopped by a very strange sight I never expected to see. The green grass below my feet is immediately cut off by charred foliage and animal remains. The stench makes me feel nauseous. Several trees are burned to a crisp, many have fallen and many still stand despite being dead.

I reach out to touch a small tree that's in arm's reach and when I do, it disintegrates into fine dust that's blown away by the wind. This wasn't caused by a natural fire. I walk into the charred land and all around me, there's nothing but death. Even the air reeks of death. I twist around in a circle and realize the burn lines form another perfect circle.

What could have caused this?

Panic slowly begins to bubble in my chest and my heart thumps rapidly. The scene around me is so twisted and terrifying, I don't know what to make of it. I've never seen something like this before in my life and it doesn't seem real.

I see the shadow once more and it glides slowly, weaving around and through the trees. Before I can follow it, I hear twigs snap behind me and I twist around to see Orion rushing towards me. "Princess Vivalda, you know not to wander far, what are you doing out here? We're not allowed to go off the trail, it's the law-" He asks urgently, out of breath from running.

"Look at this. Have you ever-" I look down at his feet and see that the ground is green instead of grey. I look at him and he stares at me, confused, waiting for me to say something. I can feel my face flush pale and cold.

I turn around and see the forest is back to normal. The trees are healthy and green, there's animals running wild and free and there's no sign of death anywhere. The instant realization makes me take a step back.

"Have I ever what? Your highness." I feel myself zone out for a split moment, confused as to what I had just witnessed.

"I don't understand. The plants, the animals, they were all dead just a moment ago." I walk around, panicking while looking for traces of dead foliage or animals. I'm pulled to a dead end when I see nothing but healthy nature surrounding us. Orion also looks around, trying to make sense of what I stated.

"Did you have another dizzy spell? Maybe it caused you to see things and-" Fearful I've made a fool of myself, I can't help but tell Orion what I saw.

"No, I didn't have a damn dizzy spell, I was completely conscious!" I shout loudly which causes my throat to sting. I take a deep breath before continuing and Orion remains standing still and composed. "I need you to believe me when I say this. Before you approached me, there was a massive burned circle with dead trees that disintegrated with the gentlest touch. There were deceased animals lying on the ground and it smelled so foul...I couldn't have possibly made it up." I look at Orion, pleading for him to believe me and he doesn't look me in the eye. Instead, he looks at the ground, unsure of what to think. He takes a deep breath and shakes his head.

"Trust when I say I want to believe, but maybe this shall be something we bring up to the king and queen when we return home. Would that ease you?" With a sigh of defeat, I agree and we proceed back to the horses and with every other step, I keep looking back to see if I'd see green turn to grey. But alas, there's no change.

We get back on our horses and make our way to Palavon. I can't help but remain stuck in my own thoughts, thinking about the forest and what I saw that Orion didn't.

Upon entering the village, we're greeted by kind faces and sweet smiles. A mother approaches me carefully, holding her young daughter up to me and she hands me a huge sunflower that was just picked from the ground. The joy of our people brings me out of the pit of embarrassment and confusion my mind is stuck in and I can't help but smile.

We find a post to tie our horses' reins to and make our way to Flame Forge. When we walk in, Riverlynn and Atticus are enjoying a conversation with Kyson and his father Rowan. They all turn their attention to us and each of them smile simultaneously.

"Do you feel better now?" Riverlynn asks and I immediately begin overthinking.

Do I tell you now or later?

I force myself to be silent about what I saw in the forest and I'd try to tell her later when we're home. For now, distractions are all I need to keep my mind at peace. "Yes, I'm fine. It was nothing a walk in the forest couldn't help." I walk over to Rowan and Kyson. They both bow but I prefer to greet them with a hug.

"You both must stop the bowing, you know how I feel about that." Kyson put on his work gloves. His face is filthy and his black hair is a mess.

"Ah, you know we're just being respectful." Kyson says flirtatiously and from behind me, I hear Riverlynn giggling to herself while standing next to Orion.

"How was the trip from the castle?" Rowan asks as he continues working on his project and slamming a large hammer onto a thick plate of silver metal. Out of the corner of my eye, I see Orion jerk forward to get his father's attention and they both walk out of the shop. I bet he's going to tell his father about what happened. I already embarrassed myself once, the last thing I need is for Atticus to know. All I can do is continue to act like nothing's wrong.

"It was lovely! The weather's really nice today." I answer quickly, almost forgetting I was asked a question.

I watch Kyson walk out of the room and down the hall. Riverlynn comes up behind me and nudges me with her shoulder, encouraging me to walk with him. After being put on the spot, I give in and follow him quietly down to the hall and into the room where they melt and mold metal.

Inside, it's warm but not too warm to the point where I'm uncomfortable. I watch as Kyson stands at his desk, carefully mending small pieces of metal together with his hands. I walk closer to get a better view at what he's making and just when I think I'm being stealthy, the wooden flooring creaks under my feet, startling him. He turns to look at me, laughing awkwardly.

"You scared me, I didn't know you followed me back here." I notice him quickly hide the metal object so I can't see it.

"I just wanted to see what you're working on, if that's alright." Kyson shakes his head nervously as I try to peer around him.

"It's nothing, I'm just experimenting with new techniques. I don't think it's worth sharing." He says bashfully.

"Nonsense! All art is worth seeing." Our eyes remain locked to each other. His shoulders relax, his jaw unclenches and his forest green eyes soften ever so slowly. A gentle smile forms on his face and reveals his project. In his hands, he holds a small chunk of metal that's been formed into an elegant sunflower. My eyes widen and my jaw drops to the floor.

"This is beautiful! It must have taken you several days to make!" Kyson hands me the flower and I observe every hand crafted detail.

"Eh, I tried my best. When I'm not crafting swords, shields and metal rods, I'm teaching myself how to make decorative pieces." I continue to look at the flower and notice each vein on the leaves and how elegantly the petals are shaped.

"This would look wonderful anywhere! Where will you put it?" I ask while Kyson cleans and organizes his work space.

"Actually, I was hoping for it to go somewhere else, outside of the forge." I look up, awkwardly and confused. I proceed to walk to the back of the room and sit on a wooden bench.

"What do you mean?" I ask quietly and he hangs a mallet on the wall over the table before joining me on the bench.

"I've been making it for you. That is...if you'd like to keep it." I feel myself smiling awkwardly as more

44

butterflies fill my stomach. "I mean, you don't have to keep it. Sunflowers remind me of you and I know they're your favorite. You know, I can just take it back-" He stutters over his words and reaches for the metal flower, but I move it out of his reach, pulling it closer to my chest.

"Absolutely not! I'd love to keep it. What makes you think I wouldn't want it? Especially knowing how long and hard you worked on it." A bashful smile forms across his face and he releases a sigh of relief.

"I don't know. Typically women prefer freshly picked roses from a garden." I hand the flower back to him and reach behind me to take the small metal flower pin out of my hair.

"I prefer to be given gifts that don't die over time." Kyson gasps quietly when I hold out the pin.

"No way...you still have that little thing?" He asks with a huge smile beaming on his face.

"Of course I do. Did you think I'd throw it out?" I take the newly crafted flower and hold both items next to each other. The sunflower is much larger than the small poppy and I can easily see the growth in his craftsmanship.

"In case you haven't caught on by now, I'm not like every lady out there. Riverlynn is the one who prefers real flowers." Kyson takes the poppy pin from my hand and carefully puts it back in my hair. He rests it back in the braid, making sure not to twist or pull any strands. Once it's back in place, he runs his hand down the rest of the long braid that swings against my lower back.

"I never noticed how vibrant the red is in your hair, it shines beautifully in the light." He looks closely at the red pieces of hair that intertwine with the brown.

"Thank you. Kids made fun of me for it when I was younger and now most of them wish they had such unique hair." We both chuckle and I find my eyes getting lost in his.

His black hair and dark toned clothing make his forest green eyes pop from the sunlight that beams from the window and I can easily see my reflection in them. His gaze doesn't move but I look at every feature on his face. From his beautiful brown freckles to his adorable dimples on his cheeks.

ι I thank him for his gifts and we make our way outside to spend the rest of the time visiting other shops and exploring the village. Our visit is soon interrupted by the toll of the evening bell, indicating it's time to go back home.

"Well, I guess it's time for you to go, isn't it?" Kyson and I stand under a tree for shade and he looks sad that we have to go.

"You know the drill, when the queen is away, we always must be home before her or else she'll send the army looking for us." I laugh and see Riverlynn and the knights approaching us from a distance, leaving one of the shops.

"Oooooooh, are we interrupting you two?" Riverlynn teases as she walks up to us.

"No, we were just having a chat before leaving. Let's get the horses ready. I'm sure they've had enough treats from the kiddos today." I gesture to the group of kids who laugh joyfully as they feed the horses apples and carrots.

"When will you be back?" Kyson turns to look at me.

"I doubt it'll be too long. It depends how busy I get with royal duties and such. If the queen allows, I'll send the knights for you. How does that sound?"

"I'd love that." I can't help but blush and feel butterflies crowd my stomach when he smiles.

Atticus and Orion approach us with the horses tacked up and ready to go. Kyson helps me up on my steed and I put my new gift in the satchel that's connected to the saddle.

"I'll see you soon, I promise and thank you again for the flower." He slowly steps back from the horse and bows.

"Of course. I'm happy you like it. Time to find a new project to work on until then." We proceed to say our goodbyes and head home and while on the road, Riverlynn trots up next to me while I zone out, thinking.

"It's painfully obvious, you know?" She says in a teasing manner.

Here we go.

I turn my attention to her, keeping my hands firm on the reins, trying to block out my obnoxiously loud thoughts that make my stomach twist and turn.

"Oh yeah? It must not be obvious to me as I have no idea what you're talking about." I respond sarcastically.

"Oh come on, you and Kyson just need to kiss already. Practically all of Palavon knows you two share a spark between each other. It's soooooooo obvious. For goodness sake, he made you another metal flower. He must really like you to go above and beyond like that." She says, beaming with joy.

Riverlynn has been teasing me about Kyson since we were children and to this day, I don't know how long it'll take me to admit out loud how I feel about him. Deep down, there's a huge spark that ignites when I see or simply think about him.

"As I've stated before, Kyson and I are really good friends. I don't tease you about Orion...out loud that is. But just because he makes me a gift doesn't mean he has a little crush on me. It's just a friendly gesture. Gifts aren't always symbols of a romantic crush." The butterflies in my stomach begin to flutter against my stomach.

Sometimes I'm scared to admit how I feel about Kyson because a small part of me worries he doesn't feel the same way. I'd hate to get excited over my feelings, only for him to continue to see us as friends. That would be embarrassing.

"Besides...I don't have time to focus on love, I have duties and responsibilities to prioritize. More tasks are added to my plate daily. Dealing with the pain and exhaustion on top of it all only makes it more difficult." There's so much more I wish to say but decide to slow down a bit and try not to dwell on it too much.

"I understand, but hey, you're strong and I'm always here if you need anything. I know I tease you a lot about childish things but it's because I try to distract you from the things that stress you out. There's a lot on your own shoulders, I can see that. You're afraid of failure, as am I, but I can assure you, we're both doing just fine. You heard what Atticus said." Riverlynn stops teasing, her tone softens and she speaks sincerely. It's not everyday she talks to me sincerely about serious or sensitive topics. It's relieving to hear her be so alert and aware about the topic that weighs heaviest on my shoulders.

The rest of the ride home is peaceful and quiet. When we passed by the area where I saw the strange green shadow, I hoped to see something strange, but everything looked the same, striking no alarm. It only makes me worry more.

Was it all just a hallucination?

I guess all I can do is wait to see if my mother will believe what I saw. But knowing the odds...she'll also think I'm crazy.

Upon arriving back at the castle, we're greeted by our father at the top of the stairs and we follow him to the throne room. Riverlynn, my father and I take a seat on our chairs as Orion and Atticus stand before us. Confusion draws across father's face as he waits for someone to speak. Riverlynn's joy is wiped by confusion and she looks at everyone individually, trying to figure out what she's missing.

After a long moment of silence, he takes a deep breath. "Is there something I must be told? Why do we stand in silence when I can tell something is potentially wrong?" I try to keep a straight face. My palms sweat and my leg bounces.

Atticus steps forward and politely bows before speaking. "I was only recently told about a small incident that happened while on our way to Palavon. Shall we wait to speak about it until the queen arrives?" Father's interest is piqued and he sits up straight in his chair to ponder to himself. Hopefully he'll say he'll wait until mother comes home.

"You may tell me about it now, I will speak with Aladora privately the moment she returns."

Ohhhhh crap.

Typically, father only handles important matters when the queen is by his side, so his response only makes me more nervous.

A door opens and immediately slams. We turn our attention to the far side of the room and see mother marching in quickly. "What is to be spoken about?" Her heels clack against the stone floor as she approaches us rapidly.

Uh oh.

My heart begins to beat rapidly and I sit frozen in my chair. She sits in the chair next to me as I slowly sink into mine, avoiding eye contact.

"What's going on, Atticus?" She looks at me and then my father while Atticus remains standing in front of everyone, anxious to speak.

"Your majesty, upon arriving at Palavon, we hit a slight bump in the road. Princess Vivalda came down with a headache and thus took a moment for it to pass." Mother immediately turns to me and all I can do is smile awkwardly without looking in her direction.

"Orion stayed with her while Princess Riverlynn and I proceeded to the village, as requested by Vivalda." He quickly glances at me before gathering his composure.

"Orion told me that-" Before he can continue, my mother raises her hand and Atticus silences.

"If you are about to reiterate what your son witnessed, let's hear from him, please." Atticus nods and he switches places with Orion, allowing him to step forward.

Orion looks at me nervously and I shake my head slowly before crossing my arms and slouching back in my chair.

"We stopped along the forest, allowing time for her headache to pass before continuing. She insisted a walk around would help ease her pain and before I knew it, she wandered off farther but requested I stay back with the horses. So, I did. I turned around for a split second and she disappeared." At this point, I can tell my parents are furious, my mother's dark red eyebrows are arched and my father sighs disappointingly.

"Thankfully, she was easily found, but when I caught up to her, she was acting a bit erratically. She spoke of seeing a strange phenomenon in the forest." He lowers his voice before proceeding.

"Princess Vivalda said she witnessed the forest being turned into a valley of death. The trees were dead and there were animal remains scattered about the terrain." The queen leans forward, keeping her eyes on me.

"Did you witness what she described?" She asks in a serious tone and I look up at Orion, hoping he will believe what I said.

"I did not, your majesty." He lowers his head, refusing to look in my direction.

"And do you believe she saw what she did?" My father interjects and I look at him, upset because I know what Orion's answer will be and it's only going to frustrate me even more.

"No. But do I believe the headache she had may have caused another one of her dizzy spells, causing her to hallucinate." I can feel my anger boiling over and I try everything I can not to leash out. "Forgive me. I know I should have brought her home, but she was adamant that-" He's cut off by me slamming my fists down on my chair arm rests.

"I didn't have a dizzy spell!" I sit up from my chair, staring at the ground. "What I saw was something, not even my imagination could make up because how could it be possible to see something so horrendous and vile if it wasn't actually there?" Orion steps back and my family looks at me, concerned.

"There was a patch of land, dead, destroyed by something so unreal. There were bodies of innocent animals lying across the ground and by the time Orion showed up...it disappeared." I look at mother, begging that she will understand and once our eyes lock, she looks at me with her brows furrowed, her eyelids lowered and the corners of her lips lifted slightly.

"You have nothing to apologize for Orion. Thank you both for bringing it to our attention. You are both excused." Both of them bow and exit the room, along with any other servants.

I release a sharp, irritated sigh and fall back into my chair.

"Why must you be so rebellious, Vivalda? You know it's forbidden to wander off the trails and go into the forest!" Father scolds loudly. "Not only have you disobeyed us, but now, you've embarrassed us by lashing out about something that wasn't there. This is why we give you direct orders when-" Mother turns to look at him and he stops talking.

"Watch your tone. She has not embarrassed us, so there is no need to scold her." She says firmly before getting up from her chair and standing in front of my sister and I. "Girls, let's go for a walk." She says as she takes both of our hands and guides us out of the throne room and into the main hall, leaving father to relax.

"I didn't mean to snap the way I did. I swear I saw what I did and I'm tired of people blaming everything on my health. Now, I'm sure you and everyone who heard thinks I'm crazy." I feel her hand squeeze mine tighter.

"Yes, you are crazy, but not the type of crazy you're referring to. You're crazy fun, crazy silly, but never a crazy burden. And I'm not upset one bit. Sure, I would have preferred you to return home when you felt unwell, but the past can't be undone, we can only change habits in the future." She speaks softly as we make our way to the back door of the castle that leads outside to the stables.

"Why are we going to the stables?" Riverlynn asks while swinging her and mother's arm back and forth.

"We're not, we are going beyond them." For some odd reason, mother's words send a strange tingle down my spine, but I have no idea what she means by that.

In the center of the horse's stalls, there's a door that I never noticed until now. My sister and I don't come around the back of the castle very often unless it's to feed the horses.

Upon following mother through the door, the smell of salt water fills the air. Several feet in front of us,

I see a line of guards blocking a large wooden bridge that goes over a wide river of flowing water.

Not only am I confused but I'm also very curious as to where we're going since I've never walked beyond the stables before since I didn't know anything would be behind them.

"Has this always been here?" My sister asks excitedly as we tread the thick green grass and I listen to the rushing water that flows and splashes over rocks and stone.

"Yes Riverlynn, it has always been here, you've just never noticed. Then again, you both were never shown every part of your home and that's my fault." We finally approach the line of guards and they clear a way for us to walk across the sturdy bridge. I want to stop and look over into the water but I continue walking forward, keeping up with my mother's pace.

Across the long bridge is a beautiful fortress of trees and other plants. Each side of the path we walk is lined by colorful flowers. The sound of trotting hooves catches my attention and I see a doe and her fawn hop across the grass. Big vibrant butterflies rest on flowers and birds sing their melodies from the treetops above us. I've never felt such peace before in my life. There's something about the atmosphere here versus the forests just beyond the castle gates. I don't know how to explain it but this place seems so much more alive and vibrant. It's so beautiful, yet mysterious at the same time.

"This place is beautiful, why did you never tell us about it?" I ask while continuing to marvel at the sight before us.

"This is Alsfield and I've been visiting this spot since I was a child when I needed time to myself. I never told you two about it because I didn't want you to wander off here and potentially get hurt or get distracted, but now I know maybe I shouldn't have kept it from you in case you also needed a space to escape." I look over at Riverlynn who disconnects from mothers hand to spin around like a child, excited to explore this new space.

After a quiet, peaceful walk, we come across an open space and in the center stands a tall stone statue that's in the shape of a person. My eyes feel like they'll pop out of my head due to how widely they're open.

"OOH! Scary rock." Riverlynn steps backwards, whispering sillily at the sight of the random statue.

"What is this?" I remove my arm from her grasp and walk closer to the statue to observe it.

"I don't know exactly. Your grandfather always told intriguing stories when I was young." Mother sits down in the grass in front of the statue, but I continue to walk around it with Riverlynn hiding behind me, fearful of the statue.

"Why must you be such a scaredy cat? It's just stone." I try to move away from her, but she stays connected to my back, holding onto my arm for dear life and I can feel her shaking her head.

"No ma'am, I'm telling you right now, that thing will eat me in my sleep. The moss juice stains make it look like some kind of infected spooky monster." I hear mother laugh at us from a distance and I can't help but laugh at how scared she is of a piece of stone.

"Anyways, what stories did he tell you?" I struggle to speak because my sister keeps pushing against my back, with her face squished against my back as she keeps her eyes shielded. I manage to walk back around and we both sit next to mother in the grass.

Riverlynn clutches to mother's side and keeps her face buried in her shoulder, trying not to look up. Mother can't help but laugh at Riverlynn and her fright.

"Well, he said that before I was born, this small island was quiet and stood still every single day. But when I came into the world, it changed. The trees and plants grew taller and faster and one day, the statue mysteriously appeared. And he too was terrified of it." Mother reaches over to tickle Riverlynn, causing her to squeal and laugh.

"Due to his irrational fear, he told me to stay away from Alsfield. But of course, I never listened. Sound familiar?" She asks, gesturing to me and I roll my eyes and chuckle.

"Hey, I'm not THAT bad anymore. I bet you were much worse than I." We both laugh and she tilts her head to the side.

"Well...true, but you're still a handful to this day."

I look at the statue while mother continues telling her story. The statue's pose is so bizarre, yet ethereal at the same time. It's hard to make out the shape because it's covered in moss, leaves and vines. All I can see are two arms with the right being held out elegantly like it floats with the breeze and the other held to its chest. I look closely at what appears to be its face and somehow, I sense nothing but calmness and contentment from something that looks so unusual.

"Do you believe what I said?" I ask quietly and my mother immediately shifts her attention to me. She lifts up her head and fixes her posture while Riverlynn uncovers her eyes.

"I believe you when you say you didn't have a dizzy spell. You know your body better than anyone. I don't think anyone can say what did or didn't happen. That's your judgement alone."

"I feel like a fool. Just this morning, we spoke about my leadership capability and now father and the knights may think I'm crazy. What if it happens again and no one-"

"Listen to me." She says sternly and reaches for my hands, grasping them tightly.

"What I said this morning doesn't change anything NOW. Life works in mysterious ways. If you say you saw what you did, I will believe you and be prepared to take whatever caution I must. But trust me when I say you are not an embarrassment." Her words help me feel better about the situation at hand and I feel all tension leave my muscles.

"And for what it's worth, I believe you too." Riverlynn says kindly, trying not to look up at the statue.

We spend the rest of the evening in Alsfield, joking around and listening to stories while the sun sets. Mother shows us around the small island and we walk down beautiful grassy paths and see more plants and animals that grow and roam. She shows us where the bunnies burrow and we find nests full of babies just starting to grow. She also shows us different kinds of flowers that grow all over the land.

Mother walks us to the edge of the land where we're met by the peaceful sea that rests several feet below the cliff. Riverlynn jumps around joyfully so much that for a moment, I thought she'd fall over into the sea. But it brings me joy to see her excited. It's nice to spend this time with my mother and sister because we don't get this chance as often as I wish.

We make our way back to the statue to find the path that leads back to the castle.

"When either of you feel stressed or you need a quiet place to relax and get fresh air, let this be your space. It's helped me as I've aged and now I hope it'll help you as you continue to mature. When you're in need of guidance and my presence isn't available at the time, you will find it here." A peaceful wave of joy washes over my body and I can't help but smile because a space such as this is just what I've needed.

"Thank you, I've needed this and it helps tremendously."

Aladora

Once we go back inside the castle, the girls go to their rooms to prepare for dinner and I go back to the throne room to find Cassius. Before opening the doors to the throne room, I hear him speaking to another knight. I lean my ear on the door to hear better.

"There's been sightings of strange dark figures all over Palavon this evening. The people request your help." My contentment and happiness is overpowered by sudden fear. I quickly barge through the door and the two knights turn their attention to me.

"What's the problem?" I ask sternly and knights continue to explain.

"We don't mean to cause alarm, but villagers have been gathering at the castle gates to send the news of these mysterious sightings. They said this phenomenon just began this evening." Before anyone else could speak, the main doors open and Atticus and Orion approach us quickly.

"People are crowding the gates frantically. What will you have us do?" Atticus asks urgently, running out of breath.

"I will-" I begin to speak but I'm caught off guard when I hear the back door open and see my daughters walk in laughing, but once they see everyone else, their laugh fades away. Vivalda's happiness instantly turns into worry.

"What's going on?" She asks quietly.

"Girls, please go to the study hall and I will speak to you both once we've finished." Vivalda's eyes furrow, disapproving my command.

"I will not. Whatever is going on, I can be informed as well." She speaks firmly, refusing to do as I ask.

"Viv, I don't think you-" Cassius begins to say but she cuts him off.

"I'm staying!" Vivalda raises her voice, causing an echo to rebound around the room and before walking over, she tells Riverlynn they'll meet in her room once we have finished talking. Riverlynn leaves the room and I approach Vivalda.

"I'd prefer if you don't join this talk, Vivalda, please."

"No, I want to know what's going on. Serious matters are what you've been teaching me to handle, so I want to be a part of the conversation." It makes me proud to hear her speak so confidently.

I refrain from getting frustrated and take a deep breath before allowing Vivalda to sit with us. While we sit on our chairs, Atticus continues to speak.

"The people describe seeing big black shadows that hide within the trees, escaping the Lion's Eye. Some go as far to say they've seen these shadows have beaming red eyes and they report hearing eerie screams and whispers beyond the trees in land they know not to step foot on, Wildevale and the Lion's Eye."

The Lion's Eye is the northern forest and Wildevale lies in the south. This news makes my skin crawl and my hands shake. I've never heard of any strange activity occurring around those parts of the land. Vivalda turns to me, holding her hands out.

"That's what I saw in the forest too! A strange shadow blending into the trees but with no face or bodily features. I told you I wasn't making it up!" She swings her head around to the knights. My panic begins to spike and my skin grows cold.

"Have any knights or guards seen any of this activity? Or is it just being reported by villagers alone?" The tone in Cassius' voice irks me because it sounds like he doesn't believe his people.

"From what I know, none of our men have witnessed anything strange or out of the ordinary." Atticus responds, gripping his metal helmet tightly under his arm.

"Maybe there's a sickness going around, causing the villagers to see silly things that aren't there. Maybe they're simply paranoid from childish bedtime stories. I'm sure-" I quickly stand before Cassius speaks another word. Before talking, I glare at him, annoyed that he has the audacity to say what he has and I can tell he has upset Vivalda as well.

A plan quickly comes to mind and I proceed to elaborate on what must be done.

"I leave for the neighboring kingdom at once. While I am gone, take a group of at least fifteen knights and scout the terrain, search for anything strange and report back. We will take care of this as if their word is true, even if we don't believe it. I won't take any chances. To anyone you see, tell them we are doing our best to take care of this and to go home and remain calm. The last thing we need is for every village far and wide to panic. We all must remain calm and vigilant." The knights straighten the postures, ready to take action.

"The moment you see or hear anything, you will report back here immediately. Understood?" The knights nod their heads.

"Yes your majesty, we will see it done." Orion responds and all men retreat outside to inform the other knights and guards.

I feel my heart beating so fast, so I close my eyes and allow myself to sit into my chair comfortably, thinking about the command I had just given and the task at hand.

"You just came back from Astryn, why must you leave again? Let me go this time instead or at least allow me to go with you." I can tell by the look in his eye that he's worried but I can't help but feel appalled over what he said just a moment ago.

"I love you darling, but if you are one to blame these strange sightings on sickness and fables, I can't trust you to take the journey. I need you here with the girls."

Cassius has never been to the neighboring kingdom because it's routine that he holds the fort here in Vassuren while I leave and he keeps everything together. I appreciate that he'd like to switch places but his place is here at home, caring for our daughters and staff.

"I need to make sure Astryn doesn't hear about this and potentially gather an army to fight a ghost. I promise everything will be fine as long as I'm the one to handle it." I hold his hand tightly in mine and seal my words with a smile in hopes of reassuring him.

I turn to Vivalda who sits back in her chair with her arms crossed, thinking intensely.

"That being said, Vivalda, until this is resolved, you and Riverlynn will not be allowed to leave the castle gates under any circumstances." Vivalda stands up to protest.

"But mother, I want to help-" I grab both of her hands quickly, catching her off guard.

"Out of all commands you are given, this one is most crucial. Do you understand me?" I quickly realize I'm talking loudly when I hear the echo of my voice fluttering in the room, bouncing off the walls.

Vivalda steps back from me, letting her arms fall limp to her side.

"Understood." She responds sourly and immediately retreats out of the throne room, slamming the door behind her.

I sit back in my chair and rest my face in my hands as my thoughts collide with my heart. I yearn to stay home with my family, but I also know I have to take care of something that could potentially turn into a big problem.

"I'm sorry for my poor choice of words, I realize how foolish that was of me." Cassius says quickly and I lift my head from my hands.

"It's alright." I nod and hold his hand.

"Please talk to her privately before you leave. Maybe that could help calm the tension."

I rise from my throne and catch up to Vivalda. I find her on the castle balcony, staring out into the bright orange sky as the sun continues to set.

She hears the sound of my heels clacking on the stone floor, and turns around, unpleased to see me. She rolls her eyes and turns her attention back to the view in front of her.

"Are you here to nag on me some more?" She hisses angrily as she taps her fingernails on the stone ledge.

I approach and stand next to her, resting my arms on the stone ledge. I attempt to hold her hand but she pulls it away before I could get close.

"No, I'm not here to nag. I wanted to talk to you before I leave. I'd hate for you to be upset while I'm gone. So if you have something you'd like to say, please tell me what's on your mind." She closes her eyes and takes a deep breath.

"I'm tired of being hidden away. Whether it be due to you being cautious of my health or not wanting me to be a part of settling problems." I immediately feel her pain and frustration as if it's my own.

"I know it's confusing but trust me, it's for a good reason. I teach you to prepare for important royal matters. This is something far more different that anything I've ever heard of. Not even I know how I will take care of this. I react the way I do because I love you and I'm trying to protect our family and our people. There's a lot you don't understand and one day you will, but for just right now, I need you to stay here where you're safe and protected." Vivalda finally turns to me, enraged like a boiling teapot.

"How exactly do you expect me to ever be prepared for the unknown? How do you know what I can or can't handle if you keep me sheltered in the castle walls?" I've never seen her so angry before and a part of me doesn't blame her.

"Everything happens for a reason, whether they be good or bad things, I don't always know. Maybe one day you'll understand better but right now, you must do as I say. If this is a situation I completely understood, I'd have you join my side. But I can't-"

"You can't risk me being hurt. You can't risk me getting overwhelmed. You can risk me panicking in the public eye. Yeah, I know. I've been told that and so much more. But maybe, one day you and everyone else will understand that I'm not just some weak link in the royal chain." The anger in her eyes and the sadness in her tone breaks my heart to the point where I'm left speechless. I try resting my arm on the back of her shoulder, but she pushes me away.

"Just go. I know Astryn awaits your urgent presence." She says coldly before turning away from me. I stand silently for a moment, thinking about what to say.

"Please promise me you won't leave the castle until I get back. I've always let you get away with things but please don't do anything foolish. Not tonight out of all nights." My body tenses because I hope to get some kind of reaction but all Vivalda does is keep her cold gaze on the darkening horizon.

When I realize there's not much more I can say or do to appease her, I walk back inside and feel tears slowly fall from my eyes. I wipe the liquid from my cheeks with my long red sleeve and feel a hand rest on my right shoulder. I let out a little chuckle when I see Lyla handing me a handkerchief to dry my tears with.

I take the white fabric from her hand, trying not to cry more. "You heard all that didn't you?" I ask as I pat my eyes and cheeks dry.

"Oh your majesty, I hear everything around here. You know this." I look out the glass door and see Vivalda still leaning against the stone barrier.

"Hey..." Lyla says as she holds both of my hands in hers.

"One day she'll understand everything you've been trying to teach." Lyla has always been good at bringing comfort in difficult times. I sniffle and finish pat drying my eyes.

"I know. Please make sure she doesn't leave the castle or do anything stupid." Lyla nods and hugs me from the side before proceeding to tidy up the rooms before everyone goes to bed.

I walk down the hall and find Riverlynn in the study room, sitting alone at the desk. I knock on the side of the wall and she turns to me, smiling. "Hello mother, I heard you're leaving again." I sit next to her and she leans her head on my shoulder.

"Yes, but I wanted to check on you before I leave. Are you alright?" I rub my hand on her back.

"I don't know exactly. Viv told me she needed some space and went to the balcony. Did you talk to her?" I inhale sharply.

"I did." She inhales sharply.

"She gave you a hard time didn't she?"

"Of course she did, but it's okay." I lean my head over hers. "While I'm gone, can you do me a favor, sweetheart?" She sits up to look at me, focused.

"Of course." I think carefully about the words I choose before speaking.

"Promise me you two will always be there for each other, no matter what." Riverlynn smiles.

"I promise."

I give her one last hug before retreating out of the room.

"I love you, Riverlynn." She hugs me back tightly.

"I love you too, mother."

I make my way to the castle entrance where Cassius and the knights wait for me. I wrap my arm around Cassius' as we walk down the stairs to the horse drawn carriage that waits at the bottom.

Cassius opens the door but before I place my foot on the steps, I turn to hug him tightly.

"Please return home as soon as possible before it gets too dark." He whispers in my ear.

"Don't worry, my love. I've done this many times. Give the girls some company if you can." He nods his head and we part ways. He helps me up into the carriage that's led by one horse and is controlled by a single knight. Cassius closes the door and I let the knight know I'm ready to leave.

As we begin moving, I look up at the castle and see Vivalda still standing on the balcony that stretches over the castle entrance. The sun sets behind the castle, casting dark shadows over Vivalda's face, making it difficult to see her but I can tell she's still upset. Although I doubt she can see me, I wave at her and whisper to myself.

"I love you."

I keep looking at Vivalda until the castle is hidden by the trees and she's out of sight.

Vivalda

I watch my mother's carriage disappear into the forest, the wheels kick up dirt, causing a dust cloud to trail behind. I keep my eyes on the carriage until it's no longer in sight. I remain leaning over the stone ledge, thinking about everything and nothing at the same time, listening to the wind howl around me.

The double doors open behind me and I hear footsteps approach me. I instantly know it's my sister.

"Are you here to lecture me too?" I ask, scoffing dramatically. She stands next to me and leans her head on my right shoulder.

"No, I'm not. I just wanted to see how you're doing." I inhale sharply, trying not to take my frustration out on her.

"There's not much to talk about." I say coldly and Riverlynn nudges my shoulder playfully.

"You're a terrible liar." I walk to the stone bench to sit down and she follows to do the same. She takes my hair down while I speak and plays with it.

"Do you remember the day we visited Palavon, a few days after I woke up?" I see Riverlynn's head drop and she tries to herself.

"Yes I remember for the most part. Why do you ask?"

As I speak, various scenes and memories play in my mind as if relieving every moment.

"Do you remember how mean some people were when they saw me?" Her head immediately perks up.

"Ah, you mean all those kids I fought with because they were rude? Of course I remember. I've always wondered if they've changed since then."

I laughed at her response because I figured that'd be the first thing she thought about. She was always proud of herself for fighting other kids, especially when she stood up for me.

"Is it silly that I still think about everything they said about me? Their voices haunt my mind everyday. Now, I have parents and knights acting as if I'm incapable of taking care of myself. Mother continues to shelter me when all I want is to be a part of the bigger picture. Back in the throne room, did you see how Orion looked at me? He alone looked embarrassed that he witnessed what he did and it made me look like-" Riverlynn peers over to get my attention.

"Hey! If anything, he's the fool for not believing because now, there's a crisis occurring in the kingdom. And yes, before you ask, I listened to the conversation from the door." Riverlynn and I both laugh.

"Of course you did," Riverlynn proceeds to play with my hair which helps me relax.

"Mother doesn't think you're incapable of anything." She says and I can't help but disagree.

"How do you know that for sure?" I ask as I feel the air grow colder. I cross my arms in front of me to conserve warmth.

"She says it with more than just her words. There's a certain look she gives us and behind her eyes, I see nothing but proudness and pride. She does everything she can to ensure we're safe and protected, even if we don't like it. It's what both a mother and a queen do. You can't blame her, nor can you give her a hard time. Maybe one day you'll be put in a similar situation and you'll understand better." Riverlynn stands up and rests her hand on my shoulder.

"One day, you'll show the world the strength you carry that has been doubted." Her comfort helps but, I can't help but feel numb on the inside.

"Try not to stay up too late. If you need some company, you know where to find me."

"I know. Goodnight." She goes inside, closing the door behind her.

The wind howls louder and the bitter cold air makes my teeth chatter and hair on my arms stand. I decide the best thing for me would be for me to go inside and prepare for bed.

Once in my room, I stand in front of my mirror while braiding my long brown hair to the side. My attention is turned to the door when I hear a quiet knock. I keep my gaze on the mirror to see who comes in and I see Lyla walk slowly into my room. I smile through the mirror and she proceeds to walk in and fix my bedsheets.

"Need I lay out your clothes for the morning, princess?" An awkward scoff escapes my throat.

"Lyla, I've told you a million times, you don't need to address me as such." She looks at me disapprovingly and laughs.

"Oh, so I suppose 'trouble maker' fits better, yes?" I laugh with her as she folds over my blue and white bedsheets and fluffs my pillows.

I can hear the wind howling loudly outside. Leaves and sticks are thrown into the window.

"What's on your mind, child?" Lyla sits on the edge of my bed and I follow.

"I don't know...a lot I guess." I respond while holding her hand. I look into her hazel eyes that are covered by strands of gray hair and find it difficult to speak.

"Well, start with the first thing that comes to mind. I have all night to listen." Each of my thoughts collide into one big mess in my mind. I don't know where to start or end.

"I feel like I'm doing something wrong and I don't know what. I mean well with my intentions and words and yet, I feel like it's all wrong. Does that make sense?" I say as I look at the floor, bouncing my left leg rapidly.

"Oh my dear, you're not doing anything wrong. You're right where you need to be. Your mind creates a timer that no one else can see. Your mind tells you the silliest lies." I feel my shoulders slowly tense up and my jaw begins to tighten.

"I don't understand myself. I want to prove that I can care for myself and hold the crown at the same time. But at the same time, I'm so scared. I'm scared of letting my mother down more than the crown. Sure, my duty is to guide our people, but my family is what comes first. Everyone, including her, says I'm doing great, but the fear of failure still lingers and I can't block it out." Releasing my words makes a heavy weight drop from my shoulders. I unclench my jaw and breathe steadily.

Lyla turns her body towards me and speaks softly while moving the baby hairs out of my face.

"Your mother is protective because she loves you. She is cautious because she cares for your wellbeing. She is scared because you girls are her very life and soul. You know that just as well as I. All you can do is take control of what you are allowed, but do so maturely." I wipe my watery eyes with my blue sleeve and Lyla holds both of my hands.

"Everything will work out the way it needs to and when the world calls for a leader, you will be there to answer." She pulls me in for a hug and gets up to leave the room.

I lay back on my bed and pull the large blue blanket over my body and slowly drift off to sleep.

Hours pass and I wake up after tossing and turning. My stomach begins to twist and my heart races rapidly. It feels like my body is trying to run a million miles an hour and it becomes so intense that I throw myself off the bed and fall to my hands and knees.

When my body crashes to the floor, I can hear a storm raging outside, colliding with my pain and discomfort. I begin to hyperventilate and feel my eyes bulging from my skull. My arms and legs are stabbed by millions of needles, causing them to feel numb. All of my pain gathers to my chest and stomach. I try holding myself and rocking side to side, but my hands are so stiff and numb to the point where my fingers flex upwards. I can feel my vision grow hazy, so I close them and try to focus the best I can to get rid of the attack.

I often have panic attacks like this, but never this extreme to where I feel like I will die where I lay.

"Please stop." I whimper quietly to myself.

I try to control the attack by taking deep breaths, but it only makes my mind even more aware that I'm in danger, therefore, making it worse.

My door slams open with the crash of thunder. I peel one eye open and look under the bed and see bare feet running quickly across the wooden floor. I close my eyes once more and feel two arms roll me over, lift me up and pull me close. Whoever it is holds me very close to their chest as my body goes limp.

"It's okay, I'm here." A gentle voice says softly over me.

She rocks me back and forth which helps me take slow deep breaths and I can feel my heart begin to slow down.

My cheeks are soaked with tears and my hair is unraveled from the braid. Once I'm in control, I look up and see two worrisome blue eyes staring down at me.

"Hi." She sniffles and moves the hair out of my face. By the concerned look on her face, I can tell she's been crying and it's not because she's worried about me.

Something is off, so I lay in her arms, silently, trying to catch my breath. When I'm ready, I slowly sit up. My ears perk up when I hear several footsteps running past my room. Pieces of metal rattle and men shout loudly.

"What's going on?" I ask urgently, turning to Riverlynn who keeps her eyes set on the hall and a single tear drop slowly falls down her face. The corners of her lips quiver and she covers her eyes with her hands.

I lean forward and lightly rest my hands on top of hers

"Hey, hey, it's alright. What's going on?" She pulls her hands down and holds mine and her eyes are swollen red.

"Mother hasn't come home." Her voice shakes and more tears fall from her eyes. My heart sinks to my stomach and I quickly get up and walk towards the door.

"What are you doing?" Riverlynn asks while wiping tears from her face.

"I'm going to see father. Stay here until I come back. I don't want you to get overwhelmed." I quickly rush out of my room and run down the hall behind the guards that are heading to the throne.

I slide into a room on the left side of the hall that leads to the kitchen and I can hear my father speaking loudly as I barge through the door.

In the throne room, several knights and guards line up in front of my father, including Atticus and Orion who peer over at me. Father stands in front of his chair, paying me no mind, continuing to give orders.

"The queen should have been back by now and has never stayed out this late. We will tack up immediately and I will take the trail Aladora forged to Astryn. We will do whatever it takes to find her and ensure she is safe!" I shield my eyes when a bright lightning strike flickers from the window. The thunder roars loudly and rain patters against the castle walls.

I slip back into the kitchen before my father has a chance to spot me and he leads the cavalry out of the castle.

I slam my back against the door and my mind begins to race dangerously.

I need to find Lyla.

I rush back to the main hall and instantly come across one of our chefs, William who is organizing cleaning supplies in a storage room.

"William, have you seen Lyla?" I ask, panting. My urgency makes him jolt and he turns to me in a fright.

"Oh, I'm pretty sure she's asleep by now. Is there something you need?" I completely forgot that Lyla has a specific sleep routine and decide not to bother her.

"No, nevermind, thank you." I continue to speed down the hall and return to my room and find Riverlynn still sitting on the floor, leaning against my bed.

"What happened?" She stands up but I remain frozen in the doorway, staring down at the floor. I look past her and see the storm continuing to rage through my window.

"Father is leading the knights down the trail to Astryn to search for mother and I'm going too." Riverlynn stomps up to me.

"Absolutely not! If father has gone with them, it's guaranteed they'll find her. Maybe the carriage got stuck in mud due to the storm and-" It's funny she'd think I'd have the patience to just sit.

"I'm not going to take that chance when I feel something calling me. Something is telling me to do this and I can't ignore my gut. What if they CAN'T find her? Father is not of royal blood, therefore, he has never been to Astryn, so how do we know he'll find his way and not get lost?" Rivelynn is overwhelmed by my tone and takes a step back while I walk past her to get ready for the storm that waits for me.

"Mother will kill both of us if you go out there. I know she told you not to do anything stupid, so why can't you abide by her word for once?! Why can't you just stay put? Sure, we've disobeyed her on occasion, but that was for fun. This is serious!" She pulls my shoulder back and I pivot to her, facing her arched brows and eyes that swell with tears.

"You don't know the trail, just as much as father." I pause to look at her silently. All I can hear is my heart thumping against my chest and the surging storm outside.

"But I know our mother." My sister scoffs and steps back.

I retrieve long black boots and slide a long black coat over my night dress. I sit at the edge of my bed to lace up my boots and Riverlynn remains standing still in the middle of the room.

"Viv, I know you want to help and prove your worth, but this isn't the way to go about it. What if YOU end up getting into trouble and there's no one to help? Imagine father's fury if he comes home and I have to tell him you're not here? Then that'll just be another problem he'll have to worry about." I slam my right foot down after lacing up the strings on my boots.

"Whether anyone likes it or not, I'm leaving. You, nor anyone else can stop me. If this will be a mistake on my part, then I will deal with the consequences." Riverlynn rolls her eyes and shakes her head, disapproving of my actions. She takes a deep breath and releases her words slowly.

"You're right I can't stop you. But I don't know if I'll be able to have your back if this goes wrong." Without saying another word, I pull my hood over my head and leave the room. I head towards the stables behind the castle, making sure to not be seen by the few guards who remain at their posts.

When I step outside, a heavy cold gust of wind slams into my face. The darkness of the night is lit by torches and lanterns that line up the pathway to the stables.

I quickly tack up our fastest horse and hook two lanterns on each side of the saddle and once we're ready, we run out of a hidden gate that leads directly to the forest.

Rain splatters against my face, making it difficult to keep my eyes on the paths ahead but eventually, I find the main path that my mother marked that leads to Palavon, which is also the same path I last saw her take when she left.

She has always told us that the way to the northern kingdom is directly through Palavon and past the mountains that lie just outside the village.

As we run through the woods, I keep my eyes peeled just in case I come across anything unusual, but the only thing I find odd is I don't see any signs of my father and the knights going down the path.

Did father lead them off the trail? They shouldn't be far from me.

I begin to hear strange sounds coming from beyond the forest. I keep myself balanced and unhook one of the lanterns from the saddle. I hold it out, expecting to see an animal but all I see are dark trees and thick bushes.

On the opposite side of me, I see a dark shadow zoom past me out of the corner of my eye and when I twist around to shine the light on it, it disappears.

An overwhelming wave of fear consumes me to the point where I'm scared to move. I knew what I was getting into, but I don't know how real or dangerous these strange shadows are. The eerie sounds grow louder and louder. It sounds like whispers, but I can't make out what's being said.

What am I doing?

A part of me debates on turning around and returning home when a sudden lightning bolt strikes the ground in front of us, causing the horse to rear up on its hind legs. I don't have time to grab onto the saddle, so I scream before quickly falling to the ground and quickly roll out of the way to avoid being kicked or trampled by the frightened animal.

With how frantic the animal lashes out, I know I have no chance of calming it down and it takes off and disappears into the woods. Before standing up, I reach over to grab the lantern that fell with me and hold it up to look around me. I stand up and my clothes are coated in thick mud.

I turn to continue down the path but I'm stopped when I see a terrifying dead tree that appears to have sprouted in the middle of the dirt road. I've traveled this road many times and have never seen a tree in the middle of the path. My fear intensifies and my skin begins to crawl. I look at the tree and see nothing else strange about it.

Shining the light towards the forest only makes the experience even more terrifying because it looks like a pitch black abyss, leaving me fearful of what lies beyond in the darkness.

I have no time to reminisce on what I've already witnessed. I walk around the tree and my eyes widen when I see a second dirt path that winds to the right, leading away from the main road. It's a path I've never seen before and is partially hidden by thick trees and thickets. I know the path that goes straight leads to Palavon, but I don't know where the other one goes.

I lower the lantern to the ground and I see two parallel lines going north and hoof prints going north east. Seeing this leaves me confused because it looks like father led the knights north east.

Water begins to wash out the prints and I decide to follow the same trail in hopes of catching up with them.

Thunder continues to roar loudly as I run down the dirt road, kicking up mud with every step. I steadily jump over fallen trees and large rocks that sink into the mud, being careful not to slip.

The eerie noises and voices return, mixing in with the howling wind, causing me to panic and run faster. I do my best to stay on the path, keeping the lantern lit as long as possible.

I see shadows zoom past me on each side. I'm so terrified that I refuse to look at them and I keep running.

Without looking, I know these weird shadows are terrifying to look at. I see small red beams of light flicker around me, but I can't tell where it's coming from or what it is.

I don't know what's more terrifying, their screams or the fact I can't see them.

I can see the shadows begin to grow in large numbers, surrounding me like a pack of wolves ready to pounce on a bunny. Instinctively, I shield my head with one arm and run with my eyes closed screaming, hoping it'll scare them off. But instead, it seems to rile them up even more. I try swinging the lantern at them but they quickly glide out of the way.

I have a hard time believing any of this is real so I come to a sliding stop and thrust the lantern forward while looking up. As soon as my eyes focus, a massive terrifying creature made of black smoke with beaming red eyes roars in my face. Its steaming breath smells so vile, I feel sick and the sight of it causes me to scream so loud, I thought my vocal cords would rupture.

The beast with two rows of sharp teeth charges at me, but I manage to quickly dive out of the way and continue to run.

I can't believe what I just saw. The shadows are more than just apparitions, they're terrifying monsters I've never thought could exist.

The bloodthirsty monsters continue to chase me. I look back and see at least five of them following me. They don't have any appendages and their bodies are made of thick black smoke. Due to being distracted, I stumble down a slippery hill. I lose grip of the lantern and my legs and arms slam against large rocks and trees while mud fills my mouth.

My stumble comes to a stop when my back slams into a tree, knocking the breath out of me. After a moment, I try to get up but instantly fall against the tree.

The atmosphere is so dark, I can't see anything. Instead, I can hear the monsters charging towards me from the top of the hill. Due to not being able to move, I wrap my arms over my face and my body tensely curls up.

I can't help but scream and at the same time, I hear a deafening boom coming from somewhere far in the distance. A ray of light shines through my sleeves and the creatures scream in agony, I keep my face covered just in case until the light fades away and the atmosphere goes back to black. Before I can uncover my face, I hear something approaching me slowly. My head continues to spin so fast, I can't tell what stands in front of me.

My entire body is in such immense pain that my eyes close and I pass out.

When I finally wake up, I see the treetops moving rapidly above me and my body is bumping up and down. My face is leaning against something wet and cold.

I give my eyes a moment to adjust before looking up and seeing a familiar face.

"Mother? How-" My voice is sore and hoarse and mother looks down at me, relieved that I'm awake.

"Oh thank goodness. Try not to move or speak okay? I'm trying to get us home." She turns her attention back to the path while looking around cautiously.

My head, chest, arms and legs hurt terribly and it's difficult to think or see properly.

I feel like I'm running through a nightmare.

Aladora

I look back to ensure we're not being followed and I try speaking in small words so Vivalda can understand me.

"My carriage got destroyed by these monsters. My guard was killed and all I could do was unhook the horse and run. I was trying to find my way home and in the midst of finding the trail, I saw a bright flash of light coming from the forest, hoping I'd maybe find your father or other knights. But instead, I found you unconscious by a tree. I'm serious, please try not to move." I keep us balanced on the horse, holding her close to my chest with one arm and gently grasping the horse's mane with the other.

I look around frantically, trying to find a trail I have marked or one that I'm familiar with. I've never been off the hill before, so I have no idea where we are or if we're going the right direction. For all I know, we could be going back north.

I hear a loud hiss behind us and I turn around to see a giant shadow-like figure zigzagging through the trees, hunting us. I urge the horse to go faster but the creatures quickly catch up.

The stories my people told are true!

I do everything I can to remain calm and not panic, but it's almost impossible.

The mysterious creatures' black clouded bodies flow with the wind as they fly. One of the monsters catches up to us and I watch as two large arms stretch out from its body and its fingers turn into thick sharp claws. My eyes widen at the grotesque sight.

"Go faster!" I desperately urge the horse and it goes faster, running past the creature. The hollowness in their deep red eyes that follows us sends chills down my spine.

I quickly realize we can't outrun them for long and I turn around to see them flying towards us at an alarming speed.

I duck down over Vivalda as they race over us, trying to grab us and attack the horse. Vivalda sees them fly over and is immediately alert.

"What are those things?!" Vivalda screams in my arm.

I don't answer because not only do I not have an answer, but I'm too focused on keeping us steady while avoiding being touched by the mysterious creatures.

We continue to run deeper into the forest and I lose track of the trails. Tree branches scratch every part of my body and I do my best to shield Vivalda from getting hurt anymore than she already is. All I can do is pray that the sun will show its face as soon as possible.

"What do you think you were doing in the forest alone?!" I yell at Vivalda while swerving around fallen trees and dodging the beasts as they continue to taunt and fly over us.

"Is now really the time?! We're being hunted by monsters, you know!" Her voice is weak and she tries to wipe her face that's covered with mud and water.

"Answer my question, Vivalda!" I yell forcefully over the sound of the beasts screeching and roaring.

"I was worried and wanted to help! I'm sorry!" She responds, while holding onto me tightly. I feel all remaining warmth escape from my body.

"What are we going to do?!" Vivalda brings my attention back to the situation at hand and more creatures appear and circle around us.

I watch them steadily as they glide with us, keeping up with our pace. They all arch their backs and charge forward at once.

I quickly lunge myself over Vivalda again, but this time, they manage to dig their knife-like talons into my back and sides.

I release an agonizing scream as I hear my flesh tearing like paper while they continue to attack. No matter what, I do whatever I can to ensure they don't put a finger on my daughter.

The open wounds sting intensely and I can feel blood trickling down my sides, mixing in with rain water. There's nothing I can do besides endure their attacks since I have no other means of protecting Vivalda. I look up to see where the horse runs and my gaze is met by another pair of beaming red eyes that stare deep into my soul. It opens its mouth and black slimy ooze drips from its gums while it growls loudly.

Before I can react, a bright thunderbolt crackles and descends from the sky, striking the beasts and immediately disintegrating it.

The thunder strike causes the horse to trip in the mud, causing us to fall off and crash onto the cold wet ground. I remain on my side, frozen because I've never felt such excruciating pain in my life.

I sit up and wrap my arms around my stomach. I feel blood continuing to trickle down in between my fingers. I try to brush off the pain and look around to see where Vivalda is. But the first thing I notice is the beasts have disappeared and are nowhere to be found.

I try my best to breathe, but it hurts to move, even in the slightest.

I see Vivalda rushing to me and she falls to her knees in front of me.

"Are you okay?" She pants hysterically in shock.

A ray of light catches my eye and I look up to see the sun beginning to peak from behind thick black clouds that slowly drift away while it continues to rain.

The sun shines dimly on Vivalda's face, uncovering her wounds from the shadows. I can tell she's in such shock that she hasn't realized the pain she's in yet.

"I'm fine. I'm just relieved I found you." I pull her in gently and rest my head against hers.

"Those things...that's what I saw in the forest. What are they?" Vivalda starts to cry and moves to rest her head on my shoulder.

I can feel her body shaking. Not due to the cold, but due to uncontrollable fear and terror.

"I don't know...I don't know." I speak slowly and feel a wave of pain throb and pulsate through my stomach, causing me to wince and gasp for air.

The pain grows unbearable. Vivalda pulls back, startled and concerned and she analyzes me to figure out what's wrong. Before she has the chance to notice the dark red blood that blends into my dress, I quickly grab her hands.

"I'm sorry for sheltering you so much. Now, I understand why you've been so angry and frustrated with me." Vivalda begins to break and cry even more. Her eyes widen, her lips quiver and her brows twitch.

"No, no, you have no reason to apologize. I couldn't even- I made it worse. I didn't stay home- I don't know where-" I grasp her face with my hands, attempting to calm her down.

"Shushhhh. It's alright. Listen, I found my way home, right here. You did what you deemed right. That's what a leader does." I continue to wipe Vivalda's tears as she cries and trembles.

"Maybe it wasn't such a bad thing that you disobeyed me." I try to laugh but instantly feel warm blood beginning to clog up my throat, causing me to cough and spit up.

"Oh no...we need to get you home. Now!" Vivalda sits back urgently and looks around the forest, trying to find a way out.

"I don't think either of us are capable of walking right now, darling. Let's stay right here until the knights find us. I'm sure they're around here somewhere if they've been searching down the path to Palavon." I push myself back up against a tree and sink into the muddy floor. My eyes feel heavy and the pain continues to surge overwhelmingly. Vivalda turns her attention back to me and crawls over to sit next to me.

"I want you to have something..." I slowly move my hands off my stomach and unclasp the gold necklace that dangles from my neck. I'm surprised it managed to stay on after all the chases I experienced.

I put the necklace in Vivalda's hand and curl her fingers over her palm so she grasps it tight and she stares at me silently.

"No, I can't take this. It's your favorite." More tears shed from her eyes at the sight of the necklace and I can feel her weakly trying to uncurl her fingers but I keep a tight grip on her.

"You can and you will. It was always meant to be yours. Let it be the reminder of your strength as it has been mine for most of my life. You are the storm to be feared and the call to be heeded." Vivalda breathes heavily and her hand shakes violently under mine. She grows more concerned than before.

"Please stop with this kind of talk, why are you..." Her gaze falls to my hands and she realizes they're coated in blood. Her mouth opens and she immediately looks down at my stomach, seeing my torn skin peeking through the damaged cloth.

"No...NO! You're fine, you're fine. We just have to find someone and get you home!" She screams frantically as she tries to get up but I pull her back down to my side.

"Will you just sit with me...please." My voice shakes as I hold back tears, trying to get her to listen.

Vivalda begins to hyperventilate and shake hysterically. The look in her eyes breaks my heart. The pain, the panic and the helplessness shatters what's left of my fading heart. She tries to pull away once more but I do what I can to keep her with me.

"Viv, just listen to me this once. Don't rebel or run away!" I cry, allowing my tears to fall.

She instantly dives next to me and holds me softly, wary of my wounds. She leans her face into my shoulder and lets out the loudest cry I've ever heard before.

"This isn't fair!" The agony in her voice hurts me more than the open gashes scattered across my body.

My vision begins to blur and my body begins to slowly go numb.

Before my eyes grow heavier, my attention is turned to the sound of horses hooves treading the ground rapidly, splashing through water. Vivlada sits up and for a split moment, I see a glimmer of hope in her eyes. She twists and turns her head, looking for where the sounds come from. She then gathers up my dress and layers it across my stomach and sides and takes off her own coat to cover me.

"Hold this here the best you can, I'm going to find help." I stop her one last time before she gets up.

"I love you." I say weakly, trying to smile. Vivalda's brows scrunch and her lips shake.

"Don't do that. Everything will be okay. I'll be right back." I can't help but stare into her brown eyes for as long as time allows me.

I don't want to let go...

I can't let her go...

Her hand slips from my grip and I watch her disappear into the trees.

"You'll be okay."

I whisper my last breath and the last thing I hear is the echo of my daughter's voice.

Vivalda

I run out to the muddy road and see my father, followed by Atticus and Orion. "FATHER!" I yell with what voice I have left and my father sees me immediately before running to me. Atticus and Orion trail behind closely. All of them are confused to see me.

"Vivalda!" My father jumps down off his horse before it comes to a complete stop and he runs to embrace me. Oh my gods, what the hell are you doing out here?!" I pull back from him and the knights get down from their horses.

"There's no time! Mother, she's-" I pull his arm to guide him to where she is.

"You found her?!" I don't answer and continue to lead him into the forest.

I look around and once I lay my eyes on her, my skin grows colder and my heart falls to my stomach. My mother looks...lifeless but I refuse to believe it.

"Aladora!" My father rushes to her side and he gently pulls her forward to his chest. Once he realizes his body is limp and she's no longer breathing, his eyes widen and he instantly cries.

"No no no, please. PLEASE! Wake up darling, I'm right here!" I stand frozen and the knights join his side, in shock.

Her hands fall limp, her eyes are shut and her chest doesn't move.

No.

My father cries over her body and doesn't stop.

"She was just...here. I was trying to find help-" Atticus turns to me but I remain staring at my mother's lifeless body.

"I tried to help, there were monsters and they-" My knees shake under me and before I can crash to the ground, Atticus catches me and holds me tightly.

"Atticus, please tell me this is just a dream! Please tell me this isn't happening!" I sob over his metal breastplate. And he runs his hand over my head, sniffling.

"This isn't your fault. I know it's not." His voice trembles and he turns me away from the view of my mother.

I wish to the gods she'll move or breathe again. I wish the gods would allow me to hear her speak again.

This night doesn't feel real.

I want to join her side one more time, but my father's sadness and anger terrifies me. I pull away from Atticus and see my father turn to look at me.

"I'm so sorry, father." His eyes are red and swollen and there's nothing anger written across his face.

"We're going home. Now." He says coldly.

Atticus leads me to his horse and helps me up. Father carries his wife in his arms and Orion helps them both on his horse.

He has covered his face with my coat and we gently make our way back home. While speeding on the trail, I keep my head resting on Atticus' back the entire way back but every other moment, I'd find myself looking at my mother, hoping to see her move, even just an inch.

At one point, I see another strange shadow move between the trees as if watching us closely, but I'm too exhausted and heartbroken to care.

Those beasts already had their kill, what more could they want?

After a while, we finally make it to the castle gates. Once the other knights realize it's us, they blow their horn to let everyone know the king has returned.

The guards quickly open the gates, staring at my father's lap in shock as we pass by. I keep the side of my face resting against Atticus' back and once we stop in front of the stairs. I hear the doors slam open and see Riverlynn walk out with Lyla and other servants behind them.

I barely see Riverlynn's eyes turn to our father and back to me, shaking her head in utter disbelief and all I can do is keep a blank stare. Riverlynn covers her mouth and falls to the floor, sobbing in her hands.

I urge Atticus to hurry and help me down so I can go to my sister. Once my feet hit the ground, everything hurts, but I continue to charge up the stairs to be with my sister. With every step I take, my muscles pinch and feel like they're pulling and tearing apart.

I fall in front of my sister and instantly wrap her in my arms. She embraces me back and cries loudly against my chest which causes me to cry with her.

"I'm sorry, I'm so sorry." My voice shakes and I look up behind her to see Lyla in shock, trying hard to conceal her own tears with a handkerchief in her hand.

I reach my hand up and Lyla takes it before joining us on the ground and holding us both. The other staff and servants around us sniffle and cry to each other.

I lift Riverlynn off my chest and hold her cheeks with my hands. I try to speak but no words form and release. Her blue eyes are bright from her tears and her skin is soaked with tears.

Father walks past us and into the throne room and once we follow behind, we see two knights uncover a golden altar that's covered by roses. My mother would use the altar to pray to the gods. Never once did I ever think it'd be a place to rest her body.

Our father kindly asks all staff to help clean her up and prepare for her burial and once her body is uncovered, Riverlynn shields her eyes.

In the light, I can see every wound that tarnishes her beautiful skin and her rich red hair is soiled with mud, twigs and leaves.

"What happened?" She asks quietly, in shock at the sight before her. I pause briefly, emotionally and physically numb, glued to the ground. One of the servants moves mother's arm and I see four large gashes slit across her side which makes my anger boil to the point where I almost break down. But before I can react harshly, I disconnect from Riverlynn and Lyla.

"I need to go." My sister tries to keep me by her side, but I break away and go to my room alone while our mother is taken care of.

"Vivalda-" Our father tries to stop me, but I ignore, ashamed to face him.

I slowly make my way into my room and proceed to the washroom. Hunch over the small counter and when I look up into the mirror, I'm met with a face that has been through absolute hell. My night dress is ragged and torn to bits. There's cuts, scrapes and bruises all over my body and my hair looks like a rat's nest that's mended by dried mud. It looks like a million blood vessels have burst in my eyes, making them red and puffy.

I pull a lever on the wall that allows warm water to run and collect in a stone bowl in front of me. I splash water on my face which causes my skin to sting. I try to clean myself up, but the pain makes it difficult. I catch myself freezing and zoning out aimlessly, watching images replay in my head over and over. From losing my horse and running aimlessly through the forest to seeing terrifying creatures and suddenly waking up in my mother's arms. I don't want to keep watching the horror come back to life. It calls for too many emotions to pile on my shoulders, weighing down on me.

The rage, sadness and confusion is too much for me to handle to the point where I almost collapse. I do my best to continue rinsing the mud from my skin and hair when I hear three soft knocks at the bathroom door.

"Viv dear, it's me." Lyla says softly.

I want to be left alone now and probably forever.

Despite preferring to be alone, I'd hate to shut Lyla out because I know she means no harm and wants to help. Now's a bad time to shut others out too because I know they're also hurting.

I open the door, refusing to look at her and she follows behind me while I return to the sink. Lyla glides behind me and walks to the tub, turning on the water, waiting for it to run hot. I stare at my reflection, falling into a endless abyss, stuck firmly in my own thoughts.

"I'm here for you...you know that right?" She asks quietly. I take a moment to respond.

"You won't believe what happened...no one will." I whisper back.

Lyla turns off the water and the warm steam stings my skin.

"You've never given me a reason to not trust your word."

I stand up from the counter and slowly step back until my back hits the wall.

"I did this..." I whisper under my breath, crying.

"What do you mean, little one?" Lyla turns off the water, keeping her eyes on me.

I stand frozen to the ground, feeling my legs shake from the heaviness of my body. I begin to hyperventilate quickly.

"I did this!" I scream before falling to the ground and at the same time, Lyla catches me and slowly slides onto the floor with me.

I breathe rapidly, trying to talk and breathe properly at the same time, sounding absolutely hysterical, unable to control myself.

"If I had listened for once- if I had stayed home, this would have never happened. She would have made it home and I wouldn't feel this pain- I can't-" I begin wheezing frantically and Lyla sits silently, trying to comfort me with her gentle touch.

I'm being surrounded by four walls that are slowly closing in.

"She's not here anymore! Those monsters tore her to shreds right in front of me and I couldn't stop them! I didn't mean for this to happen!" I snap out of my shock when I feel a terrible stinging pain. I realize that while pushing my back against the wall, I've been digging my nails into the sides of my legs, tearing the skin along my thighs.

Lyla pulls my hands back to stop me from causing more harm and she encourages me to lay on my side and rest my head on her lap. By her grabbing my hand, I begin to calm down and breathe.

"Release." She says softly while holding me close to her. Her voice breaks and she cries softly with me. "No one will hear and no one will judge. I'm right here."

I proceed to scream and cry until my lungs and throat can no longer take it. My voice rebounds around the room, piercing my eardrum and Lyla continues to sooth me with her touch.

I can feel my heart breaking apart, piece by piece. Every artery is tearing and ripping apart. It doesn't stop.

After several moments, the screaming finally comes to a halt and I'm left lying on Lyla emotionally, physically and mentally numb. I feel disconnected from reality.

"I swear...those monsters...they're real. The shadows...they're real. And I swear they're going to pay for what they've done." I say while curling my fingers into a fist. "I don't know what to do." My cheeks burn from screaming and crying.

Lyla rubs my shoulder gently, sniffling. "All we can do is take it day by day. And no matter what you think, you are NOT to blame for your mother's death. I know you did everything you could and I know you were trying to help. Let's get you cleaned up and I'll send

River in to help. You both need each other more than you know."

I nod my head and slowly get off her lap. Her once white gown is now drowned with tears and filthy with dirt. She helps me stand up, hugs me and leaves the bathroom, closing the door behind her.

I take a moment to remove my torn dress, leaving nothing but my undergarments on and steadily step into the tub.

My leg muscles shake as I lower my body down to sit down. Everything hurts. Every single part of me feels torn.

Shortly, I hear a knock at the door, followed by a muffled voice.

"It's me." I hear River from the other side of the door.

She walks in cautiously and sits next to the tub.

Riverlynn

Seeing my sister in the state she's in is like witnessing a horror story come to life in a gruesome way. I can tell by her beaten face that she's in excruciating pain. She looks at me with her head tilted to the side and she tries to smile. Her cheeks are flaming red, her hair is matted and caked with mud and her skin is torn, scrapped, cut and bruised.

I sit on the ground next to her as she lays her head on the ledge of the stone tub. My body shudders after having a crying fit.

"What's going on out there?" Vivalda asks weakly. I take a deep breath before responding.

"Father is umm...organizing her burial as we speak. He's not ready." I lower my head, trying not to start crying again.

"None of us are." I nod my head and keep my gaze on the wall adjacent to me.

"I'm so sorry." She says even quieter and I quickly pivot my head to look at her before sitting up to get on her level.

"You keep apologizing, but what for? You've done nothing-" Her brown eyes are empty and emotionless.

"But I have. I should have listened to you and mother. Everyone's going to blame me-" It breaks me to know she thinks the way she does.

"Don't think like that. I know it's impossible to NOT think, but...listen." I grab a cup off the counter, scoop up water and run it over Vivalda's head, watching mud, dirt and leaves slip into the water.

"I am not mad or disappointed at all. We all learn. We grow. We love. We...lose. But as long as we stick together, we'll be okay." I refrain from sobbing and continue to help Vivalda clean herself up.

"We need to bury her in Alsfield. I know that's where she'd want to be." She says slowly.

"I knew you'd say that and I already mentioned it to father."

I gently brush out her hair and get all the mud washed off her skin and by the time we're finished, the water is dark brown, full of dirt, leaves and blood.

I exit the bathroom and open her wardrobe where I find Vivalda's dresses, blouses and skirts that are different shades of blue with black or silver detailing.

I spot one of her favorite long sleeve dark blue dresses with silver sparkling detailing on the shoulders and bust. I take it off the rack and find a pair of silver flat shoes to bring to her. Once I walk back into the bathroom, I see her blankly staring at herself.

"I picked your favorite dress." I set her clothes on the counter and she doesn't move an inch. "I'll wait out here until you're ready." I walk out and close the bathroom door and approach the window where I see dark clouds hovering in the sky while it continues to rain. I've never felt so heartbroken and depressed before. I don't know what to do.

Everything's about to change. For the best or worst, I do not know.

The bathroom door opens and Vivalda walks out slowly, visibly shaking. When I approach her, I notice she's holding a gold necklace charm in her hand, grasping it closely to her.

"Mother's necklace." I say softly. Vivalda uncurls her fingers to show the gold sword pendant.

"I never told her how much I loved her." She holds back tears as she fiddles with the sword pendant.

Knowing our mother gave it to her brings me a glimmer of hope because I know it means a lot for Vivalda to have.

I wrap my arm around her waist and we make our way back to the throne room where everyone waits for us.

We walk down the corridors silently and we're stopped by our chef William. He turns to us and instantly hugs us. We both wrap our arms around his shoulders and torso, embracing his comforting gesture. He looks at us with deep sadness in his eyes. Seeing him so sad breaks my heart all over again.

"If you both ever need anything, I'm always here. Your mother was and will forever be one of the most amazing people I've had the honor of meeting." William is like a grandfather to us and has been here for most of our lives. Him and mother were close friends. My heart aches for him and the rest of the castle staff.

Once we join our father's side, he kneels over his wife with the guards and knights behind us, bowing, paying their respects to their fallen queen.

Even though it pains me, I can't help but look at her lifeless body. I can't believe it. I've never seen her so peaceful and silently still. I can hear her voice echoing in my mind like a haunting melody.

Her long wavy red hair is laid beautifully to her sides with small white flowers in it. She holds a bouquet of red dahlias which have always been her favorite and father dresses her in a red sparkly gown that has gold lace embellishments on the shoulders. Despite her wounds, she looks as beautiful as ever.

I feel my arm being tightly squeezed and I turn to see Vivalda staring at mother with silent tears sliding down her face.

I lean my head on her shoulder and she hugs me close to her side.

After a long moment of silence, father stands, hesitating to leave his wife's side. He turns around, his cheeks, eyes and ears are red and tears rest on his beard.

He walks up to us and hugs us gently, sniffling and whimpering softly. We both hug him back, refusing to let go and I can hear Vivalda crying in his shoulder.

He doesn't say a word after hugging us and before he goes back to our mother, Vivalda grabs his hand, not wanting him to walk away. She keeps her eye on mother's body, zoning out.

"We'll be okay." He takes a step back and turns back to the altar where Lyla lays down more flowers and her tears fall onto the petals.

She gently moves mother's hair, running her fingers through it and while she finishes tidying up the altar, the knights behind us stand up at the same time. When I look over my shoulder, I immediately lock eyes with Atticus and Orion who are at the front of the group. Atticus smiles at me and I smile slightly back.

"I sent my men to pick up Kyson and Rowan, they should be here shortly." Atticus says quietly and I'm grateful for his gesture. I know they'd want to say their goodbyes, along with the rest of the kingdom.

In order to slow down time, we sit by mothers side and tell everyone stories of her past and good memories we all share together. Father recalls the day she asked him to marry her and how it was a beautiful coincidence because he had planned to ask her at the same time. Fate brought them together at the perfect time.

Vivalda sits quietly to herself, leaning against the altar, resting her head next to mother's side. The red roots of her hair blend into mother's hair as she twists her hair around each other's.

The front doors open and I turn to see Kyson and Rowan being guided by two guards.

Vivalda continues to play with mother's hair and Kyson and his father bow to us and Kyson walks over to Vivalda, kneeling next to her. Without a single word, Kyson holds her and she sits up to lean her head on his chest. Kyson's eyes grow heavy with tears and before I can move, I feel a hand rest on my shoulder. I look up and see Rowan standing over me. He helps me stand up and he hugs me gently.

"I'm so sorry for your loss." He whispers quietly. After Kyson and his father express their condolences, Orion finds his way over and stands with me. We take one last moment to be in the queen's presence and watch as mother's body is picked up and rested into a separate wooden box that's covered in flowers.

Once father is ready, he, Atticus, Orion and other guards carry mother out of the castle and we make our way to Alsfield.

I walk on one side with Orion while Vivalda and Kyson walk together on the opposite side.

Once the doors open we're met by several people waiting patiently at the castle gates, wanting to pay their respects to the queen. The sight before us is both powerful and heartbreaking. Children, men and women of all ages with heavy saddened eyes.

I look at Vivalda whose eyes widen in surprise. She shakes her head subtly. I can tell she's not prepared to face her people. She keeps her head held low, trying not to look up.

When we reach the bottom of the stairs, I see many people holding flowers out between the metal bars. I pick up the sides of my long pink dress and I run over to them with Orion switching places with another knight so he can follow behind me.

I can hear the cries of our people the closer I get. I look at each of them and an older woman stands in front of me, holding out a bouquet of mixed red and white roses. I take the flowers and hold her hand. She smiles and I manage to return a smile as if to silently say thank you.

More people step up to the gate with flowers in hand and Orion steps up to help hold some of them. Once we've gathered every flower, a small high pitched voice emerges from the crowd. A little girl steps up to the gate, I kneel down to her level and she holds out a large sunflower.

"Can you give this to Princess Vivalda, please?" Her kind gesture makes my heart melt and I nod happily.

"I'd love to. I know she will love it." I smile at the little girl and stand up to face everyone. It takes me a moment to find my words because I simply don't know what to say.

"Thank you all for being here and sending your love that never goes unseen or unappreciated. I know my mother appreciates you all for being here today. Thank you." My voice begins to quiver and I turn back to meet up with everyone else who's begun to cross the bridge to Alsfield.

We take our time to catch up and once we do, the men lower the wooden bed down and Vivalda stands in front of the crowd next to father. I join her side and hand the sunflower to her and she looks at it confused.

Vivalda

I stare at the flower that Riverlynn holds, confused as to why she hands it to me. "A child wished for you to have this." She says quietly and I shakily take the flower from her hand.

"Thank you." I whisper and she and Orion take the bunches of flowers they hold and lay them inside around the borders of the wooden casket

I see Kyson observing the wounds that scatter across my face. "I'll explain later." I whisper to him and he nods his head silently. "Thank you for coming." I say while watching two knights digging a hole in the ground, preparing for mother's burial.

"There's nowhere I'd rather be right now. In a way, your mother was like my own. But I can't begin to imagine how you must feel." I begin to disassociate and zone out, letting my thoughts crowd my mind like parasites.

She was alive moments ago and now we're about to say goodbye.

There's no one to snap me out of the nightmare that continues to play and follow.

Once mother's burial is prepared, the king stands in front of everyone to share his last words. Kyson is hooked on my left arm and Riverlynn on my right with Orion standing with her.

"Aladora was perhaps the greatest leader Vassuren has ever had. We and our people grew from nothing and because of her strength and determination, our empire grew strong. Though it will feel impossible, she would not want us to stay sad forever."

Father joins the knights and they all work together to lift mother's casket and carefully lower her into the grave. My father picks up a shovel but by the broken look on his face, he doesn't have the heart to cover his wife, so he leaves the job to the other knights and stands with the rest of us.

Watching her body disappear under the soil tears a massive hole in my heart. Riverlynn cries into father's chest and I remain staring at the mountain of dirt.

After more long moments of endless tears and cries, father and the knights retreat back inside the castle. Rowan goes back home to Palavon with the rest of the villagers and Riverlynn, Orion, Kyson and I stay back, sitting around mother's grave.

"How does someone move on from something like this?" Riverlynn asks, sniffling and rubbing her tomato red nose with her sleeve. My eyes hurt from crying so much and I feel like falling asleep on the grassy ground.

"I don't think we do. Instead, we just...cope, I guess." I say, exhaling deeply.

"Well then, how do we cope with such a big loss? The grieving process is completely new to us." I look up at Riverlynn and scoff.

"You ask too many questions, you know that?" A small smile forms on her face.

"Hey, I got it from one of you two."

From behind us, I hear birds beginning to sing and the rain lightens up to a sprinkle. I zone out into the trees and slight paranoia creeps up my spine. But then a thought comes to mind once I remember what lies beyond the trees.

"Do you mind helping me up?" I ask Kyson quietly and he stands up to get me on my feet. I walk over to Riverlynn and hold my hand down to her.

"What?" She asks, confused.

"We're going to the safe place for a little bit." Riverlynn smiles when she realizes what I'm talking about and takes my hand.

My sister and I lead the men deeper into the forest, searching for the stone statue mother showed us. After a nice silent walk, we finally find her, surrounded by rocks and trees.

The stone is soaked and covered with leaves and other debris from the storm. Kyson and Orion analyze the statue, confused.

"Oh wow, what is this?" Kyson asks while looking up at the statue in awe.

"I don't know exactly. Our mother would come here to relax and take a breather." Kyson curiously walks around the statue and he looks like a child who's seeing the most incredible thing ever.

I continue to explain more details about the statue and its correlation to my mother.

"Am I the only one who finds this a tiny bit creepy? I mean, someone HAD to have sculpted this, right?" Kyson says superstitiously, peeking his head from behind the statue. I shrug my shoulders and sit on a boulder next to the statue, getting lost in my thoughts.

Orion sits on the wet grass and invites Riverlynn to sit next to him. I can feel my sister's gaze fall on me silently.

"Do you wish to talk about it? If not, there's no rush. I figure it's easier to speak about without others around." Riverlynn asks calmly.

Kyson hears the conversation and walks around to sit next to me on the rock.

"I don't know. I think it's too soon." I keep my head lowered while twiddling my fingers. I want to tell them what happened but I don't know if they'd believe me.

"Do you say that for our sake? Or for yours? We all saw her body, Vivalda. I'm prepared to hear the worst of it because I don't know how long I can go without knowing what happened. Soon or later, you'll have to tell father too. Starting with us might be a lot easier and I'm not here to scold or judge." Her tone is soft and gentle. I can tell she's being genuine. And she's right, telling them would be a lot easier than telling the king, which I'm already dreading.

"I don't know about the rest of you, but I have all day to listen. So, you are more than welcome to take your time." Kyson adds while getting comfortable, leaning his back against the body of the statue.

I take a moment to gather my thoughts and once I find my voice, I tell them every detail I recall that lead up to mother's death. While speaking, I find myself holding the gold necklace pendant that rests against my chest. Without breaking, I tell them everything, describe every single detail.

Once I begin to mention the shadowy monsters, all of them look at me with bewilderment. I start to feel embarrassed because I'm sure I sound absolutely insane and that I'm making up everything.

Once I finish retelling, all of them sit silently on the verge of tears.

"I know it's hard to believe. I have a hard time believing it myself. But everything I witnessed was more real than any nightmare I've ever had." Instead of feeling intense sadness, I'm left sitting in boiling rage that intensifies as time passes.

"Mother told us a silly story growing up to help us sleep. She told us generations ago that the world was flourishing with some kind of magic. I don't remember much of it." Orion thinks to himself for a moment and shrugs his shoulders.

"So, we're left to believe that silly little stories are coming to...life?" His question makes my mind fall into a rabbit hole and I'm left with more questions than answers.

"Think about it. The tales had to be witnessed by someone in order for the stories to be told. Maybe that someone was never taken seriously because they were telling the impossible. Therefore, being turned into a 'silly story' to tell children." I pause and take a moment, realizing how insane I sound because none of them respond to me or acknowledge what I say.

"I know it all sounds insane, but I swear, I speak truly and if you all were there, you'd be desperate for others to believe you too." I rest my face in my hands, leaning over my knees that are pulled up to my chest.

"So...what do we do?" Riverlynn exhales deeply and I shrug my shoulders, having no idea how to answer.

"There's nothing we can do until father hears and takes action. My pain hinders me from being able to focus properly but I think it's best we all try to rest and see what tomorrow brings." Orion stands up nervously, unsure of what to say.

"I will wait to hear orders from the king and until then, I'll inform the rest of the knights to keep an ear out for suspicious activity." I nod my head and Kyson helps me step down from the boulder.

"No matter what, nothing will bring her back." I growl before feeling Kyson's hand rubbing my back. I slowly look at him as the dim sunlight makes his green eyes pop beautifully.

"Let's get you inside to rest, okay?" He asks as he gently helps me off the boulder. Before following the path, I gently pull Kyson's hand back and he looks at me, confused.

"Will you stay with me tonight? I know that sounds really um...far-fetched but I thought it'd be easier for me and-" I begin to slow down and stutter over my words, embarrassed. An eager smile forms across his face and his cheeks begin to blush.

"Wouldn't that anger the king?" Kyson laughs nervously and I shrug my shoulders.

"I don't think so. If anything, I think he'd understand. I just don't want to be alone tonight and I know River will want Orion by her side as well." Kyson smiles and holds my hand tighter in a comforting way.

"I'd love to, as long as you're comfortable." He says sincerely and I nod my head to assure him that's what I want.

Once we get inside the castle through the back door, we walk down the halls that's boarded with gray stone walls. Upon approaching Riverlynn's room, Lyla rushes from the other end of the hall.

"Your highness, the king is requesting your presence at his throne." She says, catching her breath. I can tell she was looking for us.

"Did he say why? I'd much rather be resting right now than-"

"He says it's important and he'd like to speak to you alone." She looks calm, but her tone is urgent. I look at Kyson and he looks just as confused as I.

"I'll wait for you in your room." He whispers before slipping past me and he walks into my room.

I take off down the hall and to the throne room as quickly as I can and when I open the door, I see father pacing back and forth in front of the gold altar that is now covered by a large blanket. Once the door closes behind me, he turns around to look at me.

"There you are. I was hoping...if you wouldn't mind...um-" I approached him slowly.

"You want to know what happened." A sad smile forms on his face and he slowly nods his head.

"If it's too soon, I'd completely understand. I just can't help but wish to know." I feel my stomach shrivel up and deflate and my hands begin to sweat.

I follow him to his chair and I stand before him, hesitating to speak, but since I'm here, there's no turning back. Father can tell I'm scared to speak, so he begins the conversation by asking a question.

"Why did you leave the castle when you were deliberately told to stay put?" He speaks in a more serious tone, trying not to break. I can tell he doesn't want to get mad at me or have a reason to be. I take a deep breath, stalling up to every last second I'm given.

"I...just wanted to help find-" I'm stopped by my father holding up his pointer finger.

"How did you find her? Tell me everything." I swallow the lump in my throat and proceed to tell him everything I remember. I mention the mysterious tree, the black shadows, waking up in my mother's arms and the last words she told me. And while telling him everything, I'm too scared to look him in the eye. Instead, I gaze at the floor while holding mother's necklace pendants tightly in my hand.

"I truly believe that the creatures we saw in the forest are what our people are seeing as well. We should act fast and figure out what they are and where they come from before they have a chance to take another life-" Father gets up from his chair, holding his hand to his chin, pondering silently to himself.

"She was on her way home." He mumbles to himself quietly to the point where I can't hear him.

"What?" I ask quietly, turning in a half circle to follow him.

"You left to 'help' get your mother to return home and instead, she had to stop to help you while on her way? All because you decided to go against her command?" Anger begins to fill his tone and my heart thumps against my chest and falls to my stomach.

"Well, I didn't-" I try stepping closer to him to ease his anger and he instantly snaps around with his eyes full of tears and his hands curled into fists.

"SHE COULD HAVE MADE IT HOME!" I jolt and stumble backward from the force of his shout. "AND

YOU STOPPED HER!?" The sudden spike of intense rage frightens me. I've never seen him so angry.

"No...NO! She said-" I speak timidly, afraid of unintentionally escalating the situation but he talks over me loudly.

"You had one job...one job, Vivalda! And now, your disobedience has cost us your mother's life!" He gets close to me, pointing his finger at my face. At this point, I'm quivering so bad that I feel like my knees will buckle under me.

"Why would you say that? She, herself, said that she didn't know if she was on the right path in the first place!" I raise my voice louder, following my father as he walks around, disappointed, angry and ashamed.

"Do you really expect me to believe the tales you tell? 'Foggy monsters in the shapes of demons', do you understand how absurd that sounds?" I stomp my foot down, fed up with his arguing and him refusing to listen to me.

"You saw her body! You saw her wounds! If it were a bear or even a wolf, then I'd say so, but it wasn't. How could I make up something so bizarre if my own eyes didn't see it?" I try my best to speak in a way that makes him understand, but by the anguish in his eyes, he won't budge.

"You've always been one to have your head in the clouds, Vivalda, and now it's fogging your mind with hallucinations because you can't own up to your mistake." I almost thrash my arms down, but quickly compose myself. I keep my gaze on the ground because looking at him only frustrates me more because the look on his face shatters me into a million pieces.

Does he truly blame me for mother's death? Or is this the first stage of grief?

"I know I messed up and I know there's nothing I can say or do that will make up for my foolishness. I didn't mean for any of this to happen. To me, it's more absurd to think this is the outcome I foresaw or wanted. But there is something out there that's far more menacing than anything you could ever imagine and we have to do something before another life is taken. Our people don't deserve to witness what we did." The king walks back to his throne, shaking his head and running his hand over his beard. I stand still in the middle of the room, continuing to stare at the ground, waiting for his response.

"Your mother's life mattered more to me than commoners ever will." My eyes widen and I immediately look up to face him before slowly walking closer to him.

"You don't mean that." He doesn't say a word and instead, he shrugs his shoulders before slouching back on his chair. Now, my anger begins to rise and I speak to him in such a serious tone, but I know nothing I say will help.

I've given up trying to reason with a man who's just lost his wife. I understand his anger and his disbelief but nothing could have prepared me for the way he raised his voice at me or the fear that struck my heart.

"My mother, the queen, cared more about 'commoners' than the crown on her head. She's been gone for barely a day and you've already forgotten what she stood for. Lucky for you..." I shake my head, holding back tears, refusing to let him see me cry. "I'll never forget." I march out of the throne room and go back to my room.

From down the hall, I can hear my sister, Kyson and Orion talking in my room with the door open.

I awkwardly stand in the doorway with my shoulders hunching over, my hands curled into fists and my teeth gritted. They all turn to me and their smiles slowly fade away.

"How did the talk with father go? You look a bit...tense." Riverlynn asks while sitting on my bed and Kyson and Orion standing by the window. I shake my head and walk in the room, closing the door behind me and slamming my back against it. I look up at the ceiling while batting my eyelids to avoid tearing up. I exhale sharply and they wait patiently for a response. Once my thoughts are gathered, wrap my arms around my torso and look at my sister.

"He didn't believe me when I spoke about the monsters in the forest." Riverlynn scoffs. "I saw that coming. I figured he'd be stubborn." She rolls her shoulders and stretches.

"He also blames me for mother's death." I say numbly and everyone immediately turns to look at me in shock. Riverlynn jumps off the bed and stands furiously. "He did not." She says sternly and I nod my head.

"AND he said he doesn't care for the safety of our people so I don't think he'll be doing anything productive anytime soon." I walk over to sit in the chair that's next to my bed. I rest my face in my hand, trying to wrap my head around everything and it's nearly impossible.

"Maybe I am the reason..." I whisper to myself thinking no one can hear and Riverlynn speeds around the bed to stand in front of me.

"NO. Absolutely not. You are NOT the cause of mother's death. If you were, you know she would have dragged you down with her." She tries to lighten the situation but it unfortunately doesn't distract me from everything I'm feeling.

"It's getting late, we should go to bed. I'll figure out stuff tomorrow." I get up and walk past my sister to retrieve a long sleeve night dress from my wardrobe.

I walk into the washroom and hear Orion and Riverlynn leave the room. I find myself staring in the mirror once again. My bottom lip is cut, my arms and legs are covered in small gashes and scraps and my ribs are badly bruised. Everything hurts but at the same time, I feel numb.

After changing out of my dress, I gather my hair and twist it into a thick bun, securing it with a blue ribbon. The red spiraling streak in my hair makes me think about my mother and I can't help but reminisce about the days when I'd sit with her, playing with her hair.

I try not to dwell on it for too long because I don't want to keep Kyson waiting.

I leave the washroom and see him leaning against the wall, looking out the window at the setting sun. He looks at me and smiles softly. I proceed to sit on my bed, staring out the window with him. Dark grey clouds continue to cover the sky and it proceeds to rain.

"I know you'll disagree, but what he says isn't true. Sometimes the path of grief causes the ones we love most to turn into someone unrecognizable. But I'm sure once he's had time to process, he'll realize how wrong he is." He keeps his hands in the pockets of his black pants and I look at him without him noticing.

"You should have heard him. I've never heard him shout so angrily. The rage and overbearing sadness in his eyes, the way he approached me…I've never-" I begin to break and cry into my hands, not wanting to draw Kyson's attention, but before I know it, I sits next to me, wrapping his arm around me and pulling me to rest against his chest.

He doesn't say a single word and instead, he just holds me while I cry and once I manage to calm down, I look at him with uncontrollable tears streaming down my face.

"I don't know how to fix this." Kyson rests his hand on my cheek, wiping the tears with his thumb and his green eyes peering into mine.

"You don't have to. Not right now at least. Give it time. Nothing and no one heals in a day." He smiles and I smile back.

He walks around to the other side of the bed and I lift up the sheets to get ready for bed. Kyson instantly falls asleep next to me and I stay awake long enough to see the sun go down completely. Eventually, I managed to close my eyes and fall asleep.

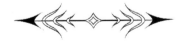

I open my eyes to bright blue skies and white fluffy clouds. I roll my head to the side and realize I'm lying on a thick patch of grass that stretches far and wide.

There's no mountains, castles or trees in sight. Just plain green grass that sways with a gentle breeze.

A shadow grows over me and the sunlight is blocked out. I look up and see a dark figure standing over me and once my eyes dilate, I see a woman look down and smile.

I know this face.

"Hello, mother." I say softly and watch as her cheeks raise, pulling up the corners of her lips and widening her beautiful smile. Her scarlet red hair falls over her shoulders and she walks around to help me stand up. I take a moment to simply look at her, emotionally. Before I can say anything, she squeals happily and runs past me

I watch for a moment as she runs through the thick green grass that stretches beyond the horizon.

"Follow me!" She shouts ahead of me and I run to join her side, laughing and giggling uncontrollably and running freely. This moment reminds me of when I was a child, running with mother down the castle halls, playing hide-and-seek.

We continue to run until we're startled by a loud crash of thunder. I look behind us and see the white clouds turn black and gather together as if to make one giant cloud. Instantly, mother takes my hand and runs off frantically. She screams in horror as I trail behind her but unable to let out a sound. I run as fast as the massive clouds begin to approach closer. The endless field of grass makes it feel like I'm running in place, gaining no traction.

Mother stops suddenly and looks at me. She squeezes my hand tightly and whispers something inaudibly.

"I don't know what you're saying." I say, looking back as the clouds fall to the ground and spread across the field, killing every blade of grass it touches and spreading like a disease. Thunder continues to rumble loudly in the sky, shaking the ground.

I look at mother, hoping she'd repeat what she said, but instead, all she does is look at me, smile and rest her hands on my shoulders. Before I know it, she shoves me backwards and a large black hole appears under me and I fall into a never-ending void. As I fall, I watch her turn around and allow the clouds to devour her and the last thing I see is a bright light caused by a strange explosion that echoes down the black pit. I let out the loudest scream as I continue to fall and the pitch-black crater swallows me whole.

Loud thunder causes me to jolt in my bed and wake up. I sit up quickly, gasping for air as if I wasn't breathing during the strange dream that just occurred. My heart races rapidly to the point where I can't control it.

I slowly turn to sit on the edge of my bed and I light a large candle that sits on my nightstand. I run my hands over my face and listen to my heartbeat pound throughout my body. My attention is turned to my window when I hear the wind raging outside, causing the frame to creak.

Once I manage to relax, I stand up and walk to the window with my feet dragging heavily on the ground. I walk up to the window so I can close the curtains, but before I do, I notice a small red flower resting on the wooden ledge. I reach over to grab it but notice its stem is growing out of the wooden frame. Due to my exhaustion and my aching pain, I don't care to pay much attention to it. For all I know, I could still be asleep.

I retreat back to my bed but before I can turn around fully, I see another red flower sprouting from the wooden floor. And when I look at my bedroom floor, I see even more flowers trailing towards my door. At first, I think they were left by the castle staff to say their condolences since it's the same flowers we buried my mother with, but how are they growing out of the ground?

I look over at my bed and see Kyson rolled on his side, snoring softly, indicating he's in a deep sleep. I quietly follow the trail of strange flowers, ensuring not to wake him up.

I exit the room and close the door behind me and when I look down the hall, I see a colorful trail of red, yellow and white flowers. The mysterious trail leads all the way down to the end of the hall to the back side door. I stare down the hall that's illuminated by lanterns and torches, hesitating to follow. I question whether I should follow or if I should wake my sister. But again, a small part of me thinks this is nothing but an odd dream, so my curiosity gets the best of me and I proceed to follow.

I walk lightly to avoid waking someone up or grabbing a knight or guard's attention. I walk to the side of the trail, avoiding stepping on the flowers and crushing them. I keep my eyes fixated on the ground, confused by why they have mysteriously shown up in the castle. I've never seen something so interesting.

Once I reach the back door, I see the small flowers grow up and scatter across the bottom of it. I slowly open the door and I'm immediately hit by the chilly breeze blowing against my face. It's sprinkling lightly and thunder continues to rumble in the sky, lighting up the darkness every other moment. Thankfully there are lanterns outside to keep the paths lit.

I look down and see the flower trail ends at the door, leaving me unsure of where to go or what to do. I take a step out, wrapping my arms around my chest, trying to keep warm. I look up at the sky, seeing the sky begin to turn blue, indicating the sun will begin to rise soon.

I turn around to go back inside, but feel my foot get caught on something strong. I try forcefully pulling my leg up, but it remains stuck to the grassy ground.

I lift the bottom of my dress up and see a green vine wrapped around my ankle. I try pulling away and breaking it, but it holds on strong as it's anchored into the muddy ground.

I crouch down to gently unravel the vine from my skin and before I can stand, something bizarre catches my attention. Out of the corner of my eye, I watch as flowers bloom rapidly before my eyes, painting a new path towards the stables.

I remain frozen where I stand, staring fearfully at the harmless plants that continue to grow and sprout.

This has to be a dream and if not a dream, a trap.

I figure I'm just being paranoid because I don't think flowers are capable of causing danger and as long as I remain on castle grounds, I should be okay.

I walk steadily as the trail of flowers continues to scatter ahead. Once I reach the stables, I turn around and see the trail behind me disappearing slowly. I begin to feel uneasy but it's too late to turn around and go back. I walk through the doors and I immediately see the flowers stretch over the bridge that leads into Alsfield. Following an unknown phenomenon into a forest late at night doesn't sound like a pleasing idea, but I'm too curious to turn around and go back inside.

As my foot touches the wooden bridge, the most incredible thing happens before my eyes. The trail of flowers begins to...glow. Each little petal lights up like a nightlight, lighting up my path. I stumble back slightly, confused as starstruck.

I squat down to touch the harmless flowers and when I barely graze a small petal, a bright flash of light emits from the forest in front of me. And I stand in absolute awe when I see the forest turn into a glowing utopia. Each and every single flower, tree, bush and blade of grass glows, erasing every inch of darkness.

I can't help but be captivated by the forest's supernatural beauty. I stay sitting close to the ground, gently holding a small flower between my fingers and a random small voice in the back of my mind that tells me to keep going forward.

I follow the glowing flowers into the forest. The trail ahead of me continues to illuminate and before I can walk deeper into Alsfield, I stop when I see my mother's grave. Tears fill my eyes when I see beautiful white and red glowing flowers scatter beautifully over her grave. Something about the sight feels so peaceful and comforting at the same time in a way I can't explain.

At this point, I'm quite certain that I'm still dreaming, but it's a dream I don't want to end. And I choose this over a terrifying nightmare.

I continue following the glowing path as I'm led deeper into the forest. Once I pass a wall of thick trees, I see a bright white light flash out of the corner of my eye. The trail of flowers leads me in the same direction and after a moment of walking, it leads me to the stone statue. I stop in front of the statue and watch the path of colorful flowers circle around the stone.

A part of me is scared to be outside the castle alone. Being in the dark made me experience the worst things I never thought possible but something deep down reassures me that I'm okay. I'm safe in this space, just like my mother was.

I observe the statue as glowing green moss begins to spread sparsely at the bottom of the statue and a few different colored flowers spread out across the figure's body. I walk around and see a large purple flower bloom at the back of the statue's head and it looks as if it ties two pieces of her hair together. Bright colors cascade across the dark stone, making it look like a decorative art piece.

Why am I here?

I think to myself and remember why my mother would come here. She'd use this space to release her stress. Maybe that's why I'm here, to unleash the overwhelming built up emotions that weigh down on my shoulders. But the problem is, I feel numb, there's no scream or cry that boils in my core.

I step on a small boulder that's in front of the statue and I reach my hand out to touch the stone figure's hand that rests on its chest.

"I don't know what to do." I take a deep breath and I'm startled when all light and color from the flowers turns off like an intense light switch.

I look around and see the glowing color of every single plant illuminate brighter than before. Before I can pull away from the statue, I feel something move under my hand. I look at the statue and see the hand moving. The fingers curl around mine gently and the bumpy stone texture slowly softens.

It still feels like cold stone to the touch, but it also moves like a normal body. I begin to shake, hesitant to look up, frightened. When I look up, I see the stone statue transforms into an ethereal woman with long white flowing hair and white glowing eyes. Her entire body has a green aura that glows around her gray skin.

Once the stone mask is dropped and it crackles away from every strand of hair and her stone dress turns into flowing fabric, she slowly looks down at me and smiles. I feel like turning and running but I take a step back, almost stumbling off the rock, but the woman keeps hold of my hand and stops me from falling. I quickly take a step down, forcefully pulling away from her grasp.

I stand still on the ground, staring at her confused and waiting to see what'll happen. The mysterious woman breaks away from the boulders that surround her feet and she approaches me slowly.

"Hello Vivalda." Her voice is soft and has a strong echo that sounds intimidating. Hearing her speak sends shivers down my spine. I try backing away from her but she follows steadily keeping her eyes on me.

How does she know my name?

"It's easy to know when I'm in the presence of a daughter of the almighty Aladora. Aside from looking just like her, you have the same curiosity qualities as her." I feel my knees grow weak and my heart races.

I feel myself slowly back up into a tree and I instantly yelp and jolt away when I feel a strange vibration crawl up my back. I turn around to see the bark on the tree trunk glow. Light blue particles pulsate in the cracks of the bark like moving veins.

"Had I known you'd be so shaken, I wouldn't have called you here and I would have waited." The woman laughs.

She looks so kind and gentle and she continues to smile softly at me. Her lips are dark gray and she has giant leaves coming out of the side of her head that almost resemble large ears.

I can't fathom how this is possible.

"Wh-who are you and how...how do you know my mother?" I attempt to bravely take a step towards her. Her face turns downwards for a split moment before she smiles once more.

"Come with me." She says before turning away with her long white gown trailing behind her.

Nope. This is definitely a dream. I need to wake up. I need to wake up.

"You're more than welcome to go, but I can assure you, you'll want to see and hear what's waiting for you." She continues to walk away.

I instantly realize she can hear every thought that floats loudly in my mind but her words pique my interest and I decide to follow her cautiously, leaving several feet between us.

I look down at the bottom of her gown and see the earth below her blooming and glowing everywhere she steps as if she walks on a path of illuminating magic. I'm dying to ask a million questions but know I should be patient and wait to see what she has to say.

Deep in the forest, she leads me to a gigantic tree that outgrows the rest. It's thicker than the width of two horses and its branches hold giant leaves. Its bark has colorful veins that grow and pulsate up its trunk and it looks like it's slowly moving, as if it's breathing.

I walk past the woman and cautiously approach the tree. Its blue veins are so captivating that I can't help but gently lay my hand on the trunk and I feel the veins moving like hundreds of small caterpillars under my fingertips. Once I'm able to focus, I can hear a faint thumping sound coming from within its body. It sounds like a band of drums beating together to create the most calming sound. It sounds like a majestic heartbeat.

The tall woman approaches my side and I instantly back away from the tree. She turns around and leans back against the tree, extending her arms to the side. As she does, the tree branches move in unison, curling over her fingertips and around her arms. Her body is pulled closely to the trunk and her back begins to morph into the tree as if she and nature are being bound as one. A whirlwind of emotions surges within me, leaving me breathless with excitement. It's as if time itself pauses, allowing me to fully absorb the breathtaking beauty that surrounds me. She's unlike anything I've ever witnessed in the most beautiful dream I've ever had.

She's created a throne.

I continue to stare in awe as she sits with the tree, not causing it any harm. She sits comfortably and looks at me, smiling. I wait impatiently for her to speak.

"I am Silva, the keeper of the forest." I step forward, mesmerized by her voice.

I sit down in the soft grass and listen. Her voice echoes softly through the air. Something about her voice feels safe and comforting and the more she speaks, the more tension I feel releasing from my body.

"How are you...here? How is all of this possible?" I gesture to the glowing wonderland that sways and dances around me.

"Explaining how I came to be is not a simple task. I came to your world thousands of years ago to protect the balance of life after watching humanity struggle for what feels like an eternity. I came to Vassuren when your grandfather was crowned king. Do you know much about him?" She asks and I shake my head.

"Not really. No one really asked about mother's ancestors. When they were brought up, there was always uneasy tension." Silva raises one of her dark grey brows and tilts her head to the side and speaks in a deeper tone.

"Aladora's father was a terrible ruler, husband and father. During his reign, the kingdom suffered due to his suffocating ignorance and ego. He put himself higher than any person in the world, including your mother, his only child and his wife. He neglected his people and raged unprovoked war. When the kingdom was on the verge of its downfall, your mother took the throne by force and banished your grandfather, ending his treacherous leadership." I lower my head, briefly thinking to myself, slightly overwhelmed by the information this new being shares.

"How do you know this?" I look up and she sits up tall.

"I was sent here by a higher being and when my body found its place on the ground, I was forced to remain coated in stone. Unable to move and unable to speak. Your mother found me here and she'd visit me almost every night. She was never afraid of my strange presence and instead, she shared with me her struggles with me and that's how I got to know about your family. She told me everything, unaware that despite my stone gaze, I could see and hear it all without being able to move." Goosebumps cause the hair on my neck, arms and legs to stand and I'm left feeling overbearing shock.

"She never told me." I say quietly, falling into my own thoughts. I look at her, confused. "The darkness of her family line was nothing she wished to speak about. She believed it was her burden and hers alone. When her father's reign ended, she made it her mission to never allow herself or her offspring to fall into tyranny ever again."

Hearing her talk about my mother makes my heart ache. It's still hard to believe she's not here.

I want to ask so many more questions regarding my mother's past, but I think it's best for a dark past to be left where it is and I don't think this being will have the answer to everything regarding my mother.

"Okay, I'm sorry but I have to ask. What you say is true, correct? This. All of this...magic is real? You are...real?" I stumble over my words, trying to make sense of everything I see and hear.

"Yes." She responds and I feel myself zoning out aimlessly, staring at the glowing flowers around me.

"If you've been here for so long, why didn't you come to life sooner?" Silva takes a deep breath and at the same time, the wood that connects to her body creaks.

"It was against my morals to come to life in front of a human." I could see the sadness behind her glowing eyes. "If it's against your 'morals', why have you come to life before me?" Silva takes another deep breath, causing the world around to breathe with her.

"I was forced to remain still until someone worthy of my presence and power could wake me. My magic called you here and by following it and believing in it, you woke me. I can hear all of the questions you have. I know you're anxious and scared, so I will try to make this quick." I sit up and forward, ready to hear more of what she has to say. I anticipate that she will talk about something else important.

"The creatures that are responsible for your mother's death are forces of dark magic. I sensed their presence while I stood frozen and I knew it was only a matter of time until I'd be awoken. The first attack that resulted in the queen's death was only the beginning." I immediately jump to my feet and look Silva in the eyes.

"I knew it. No one believes me. How do we get rid of them?" Silva cuts me off by raising her pointer finger, trying to calm my boiling rage.

"For one, patience is important. This is a situation I'm still understanding myself. But before we try to find a solution, there's something you need to know."

My shoulder relaxes and I go back to focusing on her words. My heart races with a mixture of anger and anticipation.

"There is much about your world that you have yet to learn about. Forces of magic have walked alongside you since far before you were born. Many years ago, these beings, known as Serafaes, coexisted with humans. But unfortunately, that peace was torn by a force far more evil than one could imagine. Now, there are very few of us left. Thankfully, no one ever suspected my true physical form. Not even your mother."

I slowly pace back and forth, overwhelmed, feeling like my mind is going to explode. My skin starts to tingle and my hands begin to go numb. Despite being surrounded by so many plants, it's hard to breathe.

"My mother would have told me. H-how do I know this isn't just some kind of dream that's nothing but a nightmare in disguise? Surely, I'll wake up and all of this won't be here. YOU won't be here and I will go back to-" I clench my hands to my chest, feeling my heart pound against the walls of my chest and I lose my train of thought.

"Human dreams are quite an interesting concept. But I can assure you, you'd never find someone like me in a dream." I can feel Silva's stern gaze on me as I continue pace, waiting to consciously wake up.

"Surely, you believed in those magical tales you were told as a child, right? If that's the case, then why is it hard to believe now?" I stop pacing and slowly walk up to her, refraining from running back into the castle.

"Listen. Children are only told about magic so they can have something imaginary to hold on to. Magic will never be able to fix the terror I've endured. If magic was so real and true, that night wouldn't have happened!" I shout and realize I'm glaring at her. But my stare is broken by her intimidating size. Silva stands up and the tree branches unravel and disconnect from her body. She steps up to me, towering over my height like a giant.

I feel like I'm going to start hyperventilating and I'm overwhelmed to the max. I walk backwards, shaking my head.

"This is too much." I turn around and start to find my way out of the forest but Silva follows behind.

"There is a magic force that is calling for you, begging for you to believe in it. And the proof of its existence lies within the necklace around your neck!" The mention of my mother's necklace catches my attention and I quickly turn around.

"What are you talking about?" I ask sternly. Grasping the sword charm in my hand.

"To any other human, it may be just a simple piece of metal, but in reality, it's the key to ensuring no one will ever experience what you have!" She walks towards me and the wind makes her long white hair blow backwards gracefully. The leaves in her hair shake and the glowing plants fade in and out steadily.

"That pendant was your mother's symbol of hope, now it's your symbol of strength. She gave it to you, unknowing of its hidden properties. But she gave it to you because she knew it was meant to be yours." My eyes begin to water and tears slowly fall to my cheeks.

I feel my hands shaking violently as I hold them close to my chest, trying to calm down. When Silva notices I'm on edge, she softens her gaze.

"Take the necklace off and you'll understand." I decide to humor her and do as she says, overwhelmed by her confusing words that don't make much sense. "If it means I get to wake up soon, fine." I reach back and unclip the necklace chain and hold it out with the sword charm dangling from my hand.

"Okay, now what?" I ask, holding the necklace awkwardly. Silva backs up a few feet and the forest goes silent. "Hold the charm in your hand and focus all your energy on it." I look at the necklace and back to Silva, perplexed by what she asks of me.

"I'm sorry but...what does that even mean?" I ask, annoyed and she scoffs lightly under her breath. "Humans are so strange, they can't understand the simplest of words." She teases.

I know a talking tree lady didn't just call me "strange".

"I heard that." Silva raises her voice and crosses her arms in front of her chest. I do what she says and hold the small charm in my hand, close my eyes and focus my emotions, honing in on everything I'm feeling. I think about everything I've seen, everything I've heard and everything I've felt.

I pick apart my emotions like a puzzle and piece them together again to understand exactly what it is I feel and why.

My eyes stay closed and everything around me remains calm and silent.

The air that rests between my trees is silent and
calm. All I hear is the heartbeat of the forest that echoes
with my own. I stand still with my feet intertwined with
the grass below me, waiting for something to happen. I
can sense Vivalda trying to steady her breath and focus,
despite the thoughts that overwhelm her mind. I can feel
everything she feels. I feel her pain, anger, sadness and
confusion.

She begins to tighten her fists, growing quickly
impatient when a sudden gust of wind blows through the
trees, nearly pushing Vivalda over. I remain bound to the
ground and watch thick fog follow in from beyond the
forest and wrap around her like a vortex tunnel. The wall
of fog grows thicker until I can no longer see her. A
bright flash of light emits from the vertical tunnel and
the gray fog turns bright blue and glows intensely. The
heartbeat of the forest intensifies excitedly and the
ground rumbles below us.

With a loud *whoosh*, the fog dies down and
dissipates into the air to reveal the princess coated in
dark metal. Her nightgown has disappeared and is
replaced with black metal armor that has glowing blue
designs scattered across its surface. The front sections of
her hair are pulled forward into two braids that lay over
her chest and the rest of her hair hangs behind her. A
silver halo crown resting on her head firmly and doesn't

move. The necklace charm has transformed into a full-sized sword that she holds shakily in her hand. The glowing colors from the forest bounce off the metal armor that covers her chest, arms and legs, creating a rainbow to cascade across the grassy floor.

Vivalda stumbles backwards from the weight of the sword and armor and she quickly catches her balance. I observe and listen as she looks at the armor and the sword. Her once beaten, bruised skin is now healed but her skin is pale, stained with fear. She slowly begins to hyperventilate from the sudden change. I immediately walk over to her in an attempt to help calm her nerves.

"What is this and why do I feel so strange?" She continues to panic and paces back and forth, holding the sword disgustedly. She then drops the sword blade down as it stabs the grassy ground. The moment the blade makes contact with the grass, I feel a quick sharp pain pinch my chest. After the sword hits the ground, the armor disappears and once the weight disappears, Vivalda releases a sigh of relief. The sword turns back into a necklace.

"WHAT WAS THAT?!" She asks frantically before reaching down to pick up the necklace.

"It's going to-" I try to stop her from reaching down for the item but it's too late. As soon as she picks the necklace back up, the armor and weapon return to their previous forms.

"What the hell?!" She shouts angrily. I reach my hands out, trying to ease her tension.

"Please, try to relax. Everything is perfectly fine. I know this is an incredible shock, but this is a good thing." I say as Vivalda stops pacing and stands in front of me, slapping her chest with her hands repeatedly as if trying to push off the armor.

"'Good thing'? What are you- this is not normal! What do you mean 'relax'?!" Vivalda stands awkwardly with her voice raised in a high-pitched tone.

"Your mother's necklace has been enchanted with some of the most powerful magic, gifted from the gods that watch over us. Your mother has kept it safe her entire life, waiting for it to fall into the hands of someone worthy of bearing its power. And by the armor and sword showing its true form, it has chosen you. The armor is a reflection of who you are." Despite my encouraging words, it only causes Vivalda to panic more. She pulls aways from me and walks off as the metal clanks against itself.

"No. This is not 'who I am'. I barely know who I am. What is a sword and magical armor going to do to change that?" She stops talking abruptly and a thought strikes her mind. "My mother had this the whole time? Why couldn't she use it against the monsters that tore her apart?!" I close my eyes and take a deep breath.

I knew she'd bring this up.

I speak to Vivalda calmly, trying to avoid overwhelming her even more. "Your mother possessed no power from the necklace because it didn't bind to her the way it has to you." Vivalda holds the sword out and with her other hand, she feels the braids that drape over her chest and follow the strands until her hands touch the metal crown. Once she touches it, her eyes widen.

"Is this thing anchored into my head?!" She tries moving the crown around but it doesn't budge. "Um-yes." I say, hesitantly and a look of disgust crosses her face.

"No no no no. No thank you. This isn't right. Magic? Serafaes? Dark magic? Magical armor? 'Magic' will never decipher who I am." Vivalda stares at me angrily.

"Then that means, YOU know who you're meant to be, right?" I ask softly and she looks up at me with her eyes widened. She takes a moment to respond and shake her head, irritated. "I'm just a princess who's trying to grieve for her mother. The aftermath of death shouldn't be whatever this is." This experience hasn't gone the way I intended and no matter how much I try to console her; she only ends up feeling angrier.

Perhaps, this is too much.

"Human minds have always been confusing but yours...is probably the most inconsistent." Vivalda turns to me sharply, holding her arms out to the side, keeping her legs awkwardly spread apart.

"Excuse me?" She looks at me, offended. I try listening to her thoughts but there's so much going on inside that head of hers, it's almost impossible to hear one thought alone.

"You stand strong on pride and yet, you run from it at the same time." Vivalda's scrunched face finally relaxes and she realizes how true my words are. "You want to take charge and help, but when you're given the chance, you want to run from it. Is your pride and courage just a show?"

"That's not true. You have no idea how I could possibly be feeling." She says quietly and I can tell my words ring true in her mind but she's afraid to admit it.

"I know how sudden this is, but desperate times call for desperate measures. I know how lost you feel, but here's a new journey that calls for you. Maybe this call will be the answer to everything you've ever questioned. The world needs your help." Vivalda tosses her head to the side and looks at her reflection through the sword's blade. She rolls her eyes before looking up at me.

"No. I am just a simple girl trying to do simple things in life. What help could a human possibly lend you?!" I take a deep breath, remaining as composed as possible and I continue talking to her gently.

"I may have the answer to most questions, but never all. What I do know is that you'll never know what you're capable of unless you take risks and go far beyond your limits." She looks down and shakes her head.

"A sword and armor will never balance out the trouble that rests on my shoulders. Yes, I'm on the search for my path, but this isn't it. Find someone else and tell me how to get rid of this." Her cheeks are red and I instantly feel terrible for making her feel so overwhelmed.

"By the time I return to my room, I'll wake up, you'll be gone and this will all have been an insane dream." I approach her slowly, keeping my distance. "I will not force you to walk a path you don't want. To retract your armor, release it from your thoughts and the armor and sword will disappear." Vivalda instantly steps back, a bright flash of light covers her and the armor and sword disappear. Her gold necklace dangles in her hand and she clasps it around her heck. She's back to wearing

137

her nightdress and her hair is back to being tied into a single braid.

That was impressively fast.

I thought it would have taken her longer to deactivate the armor. I'm left standing surprised yet satisfied. "I won't search for another because if I do, it means you give up the last gift your mother ever gave you and I'm sure you're not ready to let it go." Vivalda looks at the necklace and turns around to walk out of the forest. But before walking too far, she stops and turns her head to me.

"I don't mean to offend you. But there is someone out there more far more worthy than I." My brows twitch up and she proceeds to run out of the forest and back to the castle.

"I think I've figured you out." I say quietly to myself.

I lift my hands up, encouraging the glowing earth to dim and erase all of the glowing magic so it doesn't catch the attention of other humans. The sky begins to lighten and I can't help but wonder if she will tell others of our interaction. If she does, something tells me she won't be believed and I can't tell if that's a good or a bad thing.

I have time to spare, so I walk back to the ancient tree and sit, allowing the tree branches to embrace me once more. While I sit and ponder, I can't help but fear for the future to come.

"The only guidance she will follow is yours, my friend. But you left her too soon." I say as I look up at the sky that holds no stars.

The sight of no stars tells me change is coming and it's coming much faster than I anticipated.

Vivalda

I dash out of the forest as fast as I can, looking back to make sure Silva isn't following or trying to stop me. Once I reach the bridge, I look back and see the forest has returned to normal. The trees and plants no longer glow and the atmosphere is completely silent. I look up at the sky and notice the rain has stopped as well.

As soon as I cross over the bridge, a strange sensation crawls down my spine and it makes me look back one more time. Once I see nothing out of the normal, I figure I must be paranoid.

None of this was real.

Once I get back into the castle, I slowly go back to my room. Once I step through the door, I quickly notice the flowers are gone and Kyson is still sound asleep. I flop over on my bed and pull the blanket up to my chest.

Sleep feels like an impossible thing to reach, so I lay still, staring at the wooden ceiling, holding my mother's sword charm in my hand. Something feels off and it overwhelms me that I can't figure out what. All I know is these dreams aren't helping and they only make me feel like I'm falling off the deep end. I'm worried that one day, I'll fall too far.

After hours of resting with my eyes closed, I finally fall asleep.

I'm awoken by a bright light that shines in my face. I slowly peel open my eyes and see a bright ray of sun peeking through the curtains. I look over and see Kyson still sleeping peacefully.

I sit up and rub my face, trying to wake up and clean out the gunk in the corners of my eyes. Once on my feet, I wobble over to the washroom and splash cool water on my face. I reach over and grab a bar of herbal soap our healers make and I rub it gently on my skin, getting rid of any leftover dirt.

Once I'm completely washed up, I pat my face dry and when I look in the mirror, I'm left speechless to see my face clear of any cuts, bruises or abrasions. The healer's natural remedy does wonders and I'm left pleased with the unexpected results.

I exit the washroom and proceed to pick out a dress from my wardrobe. I decide to go with a simple light blue long-sleeved gown with a silver corset belt. I brush my hair and decide to keep it down for the day and I find a silver pair of flat shoes to wear. Once I'm fully dressed, I leave my room and quietly close the door behind me. From there, I wander the halls aimlessly, just trying to fully wake up and take a breather after having a rough time sleeping.

Before making it far down the hall, I hear Riverlynn and Orion talking on the main balcony. I walk up to the glass doors and once I turn the handle to walk outside, both of them turn their attention to me.

"Good morning Viv! I didn't think you'd be up this early." Riverlynn exclaims joyfully as I walk towards them. Orion steps out to the side and bows. "Good morning, your highness." He says cheerfully.

"Good morning to you both. I don't know about you but I didn't sleep very well last night. I kept having bad dreams." I walk over to the balcony and look at the beautiful view. The sun is shining bright and there's a cool breeze floating in the air.

"I couldn't sleep. There was too much to think about." I look over at Riverlynn and see the pure sadness in her eyes. "I'm sorry." I say quietly before turning back to let the view distract me. But before I can even breathe, I can sense Riverlynn observing me intensely. I slowly and awkwardly turn to her.

"May I help you?" I ask sarcastically and she looks at me with a crooked smile, tilting her head to the side and staring. I can see her blue eyes zipping around, observing different parts of my face.

"You had gashes, cuts and bruises all over your body...how has it all disappeared?" Riverlynn continues to stare, confused.

I look up and see Orion also staring at me, making it even more awkward.

"Why must you both act so strange? I've been using the healer's herbal soap as usual, I guess it has some healing properties I was unaware of." I try to wipe away the awkwardness by speaking in a more joyful tone.

"Ohhhhhhhh that makes sense! I forgot you still use that stuff. I should ask them to make me some, maybe it'll get rid of my red spots." Riverlynn says enthusiastically.

I focus on the bright blue sky, ready to take on the new day.

"Is Kyson still sleeping?" Orion asks and I nod my head.

Both of them walk over to join me at the balcony and we all look out into the distance.

Orion clears his throat and speaks softly. "The king sent a message out to Palavon last night and we were thinking about paying a visit to the people to check on everyone. We were thinking maybe you'd like to join us. But if it's too soon for you, we won't go." I lean my chest against the stone ledge, my shoulder tense up and I grit my teeth.

"You really think that's a good idea? I'm sure father won't allow it." There's a silent cry I feel throbbing in my chest. I yearn to run into my father's arms and make proper amends for what I've done. But I fear he may not want to speak to me again.

"Well as of this morning, he refuses to leave his chambers, so I don't think he'll care to stop us. Lyla says he was a bit destructive last night and he won't allow anyone in unless he's sending out messages. I think it's best to leave him in solitude until he's ready." Hearing that concerns me but I quickly accept that we all have our own ways of grieving and I agree that it's best to leave him be.

"Alright, we'll go but we'll only stay long enough to check on everyone and return home. I don't want to be a burden and possibly make things harder for others." I see Riverlynn turn to look at me and I continue to speak before she can say a word. "I'll go wake up Kyson, prepare the horses and we'll meet you down." I smile at my sister and proceed back inside my room.

Once Kyson is up and ready, we make our way outside but before reaching the main corridors, we see

Lyla walking down the hall, alone. When she sees us, she instantly smiles.

"Are you going out today, princess?" She asks softly and I let out a soft chuckle. "River and Orion convinced me to go with them to Palavon to check on everyone. Maybe joining them will lighten up my mood." Lyla's smile slowly drops and disappears, confusing me.

"My dear, don't you think it may be too soon to leave the castle? I don't want you to push yourself too hard, especially for the sake of others." I hold her hand in mine, trying to reassure her.

"Lyla, I'm fine. Maybe some fresh air will help. And besides, I'll be surrounded by those who are going through the same grief I am. But do me a favor while we're out. Please try to get father to leave his room, I don't want him to-" Lyla cuts me off.

"Worry not about him, the staff and I will take care of him. But I think you should stay home and rest for the day." I gently squeeze her hand and look at her softly.

"Lyla, I know you mean well and that you're just looking after me since mother's not here. But I promise, I'm more than capable of making the simplest decisions for myself. I'll have three strong men with me, so I'll be in good hands." Lyla takes a deep breath and I hug her before walking past her.

Kyson and I finally make it outside and we meet Atticus, Orion and my sister at the bottom of the stairs waiting with the horses. Before walking out of the gates, I look back at the knights and guards. It's strange seeing so many of them missing from their posts because father allowed them to take a break after mother's passing.

"What's on your mind?" Kyson walks by my side and I perk up my head, forcing a smile on my face.

"Nothing, I'm alright. Or- well- I'm as alright as I can possibly be." One part of me feels utterly empty and numb and the other side wants to try to enjoy the new day.

"You'd tell me if something was wrong, right?" Kyson asks, worried. I look at him softly and smile, trying to reassure him.

"Of course." I reach out and he holds my hand.

My heart begins to race when we approach the welcome sign to Palavon. The sound of soft mellow music grows louder from a distance and I can hear children running around and playing.

Once we enter the village, everyone moves slowly with saddened looks on their faces. Once they see us, they don't smile, wave or look happy to see us. I try to smile at them, hoping to bring some joy to their day but their expressions don't change. Many of them hold their heads lowly and bow slightly.

It's easy to see how much their queen's death has impacted them. Nothing doesn't feel the same.

We trot up to a horse post and tie the reins to the metal pole. Then we proceed to spend time at Flame Forge with Rowan. While walking to the building, I can sense several eyes staring at us intensely, but I think I'm just overthinking simple things. After spending time in Kyson's workroom, we hear a commotion coming from outside.

"I'll be right back. I think customers are inquiring about their purchases. This happens every now and then." Kyson chuckles nervously before exiting the room.

"Hopefully they're not angry. With there only being two workers in the shop, they can only work so fast." Riverlynn adds as she looks at the progress of Kyson's projects. There's piles and stacks of different objects including knives, hunting gear, chains and more. I also spot a few random hand-crafted items like mini figurines made of metal and glass.

After a moment, I see Kyson storm through the door, breathing heavily, panicking. I jolt back and feel my heart pound against my chest briefly.

"Oh goodness, what's wrong?" I ask as calmly as possible.

"You all need to come out here now." Kyson says urgently before running back down the hall.

Atticus and Orion immediately trail behind him while Riverlynn and I take caution and slowly follow behind. While walking down the hall, the commotion grows louder and louder and it sounds like people are angry but due to the overlapping voices, I can't tell what's going on. Once we return back to the lobby, I see multiple people crowded outside in front of the door and windows. I step forward to try to address the situation but Atticus stops my sister and I from getting too close.

"Stay here and away from the doors and windows." He commands firmly before exiting the building with Orion and closing the door behind him. Kyson sits with us as far from the door as possible.

"What's going on?" I ask firmly and Kyson walks out from around his father's desk, reading a piece of paper in his hands. He looks shocked to read whatever he sees and it concerns me.

"Were you made aware of the message the king sent out?" He looks at me with his eyes widened and his fingers start to curl over the paper, causing it to wrinkle and tear slightly. "No...why?" I ask and my voice begins to shake. Kyson looks at Riverlynn for a moment and then me. He takes a deep breath and hesitates to hand the paper to me.

Riverlynn leans over my shoulder to read the message.

"It brings me deep sadness to the news of Queen Aladora's passing. This was very sudden and unexpected. Her death came to pass due to my eldest daughter, Vivalda doing what she's always done best, which is causing trouble and disobeying simple commands. Words don't express my disappointment enough-"

Riverlynn gasps and covers her mouth with her hand, disgusted and before I can continue reading the message, I crumble it in my hands and slam it down on the ground.

"This isn't right! They can't possibly believe that!" Riverlynn shouts loudly. Rage begins to boil in my blood and I hold back tears that begin to swell my eyes.

"You know what..." I shake my head. "I can't keep fighting this. He's right. I got in the way and now, this is what I get." I say quietly and Riverlynn pulls my shoulder back so I face her.

"Absolutely not! You didn't cause any of this! You didn't know! You don't know for sure if she was even on the right path home and she was still led to-" Riverlynn begins to cry and I lift my hand to stop her from talking. "I don't care anymore. I don't care about the possibilities of what happened in the past. Now, I have to deal with the outcome of it all and I just happen to be in the center of it all."

I walk slowly towards the door but Kyson quickly stands in front of me, blocking my way.

"She's right, you weren't the cause of this and we didn't need to be there in order to know that. I know you're upset and you have every right to be. He may be king but he had no right to speak the way he did. Especially without you having the chance to talk in any way." I look at him, annoyed that's he dares to stop me and take a deep breath.

"Move." I say quietly and before I can say anything else, something heavy slams against the wall, causing Riverlynn to scream. I can hear voices begin to shout louder and louder to where I can make out what they're saying.

"If it wasn't for that menacing child, Queen Aladora would still be here! Now the land will suffer!" I hear a woman shouts angrily. I close my eyes and absorb her words like a dagger to my heart. Riverlynn immediately gets up and joins my side, protesting against the villagers.

"We cannot allow this! None of them know anything about what happened!" Riverlynn yells as she tries to get past Kyson while he remains standing firm in front of the door.

I feel my legs begin to shake and I take a step closer towards the door.

"Move." I say again but more firmly and eventually, Kyson moves away from the door.

"Please be careful. Don't give them more of a reason to explode." Kyson says softly. "They'll explode no matter what I say." After a long pause, I gather my courage and step outside where I'm met with a large crowd of angry people who all quiet down and turn their attention from the knights to me.

As I look at the faces of my people, I feel a piece of my heart break apart. This is an anger I've never seen before. It's scary. The knights move out of the way and I stand before my people, anxious and scared. I take a deep breath and try to speak and make sense of my words.

"I know you're sad and angry...I am too. But my mother wouldn't wish to see us like this-" Before I could continue, I'm cut off by an angry woman who stands at the front of the crowd.

"Your anger is nothing compared to ours! We heard the king's words!" Her words send another sharp dagger into my heart.

"The king told us what you did. He said had you remained in your place, the queen would have made it back safely!" The crowd around her mutters and agrees. My chest begins to squeeze tightly to the point where I start to feel suffocated.

"LISTEN! None of you were there! There are monsters lurking in the forests around us that are responsible for my mother's death! Many of you have claimed to see the same monsters that tore her body to shreds!" I try to speak but the people's voices fill the air once again, overpowering mine.

"The only monster around here is you!" A man yells from the back of the group. I begin to hyperventilate and my hands go numb.

They won't listen...

No words can express how hurt I feel. I never thought I'd hear anyone say that to me. My heart is in so much pain that I simply have no more pain to feel. The crowd begins to push forward, trying to reach me and I take a few steps back.

"Vivalda, get inside now." Atticus says firmly and Orion tries to push the rioting mob back. I hear the wooden door creak open behind me and Kyson grabs my hand. "Viv, come on!" Kyson shouts and tries to pull me back inside. I turn to look at him and back at the fuming mob. As they approach closer, raising their fists in the air, shouting loudly, I hear a voice in my head that speaks loudly.

"RUN."

I yank my hand from Kyson's grasp and turn to run past the knights and crowd and noise. I attempt to find solitude behind the building but I quickly hear the mob of angry men and women following me. "Your highness, come back!" Orion yells from the center of the crowd. I look around to figure out where to run and I decide to take off into the forest in front of me. I use all of my strength to charge up the hill and once I realize I'm running through the forest, I immediately get flashbacks to the dark night and my mother's voice rings in my head. But if I remain where I stand, I'll be tackled by mad people who refuse to listen to me. So I'm left with no choice but to run.

Once at the top of the hill, I grab onto a tree and pull myself up to where the ground is leveled. I hide behind a large tree and hear my sister's voice emerge from the angry crowd. I peek from behind the tree and see Riverlynn run to the front of the crowd with Orion and Atticus joining her side.

"What is wrong with you all?! Have you no shame?!" She stomps in front of the crowd and they all stop before her. "I understand your sadness but I can assure you that my sister, the one who has forever remained loyal to you all and the heir to the throne was not the cause of this tragedy!" She stomps her foot down, holding her ground, not allowing anyone to walk past her. Everyone backs up but their demeanor doesn't change.

"How would you know? Were you there to witness?!" A woman yells, throwing her hand in the air and pointing to the trees, but I remain hidden from sight. Riverlynn stands silent for a moment and I turn back to face the forest. "No, I was not...but-" She's cut off by more angry shouting.

"Then not even you know if what she says is true!" More voices begin to overlap with each other and from the back of the crowd, I see Rowan and Kyson standing, looking for me.

I turn around and slowly drop to my knees. I cup my hands over my face, resting numbly. The crowd goes wild for a moment and I hear my sister's voice shouting loudly.

"Listen! My father's words were written in grief! Just as you all speak due to sorrow! The queen would never want any of you acting this way! Yes, feel free to mourn and grieve, but not with violence. I'm sure you'd all be much gentler if the king didn't send that message. Wouldn't you?!" She shouts and the crowd stands silent.

"I stand by my sister because she'd never do anything to intentionally cause harm to someone! Especially to our mother. Now, you will all do as I say and go back to your routines! NOW!" She shouts fiercely and the angered crowd walks away, muttering.

I peek out from behind the tree once more and watch everyone retreat to the center of the village. Kyson joins my sister's side and they all look around for me. Orion comforts Riverlynn by hugging her from the side and I hear them speak quietly.

"Let's give her some space. She wouldn't have gone deep into the forest, so she'll be fine." Riverlynn assures the men and they walk back to Flame Forge.

I remain sitting with my back against the tree, trying to catch my breath and collect myself, but the internal panicking gets the best of me. And since I'm alone, I take the chance to cry to myself. I lean over my knees and hug my legs tightly to my chest. I'm ashamed, distraught and heartbroken.

Am I really the monster my father wrote me off to be?

Eventually, I have no more tears to shed. I lean back and wipe my puffy eyes. I'm scared to move because I can still hear the subtle commotion from other villagers. I stare out into the never-ending forest, zoning out, allowing my thoughts to run free until I can't make sense of them.

The wind begins to pick up and the air grows cold, causing my teeth to chatter. I gather the strength to stand and begin to slowly retreat back to the forge. My feet drag heavily on the ground and before walking down the grassy hill, I look back into the forest.

What if I just ran and never turned back?

I begin to contemplate running away into the valley of trees, but I know my place is here. I pick up my dress as I walk clumsily down the hill, pondering to myself.

The sun rays that shine slowly disappear and when I look up, I see gray clouds starting to cover the sun. The gloomy weather doesn't help me feel any better and only makes me feel more irritated.

I'm startled by the sound of birds flying out from the trees behind me. I duck down slightly as a group of black raven zoom over me, squawking loudly and disappearing in the distance.

Mother Nature isn't having it either, I suppose.

A heavy gust of wind blows against me and the leaves in the treetops begin to rattle and sway. I run down the hill to reach the back of Flame Forge. I walk over and I peek around the corner to ensure the coast is clear. Everyone in the distance is minding their own business and tending to their livelihoods.

Before I can step out, I nearly choke on air when I'm startled by a loud *boom* that causes the ground to rumble and nearly knocks me over.

"What the hell?" I slam my back against the building to keep my balance until it stops. I look over to the far side of the village and all of the warm blood flushes from my face. I see several people crowd on the dirt roads, panicking, screaming and running. I frantically look for what caused the commotion and I see multiple buildings being built up with smoke and fire. I stumble back and begin to hyperventilate.

Loose dust and dirt kicks up into the air and my eyes widen in shock when I see flames emerging from multiple buildings. I begin to panic, feeling hopeless and before I run onto the porch to go inside, Atticus and Orion charge out of Flame Forge and rush to help. The event I've witnessed is far from normal. Buildings don't randomly catch on fire.

Thunder rumbles deeply in the sky and I remain stuck, standing frozen. I grasp my mother's necklace and a sudden thought comes into my mind.

"What if it wasn't a dream?" I whisper to myself and a loud *crack* catches my attention. I look over to see raging flames growing larger. The knights run in and out of separate buildings, coughing on smoke while helping people get out. More screams fill the air and my heart pounds heavily against my chest.

Riverlynn and Kyson barge out of the building, both looking absolutely mortified to see what happens before them. They see me peeking out from the edge of the building and Riverlynn begins to shout.

"Viv, get inside, now!" I look at the chaos that continues to unravel.

"Get as many people inside as you can! I'll be back!" I shout and I instinctively rush out into the center of the village, bumping into screaming people who evacuate their shops and homes.

"Go to Flame Forge! You'll be safe there!" I encourage them as I run past them and I look back to see Kyson, Rowan and Riverlynn guiding people inside.

I stop at the stone fountain that sits in the center of the village. For a split moment, all sound around me drowns out and all I hear is the rapid thumping of my heart. I look down at the gold charm that rests against my chest and I hesitate to move.

"Please don't make me look like a fool." I whisper to myself and yank the necklace down while holding the charm firmly in my hand. The moment the necklace is detached, lightning and thunder crash over me, quickly revealing the black and blue armor I thought was made up in a dream.

It was all real...

The armor has little to no weight but the sword, however, is tricky to hold due to how heavy it is. I observe the blade in my hand and then look down at my chest. The bright blue designs on the armor beam with the rhythm of my heart. I use my opposite hand to feel the metal crown that's connected to my head. The feeling of it is very strange because it feels like it's connected to my skull and the thought of that makes me feel sick.

I put the sword in the sheathe that's connected to my hip. I've never wielded a sword and somehow...it feels like a familiar touch.

I instinctively run to help the knights however I can. I cautiously approach the first burning building. The flames burn bright and wooden debris falls from the structure. I see Orion emerge from a wall of dark smoke and once he exits the building, he nearly collapses, coughing from inhaling the fumes. I run up and help him stand, struggling to keep his limp body up.

"Thank you." He pants heavily. He looks up and once he realizes it's me, he jumps away from me with his eyes widening and his jaw dropped.

"Vivalda? What is-" I cut him off quickly before he could speak another word. "No time, I'll explain later. Where's your father?" His skin drips with sweat and he shakes his head in shock. "He's- uh- in another building." I look around and see only one other building on fire and I can hear Atticus' voice in the distance.

"Have you checked upstairs?" I turn to him frantically. He continues to look at the newly discovered armor and sword, having a hard time focusing. "Orion, focus! Did you make it upstairs?!" I shout, snapping him out of it.

"I- I tried- the smoke- it's too thick!" He shouts and we both look up at the wooden walls that creak loudly. Charred wood stuffs my nose and my chest begins to throb. From the outside, I can feel the heat of the fire and the sound of screams and embers cracking fill my ears. A strange gut feeling tells me there's someone on the top floor.

The building won't stay up for long and there's no one else to help.

I run past him and enter the building. "Vivalda, don't!" Orion's voice echoes behind me. I run into the building, the ground crunches under me and the room is covered in fire embers. Every piece of furniture, artwork, clothes and appliances are destroyed. I try not to inhale too much smoke, but I end up coughing up a storm. I wave my hand in front of me, trying to make the smoke fade away so I can see in front of me. Eventually I spot the stairs and slowly ascend up, stepping lightly, trying to avoid falling and breaking the stairs apart.

"Is anyone up here?!" I scream over until I reach the top of the stairs.

The smoke gets thicker the higher I go and I can barely see anything. I maneuver around the roaring flames as cautiously as possible. The atmosphere is extremely hot and typically fire causes metal to get very hot and essentially cook whatever is inside, but somehow, I don't feel the scolding heat that emits from the flames.

"Hello!" I call once more at the top of the stairs.

There're no flames on the top floor, but the fire from below is beginning to rise quickly.

I focus and try to pay attention the best I can, despite already feeling a bit disoriented. I hear soft crying and whimpering from inside of a closet that's in the short hall. I pull open the door and to my surprise, I unintentionally disconnect it from its hinges. I let the door fall flat on the ground and I look inside the room to see a little girl hiding behind wooden barrels. I walk into the small room and kneel in front of the girl, trying not to frighten her. She sits, curled in a ball, covering her eyes, crying.

"I want my mama!" She screams into her hand, coughing from the smoke that slowly seeps up from below us. "Hey, I'm here to help you. I can take you back to your mother if you take my hand." I reach my hand towards her.

She moves her hands from her eyes and when she sees me, her eyes lighten up. "Hi." I say softly and the wooden floor creaks under me. "Sweetie, is there anyone else up here?" I ask urgently and she looks up slowly and shakes her head.

"I promise, I'll help you get to your momma, but you have to come with me so you don't get hurt, okay?" She reaches her little hand out, I scoop her in my arms and immediately race towards the stairs as the flames grow rapidly.

As soon as I reach the stairs, the entire lower level is engulfed in a pond of fire. The stairs have disintegrated, leaving us nowhere to go. I quickly retreat to the farthest wall in the large room, trying to stay as far from the smoke and fire as possible. The floorboards continue to creak and crack, causing me to lose my balance.

"Vivalda are you up there?!" I hear Orion yell from outside. There's a single round window and I walk over to it cautiously. With one hand, I unlatch the glass panel and push the window open. I look out the window and see Orion pacing back and forth frantically.

"I'm here! I have a child with me! There's no one else!" I shout as loud as I can, hoping he can hear me over the mixed noises. Orion looks up, relieved to see me. "Can you get down the way you came?!" He cups his hands over his mouth to shout loudly. I look back and see how much bigger the flames have grown and they're slowly ascending to the floor we stand on.

"No! It's completely blocked!" I look around, trying to find another way to get us out of the building safely. The smoke is too thick and I can't risk the safety of the child. I lean my head back out the window.

"Orion, you'll have to catch this child! There's no other way!" I lean out of the window once more. Orion walks closer to the building, avoiding the fire. "I promise!" He holds his arms out and widens his stance.

"I need you to be brave for me, okay?" I calmly tell her and lift her up to the window and lift her though the small window. Thankfully, she fits like a glove.

I look at the little girl and take a deep breath. "Close your eyes for me." She does as I say and I release her from my grip and the moment I let go, I lean out the window and watch her land carefully in Orion's arms.

"Thank goodness." A huge wave of relief flushes through my body but it's too soon to relax since I remain stuck in the building, surrounded by vicious flames. "Vivalda!" Orion yells from below.

I don't have much time to think, even if I try to break through the thick wooden walls, the fire will continue to spread.

I begin to panic as walls of fire begin to close in on me. I begin to hear strange sounds emerging from the smoke and fire. It sounds like a lion growling deeply. I cover my mouth and begin to cough intensely. I kneel over and squint my eyes as they're burned by flying embers. My chest begins to throb in pain. And once I'm able to stand up straight, I open my eyes and see a massive black shadowed monster lunge at me from the dark smoke. I scream and jump backwards as it roars loudly, baring two rows of sharp, nasty teeth and bright red beaming eyes.

No! I know these eyes!

It continues to roar loudly while spitting black ooze in my face. I begin to panic more when I realize it's distracting me from escaping the building that's going to collapse at any moment. I back up farther and close my eyes, assuring myself it's not really there.

Monster bends over me and pins me to the floor. I look over and I can barely see the flames. I feel a sudden wave of energy swell throughout my arm and I see my hand ignited in blue fire. A bright blue light emits from the armor and the veins in my arm turn blue, looking like some kind of disease. The monster pulls back and opens its mouth widely, but before it can try to devour me, I thrust my hand forward and a bright blue beam of light strikes the creature, causing it to fly backwards and scream in pain. Its body clashes with the bright yellow flames and I watch its body disintegrate into burnt particles. Its painful screech dies alongside the large flames.

Once the fire is miraculously extinguished, I look at my hand and see my skin and the armor has gone back to normal, leaving me confused.

"Vivalda! Are you alright?!" I hear Orion yell from outside.

I don't have time to answer because I can feel the floorboard bending and breaking below my feet. Before I can breathe, the floor caves in and I fall through the second floor, crashing to the ground, landing on my side. I cover my head as large planks of wood land on me, splitting in half and soot gets in my mouth and nose, making it hard to breathe.

After a moment, no more debris falls and I hear Orion call for me. "Vivalda, where are you?!" I slowly get up and charred wood, stone and black dust falls off of my body. I cough and spit out as much dirt and soot as possible but the burnt taste lingers on my tongue, making me want to vomit. I slowly stand up and my body throbs painfully, especially my side. If it wasn't for the armor, I'm not sure I'd be alive.

I quickly limp out of the burnt building where I can finally breathe better and try to catch my breath. I squat down, leaning my head into my hand, coughing up more debris and smoke. I hear Orion and Atticus rush to my side.

"Are you alright? What in the gods name-" Atticus asks while observing the armor. I hold my hand up and stand. "No one believed me the first time, I'm not sure if that will change. We need to check everything and ensure the rest of the village is safe." I walk away while wiping the black dust and dirt from my face, looking at my hands, confused from the power that recently came out of my body.

I look around and only three buildings have been burnt. Whatever power that was must have taken out the rest of the fires. Either that or the knights managed to put the rest out themselves. Thunder continues to rumble and the wind blows harshly and it slowly changes course.

Something's here, I can feel it.

I remain on edge, paranoid of seeing another shadow monster. Orion and Atticus gather by my side and at this point, they've urged everyone to seek shelter, leaving no one left crowding the street.

"What are we looking for? We should go inside." Atticus urges over the loud howling wind. Orion looks at me, eyes wide and his hands shaking.

"It's those things you told us about, isn't it?" I hesitate to respond verbally so instead, I nod my head subtly while continuing to look around. I look up at the sky and see the dark clouds beginning to move quickly

"Huts don't mysteriously catch fire..." Both knights look at me as my gaze falls to the ground. Then a sudden thought comes to mind. "We need to get back to the castle, now!" I run back to Flame Forge and the men follow behind closely.

Upon entering the front door, the armor instantly releases from my body and it disappears behind a flash of light. The gold necklace falls on the floor and I crash down on my knees, feeling sudden surges of pain radiate through every part of my body. But due to the intense adrenaline rush, I'm able to quickly brush it off.

Everyone in the room stares at me in shock and Kyson helps me back up.

"We have to go home now. Rowan, keep an eye on everyone until further notice. If something happens, ring the town bell."

I grab the necklace off the floor and clasp it on while running to the horses that remain safe and tied to the post.

We run as fast as we can to the castle and as we get closer to home, the thunder and wind intensifies. It begins to rain heavily and my dress is quickly soaked.

Once we approach the castle and rush inside, we're met by multiple guards and servants in the throne room.

"Atticus, retrieve the king and any staff in the north corridors. Orion, search the south, then meet us back here. I want to make sure everyone remains together." I command the knights and they immediately disperse and heed my command.

"Will you now tell me what's going on?" I begin to pace around, looking out the large window for anything potentially suspicious and Riverlynn follows behind me. "I just saw you run into a burning building, covered in some kind of strange armor and then you came back and *POOF*, it disappeared!" She speaks quickly and she starts to get annoyed that I'm not answering while continuing to pace around anxiously. She grabs my hand and stops me from walking.

"Vivalda, answer me! Tell me what's going on!" I look at her and take a deep breath before speaking as gently as possible, despite me being overwhelmed.

"I'm almost positive that the monsters that killed my mother are also responsible for the village fire and I think they're coming here now. As for the armor...I don't know-" Riverlynn's eyes widen and she takes a step back.

Both of our attention turns to the halls where we see Orion rush in with Lyla and three other castle servants following him. Then Atticus comes through the hall on the opposite side of the room with the king and two more servants. I look at every face, making sure everyone is accounted for and safe.

Father looks infuriated to see me and he walks up to my sister and I. "What is all this racket about? What trouble have you caused this time, Vivalda?" He shouts loudly, causing everyone around us to go silent.

His hardened gaze scares me, I've never felt so small and timid while standing next to him.

My heart races uncontrollably and I'm tempted to back down but he needs to know what is happening.

"There was an attack on Palavon. Buildings mysteriously caught on fire and we did everything we could to-" Father continues to shout over me. "Who's 'we'?" I break eye contact and stumble on my words.

"Atticus, Orion and myself. I know what you're going to say but the creatures that killed mother are the cause of the attack and I have a feeling something bad is on its way here, now! It's a lot to explain but-" My father cuts me off once again, yelling even louder.

"You disturb me and the entire castle over silly superstitions? I find it hard to believe you'd ever get anything under control without causing more trouble than there was before! Do you see anything wrong within these walls? Because I don't!" His words stab my heart a million times and set my soul ablaze. My blood begins to boil and I start to lose my patience. I gather my courage and glare directly into his eyes.

"Believe me or not, but I saw its face in the fire. And if I hadn't-" He slams his foot down on the stone floor like a child, causing everyone to quiver.

"Don't speak of your mother in my presence! Your trouble is the reason she's gone!" I stomp my foot on the ground and unintentionally cause the stone below to crack and shatter like glass.

"I KNOW I'M THE REASON! That's all you and many others have said! This is why I'm TRYING to fix things and you won't listen!" His eyes widen in shock when he sees the ground cracking.

Before I can speak another word, the ground rumbles and the giant glass window shatters behind us. The blow causes a few people to fall to the ground and I feel tiny shards of glass piercing my skin. I walk around to ensure everyone is okay and I rush over to help Riverlynn stand up. I look at the window that now has a massive hole in it and black smoke begins to pour in like a mini waterfall.

"Everyone, go to the cellar and don't come out until I or the knights say it's safe to do so!" I look at my sister and hold her hands for a moment. "I need you to keep everyone together. It'll be okay, I promise. Go!" She nods with tears in her eyes and leads everyone to the cellar that's below the castle.

Orion and Atticus rally to my side with their swords unsheathed. The only other one to remain is the king and I watch him struggle to get up. He's extremely frazzled and confused at what just happened.

"What did you do?!" He asks, rubbing his eyes. I refuse to speak to him and instead, Orion steps up to him.

"Your majesty, you must go with the others to the cellar where it's safe!" Before anyone can move, a heavy gust of wind blows violently into the throne room and dark shadows fill the atmosphere, swarming around us like terrifying ghosts.

My father pivots around and once he sees the creatures, he turns to me with arched brows and curled fists. One of the beasts roars and it scares him so much to the point where he runs down the halls, towards the cellar.

I hope you believe me now.

Orion and Atticus raise their blades, standing in front of me, ready to fight.

"You must go now! You'll be safe down there!" I could barely hear Atticus yelling over the tempestuous wind that howls past my ears.

"No! I'm staying! There's no one left to help!" A low, terrifying growl rumbles the castle, causing us to lose our balance.

Then the thick shadows morph and change shape, revealing horrifying monsters. The same monsters I saw in the fire and in the woods.

"Vivalda, it's too dangerous. You must go!" Atticus yells as he and Orion spread out around the room, anticipating the beasts' attack. My heart races quicker and my legs grow weak. My mind tells me to retreat, but my gut tells me to stay. Flashbacks echo in my mind, playing on repeat. Every sound, every smell, every sight and every feeling returns to me as if I'm about to relive the worst night of my life. I can feel my heart begin to harden and my fear is replaced with growing intense rage.

The black smoke that flows around the ground and up the walls slowly transforms into hideous beasts with razor sharp claws, terrifying teeth and nostrils that release clouds of black smoke. As they move, they appear to change form. At moments, they have arms and other times, they take the form of massive bulls.

"I ran away once; I won't do it again!" I shout sternly and instinctively reach for the necklace and draw it away from my body, unleashing a blinding beam of lightning that cracks loudly through the window, striking my body and coating me with the armor once more. The lightning catches the monstrous beasts' attention and they come closer to us, circling around like a pack of bloodthirsty hounds.

My blue dress is replaced with the black and blue armor that's shaped far differently than the knight's traditional armor. I throw my right hand to the right and the tiny sword expands into a mighty heavy weapon. I find myself coated in protective armor, with a sharp weapon in hand and yet, something keeps me frozen to the ground until I see one of the monsters appear out of thin hair behind Atticus who's facing the damaged window. The bloodthirsty beast spirals and twists towards him while opening its ferocious mouth and raising one of its large claws, ready to attack.

"Behind you!" I scream at Atticus and I dash towards him. I instinctively run up to the monster and drive the sword into its vile ghostly body, aiming for its chest. I pull the blade down and hear its insides tearing apart and see vibrant green ooze leak from its body. The beast screams in agonizing pain and when I pull the sword back, the body of the brute disintegrates into fine dust particles, leaving its bodily fluids behind.

I stand tall, in disbelief of what just happened. My eyes bulge from my head and I begin to zone out. Physically, I feel nothing but intense power surging through my body. It's both an incredible yet terrifying feeling I never thought would be possible to experience.

I turn around to see three more monsters left. Orion and Atticus fight back-to-back, slashing their swords into the bodies of the shadowy monsters and one of them turns its attention away from the knights and its wicked red eyes lock onto me. This beast I face looks like a demonic slug with large claws and no legs and it hovers in the air.

I grip my sword tightly in my right hand and it rapidly charges at me, roaring so loudly that I can feel warm liquid slowly fall from my ears. I do what I can to ignore the throbbing pain I feel in my head and use all my strength to run towards the fiend. When I am inches from colliding with the beast, it swings its arm over and I react quickly enough to bend backwards and slide under its stomach. I lean on my knees and the metal scraps loudly against the stone floor. I hold the sword up and it slices through its chest and stomach.

When the creature fully passes over me, I quickly turn around and feel my feet beginning to dig into the hard ground, causing it to break under my toes. I breathe shakily and my palms sweat while holding the sword tightly.

How did that happen? I don't fight. I've never fought before.

I try to silence my thoughts so I can keep my focus on the monster. The horrifying beast cries in pain and scowls at me with its eyes glowing red. The hairs on my neck stand. I hear one of the knights shout and I look over to see Atticus and Orion struggling to fight the two remaining enemies. Time's running out and if I don't hurry, I might lose them.

Let's get this over with.

I charge at the monster once more and once it sees me, it lifts high up into the air, out of my reach. Once I get close enough, push off the ground with all the strength I have and lunge into the air, driving the sword into its chest. The beast jolts back and the blade slowly slides down its body. I look over and down to see how high I am in the air and my stomach jumps to my chest. The beast continues to flash around and I hold on as long as I can to the blade's hilt until the daunting height causes me to get dizzy to the point where I lose my grip and release the hilt, causing me to fall and hit the ground hard.

As soon as I hit the ground and land on my side, the armor and sword disappear. I try getting up, but due to the immense pain I feel, I remain on the ground. When my vision comes back into focus, I watch the monster suddenly dart straight towards me while screaming with its mouth wide open. Its bodily fluids leak onto the floor and it looks like it's ready to swallow me whole but once it's barely an inch from me, its body disappears over me. Its scream echoes and drowns out in a haunting manner and the gold necklace falls right in front of me. I quickly grab it but before I can get up, the remaining beasts stop attacking and leave out the way they came in. The bodies disappear once they get outside and I release a sigh of heavy relief.

"They're gone right? Like...GONE gone?" Orion's voice trembles as he struggles to stay standing.

"I hope so." My breath rapidly escapes my lungs. The men rush over to help me stand up and I get the necklace fasted around my neck once again.

"I'm so sorry, I didn't believe you from the start. With the dead forest, the monster you spoke of...I'm so sorry." Orion profusely apologizes but I don't see a need for him to.

"There's no need for that right now. We need to check on the others." I say as I lead them down towards the cellar.

Upon opening the door, we are greeted with a lot of commotion and everyone's voices overlap with each other to the point where it's overwhelming.

"Everyone, quiet down!" My father's command silences everyone almost immediately.

The king turns around to face me and now everyone's eyes are on me, and the knights. I can tell they wait patiently for one of us to speak, but instead, I wait to see what my father has to say.

"What do you have to say for yourself?" The king crosses his arms and before I can even breathe, Atticus steps forward to address him.

"The words Princess Vivalda has spoken are true and no one listened. You knew the villagers were witnessing supernatural events and no precautions were taken. Due to this matter, three homes were burned and the people are left scared and unprotected as we speak." Atticus' voice is stern and strong but the look on father's face disapproves of it.

"Great." He claps his hands together and his demeanor changes suddenly. "It's such a relief to hear that what was witnessed is true and you and your son were there to protect us." Atticus and Orion look at me and I shake my head. He will always be in denial that I'm trying to help.

"From here on out, we must act diligently. My priority is the castle grounds. Nothing leaves or comes in without my approval." His words make me freeze and everyone else in the room is just as stunned by his words.

"What do you mean your priority is the castle? What about Palavon and the rest of the kingdom? Did you not hear us the second time?" I speak softly and respectfully while taking a small step forward towards my father.

"You have no right to speak against my orders, Vivalda! You've done enough!" At this point, my emotions are fuming with anger and I refuse to let him walk over me like a doormat as he's continued to do so for days.

"Just as you have no right to neglect our people! When mother married you, you swore an oath. Not to the crown, but to the PEOPLE. Mother always abided by her oath, not because it's a royal law, but because she genuinely cared! Our people need us and they're just as important as everyone in this room! You have no idea what we're up against and if you continue to be ignorant, you will put the kingdom in even more danger!" My father's face slowly turns red and the veins in his neck pulsate as if he's holding his breath, ready to explode. He takes a deep breath and growls.

"Well since you think you know better than I, what will you have us do? If you conjure a plan, let's ensure no one dies this time." All the blood in my face washes away and turns pale and my heart skips a painful beat. His scornful tone draws everyone's attention to me as I stand in front of the small crowd with Orion and Atticus behind me.

I look at everyone one by one, hoping someone else would step in, but I can tell they're scared and dare not speak against their king.

Lyla covers her mouth with her hands, holding back tears. Riverlynn looks like she's ready to fight but knows better than to speak up against her own father. Kyson holds his head lowly to the ground and he out of all people in the castle can't speak up or else the king will have him punished. My father has never punished friends or family before but with the state he's in now, there's no telling what he'll do.

I try to find the right words to say, but not a single thought comes to mind. I'm not a fighter or a leader. I was handed a weapon unexpectedly and acted out instinctively as if something else controlled my body and made me fight.

I look up at my father as he stands tall with his arms crossed, waiting impatiently for an answer. He shrugs his shoulders as if to rush an answer out of me.

"I don't know." I respond quietly, lowering my head down, breaking eye contact.

"That's what I thought you'd say. Keep that in mind next time you try to be some hero to those who are less than you are."

I immediately perk my head up and feel my brows arch so tightly that it causes my head to throb. I feel the corners of my lips quiver and my jaw clenches as I firmly squeeze my hands into fists, causing my nails to dig into my skin. I look at Kyson, who is also angered and offended by his words.

"Whether you like it or not, you will obey my orders and if they're crossed, I can guarantee there will be punishments." He adds with a half-smile. I've never seen him be so small-minded before in my life.

At this point my anger fumes so intensely, I refuse to remain in the same room as him. I turn around and walk back towards the stairs so I can exit the cellar. But before I take a step up, I turn to face my father one more time.

"The duty of the crown is to its people. It's interesting how you've forgotten that so quickly." I pause briefly. "You'd think that after mother's death that you'd be doing better to protect your people, now here you are...disrespecting her legacy. Oh, how the mighty fall."

172

"You forget that you wouldn't wear a crown if it wasn't for my mother's marriage to you." I leave, not waiting for him to speak once more because I knew he'd have nothing nice to say.

I stomp heavily up the stairs and follow the halls to my room.

I never thought my own father could be so vile and blindsided. Is this his way of "coping"? Or has he always had this mindset but stayed silent out of respect for my mother?

I walk slowly, thinking to myself silently and once I'm halfway down the hall, I hear the pitter patter of feet running up behind me. I turn around and see Kyson, Riverlynn and Orion rushing to me.

"What do you guys want?" I ask coldly and for a moment, they all freeze and look at each other, hesitant to speak.

"Did you think we'd stay behind and deal with the king's tantrum? No thank you. What he said wasn't right. All of those who witnessed that agrees. We wanted to make sure you're alright. And if you need to talk about it, we're here." Riverlynn speaks softly, trying to comfort me.

"I was once told that Vassuren almost fell once due to a leader's ignorance. If the king wishes to risk the safety of the entire kingdom for reasons that are unclear, let that fall on his shoulders. Who am I to stop him from leading the kingdom to absolute chaos?" I feel numb and I wish not to talk anymore. I'm tired of trying to convince people to do the right thing while knowing they won't listen.

"I know how frustrating this is, but we can't just sit back and watch everything spiral down. Father may have ultimate control of the creed, laws, army and the kingdom as a whole but there has to be something we can do to counteract his foolishness-" Riverlynn explains.

The royal codes are nothing but rubbish in the hands of my father.

"River, I know what you're trying to do and I'm sorry but there's nothing I can do. I am nothing compared to him. His word and command overpowers mine and my words can only do so much. This is something far out of my control."

Kyson grows antsy and steps forward to speak.

"Your mother wouldn't stand for his behavior. You know this. Crown or no crown, she always fought for Vassuren and its people." Kyson speaks encouragingly.

His enlightening words make me think and I begin to step out of the negative mind space I feel trapped in.

I follow my mother's courage, not my father's ignorance.

"Not only do we have father and monsters to deal with, but I also want to know what that armor stuff was because that was-" Before Riverlynn can finish her sentence, a thought comes to mind.

"Do either of you know where Lyla is? I need her with us. I need to show you something." I ask excitedly and Riverlynn shakes her head.

"Father has all the castle staff cleaning the throne room and repairing the damages. We may need to catch up with her later. I'd hate to pull her away from father's side and potentially anger him more and cause her to be punished." She says irritated.

Of course he's immediately making the servants work on repairs. What a fool.

"Alright. I'll catch her up later. I need you guys to go to Alsfield with me. I have something to show you." I quickly lead the group to Alsfield and I feel my soul being ignited on fire as I reminisce on my father's harsh words. I can't let go of the way he looked and sounded while speaking to me. I try my best to shake off my anger, but it continues to linger.

Once we step foot into the forest, everything is peaceful and quiet as usual. Woodland critters scurry past us and birds sing from the trees. We reach the center of the forest where we see Silva's statue standing still and once we're gathered in front of her, I take a deep breath.

"I have something to show you, but you all must promise not to tell another soul about what you'll see." The three of them looked at each other confused but proceed to nod.

I know I can trust them with what they're about to see, but I still need to verbalize my precautions just in case. I turn back to look at the statue, looking at her eyes.

Please don't embarrass me.

I take a step back and the others follow my lead. I grow extremely anxious, worried that I'll make a fool of myself and maybe everything I witnessed the night before was nothing but a vision.

"Silva...if you could wake up and help me explain some things, it'd be much appreciated." I say softly, causing the others to look at me like I'm crazy. My skin begins to tingle and nothing happens.

"Silva? The statue has a name?" Riverlynn asks, confused.

"Yes. Give it a moment." After a moment, all I can hear is the sound of crickets chirping.

"Any day now would be great, don't embarrass me please." I say sharply through my teeth.

"Maybe we should just give you some space. Everything that's happened today is a lot to deal with and I'd hate to add to it." Orion says awkwardly, trying to slowly step away.

"No! I swear, I know what I'm doing. She's just taking her sweet time."

I walk up to Silva, standing on my tippy toes as if to get her attention as her stone body stands tall above me.

"Silva, hellooooooo! I know you can hear me! WAKEUP!" I scream as I jump up and down while waving my hands in the air like a weirdo, trying to wake up the statue.

"Yep, she's completely lost it." Riverlynn says under her breath and I turn to them sharply, highly irritated.

"I swear, I know what I'm doing. I'm not THAT crazy. She's just being a stubborn tree hugger-" Before I could finish my sentence, there's a sudden powerful gust of wind and the trees move unnaturally to twist together and create a canopy overhead, hiding us from the outside world.

The trees grow tall and cave over us, blocking out most of the daylight.

"About time!" I speak loudly over the howling wind.

The others stumble back, frightened and I see Riverlynn fall into Orion's arms. Before we know it, there's a blinding green light that floods the entire forest. The ground lifts and rolls over like a sea wave, I trip over a lump and fall backwards on my back.

The statue begins to crack and shed, revealing Silva's elegant figure. Grey turns into color with her skin still gray, her bright white hair has colorful glowing green streaks framing her face and her cheeks, eyes and chest are highlighted in green. She grows tall in height, stomps heavily over to me and leans over me with her eyes piercing my soul menacingly.

"Call me a 'tree hugger' one more time and I swear I'll bury you to the world's core!" Her voice echoes and booms loudly, ringing my ears which are already inflamed. Her long hair sways gently with the wind, the large leaves in her hair twitch to the side and her eyes glow white.

"Hey hey hey! I was just trying to wake you up and you weren't listening!" I say as I hold my hand up to surrender. She softens her gaze before standing up and backing away, keeping her firm gaze on me.

"Damn, you didn't have to be THAT violent with the wind and the booming. Jeez." I complain as my body throbs from falling to the floor. "You didn't answer the first time and I didn't know what else to do." I continue as I stand up and wipe the dirt and grass off my dress.

"I can't just 'wake up' on demand. It takes me a moment. Besides, I don't always expect...visitors." Silva turns her gaze to the others who begin to panic.

"Viv? What the hell is this?" Riverlynn asks as Orion holds her in his arms. Once Silva realizes they're scared, she makes the wind die down and the forest illuminates once again with the plants and trees glowing brightly, despite it being early in the evening. I look around and see small glowing orbs floating around us playfully and large flowers blooming at our feet.

"Please try to relax. I promise she's harmless. Well...to everyone but me apparently." I say under my breath, reassuring them. Silva steps forward and stands up tall. She waves her hands forward and green magic like particles glide out of her palm and fingertips. The green wispy magic flows past me and dances playfully around Riverlynn.

At first, my sister is extremely scared, but once she realizes Silva's magic is harmless, she smiles in absolute joy and wonderment while dancing around the sparkling magic and chasing it like a happy child. Once the ribbon of magic disappears, Riverlynn turns her focus back to Silva and we all gather around her.

"I mean not to scare you. It's wonderful to finally meet you, Riverlynn. I've heard so much about you from your mother when she'd visit me."

Riverlynn

I stare up at the statue that had just come to life in front of my eyes and I have a hard time believing that what I'm witnessing is real. The strange gray woman glows as bright as the north star. She slowly turns away from us while holding out a gentle hand, encouraging us to follow her. I swallow the ball of air at the back of my throat and gather my courage.

We follow Vivalda and the mysterious woman further into the forest and eventually, we come across a gigantic tree with glowing blue and orange veins that travel up its trunk. I'm in awe of the forest's beauty. When Silva wakes up, it's as if the forest awakens with her in ways I never thought possible. I can't decide whether to be fearful or fascinated.

Silva stands with her back towards the tree and the branches move and wrap around her body and arms, blending into her skin. There's a faint glowing green aura that outlines Silva's body and as she breathes, the tree and nature around her glows and breathes with her in peaceful unison.

I cautiously walk up to her and Orion joins my side with his hand resting on his sword hilt. I reach my hand out, hesitant to touch the tree, and quickly pull away.

"I promise it doesn't bite, child. But trust me when I say, swords and nature are not ones to quarrel with." Silva smiles and speaks softly with her voice echoing around us.

I slowly raise my hand and rest it on one of the branches that wraps around her arm. I can feel the tree's veins pulsing underneath the bark like a heartbeat.

"This is incredible. Did mother know about all of this too?" I ask while continuing to examine the tree and the glowing lights. I look back and see Kyson walking up next to us, astonished by what's in front of us.

"We've been told as kids that-" Orion begins to speak and Silva immediately interjects as if knowing what he'd say.

"Magic doesn't exist. Yes, I've heard all the tales and read all the lies. In a sense, some tales you've heard regarding magic and fantasy are true, while others were told in order to make my people look bad. Due to the surging ignorance of humankind, magic barely exists in the world and those who are left have remained hidden, long enough for the true tales to become nothing but human fantasies. Aladora knew the stories, but not their truths. Just as she was familiar with my stone presence, but not my true form." I look at Kyson and Orion who are just as intrigued as I am. I look back and see Vivalda pacing back and forth in front of Silva.

"As much as I'd love to talk about the pretty magic in front of us, we must talk about the spooky 'magic' that attacked the castle and Palavon." We all back up and stand in front of Silva, waiting for an answer.

"The same creatures that killed my mother infiltrated the castle. I managed to miraculously destroy two of them, then the rest just...disappeared." Vivalda explains and Silva sits up tall with a cold gaze in her eyes. Her shoulders tense and her magic beams brighter.

"The castle walls were left unguarded?" Silva asks, raising one of her dark gray brows.

"Yes, our father sent all the knights on leave for a few days to recover from the queen's death." I respond and Silva releases a frustrated sigh.

"Who knew a king could make such a grave mistake?" The deep rage in her voice sends chills down my spine.

"Do you know what those monsters are, Silva?" Vivalda asks cautiously and Silva looks at each of us one by one.

"They are known as Aerolights. They are made up of the darkest magic in the world. They are very evil, shadow-like monsters that come in various forms. Each form determines their strength and level of resilience. Their sole purpose is to kill. I don't fully understand them myself." Silva explains and Vivalda takes a step closer to Silva with the most determined look in her eye.

"Earlier, you said you're one of the few magic folk left, what else is out there besides you and these Aerolights?" Vivalda asks while clutching onto mother's necklace.

"There are a few magic folk spread across Vassuren, Palavon, Yarrin and Darali. We once coexisted peacefully with humans, until they deemed us as monsters. Even after losing many of my people, we've continued to uphold our vow of forever protecting whatever's left of the world and ALL who reside with us, even if they pose a threat. Now, after almost a hundred years, the spirits are starting to awaken once again to take down the Aerolights so they won't take another innocent life." I'm at a loss for words while listening to Silva speak. It all sounds too impossible to believe. To think powerful entities have been hiding amongst us makes me feel uneasy and I don't hesitate to ask questions.

"I saw Vivalda wearing some kind of armor that magically appears and disappears. Where did that come from?" I shrug my shoulders, feeling silly as I try to explain my thoughts after still trying to wrap my head around everything I've seen since the village attack.

"The little necklace pendant was blessed by beings far greater than anything humans have ever imagined. The pendant's power has chosen Vivalda as its wielder and now, her soul and its magic has begun to bond." I look over worriedly at Vivalda who shakes her head in disgust.

"Can you get rid of the Aerolights?" Vivalda asks sternly and Silva shakes her head.

"Not alone. And that's mainly because I don't know where they come from or what kind of magic fuels their life force. I'm not sure any other Serafae know either. That being said, we have to travel to the outer lands and gather the remaining Serafaes to see if any will rally by our sides so we can defeat them for good." Silva slowly stands from her wooden throne and the tree disconnects from her body and goes back to normal.

"Aside from that plan sounding near impossible and very outlandish, who's 'we'?" Vivalda asks, highly confused and Silva's way of responding is by staring straight at her without blinking.

Vivalda and I widen our eyes at the same time. Once we realize what Silva's referring to. Pure terror crosses our faces and I gather by her side.

"No no no, absolutely NOT. I didn't ask for the power that comes with the necklace. All I wanted was something to remember my mother by. Have someone else do it because I've been through enough turmoil as it is!" Vivalda tries to walk away and the rest of us begin to slowly follow but Silva uses her magic to make the grass wrap around her ankles, gluing her to the ground.

"Can you not be so stubborn for once? It's crucial that you understand what I'm telling you. The armor and power you possess has bonded to you. Even from afar, I sensed you summoning its power twice, is that correct?" Silva's voice softens as she tries to calm my sister's nerves.

"Yes, but that was just because there was no one else to help." Silva glides back slowly.

"Exactly, there's no one else. You're the only one who can use its power. You defeated the Aerolights and saved the village without having any prior experience in fighting. You saved the people that tarnished your name." I lower my head to stare at the glowing blades of grass that sway with the wind. So many thoughts and feelings cross my mind. So much makes sense and doesn't at the same time.

I understand Silva's point.

Maybe it chose Vivalda because she's so selfless. Unlike someone else in the castle walls.

I watch the grass unwind from Vivalda's feet and she turns to face Silva.

"I mean no offence, but I don't care if some magical force has chosen me. This isn't what I need. I already has the kingdom in disbelief that what I saw was true and now-"

"And now, many of us DO believe you. I'll admit, at first it sounded absolutely inconceivable. But once we came here and you spoke the way you did, I began to think that maybe the impossible is possible. Once I saw those beasts in the castle, I realized I should have fully believed in the beginning and maybe my father and I would have been more prepared." Orion says while resting his right hand over his heart. Vivalda smiles at him while tightly grasping the necklace.

"I've only now realized how crucial it is to prepare for not only the impossible, but also the unexpected." Orion continues and cold chills continue to crawl down my spine and my heart thumps hard and loud in my chest.

"Magic chooses its host based on their heart. Yours holds a treasuring light unlike anything magic has ever bestowed itself upon." I can feel tears make their way to my eyes and my heart begins to race. Vivalda looks at me and immediately notices I'm emotional.

"Can you show me?" My voice cracks and Vivalda quickly lets go of the necklace charm and shakes her head silently.

"Please. There's something I need to see for my own peace of mind." Vivalda looks at Orion then Kyson and they both nod their heads to reassure her everything is okay. She continues to shake her head for a brief moment but ends up giving in.

Everyone but Silva backs up just in case and Vivalda holds the sword charm before taking a deep breath and breaking the chain away from her neck.

I jump back when a huge bolt of lightning breaks through the trees and strikes Vivalda overhead, causing a huge wall of bright white smoke to circle around her like a tornado. And in no time, the lightning and smoke disappear, revealing my sister covered in black armor with bright blue glowing designs and a silver halo crown resting on her head.

An intense wave of shock buzzes throughout my body as if I was the one struck by a strong bolt of lightning.

I step closer to Vivalda, observing every inch of the armor that covers her body. The blue designs pulsate with a constant rhythm and flow. The silver bladed sword she holds has a black leather hilt with a blue crystal resting in the center below it. I carefully rest my right hand on the pauldron that covers her shoulder. The metal is cold to the touch and I look at her with teared filled eyes.

"I've seen this before." I say softly and run my fingers over one of the long red braids that rests over her shoulder.

"What do you mean?" Vivalda asks and I can tell she's so overwhelmed that she's on the verge of breaking down.

"Before you fell asleep, there was a game we'd play. Do you remember what it was?" Vivalda thinks for a moment and then shakes her head. I take a deep breath and try not to cry while I speak. "I'd pretend to be a queen in distress and you'd play the role of a fearless warrior." Her eyes widen and tears slip down her cheeks.

I feel tears filling my eyes. Vivalda's soft gaze is broken with tears slowly falling from her eyes. "Armor or none. The warrior I once saw as a child is no different than the one standing before me now." Vivalda takes a deep breath and she pulls me in for a hug, keeping the sword pointed away so she doesn't accidentally hurt me with it.

"If you ask me. As impossible and scary as this all may be, I think fate gave you this for a reason and it was all thanks to mother's choice."

"You should go." I whisper and choke on my words as they fall off my tongue. Vivalda gently leans me off of her and looks at me desperately.

"I can't, this isn't my fight, I'm not meant to-" At this point, Vivalda is softly crying but staying as calm as possible. I can tell she's overwhelmed and frightened.

"You don't deserve to carry this weight, no. BUT you said it yourself, the duty of the crown is to its people and I think you might be the only one brave enough to do something about this. I can almost guarantee you father will remain in solitude, caring only about himself. Are you going to just sit around and watch that happen?" Deep down, I don't want her to leave, not just because I can't bear to be separated from her, but also because the journey Silva speaks of sounds dangerous.

"Everything will be okay. Look...you have a giant, terrifying yet awesome spirit by your side. When we were kids, you always spoke of wanting to go on the greatest adventures possible. Maybe this is the gods telling you that this is your moment. THIS might be the adventure you've been waiting for." Vivalda looks at Silva who stands next to me. She takes a deep breath and shakes her head before looking back.

"I'll need time to think about this. Assuming things won't get worse than they already are." Silva nods her head in acceptance and as a group, we decide to spend the rest of the day in Alsfield to get to know Silva and the power my sister possesses.

As we sit in the luscious grass field, Vivalda sits next to Kyson, showing him the sword.

"If only I could make something as cool as this." He says as he examines every part of the weapon.

"I think you can. Maybe you ought to try one day." My sister says encouragingly.

I sit in between Orion's legs and lean against his chest while Vivalda and Kyson continue to chat.

"You saw my sister fighting with the armor and sword, didn't you?" I look up at Orion and wait patiently for an answer. The colorful glow casts over his skin beautifully and his hazel eyes sparkle with every light that peaks through the trees.

"I did." He says softly.

"Do you think she can hold her own?" He looks down at me and shrugs his shoulders.

"One thing's for sure, I never thought I'd ever witness a princess fight before but what I saw was quite incredible. As long as she has that sword and Silva with her, I think she'll be fine." He hugs me from behind and in his grasp, I find it easier to breathe and relax.

"Random question, Silva. Isn't the tree basket weave a bit obvious to those outside of the forest? Wouldn't others be able to suspect something strange is going on in here?" Vivalda asks as she stares at the trees that intertwine with each other.

Silva stands in the distance, bound to the ground by vines that wrap around her body from the ground.

"Humans can't see through the forest unless I want them to. There's an invisible barrier surrounding the forest that gives the illusion that the forest is completely still and normal." A silly thought comes to my mind and I observe the trees.

"Wait...if humans can't see through the barrier, why make the trees wrap around like that?" I ask curiously.

"I enjoy giving a glimpse of what my magic is capable of. Besides, it's visually pleasing and reassures the atmosphere is safe under my guidance and control." Silva says while looking around at the canopy of leaves and branches.

"We should probably head back to the castle just in case father needs someone else to yell at. I don't want to give him more reasons to be angry." Vivalda says while standing up and retracting the armor. A gust of wind flows past us and fog swirls up her body, revealing her normal figure with the sword necklace swinging around in her hand.

"If either of you need me, I'll be here, waiting." Silva leads us out of the forest and she returns to the center to turn back into a statue. Once we cross the forest's boundary, the atmosphere returns to normal.

When we cross the bridge, we hear a commotion coming from the castle and see the knights have returned and are gathering quickly around the fortress.

Did father call for their return already? Maybe he finally came to his senses.

We enter the castle through the back door and make our way down the halls. "What are you thinking?" I ask Vivalda quietly so no one can hear and she looks at the floor while walking, thinking intensely.

"I don't know. Like I said, it's not something I want to do." While we continue walking down the halls, we hear a cart rolling our way and we're greeted by Lyla.

"Oh! Princesses, I was hoping to find you both! Are you alright?" Lyla is relieved to see us and she parks her cart to the side of the hall before waddling to us slowly.

"We're fine Lyla, I was actually hoping I could talk to you for a moment." Vivalda holds out her hands to Lyla.

"I'd love to, dear, but your father ordered me to find you and tell you that he demands your presence in the throne room, immediately." She speaks quickly and by the look on her face, I can tell she's stressed. Her hands shake while Vivalda holds them gently.

"Did he say what for?" I ask and Lyla shakes her head.

"No, but I wouldn't keep him waiting any longer, his mood has only gotten more explosive and to be quite honest, some staff have thought about walking away from the castle because they're scared. But they fear that the king will punish them. I'll try to catch up afterwards."

Vivalda looks at the rest of us with anger filling her eyes.

"I'll meet you guys back here once we're finished talking." She takes off down the hall but the rest of us follow quickly behind.

"You guys never listen." She scoffs as she speeds down the hall and I can't help but reply sarcastically.

"I got that from you, sister."

Once we reach the kitchen, Kyson, Orion and I remain behind while Vivalda leaves out the door and into the throne room. From behind the door, we can hear every word that's spoken and I can't help but feel anxious to know how things play out.

Vivalda

Once I enter the throne room, I walk up to my father who sits on his chair and he orders all staff and knights to leave the room. I stand before my father and we have a silent stare down.

"What is this about?" I ask softly, yet sternly, trying not to show signs of agitation considering the fact I don't want to be around him. Being in his presence while he's obviously angry makes me feel uneasy.

"Do you realize the disrespect you've shown me recently?" He's barely said anything and I'm ready to argue back but I keep myself respectfully composed to hear what he has to say.

"I understand you're reverting to your childhood years, wanting to play the role of some kind of knight-wanna-be, therefore getting in the way of the knights and their oath. Not only that, but you dare to speak poorly of my marriage to your mother." The very few words he speaks already boils my blood. My heart fumes with rage, beating slowly, ready to explode.

"You have brought terror and fear to the kingdom and have disgraced the crown and everything we've always stood for." At this point, my anger is nearly uncontrollable.

"In what way have I disgraced you? If anything, you have disgraced everyone here. I can see clearly and somehow, you cannot. In what way have I brought such 'terror' to our land? You act as if I purposely brought these monsters to our home."

"They never showed their presence until you tried to be some kind of hero!" He shouts loudly from his chair, making me jolt slightly and then I take a step forward with a pleading voice, trying to reason with his anger.

"Father, we were told that night that the villagers were witnessing strange things and the knights were the one to pass on the message. Mother left to Astryn to ensure what the people saw were true and-" Father slams his fist on the arm rest, making me stop talking.

"And now she's dead! Who's to say what the villagers saw were true? I didn't believe it until I witnessed my castle being destroyed and you miraculously knew they were coming! For all I know, Aladora could have been arriving safely home until she needed to help you. All of this revolves around you!" I hold my hands behind my back and curl them into tight fists, trying not to lose my temper.

Cold air flows in from the broken window behind me and my shadow cascades over my father and his chair. I take a deep breath before choosing my next words carefully.

"If grief is making you think and speak this way, I think it's best to let it be known because right now, you are speaking words that are absolutely inconceivable. If you can't see that then-" The king stands up quickly, pushing the tall chair backwards, nearly making it fall over.

"Don't forget your place! You are the reason we're all in this mess!" He yells loudly, causing me to step back. His hands curl into fists and his face turns red.

"My place?! My place is with my people! I'm trying to find a way to fix it and your temper is stopping the solution from being found!" No matter what I say, my words strike more nerves than before, causing him to walk towards me slowly, trying to intimidate me but I continue to stand my ground.

"If blaming mother's death on me makes you feel better, so be it. But I won't stand by a king who puts himself before his family or his people. You disgrace the crown almost as much as you've disgraced mother." Before I know it, his hand harshly grazes my cheek, causing my head to thrash to the side. My neck and face pulsate in pain and my left cheek is left feeling warm to the touch. The muscles in my neck are tense and I feel tears rush down my face.

The internal rage I feel is overwhelming. I reach for the necklace as it swings back and forth and I'm ready to summon the armor and its power but pull back hesitantly. I want him to feel my range, my pain, my anger. But I know better, unlike him. I gather my strength and stand tall. The king faces away, staring at the floor, partially ashamed.

"This isn't the ruler our kingdom once knew. If you wish to spread lies like fire, fine. I know the truth about that night and that truth remains with me. I know you'll continue to be blinded by rage and it'll be the biggest mistake YOU ever make." I breathe heavily as I wait for him to turn his attention to me but he remains standing still, refusing to look at me.

"You'll never step foot in this room again." He growls sharply and my heart drops to the ground.

"What are you saying?" I ask quietly, scared of his response. He pivots around and snarls through his teeth.

"You will leave the castle grounds and never step foot on these grounds again." I twist around when I hear a door slam open and I turn around to see Riverlynn barge the door and Kyson and Orion follow closely behind.

"You will NOT throw such commands around like that!" My sister yells and she and the men gather by my side.

"I don't need you stepping in Riverlynn! Your sister is apparently wise enough to take matters into her own hands so now she can handle what she's being given." Our father's words continue to stab me in the heart over and over again.

"I beg your pardon!" Riverlynn snaps as she continues to walk quickly to the center of the room.

"You couldn't stay put like I asked?" I question softly as they all scan my face that's stained with pain and tears. Kyson approaches me and moves the chunk of hair that lays over the side of my face and he tucks it behind my ear.

"What did he do?" His gaze hardens as I can hear his hands curl into fists. Riverlynn is in shock once she realizes why the side of my face is red.

"Don't worry about it right now." I can tell each of them are ready to fight, but the last thing I need is my father to punish them along with me.

"What has gotten into you!" Riverlynn steps forward ferociously to approach the king but I put my hand on her shoulder, pulling her back.

"Don't. If I can't get through to him, none of you will." All three of them do as I say and step back. The king looks at us with a slight smirk on his face. I stand tall, swallow my pride and walk up to him cautiously.

"Is that your final judgment?" I ask calmly. His sunken eyes twitch and his nostrils flare.

"Yes." One simple word makes my heart drop to my stomach and my shoulders tense. We stare in each other's eyes for a few moments, I hope that in some way, he'll retract his command and come to his senses but his hardened gaze doesn't break. There's so much I wish to say but I know it won't help my situation. I pull away from my father and I can hear Riverlynn sniffling.

"Good. You've managed to help me come to my senses." He huffs and crosses his arms over his chest. I turn to the others and encourage them to follow me. "Let's go." I lead them out of the throne and before reaching the door, I stop and turn to my father one last time. He remains standing, staring at us.

"You're a coward and until you open your eyes, you'll be the greatest threat to this castle and its people. I'll forever speak of my mother and her legacy. She'd be ashamed because this isn't the noble man she married. She spoke highly of you once and now she cries in her grave." We leave the room and Orion slams the door behind us. Once we return to the kitchen, we're stopped by several knights and servants who were listening to the conversation. Lyla is in the front of the group, surrounded by tall knights with her cheeks glazed in tears.

"Please don't tell me you all heard that." I spot Atticus at the back of the group and his head hangs lowly in disappointment.

"He had no right." He speaks softly, gritting his teeth. The others around him nod and agree. I shake off pain as if nothing happened and I continue to speak strongly.

"For those interested, I'd like to have a word on the balcony. I'll make it quick before the king finds knights missing from their posts." Everyone agrees and they follow me to the balcony.

Once we're outside, I stand with my back to the stone ledge and everyone faces me. I try to wipe away whatever anxiety and stress I feel so I can speak properly.

"Whatever information I share with you right now; I need this information to be relayed everywhere. For all anyone knows, what I tell you is a speculation, that way the king will have no one to punish. It's obvious that the king isn't himself and I fear his emotions will continue to consume him ever so slowly to the point where he will continue to make rash decisions and be as selfish as he already is. But due to his command and my banishment from the castle, maybe he'll calm down. That being said, I have some important matters to tend to outside of the castle anyways. If the king won't rid the kingdom of whatever dark force this is, then I will. Or...I'll try to at least. While I'm away, I need you all to remain vigilant and on guard. I assume Atticus and Orion filled you all in on the recent events that took place in Palavon and within the castle, correct?" I look at the knights, waiting for a response.

"Yes, all knights and guards are aware of the situation and we're all just as equally confused. Where did they come from?" Atticus asks and I speak quickly, giving them whatever information I know.

"The monsters that attacked the castle are called Aerolights. They're made of pure, dark energy and their only purpose is to kill. My source of this information will remain unknown until the issue is solved. I'm going to leave the kingdom to find where they come from and bring an end to their madness before we lose more than what we already have. I fear this is a race against time and I need you all to trust me. Just because I am my father's daughter, it doesn't mean I think poorly like him." Everyone looks at each other and it doesn't look like anyone negatively opposes what I say. All I can do is hope and assume they'll do as I ask and believe what I tell them.

"Before I go, I want to leave you all with this. I'm sorry for causing all of this trouble. I'm determined to fix my mistake and I hope you all believe me on that." I look at everyone and Atticus steps forward, looking absolutely saddened.

"Between both of us, princess. I never once blamed you for the matters at hand." He smiles and I instantly feel a small portion of weight lift off my shoulders.

"Thank you, Atticus." He walks up and hugs me tightly.

"We will always rally by your side if you need us." He whispers to me before pulling away.

I dismiss everyone and they return to their posts, but Lyla, Orion, Kyson and Riverlynn follow me to my room.

I go to my wardrobe to retrieve a black long sleeve bodysuit and a dark blue long sleeve coat with Silver embellishments and a silver belt. Below the hanging clothes, I also grab my black leather boots.

I go to the washroom and change into the new outfit before returning back to the others who crowd around my bed.

"This isn't fair. He can't do that...can he?" Riverlynn's anger echoes around the room.

"Technically, yes. It's not common for a king or queen to banish their own but it's not completely unknown to happen." I tie my hair into a single braid while talking, Kyson stares out the window while Lyla sits with Riverlynn, comforting her.

"Why is he being like this?" Riverlynn cries into her hands and Orion walks over to rub her back. I sit next to her on the bed and hold her in my arms.

"He's blinded by rage and needs someone to blame for mother's death. I don't know if that's truly the case, but that's what it looks like. But like I said, hopefully once I leave, he'll ease up and do better." I stand up slowly, looking down at her.

"I don't want to be alone again." I cup her face in my hands and she looks at me with tears running down her face.

"I know. I hate this just as much as you do. I don't want to leave but I'll be back before you know it. You'll have Lyla and the men with you. They've always been there for you and that's not going to change now." Riverlynn cries in my hands softly.

"Just promise me you'll be safe. I don't know what I'd do if I lost you too." After everything that's happened, her fear is completely justified and understood.

"I promise, I'll be alright. I'll have the calming forces of nature by my side." I wink at her and we both laugh.

"Why can't we go with you?" Kyson asks softly from the window. I can feel his intense rage and anger without him looking at me.

"I need you all here to make sure everything is kept in order. Once I return, we'll all go on a trip together. How does that sound?" Everyone smiles and everyone stands to gather for a group hug.

They will never realize how much each of them mean to me. I don't know what I'd do without each of them in my life.

Lyla wipes away streams of tears with her handkerchief.

"Oh Lyla, I promise everything will be okay. Please try not to cry." I say as I bend down to comfort her.

"My heart can't take it. I don't believe in goodbyes. I know you'll return safe and sound but I don't know how long we'll have to tolerate the tyrant of a king." I hug her and she insists she should get back to work because saying goodbye to me will be too hard on her soul.

Once Lyla leaves, the rest of us make our way back to Alsfield, for what could possibly be the last time. As we walk into the forest, I can feel the cool wind blowing past the trees. When we cross the bridge and step foot into the boundaries of the forest, the plants illuminate once more and there's a bright green flash in the distance, possibly indicating that Silva has woken up after sensing our presence.

Once we reach the center of the forest, Silva stands, waiting patiently, guiding us to her with her magic. Her tall height is quite terrifying. Her white gown that's coated with green leaves, flowers and moss glows beautifully and her glowing white hair flows in the breeze.

"That was quicker than I anticipated. Have you decided?" Silva's voice echoes softly with the breeze. I inhale slowly but there's a pinching pain in my chest that causes me to flinch.

"If this is the only way to fix everything, yes, I'll go with you. It's not like I have the choice to stay anyways." I say under my breath. Silva's soft gaze is calm, reassuring and kind. I think she knows how much I don't want to leave.

"There's a long journey ahead of us. We should go now, so that we may take a rest within the forest once nightfall comes." I agree and take a moment to say my goodbyes.

Riverlynn is already sobbing uncontrollably and immediately dives to hold me. She holds me so tight; I can barely breathe and my voice is muffled. "Listen...if I don't come back-" My sister grabs me by the shoulders and pushes me back.

"Shut it. You will not say that. Not now, not ever. I'm so tired of people saying such silly things. You're going to come home and I will NOT say 'goodbye'. Save the kingdom, rub it in father's face and come home to us. Got it?" She chokes on her words as she cries at the same time. Her hysterical emotions cause me to let out a laugh.

I wish to stay locked in her arms, I don't know how long it'll be until I see them again. I pull away slowly and gently and wipe the tears from her eyes.

"I promise, I'll be home before you know it. Until then, try to keep everything organized, don't bother telling father I left and let him figure it out on his own. I plan to pay a visit to Astryn in order to get some answers regarding royal matters. But if any news or messages are to come, notify the messengers that all future messages will be handled by you and you alone. All these years of mother's lessons have prepared us for this." She nods her head and I walk over to Orion who stands tall next to Riverlynn.

"You will do everything in your power to keep my sister and the kingdom safe. I know my father will be a handful, so beat around your oath if you must. Once I return, I will rewrite the laws so you all won't be bound by death in the hands of a childish king." Orion chuckles and smiles. I pat him on the shoulder and proceed to walk to Kyson. I can tell he's in a lot of destress just by the way he has his arms crossed in front of him.

"And you, my good sir. I expect you to have a glorious sword forged by the time I come home." We both laugh but his sweet smile fades away quickly.

I can feel tears swell in my eyes. Everything's happening so fast and before I can speak more, Kyson pulls me in by my waist and holds me gently. I rest the side of my face on his chest and he rests his hand on my head in the most comforting way.

I can hear his heart beating steadily through his black shirt that's unbuttoned halfway. I release all the tension in my shoulders and sink even deeper into his hug, absorbing his comfort for as long as I can.

He's never held me like this before.

I wait for Kyson to pull away and when he does, our arms remain intertwined with each other's and his dark green eyes rest upon my own.

"Just kiss her already!" I hear Riverlynn squeals like a child causing me to laugh and break eye contact.

"There's a time and place for that, you know?" I laugh before turning my attention back to Kyson.

"For what it's worth, you can if you want to." Butterflies fill my stomach and I can feel my cheeks igniting on fire.

Without hesitation, Kyson slowly leans in to kiss me and when he pulls away, his bashfulness causes my heart to melt over and over again and I feel something

I've never felt before. My heart has never yearned to remain in a home that's no longer mine.

"Ooooooh, that was so cute!" Riverlynn squeals loudly while jumping up and down like a child, tugging on Orion's arm.

"Maybe next time, if given the chance, we'll do this without an audience." Kyson laughs softly, partially embarrassed.

"I'd like that." I slowly let go and out of the corner of my eye, I see Silva walking past us and towards the secret exit that's at the far side of the castle gates.

"I love you all so much. I'll be back soon." We all part ways and I walk away slowly, constantly looking back until they're covered by the thick trees and I can no longer see them.

When we exit the castle walls, we wander deep into the forest. Silva walks directly next to me, examining me steadily.

"They'll be okay. I know you know that, but I'll still be here to remind you. Let them be your motivation to fight through the journey ahead of you." She looks down and smiles. Something about her voice and the soft glow in her eyes brings me hope.

"Once you learn to control your abilities, things will ever so slowly get easier. We'll find the Aerolights' magic source, destroy it and you'll return home." Everything she says sounds so much easier said than done.

"I already know how to summon the armor; I've done it twice now. And I've seen the blue smoke- wiggy woo hand things." Silva laughs at me, making me feel embarrassed.

"What emotion were you feeling when you called up the armor?" Her question confuses me because I fail to understand why that matters.

"I guess the main emotion I felt at the time was...fear?" Silva nods her head and turns to face the dirt path we walk on.

"Exactly. You reacted based on instincts that were influenced by fear and the craving for revenge. Your armor and its power can't be summoned only in times of fear. I can guarantee if you were to summon the armor now, you'd fail at doing so." I scoff loudly and Silva turns her head to the side with her brows raised.

"I did it easily the first time, surely I can do it again. Watch." I stop dead in my tracks so I can focus.

I grab the sword charm and gently pull on the gold chain, waiting for the fog and lightning to appear, but nothing happens. Not even the slightest gust of wind is present.

Why isn't it working?

You've got to be joking.

Silva stands in front of me, smirking with her head tilted.

"This will be your first lesson."

I find a secluded area deep in the forest that's not near any paths or roads.

"Your power and armor relies on your emotions. The bond it's begun to forge with you is already strong and thanks to that, you're fighting instincts are already well developed. What you feel, your power feels. As the bond grows stronger, its magic will guide you and can be used for so much more than defense in battle." Vivalda stands in front of me, listening carefully.

"Alright, that'll make sense to me eventually. How do I summon the armor when I'm not...scared?" She asks while examining the necklace that dangles in her hand.

I hold out my right hand and stretch out my fingers. My magic surges from my chest, down my arms and into my fingertips, causing a green ball of powerful magic to form and levitate over my palm. Conjuring my magic is simple and feeling my power stream throughout my body is always an exhilarating feeling.

I focus my energy on the dirt ground below me and cause a low rumble to emerge from the ground. Vivalda tilts her head down, staring at the ground and she carefully backs away.

I close my hand slowly, making the orb disappear and I gracefully thrust my hand down and up, making the magic float out of my fingertips and dive into the ground. In the matter of moments, large luscious strong trees sprout rapidly from the ground. We both watch as they begin as small sprouts and transform into tall bright trees with rich green leaves. The branches stretch out as if waking up from a deep slumber and beautiful purple flowers boom around the base of the trunks. I can hear Vivalda laughing joyfully at the sight of my magic. Once they stop growing, I can feel the trees' heartbeats and my soul feels refreshed.

Vivalda is left speechless and she runs over to the tree, astonished by my magic and what little it can do. "Even in moments of contentment, you and the power you hold can grow and rebuild in the matter of moments." Vivalda hesitantly lays her hand on it as if to see if it's real.

"Yes, it is a real living, breathing tree." She looks at me and smiles.

"How did you learn to do this?" She asks while walking around the trees and observing the flowers at her feet.

"It wasn't something I learned. It's been a part of me since my beginning. It was just a matter of bonding with the gifts I was given." Watching Vivalda walk around the tree over and over makes me dizzy.

"Are you paying attention, child?" I ask loudly, causing her to stop awkwardly and peek her head out from behind the tree.

"For one, don't call me 'child' and two, you can't just show a curious human magic and not expect her to be fascinated by it." She makes her way over to me slowly, looking around the forest.

"No matter what, when it comes to magic, my advice to humans is to not question magic, no matter how confusing it may be." I turn around with my back to

Vivalda and I wave my hand over the grass and make a trail of flowers grow in the grass.

"Now that there is no danger...yet. Would you like to try?" I turn around and see Vivalda on her stomach, staring at a yellow flower as it slowly grows out of the ground. I clear my throat and get her attention, she quickly looks up with her eyes wide open, embarrassed. She immediately gets up and holds her hands behind her back.

"Try what?" She asked, looking at me confused.

I take a deep breath and kneel down to rest on the ground, knowing I'm going to be where I am for a while. "I want you to summon your armor and practice using your powers while not in a state of fear. There's no rush or pressure." She hesitates, standing awkwardly while reaching for her sword pendant. I can hear her thoughts as if they speak out loud.

She's worried about being spotted and caught by stray Aerolights that may be lurking from beyond the forest. "Don't worry, I'll know if danger is nearby. We're far from the village and human trails so the likelihood of being seen or heard is slim. If it helps you feel more comfortable, I can make the trees cover us from above." Vivalda looks up, her golden-brown eyes shine in the sunlight.

"Um- yeah. I think that would help." She says quietly and walks closer to me. I lift my hands and they're coated with green smokey magic that makes my arms tingles. The green magic floats over to the trees and grips onto them. I encourage the trees to bend and cross in front of each other, forming a weaving basket around us and a canopy over our heads that blocks out some of the sunlight. Once the canopy is formed and the trees remain still, Vivalda is once again lost in a trance, amazed by my power.

"Does that make you feel better?" I ask. Vivalda nods her head but I can tell she's still nervous and uneasy.

"When you are ready, I want you to empty your mind the best you can. Don't think about past or current events that ail you. I know it's hard but as soon as your mind is empty, turn your focus to the magic that resides in the necklace. It'll be hard to find at first, but once you and the magic find each other, you'll be able to use it." Vivalda nods while taking a deep breath.

I can sense her trying to silence as many lingering thoughts as possible. I can feel her inner peace flickering in her soul while fighting against her stress and anguish. I sit silently to myself, allowing her to focus.

Vivalda holds the pendant in her hand and closes her eyes. After a brief moment, I begin to feel a strong magical force flow through the air and gently charges towards Vivalda. The wind turns into a wall of white smoke that slowly circles around her legs.

She's got it.

My anticipation begins to pique. I can feel her magic force dance around her playfully like an invisible companion waiting to collide with her.

"Now." I whisper softly and Vivalda pulls the necklace away from her neck swiftly. The wall of white smoke waves over her like a smooth blanket, revealing the black and blue warrior in front of me. The blue symmetrical designs glow brightly and she looks around at her body, examining the armor once more.

I stand up, pleased to see she was able to summon the armor a lot quicker than I thought. Despite this, I can also tell she's still a bit weak because she has a difficult time holding the sword with one hand, which is to be expected.

"Good job. Over time, you will learn to call upon your armor quicker and you'll be able to transform more efficiently without thinking. It'll come in handy when trouble is near." I say encouragingly as Vivalda twirls the sword in her hand slowly, analyzing it closely.

"Mmhm." She says under her breath while running her fingers over the three-dimensional shapes and designs on the armor. There's a glimmer of despair in her eyes and a subtle sense of rage emanating from her soul. I conjure an idea in hopes of getting her to feel some sort of excitement.

"I want you to try something." Vivalda snaps her head up and looks at me. "I want you to move that boulder over there." I point to a large rock that rests roughly fifteen feet from where we stand and Vivalda looks at me, puzzled.

"You want me to...pick that up? What makes you think I can do that? That rock is huge!" She asks and laughs sarcastically, assuming I'm joking.

I reach my arm towards the boulder and pick it up immediately without touching it. I can feel the weight of the giant stone in my core, but in the grasp of my magic, it's weightless. I steadily move it to a different spot and drop it on the grassy ground.

Vivalda's jaw drops. "You think I can do that?! You're insane." Vivalda shouts and throws her hand out.

What a stubborn human.

"How do you know you can't do something if you don't try? You need to remember that I know your powers better than you. I can sense the power that surges through your veins and I roughly know what you're capable of. Picking up a boulder is a daily simple training task. Give it a try." Vivalda groans before sloppily turning to face the rock.

She puts her sword in the baldric that rests on her hip and stands in a comfortable position. She constantly looks over at me, unsure of what she's doing.

"Don't worry if you don't get it on your first try. You summoned the armor successfully, so that's good enough for the day." She stares at the rock. The top half of her body tenses up and her shoulders rise. Her hands curl into fists and an iridescent blue smoke slowly escapes through her tightly curled fingers.

She opens her hand while thrusting it forward and blue electric power streams from her hand, colliding with the stone and once it latches on, she struggles to move it. The hold on the boulder is shaky and her stance is uneven, causing her to lose her balance. But eventually, she's able to barely lift the rock a foot off the ground and she immediately drops it, leaving a deep crater in the dirt.

Vivalda drops her shoulders and she pants heavily. By what she shows me already, I can tell she has a strong fighting spirit, but I don't think she feels it yet and therefore feels doubtful.

"There. Happy?" Vivalda asks, unamused as she walks back towards me. It's interesting that she gets excited to see my magic, but when it comes to her own, she's disgusted.

"Yes, I am, actually. Sit with me if you don't mind." Vivalda sits down next to me slowly. Her armor plates clunk against each other and she struggles to bend down. Something feels off about her demeanor after using her abilities but I'm sure the change in her mood is from getting used to these new changes.

"Most of what you will need to learn can only be taught on a battlefield so take my words seriously and remember them." Vivalda looks at me with tired eyes. "When danger or darkness is near, you must swear on your people that you will never attack with rage. Your power, armor and weapon rely on your emotions. If you allow yourself to be guided by your own internal darkness, you'll walk barefoot on your own blade. Promise you'll never reach for that pendant when you feel your rage consume you." Vivalda's focus shifts into fear.

"Yes...I promise. Someone I once knew is making that mistake as we speak and I refuse to fall down the same path as him. But hypothetically, if I may ask. What would happen if I went too far?" Vivalda asks while playing with the blue magic that coats over her hand.

"Truthfully, I don't know, but let's try not to worry about it right now. As long as you remember that everything will work out according to plan. There's much to do and much to learn." I stand up slowly, disconnecting myself from the ground. The trees unravel and I see the sun beginning to set.

"We must continue traveling north and reach the Lion's Eye before it gets too dark. I want to reach the peak tomorrow before nightfall." Vivalda stands up, keeping the armor on and following me slowly.

We trail through the trees, continuing to steer clear of human trails, homes and pathways. The atmosphere is quiet and peaceful. Birds sing and fly overhead, the trees sway with the cool breeze and the sky is painted light orange with hints of pink. From behind me, I can hear Vivalda using her powers quietly, lifting up small rocks and tossing them to the side.

I find it entertaining to hear her playing around with the inanimate objects because I can tell she's trying to get used to it. I continue walking, weary of every step I take. We never know what could lurk within the forest, so my guard is always up just in case. My peace is disturbed by a loud cracking sound and a painful shock shoots up my spine and into my chest. It feels like I'm being stabbed by a large needle.

I turn around and see Vivalda standing stiffly and looking at me awkwardly with her right hand raised. Blue mist continues to coat her hand like a glove and I see a tree in the distance with a gaping hole in the middle of its trunk.

I slowly glare at her and the blue smoke disappears, she smiles foolishly and laughs awkwardly. "Ow." I say monotonously.

"Uhhhhh...oops." Vivalda tries to flick away the magic that coats her hand, but it doesn't move. She then quickly hides her hand behind her back as if I can't see it. "I didn't know I could do that." She tries not to laugh while continuously pointing at the tree.

"Do that again and you'll be kissing the Earth's core, got it? Warn me next time at least." I turn back around to continue walking and I can hear Vivalda snicker behind me. Her armor clanks against itself while she runs to catch up to me.

"What's the Lion's Eye? I've never heard of it until recently when we heard of villagers having strange experiences on its borders." She asks eagerly.

"Lion's Eye is a giant forest that resides north of Palavon. It stretches all the way to the northern sea." I hear Vivalda take out her sword and she carefully swings it around.

She's getting used to the weapon's weight.

"Mother never properly elaborated on why no one was ever allowed to cross into the forests. Is there a reason?" She walks slower, putting space between us.

"Well, the Aerolights are a good example as to what could possibly reside in the forest. Overall, I'm sure the laws were made to ensure the safety of-" I'm cut off by the loud sound of metal clashing with stone and I stop in my tracks, irritated.

"What did you do this time?" I stop walking and cross my arms. A deadly silence fills the air, causing me to panic and quickly turn around. Behind me, Vivalda is on her knees, her sword and gone, leaving the gold necklace laying on the grass. She pants and holds up her hand.

"Sorry, give me a moment." She says quietly under her breath and I quickly rush to her side and kneel down beside her.

"Are you alright?" I ask urgently, trying to search for what bothers her.

"Yes, I'm just tired. Walking for long periods of time is difficult for me sometimes, but I'm fine- it's fine." She quickly brushes it off and she stands up shakily. I pick the necklace off the ground and hand it to her.

"We're almost there, but will it help to rest now? We can spare a moment." Vivalda puts the necklace back on and shakes her head.

"No, we can keep going. Pushing forward is better for me anyways so I can get used to this much movement. I don't want to cause us to fall behind or potentially put us in an unfortunate situation. I'd like for this to be done sooner than later anyways."

Once the sun is down, the atmosphere grows dark and my magic lights our way. We finally reach the Lion's Eye where the trees are dark shades of purple and orange. There's a fine line where it looks like spring ends and fall begins.

"Soooooooo...I'd assume this is the Lion's Eye due to the funny colored trees. Why is everything so...dark here?" Vivalda asks while observing the different trees and plants as we cross into the new territory.

"The dark coloring of the forest keeps humans out and scares them away but typically, there's no real danger here. We'll find a spot deeper in the forest and we'll pick up our journey in the morning." Farther in the forest, I spot a large open patch of brown grass and choose it as our resting spot.

"Don't you think this is a bit too out in the open? What if those Aerolight things attack while we're sleeping?" Vivalda asks and I chuckle softly.

"Well, Aerolights don't typically cross into this territory and I don't 'sleep', so I'll be keeping an eye out if anything happens."

"So, you're going to be watching me sleep? That's a bit creepy, don't you think?" Vivalda slowly plops on the grassy ground, keeping her coat bundled over her. The grass below is soft to the touch, despite it looking frail and dead.

"No need to be so dramatic. I won't be actively watching you sleep. I'm sure I'll have better things to do than that so try to get some sleep and I'll wake you in the morning when the sun is up."

She looks at me with a silly crossed look on her face as if she doesn't believe me. But she eventually lays down on her side and gets comfortable in the grass.

Once I turn my back to her, I can sense her eyes following me cautiously. A twig loudly snaps behind her, causing her to dramatically flip over and her nerves are instantly spiked. I glance at a large bush in front of her and spot two tiny ears poking out from the leaves.

"Relax, it's just a bunny." My voice echoes softly through the trees and I wave my hand over the bush, making the leaves move, revealing a young rabbit that happily hops along.

"I promise there's no need to be scared. Try to get some rest, you're going to need it for the journey ahead."

As the time passes, Vivalda manages to drift off into a deep sleep. By the time the full moon is at its peak, deep rumbling thunder can be heard from the distance, causing Vivalda to toss and turn. To help her tune the sounds out, I use my magic to make small trees grow around her quietly, intertwining with each other, making a small dome that helps block out the noise.

The Lion's Eye is both mysterious and quiet. The green trees I grow are out of place compared to the purple leaves and foliage and brown grass.

This land isn't sick or poisoned. It's a mask.

For the rest of the night, I sit against a large tree that's close to where Vivalda sleeps and connects with the atmosphere around me until the sun begins to peak over the hills.

When the sun begins to peek through the treetops, I hear something rustling behind me.

Vivalda

I'm awoken by small birds singing right above my head and squirrels scurrying, jumping from branch to branch. I slowly open my eyes and see I'm tucked away inside of a tree dome.

"I'd like to be released from my tree dungeon now please!" I croak hoarsely, trying to get Silva's attention. The wooden cave drops and the plants sink back into the ground.

"Now that I think about it, I don't know if I'd rather be stuck in a tree capsule or have you stare at me while I sleep." When the dome drops, I see Silva standing over me, laughing.

"I didn't want the thunder to wake you. Goodness, you're just as dramatic as your mother was sometimes. I swear, there were times she'd storm into Alsfield angrily just because an ant crossed her path." Her smile and laughter slowly fades into sorrow. I feel my heart weigh heavily in my chest, yet I still find myself smiling.

"Despite being stuck in stone for what seemed like an eternity, unable to speak to your mother...I was always grateful to hear her voice. Even though my body was still, my spirit still wondered. She told me everything without knowing I was already listening and she gave me company when there was no one."

"Why were you unable to speak and transform like you do now?" I ask hesitantly. Silva's good at masking her emotions and she quickly brushes off her emotions.

215

"Magic works in mysterious ways, I've learned not to question it much when I don't understand. All I know is I woke up the moment your mother passed her necklace to you." Silva's glow dims slightly.

"Well for what it's worth, I'm grateful my mother found peace with you throughout her life." Silva smiles at me and her vibrant green glow returns once more, beating softly to the rhythm of her heart. She guides me into the forest and I can't help but let my eyes wander.

"So, where are we off to now? I thought we'd be here for a bit longer." I ask while I walk closely next to Silva.

Seeing the forest in the light is very bizarre. Everything is so dark and ominous, yet absolutely fascinating. The forest appears dead, but everything is thriving beautifully. There's deer running in the distance, butterflies perched on blooming flowers and birds singing from the treetops. Everything is golden toned.

"We're going to the fjord."

"Uhhhhh- what is that?" I asked, confused, having no idea what she's talking about.

"You'll see once we get there. Depending on how I can get us there, it may be a very long trip, so I need you to be prepared and patient. We will travel to the Lion's Peak which is far east of the forest. From there, we will make our way to the ocean." I choke on the breath I attempt to inhale.

"I'm sorry...ocean? We're going to the OCEAN?" Silva laughs and looks at me from the side.

"Yes, the ocean. You've never seen it?" She asked, smiling at me.

"If I can't step foot into an open forest, what makes you think I've been to the ocean?" I raise my brow and toss my hands on my hips.

"Good point." Silva says as she walks ahead of me, gliding swiftly over the ground like an elegant ghost.

"Are you feeling alright this morning?" She asks softly. I feel a slight pain in my stomach but it's nothing I can't handle.

"Yes, I'm fine."

While following behind her, I begin to hear strange noises following us from behind. I quickly pivot my head right and left, trying to see where the noise is coming from.

"What's that noise?" The disturbing noise sounds like two pieces of metal scraping against each other. I listen carefully, the ear-piercing screeching converts into faint, ghastly whispers.

"Try not to worry so much. It's most likely a little Taraphynx calling for its herd. Those little furballs can be quite obnoxious sometimes." Silva continues walking, but I stop in the center of the grassy pathway. I try to spot whatever creature it is she's talking about, but I don't see any animals in sight.

My heart begins to beat quickly when I see a strange red-light zip across the forest.

"Uhh...Silva?" I say quietly, trying not to tremble.

"What now, child?" She stops walking and turns around while my eyes try to stay focused on the strange light.

It looks like a thin lightning bolt bouncing and zipping between and around the trees. It begins to scurry towards me and before I know it, the light zips towards me quickly and suddenly, a large green ball of smoke shoots past me, nearly grazing my right shoulder.

I watch Silva's green magic clash with the thin light and it looks like it hits an invisible wall causing a red electric current to explode and ripple in thin air. Upon impact, a loud bellowing sound makes me cover my ears. I feel a strong force pushing against my back and I turn around to see Silva standing over me with an angered look on her face and magic ignited in her hands. Seeing Silva in some kind of battle mode scares me. Upon realizing we've stumbled upon danger; I reach for my necklace but Silva holds out her hand.

"Not here." She speaks in a deep tone. I do as she says and when I look forward, I see a massive wall of black smoke with red electricity sparking around it. A monster in the smoke continues to roar and screech, but I can't see a face or figure.

"We must go now! We're almost to the edge!" Silva shouts in a calm manner versus panicking. I'm confused why we're not fighting whatever it is but I don't bother asking and I take off running in the direction she points.

"Don't draw it's attention and don't look back. It shouldn't chase us out into the open. We can't risk fighting or else it'll call for reinforcements. We're too close to the village to risk attacking and scaring the humans." Silva glides alongside me like a graceful ghoul.

"Is it an Aerolight? I thought you said they don't enter this territory!" I shout loudly while she looks back, keeping an eye on the creature.

"Yes, and I tell no lies when I say the Aerolights' magic can't cross the Lion's borders! This one might be stronger than others!" I keep with Silva and pace myself by steadying my breathing to conserve as much energy as possible, but ultimately, I grow tired quickly. Shortly, I feel a sudden pain stab me in my chest that's so intense that it causes me to stumble heavily onto the ground.

My stomach is on fire and the sensation travels down into my hips. The slightest movement makes everything hurt worse. I remain on my knees and out of the corner of my eye, I see Silva quickly stop and rush to me.

"What happened?" She asks, panicking, jumping her gaze back and forth between the creature in the distance and I. I try to answer but no sound comes out because I'm trying to conceal the pain I feel.

The fall and agonizing groans have caught its attention, making it transform. This monster has two legs and arms and hunches over in a terrifying manner like something out of a nightmare.

Silva stands up and throws both of her hands up, creating an iridescent green barrier that grows from the ground. The Aerolight slams heavily into the shield, creating a loud warbling echo that rumbles throughout the forest.

"Change of plans. It has to be destroyed NOW. Once it calls for backup, the forest and the village will be in danger. Stay here, I'll take care of it." I watch Silva take off and I begin to feel sick to my stomach. I start to overthink and feel terrible that now Silva has to take care of a monster because my body decided to flare up.

I slowly stand up while keeping pressure on my stomach to help ease the pain. I try to steady my breathing and calm down as much as possible.

I need to be calm. I need to be calm.

I talk to myself and try to conquer the raging fright I feel deep down. Once my chest doesn't feel as tight, I slowly reach for my necklace and take a deep breath.

Please work.

I tightly close my eyes and reach up for my necklace and while hunched over, holding my stomach, I yank the metal away from my neck, breaking the chain and in the blink of an eye, under a crash of lighting, the armor forms over my body.

I peel open my eyes and I'm relieved that the transformation worked. I stand up straight and instantly realize the pain has mysteriously disappeared. The creature is close to breaking through Silva's barrier, so I rely on my instincts to kick in and instinctively run over to join Silva's side.

"Vivalda!" Silva yells for me as I dive through the barrier and drive the sword across its side. The monster wails and when I turn around, it's gone.

Where did it go? Did I kill it?

I circle, looking around, waiting for a sign of its whereabouts because I find it hard to believe I killed it that easily. I take a few steps back and hear a deep muffled growl crawl down my spine, causing the hairs on my neck to stand.

As soon as I turn around, I'm hit by an invisible force causing me to slam my back into a tree. The impact is so violent, the tree trunk snaps and falls backwards, causing me to land on top of it. I rub the sides of my temple and when my eyes come into focus, I jolt when I see Silva standing in front of me. "I told you to stay back. This Aerolight can go completely invisible whenever it pleases!" She speaks quickly and helps me stand up.

"Yeah, I think I got the whole invisible part." I stand up, coughing and grunting in pain. Silva and I look around, waiting for the beast to attack again.

"This one can only be seen when it's attacking or when it's being attacked. For this, we must be patient. If you focus hard enough, you can see its translucent figure shine in the light." Silva keeps her eyes on the forest, ready to attack with green magic floating around her hands. A green orb forms over her palm and I can feel the intense wave of her magic flow around me. It's like I'm standing close to a fire and feeling warm waves of heat brush past me. Her magical flames dance excitedly around her hand and in the blink of an eye, she sends the magic ball flying into the forest and it clashes with the invisible Aerolight. When her magic crashes against its body, it releases a loud and terrifying scream. Its invisible mask is dropped and it looks like its body glitches in and out, rapidly appearing and disappearing. Once it shocks itself, it locks its beaming red eyes on us and grows menacingly while releasing an intense roar that almost sounds mechanical.

"Go!" Silva yells and with no hesitation, I run as fast as I can towards the monster and slash the sword diagonally across its chest, causing red goop to ooze out of the wound.

The beast thrashes its body around like a bucking horse. It holds its hand low to the ground and a dark red ball of power forms in its hand. Its magic crackles and it thrashes its hand out, sending the ball racing towards me.

I block its attack by crossing the sword over my body and deflecting the attack. The dark magic brushes past my cheeks, making my heart race rapidly. I almost didn't block it in time. I observe the monster. It looks like a sewer monster made of smoke that drips like thick liquid and dissipates onto the ground. Its wounds glow red and its blood leaks to the ground, staining the forest floor.

The beast begins to heal and Silva darts past me, unleashing her fury on the monster. I stand back to catch my breath and watch how smooth and effortlessly she fights. Bright flashes of green and red nearly blind me. Watching nature fight against darkness is a suspenseful sight to behold. Silva doesn't appear to take any damage and is inflicting a lot of pain on the Aerolight that only makes the brute grow more and more angry.

What should I do?

I grip the sword tightly in my right hand and before I can step forward to help Silva, she stands over the beast as it lies on the ground and digs her hand into its chest. She and the Aerolight shout at the same time and she gruesomely pulls out a strange object out of its chest that looks like a bodily heart. It's black with thick green veins that pulsate around the organ. The Aerolight screeches and tries to reach for its heart, but before it can do much, Silva angrily slams it into the ground, causing a small smokey explosion. The heart disappears and eventually, so does the Aerolight's body.

Its screams echo in the wind as it dies and Silva stands strong with no wounds on her body. Her hands remain engulfed in green smoke but when she closes her hands into a fist, it disappears. She turns around, breathing heavily.

"Are you alright?" She asks sincerely as I stand frozen in place.

"Yeah, I think so. You're okay...right?" I look up and down, analyzing her body and see no sight of injury or distress.

"I am fine. There's no reason to worry." Despite her reassurance, I can't help but zone out while blatantly staring at her.

Silva walks up to me with a soft gaze and kind reassurance in her tone. "Hey...I know what you're thinking. I promise everything is alright. I am okay. You are okay. You've done really well." Silva rests her hands on my shoulders, trying her best to reassure me and as much as I want to believe her, I can't help but NOT feel okay.

My heart thumps against my ribs and I realize I was dwelling on the past and rewatching my mother being torn apart by those demons. Watching Silva tear the heart out of the monster's body reminds me of seeing my mother's torn skin.

"I don't know if I can do this. I want to go home." I whisper and for a split moment, I feel slightly uncomfortable standing next to her because everything continues to feel unreal.

How does the average human cope with all of this?

Silva bends down to talk to me and continues to speak softly. "No road is an easy one. But listen when I say this. Not everywhere you walk will you find pain." I feel a smile begin to creep across my face. "Once our deed is done and your kingdom is safe, you'll be free to return to the life you see fit." As much as I wish to argue with what she says, I can't deny that her kind words help me feel better, even in the slightest.

Despite the continuous overwhelming doubt I feel, I manage to relax and release the armor. When it disappears, I catch the necklace after it transforms back into a charm.

Silva leads us to the edge of The Lion's Eye where we're met with a beautiful ocean view below a tall cliff we stand on. I speed walk to the edge, making sure to stay a safe distance from the edge. Despite my terrible fear of heights, seeing the ocean for the first time is so surreal for me. The deep blue ocean waves below us softly and calmly while the sky is bright and clear with the wind howling against the mountain.

"It's so beautiful." I continue to stare at the water and listen to the sound of waving water that crashes over the shore under us.

"What are we supposed to do now?" I ask, looking up at Silva.

"We will travel east." She looks out into the horizon and steps closer to the edge, making me nervous.

"Uh- you mean north right..." I laugh awkwardly while pointing the adjacent way.

"No, we will be going east." Silva moves my stiff arm so that I point in the direction she is referring to. I awkwardly laugh and pull my arm to my side.

"Uhhhhhh. How exactly do you expect us to get down and cross the water? Where are we expecting to go? For what I know, there's no land for days and no one sails regularly anymore. And I don't know about you, but I'm not waterproof and I don't swim." I speak quickly and Silva rubs her temple with her fingers. She sits on the edge of the cliff with her long hair and dress swaying with the wind and she looks down.

"What do you suppose that is?" She taunts humorously as if I'm a child. I slowly inch to the edge and look over carefully, trying to spot what she sees. As I gaze down at the beach, I see a giant pirate ship docked below us on the shore with no one in sight.

"Woah! I thought all pirate ships were ordered to be destroyed." When I was a teenager, the king declared piracy to be illegal after news spread about the mainland that an entire crew was killed out at sea due to reckless sailing.

After a long moment of feeling nothing but shock and excitement, my smile drops when I realize why Silva pointed at the ship.

"You cannot possibly be thinking what I think you are." Silva smiles and tilts her head to the side.

"How else do you expect to cross the great ocean?" She looks at me with a mischievous smile on her face. I stomp my foot down and retreat from the edge.

"No no no no no, absolutely not! I'm not going to hijack someone's property just to sail into the unknown! Have you lost your mind?" Silva stands up and I awkwardly trip over my own feet.

"The ship's captain is wandering in the forest as we speak and will board the ship at any moment now. I sense no danger, so we're going to stowaway in the lower deck of the vessel." I look at her, unamused.

This plan has so many flaws.

I have no choice but to trust Silva and her judgement.

"Well, if it's the only way across, I won't argue against it. But how do you expect us to get down?" Silva waves her hand over the ground and makes thick, long vines sprout from the ground and she pushes them over the cliff. I immediately know what Silva expects me to do and she looks at me, smiling cheekily.

"I am NOT sliding all the way down a darn vine. Do you see how high up we are?!" Silva chuckles under her breath and without saying a word, her right arm is bound by multiple thin vines and I watch as she gracefully glides off the cliff.

I look over and see her swaying with the vines so gracefully as if she dances with the breeze and lowers down slowly towards the ground, but she stops once she's about halfway down. She looks up at me and waves her hand, telling me to join her.

I sigh heavily and reach down to pick up one of the vines. My palms begin to sweat, causing me to have a hard time gripping the plant. I drop the vine over the cliff and see Silva swinging back and forth in the air, sitting on a looping vine, waiting for me. I almost feel like laughing because I wasn't expecting to see her looking like a joyful child playing on a swing.

"Psst. I don't think I can do this." I whisper loudly in order to get her attention.

Silva looks up and waves her hand up and I feel something heavy gently wrap around my hips and stomach. She makes the vine lift up and wrap itself around the top half of my body.

"It'll carry you down so it's easier for you. It's safe, I promise." Her voice echoes quietly. I hesitate before sitting down slowly and pushing myself off the mountain. The vines hold my weight and I grasp onto two vines that stretch over my sides. The vines carry me down swiftly and I can feel my stomach slowly bouncing to my chest, causing me to feel nauseous from the daring height.

Silva makes the vines lower us down to the ship and land directly onto the top deck. Our landing causes the wooden floor to creak quietly. I stand stiffly on the wooden floorboards because I can hardly believe I'm onboard a real pirate ship. I can barely contain my excitement but quickly remember that we're on a timer.

"There's no way we're NOT going to get caught by the captain. If he catches us, I'm sure he and his crew will try to kill us or something." Silva walks towards the back side of the ship, looking out to the horizon.

"Oh, I won't be caught, YOU might though and if you do, we'll simply see what happens."

Well, that isn't reassuring at all.

Silva chuckles and guides me to a door that leads to the lower deck of the ship. She opens the door and I walk through, beginning to descend the stairs. Before Silva can join me, something catches her attention and she looks out into the distance where the sun begins to set.

"What's wrong?" I turn around, standing on the stairs.

"Nothing. There's some dark storm clouds in the distance. We might hit a storm on the way there."

Silva finally follows behind me and we wait for the captain to return. The lower deck is filthy and full of cobwebs and dust. It looks like hardly anyone is ever down here.

I look around the room, making sure there's nothing dangerous or worrisome, finding nothing but dust, dirt and sand. I feel a very strong, powerful force but I can't tell where or what it's coming from. I think being in a smaller space with Silva makes me realize how intense her magical power truly is.

"We will hide here until the captain falls asleep and we are close to the fjord, we will disembark." Once again, Silva feeds me a plan full of flaws.

"How will you know when we're close? We can barely see anything out of these tiny windows." I gesture to the small round windows that line the sides of the wooden walls.

"Trust me, I'll know. It's hard for me to miss." Silva looks out the window as small waves wash past the boat.

"So, this...fjord...what are we going there for exactly? You haven't really told me much about it. Is there a reason?" My curiosity continues to pique as I try to imagine what this place is.

"It's a hidden place no human has ever been to. That is where your next lesson lies and once we're finished there, we will travel south."

SOUTH? Is this crazy woman trying to sail the world?

"If you wish to criticize my judgment, please do so out loud. Your thoughts tend to be obnoxiously loud sometimes."

Dang it, I forget she can hear my thoughts. That's so creepy. It's not like I can just turn off my mind.

Silva glares at me with her glowing white eyes. "Okay okay, I'm sorry." I laugh, embarrassed and she also cracks a smile before quickly turning her head to the window, inspecting something outside towards the shore.

"The captain has returned. We must remain as quiet as possible." She says while she backs away from the wooden wall.

"Wait! What do we do if we get caught by the captain or one of his crewmates?" I hiss quietly and Silva cuts me off.

"Oh relax, you'll figure something out. I don't think they'll come down here anyways and if they do, I know beforehand. Now try to relax and get some sleep. I'll alert you if anything happens."

Soon after the ship takes off, I find myself sitting in a hidden corner, staring at the wooden walls, trying to not feel nauseous from the bouncing waves. Occasionally, I'd see Silva gliding back and forth, sprouting small plants from her fingertips and planting small seedlings in the floors and walls. I'd assume she's bored, or perhaps she's simply relaxing as much as possible until we reach our next destination.

Every time I hear footsteps creak from the top deck, my heart skips a beat and I shift my attention to the ceiling, prepared to hear someone walk down the stairs. I've heard pirates are known for being absolutely ruthless to those who cross their paths but hopefully those rumors and tales aren't true. At this point, I don't know what fairytales are true or not.

After not being able to sleep, I walk up to the windows to see the view outside. The waves roll gently as the sun begins to set. The ship slowly sways back and forth and with every wave that rolls, the wooden floorboards creak.

"I never thought I'd sail the seas in my life." I say quietly as Silva continues to fiddle with her blooming flowers.

"If I'm not mistaken, I believe you're the first royal to ever go out to the sea. The creeds written by noble blood made pirates look bad and now, any that remain are hated and even targeted. Since your mother was roughly your age, she always disapproved of such hatred against pirates and the sea. She talked to me about it when it crossed her mind. She once told me that it was her dream to experience sailing." She gets up and looks out the window next to where I stand. I can tell by the look in her eyes that she's in deep thought about something.

"If I may ask. What else would she talk to you about?" Silva looks at me with soft eyes and a gentle smile.

"Just like you, your mother was never silent. She always had something on her mind. Whether that'd be about her royal duties, the people, her family, or just you. You should have heard her cries every night when you were sick. There's nothing more powerful than the cry of a mother. No matter the struggles she encountered, she was always ready to put up a fight. She loved you and your family so much." I can't help but smile while she talks about my mother. I miss her so much, it still feels like it was just yesterday that we lost her.

"Hopefully one day, I can make her proud." I continue to look out the window, watching the water splash against the side of the ship.

"I can guarantee you that if she was here, she'd tell you that you've always made her proud." Her words cause an even bigger smile to form across my face.

"I hope you speak truthfully."

"I do." She responds and as the moon begins to rise, the pitter-pattering footsteps above have gone quiet.

I walk towards the stairs that lead back up to the main deck, but Silva quickly stops me.

"What are you doing?" Silva whispers and I turn my head to the side to see if I can hear anything from above and sure enough, it's completely silent.

"I don't hear anything." My curiosity peaks more and more as I slowly ascend the stairs.

"I know what you're thinking...literally and it wouldn't be wise to go up there. Not yet at least." Silva doesn't do much to stop me from walking further up the steps.

"I'm just going to take a quick peek and I'll come right back. I think the crew went in for the night or something." Out of the corner of my eye, I can see Silva shaking her head side to side but I'm too intrigued to care.

"It's not the crew you'd need to worry about." Silva whispers under her breath to where I can barely understand her.

"What did you say?" I turn to ask and Silva shakes her head and shrugs her shoulders. I slowly ascend the stairs, trying to avoid making the wood creak.

When I reach the door, I slowly turn the knob and peek through a small opening. There's multiple lanterns lit on the deck that illuminate the entire ship. At this point, I thought I would have seen a crewmate pass by, but I assume they all may be sleeping in a different section of the large ship.

Once I determine that the coast is clear, I step past the door and close it quietly. I walk lightly on my toes while constantly pivoting my head around to ensure no one can see me. I find myself standing awkwardly out in the open, in the middle of the floor.

The air is salty and the breeze is chilly. The waves crash loudly all around me, sounding like a peaceful melody I never thought I'd hear in my life. I look past the back of the ship and can see the mainland shrinking as we sail further from home.

No one would believe me if I told them I was here right now.

I walk to the nose of the ship and stand at the edge of the wooden rail, seeing the never-ending body of water rushing below the ship. The wind brushing against my skin feels so relaxing and I allot myself a moment to take in this feeling of being free.

My relaxation is cut short by a hand pulling my right shoulder back and my back is slammed against a firm wooden post. Before I could attempt to move away, I see a sharp dagger held to my throat. Its golden metallic glare shines from the lanterns that swing above my head.

"What the hell are you doing on my ship?" The woman's voice is low and intimidating.

Her hat creates a shadow that cascades over her face and her hair is bright red. She wears a red corset over a black long sleeve top and her hold on me is very strong.

I'm in shock, left standing frozen to the wooden post, terrified. I'm unsure what to do because if I make one wrong move, her knife will easily penetrate my skin.

"If you don't answer me, I'll have no problem feeding you to the sharks." First her weapon threatens my life and hearing a second threat causes my blood to immediately boil.

"Do you have any idea who I am? I highly suggest you-" My response angers her more and pushes the dagger closer to my throat to the point where I can feel it resting lightly against my skin, close to grazing it. Even the slightest breath brings me closer to her sharp weapon.

"I know exactly who you are and you have no jurisdiction around here after your spoiled family practically shunned the sea and my people from society. Now, last chance. What are you doing aboard my ship?"

The breeze pushes the lantern over and it illuminates her face. The shadow drops, revealing two icy grey eyes staring at me intensely. Her red brows arch down and when I try to move, she keeps her left hand on my shoulder, pushing it against the post and her right hand holds the blade. To avoid more trouble, I have no choice but to submit and tell her what she wants to know.

"Let's not go crazy with the pain and threats okay? I don't mean to cause a disturbance." The pirate leans to the side, squinting in disbelief. "I needed a way across the sea and...stupidly thought to climb aboard because I didn't know what else to do." I laugh and smile nervously and the pirate doesn't appreciate it.

"You really thought a captain would approve of that? A runaway princess ASSUMING she'll be welcomed aboard one of the last remaining ships in all of Vassuren? Cute but not surprising considering how rotten you royals can be." She sneers coldly and I try to stay collected.

"Please, if I could speak to the captain regarding my purpose here, I'd greatly appreciate it. I'm kind of on a timer currently and I'm not good for anything if I'm dead." The woman instantaneously erupts in laughter and she pulls her dagger back and sheaths it in her belt. She fixes her black hat that nearly falls off her head from laughing and once collected, she stands tall in front of me with her arms crossed.

"You're talking to the captain, princess. I'm surprised the clear deck didn't give it away." She laughs and I feel my cheeks go cold.

She's the captain?!

I really hope you're listening, Silva.

I'm shocked in the most positive way. I've never heard of female pirates.

"You look like you've seen a ghost." The captain's demeanor drastically changes but I can't tell if it's a good or bad thing. At least she's no longer holding a knife to my throat.

"Eh, I wouldn't know what a ghost looks like. But anyways. If you're the captain...where's your crew? Or I mean- shouldn't you have one?" The captain scoffs with a straight face.

"If I had a crew, let alone NEEDED one, you wouldn't have been able to successfully sneak onto my ship." She says monotonously and my eyes widen in surprise.

"Wow. I've never heard of a female pirate, that's-" Before I can continue, she walks over to the side of the ship to tie off some ropes and I proceed to follow her, keeping a respectful distance.

"If you're thinking about saying anything snide, I'd shut it before my dagger meets your eye." She says coldly.

What is with this defensive attitude of hers?

"Well, if you'd let me finish. What I was going to say is I think that's incredible. I never thought I'd meet a female pirate. Do you really sail and keep up with the ship all by yourself?" She finishes tying the thick ropes and leans against the latter netting that climbs up a wooden staff.

"What do you think? We just established that I don't have a crew." I chuckle nervously and she takes a deep breath. I can tell she's really irritated to talk to me. "The name's Calypso and I've been captain of this ship, the Nightwalker since I was young." She continues to tie off ropes and light unlit lanterns.

"I'm Vivalda. It's a pleasure to meet you." Calypso looks at me and shutters in disgust.

"Now that's out of the way, what are you doing here? You're quite far from home now." She asks as she leans against a wooden post.

"Well..." I laugh nervously before continuing. "I need to go somewhere. I know where but I also...don't at the same time and I doubt you may know where it is so I'm just waiting to find land I guess." I sound silly trying to explain without doing so properly because I'm sure she'd throw me overboard for speaking about the magical forces I've met up until this point.

"I've sailed far from Darali and have explored most of the open waters. Maybe I know where you're trying to go."

Silvaaaa, I could really use your help right about now. I don't know what to say!

I giggle skittishly, unsure of how to respond. "Uhhhhh there's an umm fjord that I hear is out in the middle of the sea and uhhh-" Calypso looks at me highly confused. One of her brows arches higher than the other and she taps her pointer finger on her arm that's crossed in front of her.

"You're not giving me much to work with. I think it's best to circle you to Darali or go back to the eastern shore so you can go home." I follow Calypso as she speed walks to the back of the ship where the steering wheel is.

"No no no, I can't go back, I have to reach this fjord because if I don't- if I don't, I won't be able to rid the kingdom of a darkness that's poisoning our way of life and there's a forest spirit under your ship and-"

Calypso's eyes widen and her mouth gapes open. It was at that moment, I realized I spoke too much.

As I stand on the top deck, keeping myself hidden under my own invisible barrier. I keep my distance, monitoring the interaction between both women. This newly discovered captain who sails solo has a very strange demeanor to her that I don't completely understand.

Once Vivalda mentions the kingdom's darkness, I approach them just in case things escalate.

I personally wouldn't have started the conversation with that but I'm intrigued to see where it goes. At least Vivalda is trying to be honest and I can tell she's trying to win over the captain's trust.

"You speak a bit too oddly for my liking." Calypso walks to the back of the ship where the wheel is and she stops halfway up to turn around and look down at Vivalda.

"I know, I've been told that a lot." Vivalda says and she takes a deep breath. I can hear her mind quieting down and she's trying to find the right words to speak. "I know this sounds insane but have you ever experienced strange, ghost-like shadows floating around, causing mayhem and turning livelihoods upside down? Or have you never seen the sky turn black in the blink of an eye?" Vivalda's desperate to not sound crazy. Calypso's shoulders drop and the visible tension in her body loosens.

"Well now you're making a bit more sense. If it's so dire to know, yes, I've witnessed such things, but I thought I was just imagining things. After my island heard news of the queen's passing, the sea changed in ways I can't explain. At night, I hear eerie sounds glide over the water, but I thought it was just the wind playing tricks on the tide. People at home think nothing of it, if anything, they blamed the odd occurrences on you and saw it as a bad omen." Calypso words pierce Vivalda in the chest. I can feel her pain spike, but she remains composed.

I want to tell her I'm here but I have to be patient and let things play out on their own.

Vivalda takes a deep breath and pushes aside her emotions before standing up straight and inching closer to Calypso.

"I've been told to go to this unknown fjord for reasons I don't know. All you must do is get me close enough to disembark on land, drop me off and you'll never see me again." She tries her best to convince the captain but she doesn't look like she's close to budging.

"No, I can't, I'm sorry. I can't get caught up with more problems than the ones I already deal with. The last thing I need to be mixed up in is some silly little fairytale where the 'daring' princess needs to voyage across the seas in order to prove a point. I'm taking you back to the eastern shore." Calypso proceeds to walk to the ship's wheel and she begins to turn it, changing the ship's course.

Vivalda desperately runs to her side and stops Calypso from turning the wheel and by doing so, it enrages Calypso. Her furious temper sparks, she unsheathes her dagger once more and threatens Vivalda with it. I immediately rush and jump in front of Vivalda and drop my invisible cloak, revealing my presence and causing Calypso to bump into me.

I thrust my hand forward and make a small vine sprout from the ground and wrap around one of her ankles. I form my hand into a fist and pull my elbow inward to make the vine pull her backwards. Calypso trips, falls on her back and her dagger flies out of her hand, landing out of arm's reach. I stomp up to Calypso and lean over her.

"YOU out of all people should know these 'fairytales' have always lied under your nose since the beginning of time!" I shout deeply, causing the floor to creek softly below us.

Calypso looks up at me, paralyzed in fear, her pupils are dilated and I can tell she tries to fight the rising panic that torments her. I take a deep breath and unwind the vine from her ankle. "Looks like you've seen a ghost." I say with a smile, ensuring I mean no harm.

"Were you hanging around the entire time? I had it under control, you know." Vivalda walks around from behind and scolds me. I look over and see her cross her arms and slouch to the side, visibly irritated.

"That blade she held to you was really reassuring. Besides, I'm always looking forward to seeing the look on human faces when they see me." A smile peeks through Vivalda's lips and she shakes her head. I back up and we both watch Calypso struggle to stand up.

"What the hell? Someone best tell me I'm dead before I lose my mind." Calypso keeps her light gray eyes locked on me, looking up and down, analyzing every part of my body. I step closer to her and hold my hands out, trying to reassure her I won't harm her.

"I'm Silva, the very heart and soul of your world. How's that for a fairytale?" I tease and easily, Calypso's fear turns into curiosity and fascination. She walks closer and circles around, observing me cautiously.

"Wow, this is really real...you're real! Oh crap, I'm sorry, I didn't mean to get so angry, it's been really rough lately. But if it makes you feel better, princess, I wasn't actually gonna stab you, I was just trying to scare you." I hear the sincerity in the captain's voice and her eyes show much remorse and pain. I'm not sure what she's dealt with, but I can tell there's a lot of weight on her shoulders. Just like Vivalda.

While Calypso stands in front of me, I hold out my hand as a giant white and gold moonpine flower sprouts from my palm. Both women watch in wonderment as the flower blooms. Bright sparkling magic flicks off its petals and it shines bright in the dark.

"This is moonpine, it only blooms when the moon shines and hides in the day." Calypso hesitantly picks the flower from my hand and gently touches its petals.

Its glowing white stripes illuminate her face and her deep red hair shines vibrantly. The magic of the flower helps ease the tension she feels. She looks out into the horizon and turns back to us as if making a silent decision. Once her decision is made, she walks back to the wheel and has us continue to sail east.

"I'm sorry about the scary dagger and the anger. It's been a long time since I've talked to someone who didn't immediately pose a threat to me or my ship." Vivalda walks over to the dagger that remains on the floor, she picks it up and returns to Calypso. She appreciates the kind gesture and slides it back into the sheath that rests on her hip.

"Well, now that you've made yourself known, what is this journey you both are on and how far east are we sailin'?" The captain asks.

"There's something on a fjord that we need, if I were to tell you what it is, neither of you will believe me and one of you may faint. As for you, captain, you mustn't tell a single soul about us or what we're doing. If you do, I will know and I'll sink your ship to the bottom of the sea." Vivalda's eyes widen and Calypso glares at me as if she doesn't believe me.

"Mmmhmm, whatever ya say. Ya giant walking stick." She says the last bit under her breath, humorously.

"Want to run that last part by me one more time?" I ask and the captain turns her attention forward to focus on steering.

"Oh nothing! I was just saying how ridiculous ya both sound but I look forward to...whatever this is." She says in a fake cheerful tone with a half-smile on her face.

"Wonderful. I'll let you know when we're close. It shouldn't take long."

Vivalda and Calypso spend the rest of the night getting to know each other while I listen in on their conversations from a distance.

"How did you learn to sail a giant ship by yourself?" Vivalda asks while observing Calypso tend to the ship.

"I learned everything from my father. He was known as the 'Iron Captain'. He was perhaps the greatest most fearless sailor known to man. He gave me the Nightwalker the moment I was born. He said he knew my soul would one day belong to the sea." There's a strange sadness in Calypso's tone while she speaks.

"What do you mean 'was'? Did something happen?" Vivalda's curiosity grows stronger and stronger, but she remains respectful, avoiding crossing the stranger's boundaries.

"Surely you recall when King Cassius forbade all future sailing and wrote it in law after an entire ship of people went missing, correct?" Calypso asks and Vivalda nods her head.

"My father was the captain of that ship and I've been searching for him and his crew for years. This is the fifth time I've circled around the main lands, trying to find whatever remains of them or the vessel, DayBreak." I feel Calypso's heart aching from where I stand. Now I'm beginning to understand where her anger and impulsive actions stem from.

Vivalda looks at her sympathetically, following her to the far side of the ship where they both lean over the ledge, staring at the water.

"After several days and no return of my father or the crew, the people of Darali immediately presumed the crew to be dead. My father had a fascination for ancient stories and he was always determined to debunk them or find the truth. Due to his fascination, people considered him to be dangerous and ultimately blamed him for the 'death' of his own crew. My friends lost their family and the village lost good friends, so...they needed someone to blame. Since the captain never came home, the next closest thing they could take their anger out on was me. And from there, it only got worse and more trouble came my way." Calypso's cold tone soars bravely with the salty wind while she stares out into the distance.

"Now, I sail every night, hoping to find somethin' that remains of my father, the crew or the ship. I know somethin' happened and it wasn't my father's fault. Even he wouldn't make mistakes as big as the ones I've made. But I still feel like I'm further and further from the answers and closer to losing hope."

She pulls out a glass bottle from a woven basket that has rolled up paper inside it and throws it overboard.

"What was that?" Vivalda asks as she watches the bottle bobble up and down with the waves.

"I guess you could say it's my prayer, but it's of no importance since they're ignored every night." The captain stands emotionlessly with her arms crossed in front of her.

"You know...you and I have something in common." Calypso looks at her confused and slightly disgusted.

"What's that?" Calypso asks.

"We're blamed for the impossible." Calypso thinks to herself for a brief moment and I can feel her heart begin to lighten, but she doesn't show it on her face.

"I guess you're right. People like to spread rumors about us too and I think that's probably the most difficult thing to deal with. Ya can't reason with stupidity sometimes." The captain says compassionately. Vivalda's slight smile drops.

"I assume my father's message traveled overseas?" Vivalda expresses her disappointment by shaking her head and lowering it towards the ground.

"He has knights sail out to deliver the news. But if it makes you feel better, I never believed what the king said. Something about his message was off. It came across like he just needed-"

"Someone to blame." Both women say at the same time and they both smile.

"Yes. But if I may ask, just for clarification purposes. It's not true ye lead the queen to her death, right?" Calypso speaks cautiously because she can tell Vivalda is sensitive to the topic. I think about stepping in to change the conversation, but I wait for Vivalda's response.

She looks at the captain, slightly offended by the question but she quickly takes a deep breath. Her eyes are full of sadness and frustration but she speaks with a calm tone that masks her emotions.

"I didn't kill my mother but I know what did. They're massive monsters made of dark magic. I'm trying to find the force that brings them to life so I can bring an end to their kind. I loved my mother more than the world did. She fought so hard to make it through that night, but ultimately, I couldn't stop it. I was-"

"Helpless?" Calypso chimes in and Vivalda lifts her head up. Her brows raise and the corners of her lips turn downwards.

"Yeah...helpless." Vivalda's voice shakes but she still manages to smile faintly. The two young women don't realize they are beginning to form a very special bond and it brings my soul much warmth and hope. Vivalda hasn't had someone to relate to since the journey began. I can tell this is something she's needed.

"I don't think I'll ever amount to my mother's greatness. No matter how hard I try, I always end up unintentionally messing things up." I slowly approach behind and stand next to her.

"You're right, you'll never amount to your mother." My voice startles Vivalda and she quickly turns her head towards me, annoyed.

"Wow. Thank you so much for the reassurance, I really needed that." She tosses her braid back and leans over the rail. I snicker quietly, turning my head to the open waters that roar around us.

"You will never amount to Aladora because there's no bar to rise above." Vivalda turns around and smiles.

"I appreciate that." I look over and see Calypso staring at me.

"What exactly are you? Are you a walking tree or somethin'? Wait- you can't be because you appeared out of thin air and last, I checked...trees don't naturally do that." Her deep silly tone causes Vivalda to burst out laughing and she covers her mouth with her hands.

"I am a Serafae, a keeper of your world and my purpose is to keep it alive. When I breathe, the world breathes with me." The glow from my body reflects across their faces.

I walk over to the wooden railing, I place my hands down and thin green mossy vines eject from my fingertips. The greenery swivels around the wooden poll and reaches to where Calypso stands. She gently rubs her hand on the vines and is surprised to see that it's real and not some kind of illusion.

"No one back home would ever believe this." She runs her fingers over the moss as if it's a pet and her eyes widen when a thought comes to her mind. "Wait! So if you are the soul of the world, if you die...does the world die too?" Her question takes us by surprise and Vivalda looks at me worryingly.

"I am not one who can die. I have no heart. You can take that dagger of yours and try if you wish to test me." I draw the vines back and hold my arms open to see if she takes the offer but ultimately, she shakes her head and refuses.

"Oh no, I think I'm good. I'm already on the bad side of hundreds of humans, the last thing I want is to be on yours." The captain stands stiff, laughing nervously.

The sound of thunder rumbling catches my ear. I turn my head to the sea, searching for a nearby storm but see no evidence of one brewing.

"Is something the matter?" Vivalda asks as I keep my sight glued on the sky. I feel an invisible force tug on my chest as if drawing me near.

"We're here, but somethings wrong." My gut clenches as I still see nothing strange in the sky or water.

"What do you mean? I sail these waters all the time, there's nothing but endless miles of water." Calypso tries to spot what it is I see and hear.

I quickly glide to the nose of the ship and stand on the ledge while holding onto a wooden pole.

"What are you doing?!" Vivalda yells as she and Calypso run, catching up behind me.

There's a strange force of energy coming from in front of the ship but I can't pinpoint where exactly it's coming from. I wave my hand in the air, over the water and a green river of magic flows elegantly from my palms. It flows down the side of the ship and pours into the water like glowing seafoam.

The glowing particles illuminate the sea, revealing nothing out of the ordinary but deep down, I know something is wrong.

"Ah, you have a bad feeling and your way of overcoming it is by polluting the ocean. Got it." Calypso sneers but I ignore her sarcasm.

I take a deep breath and feel my magic surging throughout my body, feeling like a refreshing blow of icy cold air and I keep my eye on the distance, waiting patiently.

"Why won't you tell me what's going on? You're worrying me."

Vivalda thinks to herself silently.

My gut is never wrong.

In the near distance, my magic suddenly slams into an invisible barrier, causing a glowing green wave to rise into the air.

There you are.

I see an invisible barrier glimmer iridescently from my magic's light. I get down from the ledge and keep a safe distance from Calypso and Vivalda before throwing both of my arms in the air to force the barricade to part open. Calypso and Vivalda shield their eyes from the bright flash of light and once the tear in the barrier is large enough, I'm left shocked at the sight behind it.

Behind the transparent wall, there's a huge mountain engulfed in bright orange flames, surrounded by multiple Aerolights as they hover around maliciously.

"Silva, what is that?!" Vivalda screams.

The mountain is under attack.

"Steer towards that opening now! Take us to the mountain and I'll push your vessel out so you don't get stuck in this!" I yell at Calypso and she immediately runs upstairs to the wheel.

I have every ability to abandon the ship so I can get to the mountain before them but I don't want to leave Vivalda behind.

"Aerolights? Silva, did you know they'd be here?!" Vivalda looks at the hidden world, scared and in shock.

"Of course not! They've never entered the fjord before! We have to get rid of them before they escape outside of the barrier. Are you ready?" I ask Vivalda and I can immediately sense her uneasiness. She breathes heavily, keeping her eyes on the inflamed mountain that draws near.

"Just remember everything I taught you so far. Stay on your feet and you'll be okay. I promise. If you must, seek safety in the forest and I'll take care of the rest." I reassure her calmly; I don't want to frighten her any more than she already is. She nods her head slowly in an unsure manner.

The boat widely turns and the ship aims for the opening in the wall. The waters grow strong and resilient as we get closer and the water from inside rushes against us.

"We're moving too slow." I say quietly and before Vivalda can turn to me, I disappear and teleport to the back of the ship. The wind howls loudly, thunder rumbles in the sky and the waves crash against the ship.

"Where'd you go?!" I hear Vivalda shout and Calypso snaps her head back to see what I'm doing. I walk to the farthest ledge and bind myself to the ground and the rail with strong vines. Vivalda approaches behind me rapidly.

"What are you doing?!" She shouts over the roaring winds that unbinds her braid and her hair floats freely in front of her face.

"Both of you, hang onto something!" I yell to them and Calypso holds onto the wheel tightly while Vivalda holds onto a wooden post right next to me.

I pull my arms back and feel my magic charge and once it's ready, I push forward and use my magic force to push the ship forward. My powerful magic hits the surface of the water and the push is so strong, it nearly makes the nose of the ship lift out of the water. Both girls shriek loudly while they hold on tight, trying not to let go or lose their balance.

In order to get us moving properly, I have to focus to ensure my magic pushes against the surface of the water and not sink into it. I tighten my core and remain resilient until we enter the barrier.

When we pass the gap, the atmosphere changes rapidly. The sky goes from being pitch black to raging fiery red. It's like we've entered the depths of a terrifying Hell I've never seen before. I keep pushing my magic forward until my focus is broken by Vivalda screaming loudly beside me.

"Silva, hurry, I'm slipping!" I quickly look over and see Vivalda struggling to hold onto the post. Her fingers are beginning to slip but I can't risk shifting away from my magic, because if I do, I could put the ship into distress. Vivalda's right hand disconnects and she loses all of her grip. She's immediately thrusted backwards towards the rail, but before she could completely fall overboard, I immediately throw out my left hand, and grab her arm.

My magic wraps around her and her weight tugs on my shoulder. I feel the ship rattle while magic continues to pour from my opposite hand.

I struggle to balance both weights. On one arm, Vivalda is pulling me to the side and the other the sea is pulling me forward towards it.

"We're approaching the mountain!" Calypso shouts and I look back to see how close we are. Due to the close proximity, I release the magic that pushes against the ship and I make the vessel balance on the water.

I pull Vivalda up and she instantly falls to her knees, extremely shaken up and I quickly help her up before pulling her into my arms, reassuring her she's alright.

Our attention is turned to the sky when we see a small group of Aerolights dive over the mountain and slam into the side of it, causing a piece of the mountain to crumble. A loud ferocious roar emerges from the stone and makes Vivalda jump.

"That's not what I think it is...is it?!" She shouts loudly as we watch a large black and red dragon take off from behind the peak. Bright burning flames reflect across the gold scales that cover the dragon's chest as it majestically soars over the trees.

"You've gotta be kidding me! SINCE WHEN WERE DRAGONS REAL?!" Calypso shouts dramatically, nearly steering the ship the wrong way.

The dragon chases the vile creatures and it pulls back its head to release a violent tunnel of spiraling fire that sets a couple of Aerolights ablaze. The monsters scream in pain as they fall from the sky and fade away into fine dust. I feel the ship begin to rock violently.

"This is the closest I can go!" Calypso yells as she struggles to keep the helm steady.

"We must go now, Vivalda!" She follows me to the side of the ship and upon looking down, there's a lot of big boulders close to where we've stopped.

"Swim to those rocks and I'll help you get to land!" Vivalda retreats back a few steps, panicking.

"Absolutely not! I can't swim!" She looks up at the dragon, watching it continue to chase and attack the Aerolights. I cautiously step closer to her.

"And I told you multiple times, your armor and power reacts based on your instincts. Even with your armor gone, your power remains. Your power trusts you, now you need to trust it." Her eyes twitch and she takes a deep and shaky breath before nodding.

Vivalda

I watch Silva disappear and turn into a sparkling green stream of magic. She floats off the ship and swoops down to reach the beach, waiting patiently for me.

I peer over the side of the ship, terrified of the depths below. The water continues to roar and crash against large boulders that stick out of the water.

What if the tide takes me out?

What if I can't swim?

Surely Silva could've got me on shore a lot safer and quicker.

"Your highness, you must go now! I can't fight the current much longer!" Calypso yells frightfully, straining to keep control of the giant ship.

I quickly step up on the rail and dive into the water. Once my body hits the water, my bones nearly lock out from the freezing temperature. I quickly remember what Silva said so I don't end up drowning. I quickly swim up to the surface and once my head is out of the water, I lock my eyes on the nearest rock to climb on. Thanks to the necklace's energy, I almost instantly know how to swim and I make my way to the nearest boulder.

I try my best not to panic due to the fear of the water and the overstimulating noises. Not to mention that I'm worried I'll be spotted by one of the Aerolights before reaching the shore.

Before I could touch the rock, a harsh wave slams my body into the large rock and due to the excruciating pain, I struggle to grip onto the rock but eventually, I slowly climb up and flop on top of the boulder. I steadily get to my feet, trying not to slip back into the water. I hold my side with my arm and I can't help but grunt and cry in pain. My attention is caught by the dragon who continues to roar and bellow.

I can't believe it...they do exist. But how?

My thoughts are snapped away when I hear Silva shouting for me.

"Jump across the rocks! I won't let you fall!" I turn around and see her waiting, standing between the trees on the shore, waiting for me to get across.

I search for the nearest rock and before I have the chance to jump, Calypso's ship creaks loudly behind me. I turn around to see it being pulled closer to the shore by the untamable current.

I react quickly and jump onto the next nearest boulder. I see two thick streams of green magic flow past me and latch onto the boat to push it back so it can exit the barricade smoothly.

I release a heavy sigh of relief and I lock eyes with Calypso one last time before she runs out of sight to tend to her vessel. Once the ship exits the barrier, Silva closes it and I continue jumping on the boulders until I eventually reach the shore.

Once my feet land on the soggy mud, Silva reaches down to help me stand up. The constant jumping causes my legs to throb and the right side of my body is in terrible pain. Even breathing only adds even more pain.

"Are you alright?" She asks as I hold the right side of my stomach.

"You said we were going to a fjord. Never once did you mention there'd be a dragon involved! We have more of a chance of being eaten by the dragon than we do the Aerolights. What the hell are we doing here?!" I raise my voice and Silva looks at me annoyed. I can't help but ask questions due to the insane adrenaline rush.

"I didn't think I'd have to introduce you to the fjord under these circumstances! Trust me, it was supposed to go a lot smoother than this. The first thing we're going to do is help the dragon by getting rid of those Aerolights and then I'll explain more afterwards. I'm going to take care of the ones in the forest and you'll take the ones that wander at the base of the mountain, they shouldn't be too much to handle. Can you do this?" I stare at her silently for a brief momentum in utter shock and confusion.

Everything is moving too fast. I'm not ready to fight with a huge dragon flying over my head, unsure if it poses a threat to us or not.

"I guess I don't have much of a choice." I protest.

"I'll be there the moment you need me." Silva says as she mysteriously disappears into the forest with her magic trailing behind her.

I try taking a few deep breaths but another roar from the dragon catches me off guard. I climb up the mountain to get a better view of the battle playing out before me. I reach a flat cliff that overlooks the fight but I stay hidden in the trees to avoid being seen.

I watch as the dragon annihilates each Aerolight one by one and my thoughts continue to race. I can't help but be terrified of what I'm witnessing. One by one, the Aerolights throw powerful attacks and the dragon isn't affected.

Are its scales indestructible?

One Aerolight rushes out of the forest and joins up with the other three in the sky. Once they're together, the monstrous black cloud demons gather together, they combine their power and attack the dragon with a bright laser-like beam of energy that hits the dragon hard and causes it to bellow and roar loudly in pain. My heart drops as I watch the dragon turn into a burning ball of fire and plummets onto the long-ranged cliff in front of me.

The Aerolights fly off and dive into the far side of the mountain behind me and once they're out of sight, I rush out from the trees to see what remains of the giant beast. Once I reach the bundle of fire, I hear something snar! behind me and I turn around to see an Aerolight slowly walking out of the forest, walking on all fours like a massive wolf, baring its sharp teeth. I freeze in place and my mind goes completely blank.

I'm too scared to shout for Silva or make a single noise. All I can do is keep my eyes on the monster as it slowly walks towards me with black saliva oozing from its mouth. Without thinking, I instinctively reach for my necklace and the creature charges at me. But before I can react, the burning pile of flame that rests on the cliff quickly shoots off into the air and slams down on top of the Aerolight, coating it in flames and killing it instantly.

I shield my eyes from the burning embers that fly past me, stinging my skin and burning my eyes. In front of me, a tall wall of fire remains burning brightly. I cautiously walk towards the flames, feeling the air get hotter. The blaze roars louder as I get closer and the fire on the ground rises once more.

Did the monster manage to survive the blast?

I reach for my necklace, grip the charm firmly and pull it away from my neck. The blade rests firmly in my hand and I walk closer to the flames that no longer burns my skin due to the armor's protection. Once I'm inches from the fire, I hold the sword in both hands with the blade facing downwards and lift it over my head, ready to drive it through the burning beast to destroy it for good. But before the tip of the blade touches the fire, the flames rise up and the fiery wall drops, revealing the impossible.

It's no monster.

It's a woman.

The dissipated fire uncovers a tall woman standing in front of me. Her skin is deep shades of red and orange and her body is covered in black dragon scales. She has long wavy golden hair and two large black horns growing out of the side of her head. In between the horns that curve upwards, there's a small beaming ball of fire that balances in the air, keeping up with her movements.

Her hands look like they're made of black stone with thick long claws connected to her fingertips. Black burnt scales cover parts of her arms, legs and chest. Upon looking closer, there are bright red and yellow veins that look like lava flowing underneath the charred parts of her skin.

I'm in such shock that I can't find proper words to describe the incredible creature that stands before me.

I cautiously take a step back and the metal that covers my feet clanks against a rock, catching the woman's attention and causing her to turn around.

I feel my heart drop to my stomach and my body tenses up in fear. I don't know if she has good intentions or if she'll want to kill me. Her fiery golden eyes lock onto mine and I can't help but silently stare back. Her shoulders are covered in black spines and spikes and smaller black scales cascade around her right eye.

"Took you long enough princess." The woman's voice is deep and raspy with a subtle growl.

Silva, I'd greatly appreciate it if you'd find me before I faint.

"Uh- who- um how do you know I'm the princess? Who are you?" I stumble terribly over my words.

The scaly lady walks closer to me and looks me up and down, analyzing my features.

"I know an outsider when I see one. Besides, it's not every day I witness someone baring Ves-" Our attention turns to the forest when a loud explosion erupts in the distance.

"Hold that thought. It's not over yet!" The woman turns around and I watch two large black scaled wings spread out from her back. With one heavy flap, she takes off into the air and dives into the forest.

Once she vanishes, a bright green light escapes from the depths of the woodlands.

Yeah, yeah, I'm coming.

I rapidly dart into the forest as quickly as I can and I immediately hear tree trunks snapping and explosions rumbling the ground. Once I approach the battle, I see Silva dive onto an Aerolight, tacking it to the ground and she thrusts her hand into its chest, tearing its heart-like organ out of its chest and squashing it in her hand.

I look to the opposite side behind her and see the dragon-woman handling two other Aerolights but it appears she's defending versus attacking like Silva is.

I know Silva doesn't need my help, so I proceed to help the other woman. I sneak around quietly in order to get behind the giant bodies of smoke so I can take one of them by surprise.

By the time I reach their tails, I see the dragon woman's hands are ignited on fire and in the center of her palms, she holds a large ball of fire, gripped by her long black talons.

She rapidly shoots fire from her palms and fingertips; she also uses her flames to block the Aerolights' poisonous attacks. Her raging fire brushes past me and carries the scent of the creature's burning flesh. The smokey monsters counterattack with raging beams of dark energy and the dragon manages to swiftly avoid the attacks by waving her hands up and down, disintegrating their strikes with strong waves of flames.

I grip the sword tightly in my hand and lunge myself onto the Aerolight on the left, landing on its back and stabbing the sword through its back and I puncture the dark heart that lies in its chest.

The other Aerolight roars and the dragon takes advantage by using both of her hands to fill its throat with scorching fire, drowning it with her power.

As it burns, I use all my weight to drive the blade deeper into the beast's back while being bucked around. Despite being bumped around, I manage to stay on it firmly until I'm dropped to the ground and both Aerolights disappear, indicating they've been defeated. I stand up in front of the dragon and the fire on her hands extinguish. I look past her and see Silva finish off the last remaining Aerolight before swiftly approaching us.

"That's the last of them. Thank you both, I owe you a great debt." The dragon lady says kindly before I stomp up to Silva with a pulsing pain in my side and her gaze falls down on me.

"Explain everything now. Why are we here? How is this place hidden by an invisible barricade? And...who...is this?!" My growl grows into a whisper because I don't want this newcomer to assume I speak badly about her.

"I think I can answer a few of those questions for you." The scaley lady steps up and stands next to Silva.

Heat radiates off her red ashy body and her golden eyes remain glowing. When she breathes out of her nose, I see the smallest clouds of charred smoke puff out. I find myself awkwardly staring at the fireball that levitates between her horns.

"My name is Phoenix and I'm the protector of my home, Dragon's Fjord." While she speaks, I can help but keep my eyes on her because I'm still in shock that she's real. Silva remains standing still, listening and observing the conversation.

"The fjord was barred by Silva's magic to ensure its treasure and my people are hidden and protected from the human world. Silva casted these barriers nearly hundreds of years ago after humans attacked my first home, unprovoked." Phoenix's tone is strong and proud and the growl in her voice is intimidating but it's also easy to understand her.

"Just like the barrier over Alsfield back at home?" I look at Silva and she nods her head.

"Who exactly is 'your people'? Are there more...people like you here?" My question causes Phoenix to laugh and a cloud of gray smoke escapes through her sharp teeth.

"No, I'm the only one who can change form. Though...I've always questioned why this form resembles a...human. But my people rest within the mountain for protection and they only come out when I deem the mountain to be safe." She looks at Silva and she nods her head as if giving approval for something I'm unaware of.

The ground below us begins to rumble and I hear a subtle bellow coming from beyond the trees. Phoenix leads us back out towards the cliff and I look around, trying to figure out what's causing the noise. Phoenix stands in front of us and lifts her hands up towards the deep red sky. Her skin glows bright orange and she pulls the fiery sky fumes from the atmosphere, absorbing the fire into her body. The red sky is replaced with bright blue and white fluffy clouds and I'm able to see the iridescent shimmer of the invisible barricade.

Phoenix pulls her arms to the side and she looks back at me, raising one of her scaly red brows.

"You may want to cover your ears, princess." Phoenix smiles mischievously before releasing a very low, yet loud roar, causing me to cup my ears with my hands.

Once her roar comes to an end, I'm confused, not understanding what the purpose was because everything goes silent and still. But slowly, I begin to feel the ground shake below my feet and I struggle to keep my balance while Silva and Phoenix remain standing tall and unphased.

Another deep growl protrudes from inside the mountain and my attention is drawn to the sky when I see more dragons emerge from the base of the mountain.

I follow the creatures with my eyes as they roar happily in the sky. I run to the edge of the cliff and watch the magnificent beasts fly over my head with each of them being a different shape, color and size than the next.

I hear a high-pitched roar that almost resembles a musical melody and I immediately lock eyes with a huge black dragon with dark purple scales that scatter across its belly, chest and tail in the shape of a sharp spear. The moment it sees me; it rapidly swoops down towards the edge of the cliff. I stumble backwards, giving it space to land, not knowing whether to run or remain where I am.

The dragon lands heavily on all fours, shaking the stone beneath me. I keep my gaze locked on its bright blue feline shaped eyes. In its reflection, I can see my own wonder and fascination which seems to match the temperament of the beast in front of me.

Black smoke slowly pours out of its nostrils like a gentle waterfall. I'm tempted to reach my hand out, but worry it may eat me in one bite.

Its nose is just inches from my touch so I slowly reach for its sharp nose that curves back and up towards its face. I steadily reach my hand up and the dragon leans its head down, allowing me to touch it.

"I'd be most appreciative if you won't eat me." I whisper and laugh softly and the dragon murmurs as if it can understand me.

I run my hand across its cheek, feeling its smooth scales under my fingertips. "When I was a child, I dreamed that you were real. Now, here you are." Seeing that the dragon is content, I walk around to see more of its physique. It has four strong muscular legs, wide scaled black wings that rest to its side and a sharp, deadly tail. While walking around cautiously, Phoenix and Silva approach me.

"It's not every day a Dark Torrent accepts someone's company, let alone a human's. He really likes you." Phoenix says as she walks next to me. I don't know what's more terrifying, the fact that she's nearly two feet taller than me or that I'm standing between two dragons.

"This is Indarri. Despite his large size, he is one of my youngest." She walks up to his face and he rubs against her side like a giant cat, purring in a low tone.

"Wait, so you- these came from-" I fumble trying to find the proper words to use, but in the end, nothing but silly gibberish escapes my tongue.

"No no no. While yes, I raised most of them on my own, I found most of them as hatchlings and others I rescued from hunters. I formed this colony thousands of years ago and now, they all look to me for leadership.

They've been my family since I was born. There's not many of us left, but I cherish and protect those who remain." Phoenix pets Indarri, making him purr loudly. The way she's so gentle and caring with Indarri makes me smile.

"As incredible as this is, I still don't know why we're here. Surely it wasn't to gaze at dragons." I look at Silva, expecting her to answer, but instead, Phoenix continues to talk to me.

"Next to Silva, I am one of the last remaining Serafaes. I will join you on your journey and help you defeat the Aerolights that plague our homes. I'm sure by now, Silva has begun to teach you about the connection between your emotions and your power but I will teach you how to hone in on your strength and courage."

I've just met Phoenix and I'm already seeing similar attributes between her and Silva, despite them being different elements.

"I mean...is that really necessary? I already know how powerful my abilities are-" Phoenix's eyes glow brighter and she steps closer, causing me to shutter and step back.

"Even when you think you've learned it all, there is still much to teach. There's a difference between power and strength. You have the adequate strength but you lack the confidence to use it. Once you've mastered these tasks, you may find yourself fighting alongside me successfully without freezing in the middle of a fight." She laughs, teasing and her eyes stop glowing, revealing vibrant red eyes.

263

Something tells me I can trust her.

"Hey, I only froze because the impossible is unraveling before my eyes as each day passes. Never in my life did I think it'd be possible to witness monsters, a scary fairy and dragons. How else am I supposed to react?" I look at Silva who stands still by herself, smirking.

"I don't understand. Humans imagine the strangest things for self-entertainment, but once it stands before their eyes...they're confused." Phoenix and Silva laugh in unison.

As much as I hate to admit it, she does have a point. I take a deep breath. "Alright, how do we begin?" I ask Phoenix while my hand rests on the hilt of the sword that's tucked away in a baldric.

Phoenix signals for the dragons to leave and they all take off, following Indarri back into the mountain. Silva steps back towards the forest, binding herself comfortably to the trees around her. Phoenix who stands with her back to the edge of the cliff, facing me with a smile on her face, baring the tips of her sharp canine teeth.

"You've fought the Aerolights on land, now it's time to see how well you do against those who roam the skies." Phoenix raises both arms out to the side and falls backwards off the cliff. I rush to the edge and watch her disappear under a thick blanket of fog.

Where did she go?

I look around, worrying when I hear a loud roar echo through the air, booming from behind the clouds. I look up and see a large shadow shoot up into the air and Phoenix flies through the clouds.

She swoops high into the air before diving down and hovering above where I stand. Her wings flap heavily in the air, blowing away the fog and remaining smoke.

"Our foe is quickest when in the air. It allows their attacks to be more precise and their field of vision to be wider. When an enemy is airborne, your sword is of no use. You must rely on your other abilities."

I instantly think about what Silva has taught me so far. I look at my right hand, close my eyes and take a deep breath, waiting to feel the slow rush of power fill my veins. I stand calmly, listening to the waves crash against the base of the mountain. Eventually, a cold sensation washes over my body and I open my eyes to see the subtle green veins in my hand turn bright blue. Electricity cracks between my fingers and in my bloodstream. I twiddle my fingers around and watch the tiny blue currents bounce around my skin.

Phoenix peers down and nods satisfyingly. She flaps her wings slowly, keeping her levitating still in the air. She forms a ball of fire in each hand and I instantly hear the flame's roaring.

"First, I want you to focus on deflection and shield yourself in a timely manner. Are you ready?" Phoenix's deep majestic voice roars through the air. I hesitantly nod my head and prepare myself.

I move my left foot slightly farther than my right and I hold out both of my hands to the side, anxiously waiting to duel against her.

She raises both hands, with her left hand held forward and her right pulled back. Her body radiates with power so strong, I think about backing down, but I know that by now, it's too late and I don't want to make a fool of myself.

Phoenix thrusts her right hand forwards, sending a single raging ball of fire directly towards my face. I quickly cross my arms in front of my face to shield myself. Her fire slams strongly into the metal bracers, causing her attack to instantly explode, sending the flames roaring past my ears and over the metal halo that's connected to my head.

Once the fire vanishes, I slowly lower my arms down and peek over to see Phoenix with a surprised look on her face.

"You react well to fire being aimed at your face and yet you freeze at the sight of an Aerolight? Interesting." She teases and smiles snidely, snickering quietly to herself and turning her attention to Silva.

"I didn't freeze at the sight of them. I froze at the sight of you!" While she continues to look away, I use the opportunity to take her by surprise and reciprocate by throwing a blue ball of positive energy at her. Without looking my way, her right wing covers her body, shielding the attack.

"I find being attacked by fire versus giant monsters to be completely different." I stand tall, holding my right hand out, holding a second ball of blue electrical smoke that makes energy sizzle between my fingers.

"In my past experiences, humans saw that as the same thing." Her statement confuses me, but I don't think much of it.

I look down at my hands once more. I'm still getting used to this power I possess and the strength I feel from using it. I'm understanding more and more what Silva means when she told me Vessoria and I have to work together.

The flapping of Phoenix's wings goes silent and when I look up, she's gone. Thick grey smoke fills the air and I look around trying to find her but all I can hear is her booming voice.

"Some Aerolights can blend into the clouds, fog and smoke. And some can go completely invisible. It's critical that you listen carefully. Even their silence can be heard if you pay close attention."

Did this just turn into some kind of metaphorical lesson?

I assume that's her way of indicating that way I'll find where she's hidden. I walk closer towards the edge of the cliff and I stand completely still, listening very closely to the smoke in the sky.

I close my eyes and tune out all irrelevant sounds such as the tree branches blowing with the wind, Silva's vines twisting and turning around her and the metal layers on my body softly clinking against each other.

In the midst of the meditated silence, I hear a fire ignite quietly in the sky. I keep my eyes closed, deciding which direction it comes from and I feel my body being tugged a certain way. I hold my hands out in front of my chest with my palms turned inwards. Magic buzzes and swirls around my fingertips, ready to blow. Once I'm ready, I open my eyes and I push my hands forward, releasing a radiant ray of bright blue energy that clashes loudly with her fire that barely begins to peak out from the smoke.

I can feel her power pulling me forward, dragging me towards the end of the cliff, causing my feet to dig deep in the stone floor, making it crack. I use all of my strength to try to pull her down from the sky, but I've already underestimated her incredible strength. My knees begin to buckle and quiver as I get pulled farther and farther to the edge. The blue magic slowly eats away whatever fire she creates, but it's not devouring it fast enough.

She wouldn't pull me off the edge...would she?

"You're stronger than this, push harder!" Phoenix's voice booms in the distance as she continues to hide behind the clouds.

I look behind me to see I'm just a few feet from the edge and that's when the panic begins to settle.

"Fight with your fear!" Phoenix says encouragingly and it only makes me overthink more than I already am.

"WHAT?! This entire time, Silva has told me NOT to fight with fear!"

"You misinterpret my words. I tell you to not act out irrationally DUE to your fears!" Silva chimes and I instantly understand what they mean.

Fear can be a strength but also a weakness.

Determined, I look closely and see the faint outline of Phoenix's body. I shift my weight and carry my powerful beam with my right hand. While holding off the fire with one hand, I use the other to shoot a second ray of energy at her, aiming for her wing.

The blue magic slams hard into the inner part of her wing, causing Phoenix to unleash a loud roar and fall out of the sky and towards the sea. Her tunnels of fire retracts, allowing me to release all magic which relieves a lot of tension, allowing me to catch my breath.

I rush over to look over the cliff's edge to find Phoenix, but once I peer over, she's nowhere to be found.

Please tell me I didn't kill her.

The atmosphere goes completely silent for a split moment but that silence is broken by something slamming down onto the ground behind me. The floor shakes so violently that it makes me lose my balance and slip off the cliff. I release a loud scream before feeling something grip my arm tightly.

My heart pounds out of my chest and my stomach drops when I look down and see my feet dangling high in the air over the strong rushing waves that crash into sharp rocks. I quickly look up and see Phoenix looking down, smiling mischievously. She quickly pulls me up, helping me stand on the mountain. I instantly run far from the edge and turn to scream at her.

"Was that really necessary?!" I bend over, leaning on my knees, trying to breathe. Silva unbinds herself from the trees and vines and approaches me.

"Apologies, if you wish for me not to help you next time, I shall let you figure it out on your own. I don't suppose you have wings hiding between your shoulder blades, right?" Phoenix says sarcastically, looking around at me.

Who knew a dragon could be such a pain?

"I was talking about you swooping down and scaring me, which caused me to trip and fall. Did you have to dramatically appear like that?" Silva and Phoenix both laugh.

"It's all part of the learning experience. Now, you know to keep your guard up and not immediately assume your opponent is dead." Silva remarks, peering down at me, smiling. I shake my head and wipe dirt off my armor. I lean down and onto my knees, trying to catch my breath and calm the lingering panic that slowly goes away. Phoenix steps up to me and I see the tips of her sharp clawed feet come near and I pop my head up.

"I didn't mean to cause such a fright. I didn't think it'd scare you that bad." I nod my head and accept her apology. "Let's rest at the base of the mountain and I'll answer some questions you may have." Phoenix says softly, tucking her wings behind her back and she leads us down to the base of the mountain.

Phoenix and I sit on a couple of large boulders that stand tall on the shore, above the gentle waters. We both watch as Vivalda walks along the shore, staring at her reflection in the water. Phoenix takes a deep breath and a small flame escapes her mouth.

"You're unsure of something." I say quietly, looking at her over my shoulder.

She takes another deep breath and keeps her eyes fixated on the Princess. "I don't mean to sound like a broken record. We've been through this before. I know you've spent plenty of time with her up until this point but...do you truly think she's the one?" She keeps her gaze focused on Vivalda, studying her carefully.

"I know she is. Why? Do you doubt my judgment, old friend?" I move my long white hair out of my face that's blown by the salty wind.

"Of course not. Times must be darker than I thought in order for Vessoria to choose a human host. She's having to learn so much in such a short amount of time. I worry, that's all." Her bright red eyes turn to me and I instantly sense her paranoia.

"I understand your worry, but I know we are on the right path. Once Vivalda masters her powers, we'll find the Aerolight beacon, destroy it and everything will go back to the way it used to be."

"You mean we'd go back to hiding?" Her tone sadness and I look at Vivalda who continues to look at herself in the water's reflection.

"I think this time, our future will play out differently. As long as we can gain the princess' trust and she has ours, everything will play out the way it needs to." Vivalda runs up to us, stomping in the soggy mud.

"I must ask a question or two because if I don't, I think I may lose what's left of my mind." Vivalda walks up to Phoenix, itching to have her questions answered.

"Why do you not look like a typical dragon? I'm not saying the look is strange, but in no story have I ever heard of a humanoid dragon." Vivalda asks awkwardly, having a hard time asking her question, worried she'd offend Phoenix.

"Why don't you sit with us? I'll explain the best I can." She invites Vivalda to sit on a rock in front of us and her armor clanks loudly against the stone. She must really enjoy being geared up since she's kept it on this entire time or maybe she's still getting used to it still. The princess sits anxiously like an excited child about to be told a bedtime story.

"Thousands of years ago, a red dragon egg was found by humans here on this mountain, hidden within the forest. No one could pick it up or touch it because if anyone tried to lay a finger on it, their body would disintegrate. The egg stayed in place for a very long time until one night, a strange phenomenon occurred. The moon turned red and it summoned a herd of dragons that didn't have a home. Once the dragons were drawn to the egg, they sheltered and protected it while making the fjord their home. Unfortunately, even though no dragon ever showed humans any hostility, it didn't take long for humans to feel intimidated by the dragons' presence. Due to the human's irrational fear, they sailed from the mainland and began hunting and killing the beasts one by one. They grew in numbers until exactly one hundred and one men invaded the mountain and gathered around the red egg and they tried destroying it with their weapons, all to no avail. The dragons did everything they could to protect it and eventually, the egg began to crack open, not because of human weapons but because the beast inside was ready to rise and protect the innocent. I was the beast in the egg." Vivalda's eyes widen and her mouth hangs open in surprise.

"A hundred dragons died that night and in return, I killed a hundred men but spared one. The man I sparred looked at me like I was the monster and he called me 'the devil'. I let him live so that he may always remember the face of the beast he tried to destroy."

After Phoenix finishes speaking, Vivalda jolts back and she strikes a curious thought.

"Wait- that sounds like a fairytale I heard about when I was a child, but the monster was called-" Phoenix looks down, disappointed and interrupts.

"'The Flaming Demon'?" She looks up at Vivalda, upset.

"Yes. When I was a child, I vaguely remember villagers talking about the story of The Flaming Demon. But that's not how they told it." Phoenix shifts her eyes up, startling Vivalda. She's interested in what the princess has to say.

"How would they tell it?" She tries to ask softly but is unaware her fangs are bared and a ball of fire sparks between her horns. Her pain and sadness radiates hotter than the scorching lava that flows in her veins. Vivalda can sense her range and yet, she remains calm and talks to her gently since she knows Phoenix means no harm.

"The story told that dragons once attacked human villages, unprovoked, costing the lives of many innocent people. From there, dragons were always seen as dangerous 'demons' and 'monsters'. I will say, I never enjoyed listening to those stories." The fire fuming from in between Phoenix's horns extinguishes and she smiles slightly. I can sense that Vivalda's fascination and kindness has helped heal a small portion of the dragon's heart.

"The telling of that tale is just as interesting as it is foolish. It's fitting if it's coming from the mouths of ignorant humans." Phoenix smirks, trying to shake off her pain.

"For what it's worth. Not all of us are ignorant and foolish." Vivalda smiles brightly and Phoenix joyfully nods her head.

"The tale of that night turned into nothing but a scary story for human children and the truth of that night died with the man who was spared." Phoenix continues, speaking softly.

I look out into the distance and see the sun beginning to set in the horizon. "There's plenty of time for more questions as we travel. We must leave for our next destination before it gets dark." Vivalda zones out for a moment, taking in everything thought, feeling and emotion.

"What are we traveling for? I've already managed to gather a magical giant and now a dragon, what more could we possibly need?" Phoenix and I look at each other with our eyes widened. Phoenix tilts her head towards Vivalda, waving her brows up.

"We have just one more moment to spare." I begin to speak and Vivalda sits more comfortably with her hands held in her lap. "There's much more to our journey than just finding where the Aerolights come from. Your sword is called Vessoria and as mentioned, it's not often Vessorian magic bonds to a human. The Serafaes' goal is to help you reach your full potential and master your power and abilities. So, that being said, we are gathering some of the last remaining Serafae to assist us. Once we have what we need, we will explain further. Until then, our next stop is Yarrin, so do your best to prepare yourself, it's going to be a very cold trip." Vivalda shifts her attention to the distance where we entered the fjord.

"Why don't we call for Calypso and have her come back through the barrier? Maybe she can take us there! I'm sure we'd get there much quicker and she's said she's sailed all around the mainland, so surely she's been to Yarrin before." Phoenix growls, catching Vivalda and I off guard.

"A random human knows of my home?" She asks furiously, eyes narrow and brows sharp. Her large black claws curl into a fist and smoke seeps from the cracks of her skin.

"I didn't expect the mountain to be under attack and for you to be out of hiding. So, due to those circumstances, she helped us get to the mountain. If given the chance, I promise you can trust her. She holds zero malicious intent." My words help calm her nerves and her shoulders relax.

I don't blame Phoenix for feeling uneasy when it comes to humans. She only trusts Vivalda because she bares Vessoria. She has had her walls up for so long, she doesn't know who she can fully trust when it comes to her home.

"Alright...we will travel with her, but the moment I am threatened, I won't be afraid to let the fire dance."

From the shore, I open the barricade slightly and we can see Calypso's ship peeking from the outside. I'm surprised to see the vessel because I didn't think Calypso would linger around. I stretch my arms out and wave them forward to encourage the waves to draw the ship towards the base of the mountain.

"Don't tell me I have to swim across the water again. It was quite scary last time and I'd prefer not to go through that again." Vivalda peers over the water between the shore and the vessel.

"I can help you with that." Phoenix walks up and stands behind Vivalda and she wraps her scaly arms around her torso.

"What are you doing-" Before she can release her breath, Phoenix's wings stretch from her back and she takes off from the ground, holding the princess firmly to her chest.

Phoenix flies over to the ship and lands safely on the top deck.

I can hear Vivalda shriek loudly which makes me laugh. Once they're onboard, I vanish into the cool air and teleport to the ship effortlessly. Once I shift back to my normal state, I see Vivalda clasped to Phoenix's torso as if she thinks they're still in the air and she's afraid to let go.

"You can let go now your highness, it wasn't a far flight." Phoenix says, holding her arms out awkwardly to the side. Vivalda slowly opens her eyes and lets her go, stepping down one foot at a time.

"Warn me next time you do that. I didn't think you could take off so fast." Vivalda leans on her knees, catching her breath. From behind, we can hear boots quickly treading against the wooden floorboards.

"Ahoy mates! I didn't think we'd actually see each other again!" Calypso runs up to us and stops dead in her tracks at the sight of Phoenix, nearly falling backwards. Her eyes widen and her mouth gapes in disbelief.

"Uh, what- who, HOW- woahhhhhhh." Calypso stutters over her words and Vivalda rushes to her side in hopes Calypso won't say anything that could potentially set off Phoenix.

"Ah, Calypso, this is Pheonix. The guardian of Dragon's Fjord. Phoenix, this is Calypso, captain of the Nightwalker." The captain walks past Vivalda silently with her mouth still gaping open.

She generously keeps her distance and both Calypso and Phoenix analyze each other carefully. Calypso suddenly squints her eyes, drops her brows and crosses her arms over her chest. It looks like she doesn't believe what stands before her and Phoenix glares at her, waiting for Calypso to say something foolish.

"Nah, I'm not fully convinced." Calypso says in a snarky tone, shaking her head while Vivalda laughs nervously from the side.

"What do you mean?" Vivalda asks, taking a step back. She's worried Calypso will overstep Phoenix's boundaries before having the chance to get to know her.

"You're the Flaming Demon, aren't you?" Calypso asks skeptically, dramatically tilting her head to the side. Phoenix's eyes widen and she looks at Vivalda for a split second before shifting her gaze back to Calypso.

"You know that story as well?" She asks quietly and Calypso nods her head, slowly arching her brow. The mischievous look on Calypso's face tells me she's ready to cause trouble.

"If you really are some kind of guardian, can you prove it in some way?" Seeing Calypso's cold gray eyes clashing with Phoenix's bright yellow eyes is like watching a dance between fire and ice.

On one side, I can tell Calypso is just trying to get a reaction from Phoenix for her own source of entertainment and on the other, I can tell Vivalda's stressing out, worried something bad will come from the pirate testing the dragon. I, on the other hand, remain content, ready to see what happens.

Phoenix's tightly sealed lips curl into an impish smile and vicious flames escape her fingertips. She rolls her hands over each other, forming a large ball of fire to levitate between her hands. Calypso backs up cautiously at the sight of burning fire levitating over her wooden ship.

Phoenix curls her claws over and around the ball, grasping it firmly before throwing it straight into the air. Once it's high into the air, the fireball explodes, causing sparking embers to descend into the sea, dissipating before causing a single ripple.

I look at Calypso who's standing still, unphased, waiting patiently. Phoenix turns her ear to the mountain and suddenly, the ship begins to rock and rumble at the sound of her dragons roaring in unison from the depths of the mountain, inside the hidden cave. Vivalda trots up to Calypso and rests her hand on Calypso's shoulders.

The princess laughs excitedly. "Come on now, you're being a troll. There's no way you don't believe her just by her presence!" She shouts loudly as the roars die down and the ship stops rocking.

"You think I'm that dumb? I believed it from the moment I saw her in the distance. I just wanted to know if there were more dragons here." Calypso laughs proudly of herself. Phoenix is left dumbfounded and yet satisfied at the same time. I don't sense a spark of hatred or anger in her heart.

"Now that you know the tale of the Flaming Demon, I want you both to remember something that no other human was ever able to understand…though my skin may be red and my horns turn into fiery torches, I am no demon. Understood?" She asks softly and both Calypso and Vivalda smile and nod in agreement.

Calypso steers us out of the fjord and I close the barrier behind us once again. I can feel Phoenix's sadness due to leaving her home. I don't think she's ever been away from her colony before.

"Where are we headed?" Calypso asks as she and Vivalda stand at the ship's wheel. Vivalda tells Calypso about our plans and next destination while Pheonix and I remain talking to each other.

"You'll return sooner than you know and until then, they'll be safe. Even then, if something were to go wrong, the dragons can take care of themselves, especially with Indarri watching over them." I say softly. Phoenix smiles and nods and a quick thought pops into my mind, raising slight concern.

"Now that I think about it. How did the Aerolights get past the barrier in the first place? Did you witness it happen?" I ask and Phoenix immediately turns her head and looks at me, concerned. She thinks to herself for a moment before answering.

"I don't know. I saw the wall covered by a dark shadow, I assumed it was you opening it and they simply seeped in and broke through." I think back to when Vivalda and I boarded the ship and I saw the storm clouds in the distance before the sun went down.

"The clouds..." I begin to speak, but get lost in my own thoughts. Phoenix peers over, looking at me, worried. "Before we began to sail, I saw dark clouds in the distance. I only realize now that they weren't storm clouds. The Aerolights began invading the fjord long before we arrived." I continue to think to myself and slowly begin to realize a strange pattern with the Aerolights and their scattered attacks.

"We're being watched and they know where we're going. Before leaving the Lion's Eye and boarding the ship, we were attacked by an Aerolight. They knew where we were headed and got there before us without me mentioning where we were going or what our mission was." Phoenix's eyes illuminate and her hostile glare pierces my soul. She bares her teeth and growls quietly before taking a deep breath.

"I assume they know the rest of our plan and that we're headed to Yarrin." Phoenix looks down at the ground, angrily.

"I've never seen one get close to the frozen lands, but then again, I said the same thing about the Lion's Eye. Maybe this time luck will be on our side and maybe my suspicions are wrong." Despite trying to hold on to a small bundle of hope, there's still a lot of concern that remains glued to my mind.

"Silva, don't you think we should tell-" Phoenix's is cut off by Vivalda letting out a loud and painful scream in the distance.

Phoenix instantly spreads her wings and takes off and I follow behind. Once we land on the helm, we see the princess hunched over, groaning in agony. The armor has vanished and the golden necklace lies on the floor many feet away from her.

"What happened?!" I ask loudly, looking at Calypso who is just as shaken and confused.

"I- I don't know, she said she was ready to put the armor away and once it disappeared, she fell down, screaming!" Calypso inches to help the princess but hesitates.

"I'm fine, just give me a moment." Vivalda groans and struggles to speak as her face rests in her hands with her body hunched over her knees.

I slowly bend down and hold one of my hands over her body, allowing my power to flow over her and I attempt to see what's causing pain, but before I can say something, she holds out her shaking hand and brushes mine away.

"Like I said, I'm fine. I just need a moment. This happens more often than people think." She slowly sits up, breathing heavily and her eyes full of tears.

"Do you know what's ailing you?" I ask quietly, leaning closer to her, trying to comfort her.

"I don't know. Every time I disconnect from the armor, I'm overcome with this pain and it's gotten worse each time. I'd typically feel something like this only on occasion, but it's gotten more consistent since I first wore it." She scowls towards the necklace that remains on the wooden floor. The bright light that beams inside my soul flickers quicker and quicker as if matching the rhythm of Vivalda's heartbeat.

I shake my head feeling a bit overwhelmed and flustered. "It's not the armor causing this, I would know if it was. Typically, if enchanted emblems don't like its host, it'd kill them instantly or simply not work. I'm not sure what it is but until we know the cause, keep the armor off unless it's absolutely necessary to use it. Do you understand me?" Despite Vivalda looking annoyed, she agrees. I reach over to grab the necklace and when I hand it to her, she hesitates to pick it up. Instead of putting it on, she puts it in her dress pocket.

She stands up on her own, wincing and twitching in pain. I try to help her but it adds to her frustration. "Silva, I'm fine. I'm sure it's just my illness flaring up as it does every so often. I'm used to it." The princess says monotonously while suppressing the pain that pulsates through her muscles, tendons and bones.

She walks away from us and goes to the nose of the ship to lean against the ledge and look out into the horizon.

Vivalda

I slowly breathe through the aching pain that eventually fades away. My stomach feels like it's being slashed by thousands of tiny axes and my bones and muscles feel like they're being crushed by mallets. My chest feels heavy, and my head feels light and cold. I do what I can to snap out of it and focus on the matters at hand. I feel a finger tap me on the shoulder and I look over to see Calypso handing me a wooden mug filled with water.

"Don't worry, there's no fish dung in it if that's a concern ya have." She jokes lightly. I take the cup from her hand and consume it slowly. Calypso sits on a wooden bench next to me.

"Thank you." I say, wiping water from the corner of my lips. Calypso leans back, pulling her black hat over her eyes and bringing her arms around behind her head to rest. A light glare catches my eye and I peer over to see Calypso's dagger shining in the sun.

"That's a beautiful dagger you got there." Calypso peeks down, looking at her weapon.

"Aye. It was my father's before he disappeared." She unhooks the sheathed blade from her hip and hands it to me.

The dagger's sleeve is made of black leather that's covered with gold details that sparkle in the sunlight. And its hilt is black with a golden topper to match. Once I pull the blade out, the shape of the blade is very unique compared to others I've seen before. The gold blade is sharp on both ends and it waves like the sea, making it very dangerous.

"This blade is quite fascinating. Did your father craft it himself?" I ask curiously as I continue to fiddle with the dagger.

"Oh goodness no. That man couldn't craft a weapon to save his life. He tried many times and he always managed to make the strangest pieces of metal." Calypso laughs. "He got that one from a blacksmith in Palavon when he was around my age, maybe younger. Eh, time be irrelevant in my eyes." I chuckle and carefully slide the knife back into the sheath before handing it back to her.

"If you don't mind me asking. Did your father ever tell you the name of the forgery by chance?" I ask awkwardly, hoping for a certain answer. Calypso sits up and thinks for a moment.

"Ummm, I believe he mentioned it just once. I think it had the word 'Forge' in its name, but I could be wrong." She shrugs her shoulders.

"Do you think it could have been 'Flame Forge' by chance?" Calypso quickly turns to look at me, surprised.

"Yes, I believe that's correct. Are ya familiar with the place?" She asks curiously and my heart beats with excitement, making me think about my friends and family back at home.

"I am! I'm really close to the owner and his son!" A smile forms on her face and then her bright gray eyes widen.

"They never mentioned an old sailor, did they?" She sits up quickly, leaning on her knees, intrigued and beaming with hope. The hopefulness that swells in her eyes makes me feel sad after knowing my response.

"No, I'm sorry. Since piracy is shunned from the kingdom, I don't think they would have ever mentioned him. They wouldn't have risked him being caught or punished." Calypso wipes her hands over her face and brings them to rest against her lips as if she prays silently to herself.

"I'm so sorry. I know that's not the answer you were hoping for." I rest my hand on her shoulder and I see a kind smile peek from her stained black lips.

I look over at Silva and Phoenix who stand talking amongst themselves quietly. I randomly stare at Phoenix's black shiny wings that glisten in the sunlight and it makes a thought come to mind.

"Pardon me, the both of you. Phoenix, I have a question if you don't mind me asking." I begin to walk towards them and Phoenix turns around to give me her attention.

"Of course, princess." She walks closer towards us and Silva glides closely behind.

"When you were in your full dragon form and you-"

I hear something thud behind me and when I turn around, I see Calypso has clumsily fallen off the short bench and shouts excitedly and loudly. "Dragon form?!" She gets up, holding onto her hat so it doesn't fall off and she jogs over to me.

"Yes, give me a moment." I respond, holding my hand out to quiet her excitement, all to no avail.

"WHAT?! You didn't mention she can turn into a dragon!" She pauses, looking at Phoenix for a brief moment. I can tell she's looking at Phoenix's wings, observing them closely.

"Well, actually...that makes sense. Never mind, carry on." Calypso says as she proceeds to lean against a thick wooden beam. I try to hold my laughter in but it quietly slips out and Phoenix crosses her arms, tilting her head, highly unamused with Calypso's sense of humor.

I clear my throat and proceed to ask my question. "Anyways. When you were fighting the Aerolights, what caused you to fall from the sky and crash onto the mountain?" Her eyes widen and she swivels her head around in a circle as if to relieve tension in her neck.

"I can only stay in my beast form for a certain amount of time. It all depends on how much energy I have. I'm strongest when in beast form and by the time that fight began, too much time passed by. Aside from that, I had to draw them to the ground anyway. Fighting Aerolights in the air can be quite exhausting and difficult." Calypso scoffs and the rest of us glare at her simultaneously.

"So, what I'm hearin' is, ya ran out of energy, went ka-boom and your excuse is you needed to draw them elsewhere? Got it. Sounds like ya may be a wee bit embarrassed, yeah?" She says with a cheeky smile forming across her face. When she looks up, she notices we're all staring, she sucks in the sides of her cheeks and releases them, causing a *pop* to escape her mouth.

"What?" She tosses her hands up in the air and a beam of light shoots over Calypso's head, causing her to fall over. Calypso quickly looks up to see what damage was done to her ship and before she can get angry, we both notice there's no burn marks on the wood. Calypso jumps back up and we look at Phoenix's hand as white smoke seeps out of her fingertips.

"What the hell mate?! Ya could have set the entire ship a blaze."

Phoenix snarls with a slight smile on her face. "But I didn't. Your sarcasm and jokes fail to make me laugh." Calypso holds her hands up as if to surrender.

"Alright, I get it."

I chuckle nervously and I look at Silva who's unamused. My shoulders and hands tense and curled.

"I am so sorry."

Silva smiles and nods and Phoenix returns to standing with her arms crossed in front of her, satisfied with her warning shot but over Calypso's sarcasm at the same time.

"Remind me not to continue to give into the human buffoonery." Phoenix says to Silva.

It's nice to see everyone getting along in a humorous manner, despite knowing each other for a handful of days. I think I'm starting to enjoy this space and the company of these new acquaintances. A dragon, a forest fae and a pirate captain. Whoever thought I'd wind up here in life?

"OH! Ya say we're goin' to Yarrin right? I don't think the princess will hold up under the freezing weather wearing whatever...that is." She gestures to the thin long sleeve over dress I've worn since leaving the castle.

"Hey, I didn't exactly know what I was getting into when I agreed to go on this journey, okay? Cut me some slack." Calypso raises her brow and gawks at Silva.

"Ah, so this is Silva's fault, I get it now." Silva begins to raise her hand as it engulfs in light green magic. "If you ever plan on firing some kind of magical spell at me, please don't sprout trees or anything like that from my ship, I have allergies." Silva closes her hand and shakes her head.

"Didn't I give you a Moonpine last night? I didn't sense any signs of allergies then." Silva smirks.

"Oh yeahhhhhh, I put that thing in my hat." Calypso reaches behind her head and plucks the colorless flower out of her hat.

I didn't think she'd actually keep it, nor did I realize it was connected to her hat. Calypso fiddles with the petals, brushing her fingers over the plant, looking at it concerned.

"Uhhhhh I think I broke it." She twists and turns the flower around, confused why it's no longer colorful. "Why is it grey and ugly?" I can't help but laugh because she looks so silly while she shakes the plant as if she's trying to wake it up from some kind of slumber.

Silva takes a deep breath. "It's called 'Moonpine' for a reason. It's not broken. It lights up with the moon." Calypso's face cringes at the flower.

"Well, that makes sense. Anyways, as I was sayin'. I only judge your attire, Vivalda, because you're gonna freeze your precious toosh off if we don't get you warmer clothes. I suggest we make a quick stop on Darali since it's on the way. It won't take us long to grab some essentials." Calypso looks at Silva and Phoenix for approval. They look at each other, unsure of something, but they ultimately agree.

Calypso sets a course for Darali which is an island far southeast from the mainland. I've never been there before but have met many people in my life who travel from there to Palavon for trading and market goods.

We spend the next day getting to know each other and I open up to Phoenix and Calypso about recent altercations with my father. While talking about serious manners, Calypso lightens the mood with her enormous sense of humor.

I sit on a large wooden rectangle platform that reaches over the side of the boat, almost like a balcony that allows me to sit over the water. I hear Calypso's leather boots stomping my way and I turn around and look up as she leans over, looking out into the sea.

"I wanted to warn you about somethin' before we dock." I hear Calypso walk up behind me and she leans over the ledge above me. I look up while she looks out into the horizon. The breeze blows her hair back and makes the peacock feather in her hat flutter. "The people of Darali aren't very friendly towards me, simply because of childish rumors and accusations. And the fact that they despise pirates sort of makes it worse. That being said, I wouldn't be surprised if they treat you the same way, so try to prepare yourself but pay them no mind."

I can tell Calypso does everything she can to hide her emotions and the pain she feels. I think there's so much more to her anger than what she talks about. But I appreciate the fact that she cares enough to warn me. "I'm sure it won't be that bad. Besides, I think I'm used to it at this point. You should have been there to witness my father's last outburst. I'm sure it would have rattled you up after the things you've been through, alone."

Calypso jumps on top of the wooden ledge, sitting down and dangling her legs off the boat while holding onto a wooden post.

"I'm sure my fist would have immediately connected to his face. No offense to your father, but he's no king if he treats his own like that. My father would never react in such a way, no matter how angered he was." She begins to kick her feet as if she's itching to ask something but is nervous to do so.

"If you don't mind me askin'...what exactly happened to the queen? Don't bother if it's too much." She asks cautiously. Making sure not to overstep. My heart skips a beat, causing my chest to feel queasy.

"Eh- I've had experience with others not believing me. I don't know-" Before I can continue, Calypso chuckles loudly.

"PSH! You think I won't believe ya after meeting these magical bozos? Come on." She points her thumb back towards the Serafaes and we hear Phoenix snort loudly behind us.

"I'd be careful. All Phoenix has to do is sneeze and your ship will be blown into tiny splinters." Both of us laugh and turn our gaze back to the sea.

"My point is, if a forest fairy and dragon have existed among us for centuries, I'm sure I'll believe whatever you tell me. Surely it can't be any crazier than that. But like I said, you don't have to tell me if it causes ya pain." Calypso's words are genuine and I appreciate her kindness. I'm not sure how many times I can retell the story without losing more pieces of myself. But if it means it helps clear my conscience and gets others to understand...I guess it's worth it.

I inhale slowly and tell Calypso what happened and as I recall the traumatizing events, I find myself zoning out, staring at the sea while speaking. And for the first time...I feel no tears swell my eyes.

Once I finish talking, Calypso looks absolutely distraught and heartbroken. "Wow, he really is a moron. Then again...most men are." Calypso says snidely.

"I've never seen or heard him act so cruel and ignorant. My mother's death is taking a toll on him, and I don't blame him. But I'd do anything to take back that night. No matter what my heart knows, I still think I'm partially to blame. Had I never left the castle, maybe it wouldn't have happened and maybe she would have returned home safely." I flinch back when I see a green leaf fall in front of my face, swaying with the breeze. When I look up, I see Silva towering over behind me, standing next to Calypso.

"Oh hello there. Creepy much?" Silva's upside-down face stares at me happily. I stare at her for a brief moment, and she tilts her head to the side as if listening to me without a single word being spoken. Her giant green leaf ears twitch back and forth, listening to my thoughts.

"What's your question, child?" She asks softly and smiles. I swivel my body around to face her, sitting over my knees.

"Why did you call me to Alsfield that night and how exactly did you know my mother had died?" I look over and see Calypso's eyes widen. Silva's head drops slightly.

"Death is something I feel every day. With each passing moon, I feel the world cry. I feel when every tree falls and when the world burns. Our souls intertwined without knowing it was possible. I know Aladora felt the same after finding comfort by speaking to stone and unleashing her pain and stress. The moment I felt her heart stop, my stone skin cracked, and the world stopped moving for a split moment. I called you to me because the world needed to be saved, and you were the one to undo what's been done." Silva's green glow slowly fades in and out.

"Maybe if I had never left, you two would have had the chance to speak to one another." Silva leans over the wooden railing, staring deep into my soul and I can't help but keep my eyes fixated on her.

"There was no telling what would have happened if you WEREN'T there, and I think that's one of the worst things to not be able to know. You were the one who found her and without you, we don't know if she would have been able to make it home in the first place. You know that." I zone out and get lost in my own thoughts and memories.

"That's just it. I didn't find her...she found me." I recall the moment I wound up in my mother's arms on a horse. I do my best to shake off the memories so I can focus. Calypso jumps up on top of the railing, holding onto a rope that dangles off that side of the ship and leans all the way over. For a moment, I'm worried she'll fall overboard but the confidence in her eye tells me being a daredevil is something she enjoys.

"We're close to Darali! Will you magic bozos stay below deck and watch over the ship, or do you wish to conceal yourselves in the forest?" I scoot off the platform and crawl through the opening behind me to stand next to Silva and Phoenix. We look out into the distance and see the island that's slowly approaching.

"We'll stay hidden within the forest so we can keep a firm eye on you both. But I must warn; if there is to be any signs of Aerolights, Phoenix and I won't be able to help as much because if we are seen by other humans, all hell will break loose worse than it already has. In the beginning, Vivalda was the only one who was supposed to know about us and now that we have a sarcastic pirate on our hands, we can't risk anyone else knowing or joining this voyage." Calypso pulls her hat, glaring at Silva.

"Aye, I'm right here ya know. Ye overgrown green bean." She puts her fists on her hips while leaning her weight on one side.

I laugh hysterically at her insult against the Serafaes and before we know it, a loud *CRACK* comes from behind us on the deck. Calypso jumps back and we watch as a small tree sprouts from the wooden floorboard. The tree grows large enough until a branch is long enough to stretch over and smack Calypso's hat off.

The captain's eyes widen and twitch. She stands still, annoyed and creepily turns to look at Silva. "I hope that thing grows apples or somethin' useful, cause I don't want there to be a big ol' useless plant just staring at me." I can tell she's trying her best from losing her temper and she looks so silly, I can't help but continue to laugh.

I clear my throat and compose myself before returning to Silva's attention. "Apologies. As you were saying?" She glares at me menacingly and I can't tell if she's genuinely annoyed or not.

"Why do you always stare like that? It's quite terrifying sometimes, you know?" I ask and Silva's eyes soften and her gray lips curve into a sweet smile.

"If I'm deemed terrifying in the eyes of mortals, there's a lesser chance of them getting on my bad side. So far, you, Vivalda, are doing very well. However...I can't say the same for the pirate." Silva gazes at Calypso behind her and sees her fumbling around, trying to fix her ruby red hair.

"Aye, what can I say? Getting on peoples- I mean...fairies' bad sides is fun." Phoenix huffs and interjects.

"Serafaes are far more powerful and sometimes sinister than fairies from silly human tales." She says under her breath.

"I know that now, firebutt. I was just jokin'." Calypso glares at Phoenix.

There's a loud screech that comes from above, so we turn our attention to the sky and see a gorgeous large brown falcon fly over the ship. The majestic creature sings while flapping its wings against the wind. Its feathers shine in the sunlight as it flies away.

Once we approach closer to the island, Calypso runs back to the wheel and turns the ship slightly to dock at a certain side of the island.

"When we get there, please be as quick as possible. I don't want to-" Silva begins to speak but I politely cut her off to reassure her.

"We'll be in and out in a heartbeat. Were there for supplies, not socialization. Not like anyone would want to socialize with me in the first place. Besides, I'm sure we're more likely to get bombarded by angry villagers than we are to be attacked by Aerolights. I'll ensure we'll be back on board hastily."

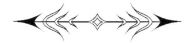

Once we approach the side of the island, Calypso drops the ship's anchor, and the vessel begins to slow down. Silva and Phoenix look around, keeping an eye out for humans, but thankfully there's none in sight that would be able to spot them. Once the ship comes to a stop, Calypso throws a ladder over the side of the vessel.

I climb down the wooden steps and land on a wooden platform that stretches to the forest beach. From a far distance, I can hear music playing. The sounds remind me of home and a small part of me gets excited to be within civilization, but I remind myself not to get my hopes up. I know how I'm going to be treated.

I look up and see a green wisp of magic dive off the ship and zip into the forest at the speed of light. Once it touches the ground, Silva forms and walks beyond the trees to check that the coast is clear. Phoenix swooping down and landing next to me. She looks disgusted to be on a human island.

There's a small flame lit between her horns and her eyes begin to glow yellow. Her nose wrinkles in bitter annoyance as she keeps her spiky ears turned outwards. I can instantly sense her boiling anger to be on a human island and I don't blame her. I think our anger is decently matched.

"I'd rather my body be turned to ash and sink to the bottom of the sea than be near more humans than I must." She growls with every word she speaks, and I instantly feel bad. I only know a fraction of her story and her anger is more menacing than I thought it could be. When Phoenix sees I'm a bit tense, she calms down and it looks like she feels bad.

"It's nothing against you...or the pirate. The both of you are the most civil and polite humans I've ever encountered. I'm sure there's more like you out there, but I must keep my walls up just in case." I feel terrible for what humans have put her through and I don't blame her for her walls being kept up and guarded.

Out of the corner of my eye, I see Calypso swing down from a rope and tie it to a tall and thick post that sticks out of the water.

"Aww shucks, was that a compliment I just heard?" She shouts in a high-pitched tone.

Phoenix runs her hand over her scaley, orange face and snorts out a puff of smoke from her nostrils.

"Savor it because I guarantee it won't happen again." I can hear Calypso chortle and laugh quietly to herself while she continues to tie the boat.

I walk with Phoenix down the wooden platform while Calypso continues to tend to the ship and tie it down. "I know you don't want to be near humans, so why not stay on the ship? I'd assume it'd be better than being even closer. Right?" I can feel blistering heat radiating from her body as the bright orange flame continues to dance between her shiny black horns. I'm sure she could set the entire island on fire if she wanted to.

"I'm not one to follow others, but I stay with Silva to ensure you, and your friend remain safe. We just want to ensure you finish this journey and we can't take any risks. Whether it lies within humans or magic, darkness lurks everywhere, so we have to be vigilant." Her speaking about my safety sounds genuine, but when speaking about random humans, her tone changes drastically. And despite her raging anger, I feel safe standing next to her.

Phoenix turns to look up at the forest ahead of us, searching for something beyond the trees and she speaks to me quietly. She quickly steps in front of me and looks down. The flame in between her horns extinguishes and the glow in her eyes fades away. She speaks quickly and there's worry behind her eyes.

"Listen, there's something you need to know-"
Phoenix peers back to look at the forest before turning to look back at me. I think she's ensuring that Silva doesn't hear her, other than that, I don't know what else she could be looking for. But the urgency in her voice is making me feel uneasy.

Before she can continue to speak, I lean over when I see a bright light come from the forest. Phoenix squints her eyes, shakes her head and takes a deep breath. "If you get even the slightest feeling something's wrong, please call for us."

"Psh, everything will be fine. If something were to happen, I'm sure I'd be able to handle it anyways."

Once Phoenix turns around and moves out of the way, we see Silva standing at the forest edge, waiting for us to catch up.

Once the others meet me in the forest, Calypso and Vivalda stand before me, ready to leave for the village.

"Find what you need and meet us back here as soon as possible. The longer you linger in the village, the more likely we are to be spotted." I explain, keeping both young women's attention and they both nod and agree.

"Silva can disappear into thin air, but I, however, cannot. The moment a human catches my gaze, I can't guarantee what'll happen from there." Phoenix's paranoia begins to get the best of her.

It's not humans she fears, it's destruction and confrontation she wishes to avoid.

"Don't be so wary. No one comes into the forest, they're too scared and have no business being over here anyways. I promise we'll be quick, but the more ya give us these paranoid pep talks, the longer it'll take for us to get it done." Calypso says as she sways back and forth on her toes, impatiently waiting to leave.

I nod my head and in the blink of an eye, they quickly disappear behind huts and tents, all I can hear is Vivalda's quiet thoughts.

I turn to walk deeper into the forest, keeping my gaze on them, following them down towards the village, but remaining hidden in the trees and Phoenix follows closely behind. I take deep breaths in an attempt to free myself from my own anger that begins to boil in my chest. Phoenix walks up closer behind me and speaks quietly.

"Silva, I wasn't-" I hold my arms up, cascading a temporary silent and invisible barrier over Phoenix and I. Once the barrier is formed, I immediately snap around to confront Phoenix, causing her to step back. I walk towards her, growing in size with every step I take, causing me to stand taller over her.

"I know exactly what you're trying to do! You know very well that you cannot be telling the princess the details that you're itching to share! Not yet at least. If she finds out sooner than planned, then this will all be for nought. Right now, our priority is getting her to her full potential and ensuring she stays alive. Understood?" I feel the stone skin around my eyes begin to crack and I quickly realize I've overstepped and I'm acting too rash. Smoke rises from Phoenix's hands and she looks at me angrily, ready to strike. She's focused on my skin that continues to break but once I am more composed, it returns to normal. I lower myself back and take a deep breath. I turn around and continue walking into the forest.

"You're going about this wrong, you know that, right? She has trusted us quicker than any other human has in our lifetimes. I never thought I'd witness a human's kindness being taken advantage of by those of us who are seen as 'lesser'." A gust of wind slams into my chest, causing me to come to a halt. I turn around once more, but this time, calmly and I don't move closer to her.

"I know how to approach this situation. I've had it planned for a very long time now. If handled differently, she wouldn't trust us, and we'd be in even more trouble. I understand your concern, I'm just as worried as you are but everything will be fine as long as the plan stays in motion." Phoenix looks at me with a cold eye, keeping her distance and I instantly feel bad for being so harsh with her.

I take a deep breath. "I'm sorry. Can you forgive me for my outburst?" Phoenix shakes her head in defeat but ultimately submits because she has no other choice. She sighs heavily and walks towards me cautiously.

"If this goes wrong, I can't guarantee I won't let the fire rain down on your forests." She says in a menacing tone with her sharp teeth bared and the fire ignited between her horns.

We put our dispute to the side and continue to follow the princess and captain as they stroll along in the village.

Vivalda

We finally exit the forest and enter civilization. I walk into the village with a smile on my face in hopes to avoid negative interactions. Calypso and I walk on a wide dirt path that is lined with shops, huts and small homes, similar to Palavon but more crowded and the people are much more energetic. People fill the walkways, chattering and shopping. Music can be heard playing inside the taverns and other musicians sing in the road, dancing around with their instruments.

Darali is much smaller in size, but something about it reminds me of home. I smile at people who look at me and pass by while following behind Calypso as she leads me through crowds of people that stare at us uncomfortably. Every time Calypso looks back, I can see the disgusted look on her face.

I begin to feel more and more uncomfortable when people begin to slow down and crowd around us. I hold one arm over my stomach while my other hand dives into my pocket to hold Vessoria. I try finding comfort in holding the piece of jewelry, but unfortunately, it doesn't help as much as I wish.

"Ignore them and stay close to me. If they dare make a move, my dagger will pierce their eye before they get a chance to blink." We walk faster through the crowds, and I begin to hear what the villagers are saying.

"That's the princess, that's responsible for the queen's death." A woman whispers to the others around her.

"I used to want to be like her." A child is pulled to her mother's hip as if to shun her from my gaze.

I slow down and come to a stop, looking back at the child and her mother. I feel my heart shatter and my eyes begin to water.

Even the children are being manipulated into lies.

I begin to walk towards them when suddenly, I feel something solid slam into the back of my shoulder. I stumble forward and when I turn around, I see a tall burly man looking down at me, furiously, as if I had gotten in his way when he's the one who bumped into me.

"Watch where you're going traitor, wouldn't want your pretty little face to get damaged now, would we?" Spit flings from his dirty mouth while he speaks. I can't help but cower because I don't wish to cause a scene, even though I saw this coming. From the corner of my eye, Calypso stomps up with her arms crossed in front of her.

"Aye why don't you carry on yer way and take ya pathetic threats elsewhere, dirtbag." Calypso walks up to him and pushes his shoulder to the side. Despite his large size, she manages to make him take a few steps back. He laughs at the sight of her and bares his brown broken teeth, wiping away the saliva that drips into his bushy brown beard.

"Well, if it isn't the scum of Darali? It makes sense seeing two murderers out and about together." He scoffs as he cracks his thick knuckles in his palms. I freeze in place upon hearing the words 'murderers'. I turn to look at Calypso whose hands curl into fists and her eyes narrow. She looks like a predator ready to pounce on its prey.

"Calypso? What is he talking about?" I ask quietly and she looks down, shaking her head.

"Nothing. He's just tryna piss me off." The man approaches Calypso and gets close to her face, but she keeps her composure, furrowing her brows.

"Oh, the pirate scum didn't tell ya? Shocking. I thought she ran off with you for a reason." I trust Calypso's word and I try to ignore angry man's nonsense.

I try to inch myself away to get out of his sight, but a large crowd of people circle around us, blocking Calypso and I from leaving.

She looks around, angered at the villagers and her hands curl into a fist. Raw, intense anger shoots through her and she can barely stay still. I can tell she's eager to let off some steam by swinging her fist into the man's face. The people around us slowly begin to cheer, begging for a fight.

"Show 'em why they should never step foot on Darali again!" A woman from the back shouts, throwing her fist in the air and causing the rest of the crowd to roar louder.

The shouting causes me to go into a state of panic. I cover my ears with my hands. My chest feels heavy, and it becomes difficult to breathe properly.

The overwhelming sensation makes me want to crash down and cry, but the last thing I need is to make a fool of myself and show how weak I can be. Calypso notices me beginning to panic and she instantly fixes her angry posture in an attempt to de-escalate the commotion.

303

"Listen, all of ya can cause a frenzy with me, but don't drag the princess into matters that have nothing to do with her! She's done nothing to ya!" She shouts to the suffocating circle of villagers as they laugh in her face and spit at her feet.

"It's so sweet seeing the failed captain's daughter trying to stick up for someone as low as she is. She ain't no princess. The royal family practically disowned her for causing the queen's death. Now, she has no royal status or knights to protect her and there's no 'home' for her to run to." He laughs and looks around the crowd, flattering himself over his insults and hatred. I can tell he's only being so nasty to get himself positive attention.

I quickly wipe my eyes to avoid anyone seeing me be affected by his terrible words.

"Listen, we just need to pick up a few things and we'll be on our way alright?" Calypso raises her hands up to surrender her rage. She looks defeated while trying to calm the situation down and I'm sure she's looking forward to a fight. She walks over to me and my gaze falls to the floor. She stands in front of me waiting for a response from the man.

"Psh, whatever. We best not see your faces here ever again!" The crowd boos and moans because he allows us to walk away.

I walk in front of Calypso, and she guides me out of the chaotic ring of angry people. I wipe the remaining tears from my eyes with my long sleeve and then I immediately feel a strange sensation that causes the hairs on my neck to stand and my ears to perk.

I turn around and time suddenly slows down when I see the man following behind Calypso with his fist raised, ready to punch the back of her head. I dart around her quickly and get between both of them and as soon as time returns to normal speed, I firmly catch the man's curled fist in my right hand and I stare deep into the man's eyes, leaving him shaken to his core when he realizes I'm standing in front of him. He tries to pull his hand back, but it's locked tight in my grip.

"Hey- what the hell is wrong with you!" He shouts frantically, confused and scared, catching the bystander's attention. I hear the collected gasps of people, shocked to see me standing up to him, counteracting his violent act.

My fiery rage springs to life and my heart beats loudly in my ears. I've never felt so determined to put someone in their place. I can feel the Vessorian magic pulsate through my vein, but I make sure it's unable to be seen by those around me. After keeping a cold gaze on him for a moment, I speak firmly to the man in a low voice.

"You'd really lay your hands on a woman? For what? Over the fact that you all are blinded by rumors and false narratives? All you want is a 'valid' reason to fight when you're not head over heels drunk. You're no better than the king who's letting this kingdom down as we speak." I pant and look around at the crowd, angrily, but making sure to keep my tone as cool as possible. "Do you know where he's been since the night the queen fell?" I ask and he and others shake their heads. The man continues trying to pull away from my grip, gritting his rotten teeth and sweating anxiously.

"He's been in his chambers, avoiding his royal calling, prepared to protect his throne before his people." I look around at everyone else who's astonished by my words. They look at me as if I disgrace the king with my own false narratives. "Don't believe me? Travel to the gates and ask my sister. The one who's NOT responsible for a death. Do that and then find me to tell me my word is wrong." The man quivers as I hold his fist steady, not moving a single muscle.

"Okay, okay! I get it! WE get it." I dig my nails into the top of his hand, tearing his skin and he winces in pain. I lean in closer to look him directly in the eye.

"You don't get it, and you never will. I was there that night. Not the king or knight and none of you were there to witness what I did. It's foolish of you to think that just because I'm a lady that it means I need a strong manly knight by my side to protect me from fools like you. Don't make that mistake again. Cross Calypso or I like this again and I'll make a bigger fool of you in front of these people who are no better than yourself." While still locked in my hand, the man falls to his knees, quaking, weighed down by embarrassment. He catches his breath and breathes through his words slowly.

"I'm sorry princess, it won't happen again! I swear on my life!" I sense no sincerity in his voice. His ego is bruised, and he can barely look at the crowd that surrounds us.

I slowly release his hand and without another word, I turn around, walk past Calypso and away from the crowd.

I refuse to look back to see anyone's reactions. All I know is my heart feels like it's on fire and once again, my emotions are piled up on top of each other like an uneven tower ready to collapse. I feel terrible for hurting that man, but at the same time, I needed to protect us both.

I hear Calypso's boots scuff behind me and she catches up, wobbling around. "Holy mother of- are you alright? I figured you'd snap while we're here, but I didn't expect to see you so angry." I take a deep breath, steady my heart and try to brush off the rage I feel.

"Yes, I'm fine. I'm sorry. I shouldn't have reacted like that. I hope I didn't make matters worse for you." My tone is numb and soft. Calypso laughs and throws her hands behind her head. I reach down into my pocket and pull out the necklace to clasp it around my neck in case we run into any more trouble.

"Ha! Are ya kidding? That piece of dirt has been ticking me off for years. It's about time someone else stood up to him and put him in his place. The rat got what it deserved. Wait..." She pauses before shuffling in front of me and stops me from walking. I look up and see her looking at me weirdly, tilting her head side to side.

"May I help you?" I ask monotonously and she walks uncomfortably close to me, staring into my eyes uncomfortably.

"Why do your eyes do that?" I pull my head backwards, confused.

"What are you talking about?" Calypso pulls out her dagger from her belt before handing it to me sideways.

"Just look! And don't tell me this is something completely normal." I look down at the reflective blade and immediately realize my eyes have changed color. Instead of being golden brown, they're now a deep sapphire blue. It startles me for a slight moment before I quickly realize why they've changed color.

"Oh, right. I unintentionally summoned Vessoria. Yeah, I guess in a sense, it's completely normal." I hand her back the weapon and she puts it back in its sheath. She looks at me dumbfounded as I walk past her.

"Ohhhhhhh, duh, that makes sense since your armor is blue." Calypso whispers quietly, making sure no one can hear us.

"Yeah, but that's my first time seeing my eyes change color. I'm sure it'll wear away shortly once my anger is beginning to subside. Silva told me that the armor and its power reflect on my emotions. My anger must have summoned it." Calypso bursts with excitement and curiosity.

"That's awesome! I wish I had somethin' like that. Well, I mean...I have my father's sword hiding in the Nightwalker, but even then, it doesn't do anything special. But if I had what you do, I'd be able to show these dirtballs what I'm made of." I appreciate her enthusiasm, but it leaves me thinking.

I'm not sure how much longer I want this "gift". All it gives me is more trouble as the days pass.

"Well if it makes you feel better. You definitely don't need powerful magic in order to make a difference for yourself. Your burning passion and determination are strong enough on its own." Calypso smiles and bumps my shoulder playfully.

"I appreciate that, mate."

We continue walking down the dirt path, looking at the shops that line the roads. When I look over, I see Calypso with her head hanging low. She looks distraught.

"You're hiding something, aren't you?" Her attention turns to me and her eyes widen.

"Eh, I always have somethin' to hide. It's not important right now. That dung for brains over there will do and say whatever he can in order to get under someone's skin." She looks over and a shop catches her eye. "Anyways, let's go into this shop." Calypso leads me into a small shop called "Blizzards Beak" and judging by the name, it's where we'll find what we need. I follow her through a white door and immediately see a ton of winter clothing dispersed throughout the shop.

"Hello, welcome- oh...it's you two." An elderly woman says from behind a desk, disgusted to see us. Calypso ignores and looks through the clothes and I do the same.

Everything is a bit too colorful for my liking but I eventually find a thick black hooded cloak that is lined with what looks like fox fur. I take it off the rack and try it on. I walk over to a tall mirror to see how it looks. It reaches my ankles and fits perfectly.

I look closely at my reflection and watch as my eyes fade from blue and back to brown. Watching the blue dissolve is both satisfying and unsettling at the same time.

I take off the coat and search for gloves and boots which are hidden in the back corner of the shop. There, I find a simple pair of boots, gloves and earmuffs just in case. I've never been to the south before, so I can't imagine how cold it gets down there.

I hold all of the items over my chest, nearly struggling to hold everything. Calypso stands behind me tapping her foot on the floor while carrying a simple red and black long sleeve cloak.

"You've really never been to the southern islands, have you?" I laugh nervously and she guides me to the front desk.

"Oh wait, I didn't bring anything with me. Leaving home was so sudden, I don't have-" Calypso raises her hand and she puts all of our clothing on the counter before reaching into a sack that's connected to her leather belt.

"Relax princess." My face immediately cringes at being called "princess" instead of my own name. It only reminds me of a past life I don't think I'll ever return to.

"You must take me for a fool if you think I'll allow you to purchase this clothing!" The old shop owner croaks and refuses to allow Calypso to pay for the items.

"Oh shut it ya old toot." Calypso tosses several gold and silver pieces on the desk and upon counting the currency, it looks like she overpays, but I assume it's to make the old woman happy so that we can walk out with the clothing that we absolutely need.

Calypso folds all the clothes neatly and carries them out. While we walk, we ignore the remaining whispering and staring from the villagers.

"Well, while we're here, why don't we stop by my favorite place before heading back?" Calypso asks excitedly.

"You're the one who said this would be a quick trip, I'm sure Silva and Phoenix are expecting us back soon and they'd be enraged if they heard us taking a side quest. I'm sure we're on a tighter time crunch after running into that crowd." As much as I'd love to spend time with Calypso and explore her home, something tells me we need to head back.

"Oh come on, it'll only be for a moment. We'll say hi to someone and be on our way. Easy." I eventually cave into her excitement and agree to go with her.

"Okay fine. Let's make it quick and avoid more crowd confrontations. I don't want to accidentally blow up a shack or something because people infuriate me." Calypso laughs loudly.

"Oh yeah, sure. I'm not sure you'd be capable of that in the first place."

Don't test me.

Calypso leads me to a large tavern called "The Drunken Fox" and from several feet away, I can hear glass breaking, people shouting and music playing all at once.

"Well, that sounds...lovely." I feel uneasy and am unsure about entering a tavern full of intoxicated villagers as if the sober ones we've encountered weren't already a lot to deal with.

"It'll be fine. It's not as bad as it sounds. I'm practically here every night I return home from the sea, and I always leave unscathed." I trust her judgment and follow behind her.

The rambunctious noise grows louder until we enter the building. The atmosphere is wild and chaotic to the absolute max. I'm so overwhelmed by sounds that I immediately want to walk back out, but I figure Calypso would drag me right back in.

I stay close to Calypso and out of the corner of my eye I see a glass cup fly towards the side of Calypso's face, but she reacts quickly and catches it with her left hand without looking. She looks for the one who threw it and immediately locks onto a man standing stupidly between two tables with his trousers beginning to fall down.

"Oooh, you messed up mate" One of his friends says with a thick accent. Calypso flips the bottle in her hand, catching it by the neck, and throws it at the man. The bottle breaks once it collides with his forehead, and he falls backwards over his chair. His pals around him laugh uncontrollably before checking on him.

Calypso laughs and continues to lead me through the tavern. "I can't believe people can be so vile." I say softly while walking next to her.

"Eh, don't worry about it. I'm used to it after all these years. They still underestimate my resilience, giving me opportunities to deck a moron in the face." I can tell she covers her pain with a forced smile.

"Well just because you're used to it, doesn't mean it's right and justifies their actions. Hopefully by the time this is all over, I'll be able to bring an end to this and hopefully they'll find their kindness and treat you better." I try to reassure her, but she shakes her head and scoffs.

"Princess. The only thing that will bring an end to their foolishness is my father coming back to tell everyone the truth to what happened to him and his crew. Until then...I can deal with it." I figure it's best to bite my tongue.

"In that case, I hope your voyage after taking us to Yarrin will be successful. And for the love of the gods, stop calling me 'princess'. My name is far more suitable for my liking. 'Princess' just sounds like an insult sometimes. And when it comes to you, I can't tell if you're being rude or not." We reach the bar at the back of the building and Calypso slams the heavy clothing on the table and laughs out loud.

"Insult? Pff, I'm just tryin' to be respectful. But fine *VIVALDA*, your wish is my command." She mocks me in a silly manner, causing me to laugh with her. Our attention is drawn to a male voice coming from the far side of the bar.

"Well, if it isn't my favorite customer!" A bartender speaks to Calypso and walks over to us. He's tall and wears a ruffled white long sleeve top with the sleeves rolled up to his biceps. He brushes his blonde wavy hair out of his face and ties half of it up.

"It's been a while, stranger!" Once he realizes I'm with Calypso, he almost loses his composure.

"Oh! Your highness. It's a pleasure to make your acquaintance." He bows respectfully, nearly shaking, causing me to giggle.

"There's no need for that." I say happily while raising my hand.

"Vivalda, this is Elias, the tavern owner. We've known each other for a very long time and he's practically the only one with a good heart around here." Elias keeps his eyes on Calypso and a gentle smile forms on his face.

"I heard from a couple of drunk morons that you got held up by that big oaf Bronwyn...again. And this time, the princess managed to tell him off. Is that true?" Elias takes out a rag to wipe down the bar.

"Oh yes, that. I think I may have gone a bit far there." I laugh nervously and Calypso playfully bumps my shoulder.

"Are you kidding? He deserved that and worse. Don't feel bad!" Calypso says enthusiastically.

Elias pours a dark liquid into a wooden mug and slides it over to Calypso. He offers me a drink, but I politely decline since drinking isn't something I fancy.

"It's true. It's refreshing to hear someone else besides Calypso stand up to him and his cruelty. Calypso has been kicking his pathetic arse for years and even then, he always comes back for round two. He thinks he is the big shot of Darali and people rave over his disgusting behavior towards 'outcasts'. But besides all that nonsense. What brings you two here? Last I heard, Calypso here doesn't typically run with the royals." I look at Calypso as she glares at Elias while slowly sipping her drink. Elias continues to clean glasses and serve drinks to others while we continue chatting.

"Ah, we're just rebelling against the kingdom and its people of course! It doesn't get better than that!" Calypso exclaims loudly, causing people's heads to turn and she smirks at them, purposely trying to get them off. I slam my elbows onto the bar and throw my face into my hands, groaning.

"You're making it worse." I slide my hands down and scold Calypso who can't help but laugh, full of herself.

"Okay, okay, I'm done. But in all seriousness Elias, I'll explain everything next time I come back. We're on a time crunch." The way she and Elias look at each other reminds me of myself and Kyson. I miss him, Riverlynn, Orion, Atticus and Lyla so much. I can't help but wonder how they're doing and pray everything is alright back home.

Hopefully my father is doing better than he was before but I wouldn't be surprised if he's still sulking in his room, ignoring the rest of his family and kingdom.

I end up losing track of time while Calypso continues to talk to Elias about her travels, leaving out the bigger details about our voyage. I can hear people picking on Calypso and talking nastily under their breath, which eventually turns into a brawl. I watch as Calypso throws herself into a crowd of angry, drunk villagers. She messes with them humorously and tussles while others around them cheer on the fight. Elias watches from the bar, entertained. From where I remain seated, it's obvious she's capable of taking care of herself and I have no reason to intervene.

Calypso runs and dances around piles of men, smacking glasses over their head and dodging their sloppy punches. I can't help but laugh so hard to the point where my stomach begins to cramp.

My laugh is cut away when a strange sensation fills the air. A strong magnetic force tugs and pulls on my body. For a split moment, I begin to overthink, paranoid there might be an Aerolight lurking around. Upon looking around, I don't see anything out of the ordinary. I try to ignore the strange feeling but the moment I do, I look out a window and see the sun is almost completely out of sight. My heart skips a beat and I feel foolish when I realize the day has washed away. I didn't realize how much time had passed. After reassuring Silva and Phoenix we'd make the stop quick, I failed at keeping my own word.

I've made a mistake.

The ground begins to gradually rattle and rumble violently. Cups on the bar shake, causing some to slip, fall and break. I hold onto the edge of the table, using my core strength to keep myself up. I look at Elias and others around me and they're completely unphased.

"No need to fret, princess. It's just another landquake. We get them pretty often around here and they don't last too long." Elias says before collecting as many bottles and glasses as he can to store them safely.

Everyone around me holds down their drinks and remains seated as if it's completely normal. I've encountered quakes like this before but something about this one feels different. I quickly gather the heavy clothing off the bar before standing from my chair, trying my best to keep my balance.

"It was a pleasure meeting you Elias, I hope to see you again! I have to go!" I shout at him over the loud sounds of people screaming and the building creaking.

I immediately take off from the bar to find Calypso amongst the crowd. From within the angry pit of people hurdled over each other, I spot Calypso in the center punching a random man over and over again.

I carefully reach my arm into the pile of fighting villages and grab her shoulder to guide her out. She stumbles back after being drawn away from the crowd and looks at me, annoyed.

"What was that for? I was havin' fun!" She tries to run back into the crowd but I instantly pull her arm back.

"We have to go! The landquake-" Calypso yanks her arm out of my hand and scoffs.

"Relax, we get 'em all the time!" She tries reassuring me but I refuse to be brushed off.

"It's Silva!" I yell in her ear and her eyes widen, nearly popping out of her head.

"Oh crap." She immediately runs with me towards the exit but before leaving the building, she turns around to wave to Elias.

We run straight towards the forest, darting aimlessly into the trees. Once we reach the forest, the ground stops shaking and the trees return to standing silently still. I take a moment to breathe and I feel a throbbing pain shoot down my legs.

"Where are they?" Calypso asks as she tries looking for them.

We walk deeper into the forest, making sure we're not seen by anyone.

"Phoenix! Silv-" I begin to whisper when I'm suddenly thrown back by a strong gust of wind. I fall back on my bottom and drop the clothes on the ground.

Immense fear overcomes me when I see Silva towering over me angrily. She grows two times the size in height, causing my heart to nearly stop. I haven't seen her grow into such a terrifying giant before. Her hair blows dramatically in the wind and her green magic illuminates the forest around us, hitting the surface of an invisible barrier dome she casted while we were gone. And once I look closely at her eyes, I see her skin looks like it's cracking. Dark cracks form from her eyes and her light gray skin wrinkles and her veins turn dark gray.

"What is your problem!?" I yell while the forest roars loudly around us. I can hear thunder crashing faintly above us as the sky grows darker and lightning flashes through the treetops.

Silva's vibrant green glowing eyes pierce my soul and her dark grey brows arch over her eyes. She's furious and I don't understand why. Surely it's because we arrived back later than anticipated, but there has to be more to her raging anger.

I look over to the side and see Phoenix keeping her distance behind Silva. A fire rages between her horns and her fingertips drip with molten lava. Her anger almost matches the way Calypso looked during the dispute with Bronwyn.

"You both told us this would be a quick stop! What took you so long?!" Her voice booms and echoes through the air, causing me to cup my hands over my ears.

"Silva, let's just take it easy. It's my fault, I convinced Vivalda to stop at the tavern with me and-" Silva shifts her attention to Calypso and the captain instantly goes silent and steps back, scared to push her anger even further.

"Enough with the shaking, the wind and yelling! Let's just talk about this calmly please!" I try to calm Silva down but it doesn't work. She stands tall over me and thunder flashes behind her.

"Due to your mindlessness, the Aerolights may have already made their way to Yarrin!"

Her words feel like a familiar stab to the heart.

In the blink of an eye, sadness melts across Vivalda's face. Her thoughts are silent, as they were before. And her heart beats slowly and heavily. I instantly realize I've stepped too far out of line once again. I slowly back away and put an end to the chaos that rumbles throughout the forest.

I stare at the grassy ground and feel nothing but guilt and regret. After everything I've taught Vivalda about anger and power, I've gone against my own word. Vivalda remains laying on the ground and Calypso looks back and forth between us both, confused and scared to speak.

I slowly recede back to my normal size and remain frozen. It feels like I've punched myself in the chest and now I feel the pain I've given. I turn to look at Phoenix, her gaze is firm and cold and her fires dissipate from her horns and hands. Calypso helps Vivalda stand up and they also stare at me silently.

"I'm sorry, I didn't mean to get so angry. Not at you. I'm just worried." Vivalda walks up to me with distraught in her eye and betrayal in her heart.

"No, hold on. What do you mean Aerolights have made it to Yarrin-" I stop Vivalda from talking and I turn around to look at the ocean in the distance. The tide is coming in fast and lightning calmly strikes in the sky.

"I have a feeling the Aerolights have already made it to the island and I'm hoping my gut is wrong."

We retreat back to the Nightwalker, Calypso unties the vessel, we all climb on board and begin traveling south.

Once our course is set, I remain standing at the front of the boat while Calypso goes underdeck. I hear Vivalda walking my way and quickly gather my composure and do what I can to release the tension in my body. I can hear the thoughts in her mind wandering loudly.

"While you and Calypso were in the village, I felt a disturbance in the distance. I don't know where exactly it came from or what it was. All I could do was assume the worst. Phoenix and I couldn't leave the island even if we wanted to and that alone overwhelmed me more. I wanted to arrive in Yarrin as soon as possible and once I saw you both enter the tavern, my patience wore thin." Vivalda walks closer to me, cautiously while listening to me.

"I think the island has been attacked. I'm not fully sure, but if it did get attacked, I'd hate to feel that if we had left sooner, we could have defended it. But for once, I hope I'm wrong. I didn't mean to take it out on you. I figured you would have wanted to spend time there and I should have been more gentle about it." I can sense Vivalda's worry and guilt and despite my angry reactions, I don't want her to feel that.

"Even though it's not her fault either, I shouldn't have let Calypso persuade me. I thought nothing of it. I promise to do better next time." Vivalda looks at me with a half-smile, I attempt to smile back but can't due to my paranoia.

"And I'll make sure not to explode like that again. Can you forgive me?" I ask gently in hopes she may respond. Her eyebrows scrunch together and her head tilts to the side.

"I'll accept your apology if you answer a question." I nod my head, anticipating what she'll ask.

"When you were mad, why was the skin around your eyes cracking?" My eyes widen slightly and for a brief moment, all the noise in my mind goes silent.

"It was simply just my veins protruding from under my skin. That typically happens when I feel angry. Doesn't the same thing happen to some humans when they're angry? I've seen a human's face turn so red, I thought it was going to pop off their body." Vivalda laughs. Warmth begins to fill my heart and I can feel the light inside me beginning to beam once more. Vivalda smiles softly and we both turn around simultaneously to see Calypso walking up to us.

"Awwww look at you two making up! That's so sweet!" She mocks while swinging her hands in front of her like a bashful child. Vivalda laughs and I lift my hand up, ignited in bright magic.

"Don't make me spawn in another tree. The next one will be big enough to sink your precious ship." Once again, Calypso isn't fazed and laughs instead before looking at me seriously, dropping every ounce of humor.

"Stop threatening my ship or I swear, I will lose my mind as if I haven't already." I find myself smiling and laughing.

Calypso and Vivalda walk to the helm of the ship to chat while I remain at the nose of the ship and Phoenix goes underdeck to rest.

Vivalda

While at the helm with Calypso, I itch to ask her so many questions, but I worry I might unintentionally overstep.

"Can I ask you something?" I ask her and she takes a deep breath as if already knowing what I'll ask. Without saying a word, she nods her head and I choose my words carefully.

"That man...back on Darali- what was he talking about? When he said 'murderers', he wasn't referring to me alone." Calypso tightens her grip on the wooden wheel and taps her nails over the handles.

"Well first, I want to clear something up." The tone in her voice is very serious. I walk a couple feet forward to lean my back against a wooden rail so I can give her my undivided attention while she talks.

"Typically, I'd gouge out the eyes of strangers that try to stow away on my ship or give me trouble. But after I heard what everyone was sayin' about you and how ye were the cause of the queen's death, I thought you'd be someone I could trust." She stares out into the dark horizon and rolls her shoulders back.

"Mmm. The dagger to the throat was really reassuring." I tease and she scoffs humorously.

"I know, I'm sorry. I tend to be a bit hostile so that people don't try to piss me off. I also panicked because for a split moment, I thought you'd report me to the king. But that was before I knew how he treated ya." The sad tone in her voice makes my heart feel heavy. Since meeting her, Calypso has always come off like she has a heart of stone, but the more I get to know her, I realize why her heart is so guarded.

"After my father disappeared, all he left me was the Nightwalker, his sword and his dagger. I sat around anxiously waiting for so long, I eventually took matters into my hands because no one else would. I gathered a crew and we sailed a ship that was smaller than this one. To make a very long story short, my determination got the best of me. One night, we were pulled into a gorge by a terrifyingly strong tide. I thought I could navigate us out of it and..." Calypso's voice shakes and her eyes glisten with tears. My heart immediately sinks to my stomach and I immediately get emotional.

"Let's just say...I went too far." I cross my hands over my stomach and look down at the floorboards, trying not to cry and hiding the urge to run and hug her. "And it costed me everything." Silence fills the air and my heart slowly thumps against my chest like a heavy drum.

"They say 'a captain always goes down with his ship' and ya bet yer princess toosh, I tried." She shakes her head and clears her throat. "But I guess since I am no man, the gods had other plans." Calypso wipes the tears from her eyes and shakes away her sadness.

"That's all the more reasons as to why my home hates me so much. I've made mistakes and no matter what I do, I can't fix it. Now, the reason I tell ya all this is because I thought maybe I'd have someone to talk to about it after spending all these years in solitude. I sail solo so that I'd never put anyone in danger ever again." Once the ship is completely steady, Calypso stretches out her arms and cracks her knuckles.

"Well, whatcha gonna do about it? The world sucks but at the end of the day, it's nice to have company around here." Calypso's demeanor changes. I can tell she's trying to push aside her feelings in order to not feel awkward after telling me what she did.

"You can't control the sea...you know that right?" I say softly and her gaze meets mine.

"And you can't control this darkness. You're not the cause of it." Her black lips curl into a gentle smile and she walks up to me, resting her hand on my shoulder.

"We both tried to do something good and the universe decided to kick our arses for it, but we shouldn't let it be the reason we give up." I do everything I can to swallow my tears because the last thing I want to do is cry in front of a badass pirate captain.

"Well, the difference between us is you seek the journey ahead of you. I, however, was forced into mine and I have no choice but to carry that weight." Calypso looks past me and gazes at Silva who minds her own business, but I know for a fact she's been listening to the conversation this whole time.

"Sometimes, fate calls us to fight battles much bigger than ourselves. Maybe the gods know we're capable and we just don't see it yet. And all we can do is run or fight." Hearing such uplifting words from Calypso was something I wasn't expecting to hear from her but it helps me feel better.

"Why does every treacherous journey have something sappy to teach regarding 'fate' or 'destiny'?" I say sarcastically, which makes Calypso and I both laugh.

"Your guess is as good as mine." She chuckles. "All I know is that it helps to hear when hope feels out of reach." I look at her, continuing to smile, feeling grateful for her kindness.

"You're right, it does help. Thank you." Calypso smiles and shrugs her shoulders.

"Nah, no need to thank. Instead, I owe ya for listening to my nonsense. It's not every day I have someone civil to talk to." She gives my shoulder a nudge before heading downstairs to tease Silva about the tree growing in the middle of the deck.

I make my way down and go down to the bottom deck where Phoenix is. Upon reaching the bottom floor, I can hear Phoenix breathing loudly and fire crackling. I look up at the roof and see thick emerald green roots bending around the wood from where Silva's tree stands. The vines move slowly and intertwine around each other, forming twists and braids that are strong and intricate.

I peer around the corner and see Phoenix huddled in the corner and her large wings wrap around her while she plays with small fires that dance on her fingertips. She looks up, noticing my gaze and she quickly curls her sharp fingers, extinguishing the flames.

"Hey. I just wanted to check on you and maybe have a little chat if you don't mind." I respectfully kept my distance, not wanting to make her uncomfortable. She smiles, and I catch a glimpse of her pearly white fangs peeking out from her lips.

"Of course. What would you like to speak about?" She invites me to sit in front of her and I happily join. I sit with my legs bent under me and I move my overcoat out from under me. Once I'm comfortable, I can tell by the look on Phoenix's face that she's very eager to talk to me.

"What were you going to say when we were on Darali?" Phoenix's smile slowly disappears for a moment and reappears. She stretches her wings out to the side and they curl around her once more.

"I know Silva probably puts a lot on your shoulders, but she means no harm, well...I don't think she does. Sometimes, she can be a bit much when it comes to her emotions. She wants to ensure everything goes right and though she may not admit it out loud, she fears errors and mistakes. Maybe that sounds a bit familiar to you?" My eyes widen once I realize Silva and I share something in common and I never really thought about it until now.

"Yes. I guess that's why I didn't take her outburst personally. I know how she feels. Back at home, I always strived for perfection because I didn't want to disappoint anyone." Phoenix nods, sits up and leans closer to me.

"You both have weight on your shoulders you're trying to balance. Silva is trying to protect the Serafaes and you're trying to protect humankind. Both of you will find balance." I really enjoy talking to Phoenix. Despite her intimidating appearance and her deep beastly voice, there's something simply comforting about her presence.

"Will you two find balance?" Phoenix's flaming red eyes widen and white smoke puffs out of her nose. "I only ask because I can tell you both have some kind of grudge against each other." Phoenix, glaring at the moving tree roots above, takes a deep breath and relaxes her tense shoulders.

"She's always been a good friend to me. I've always strived to maintain civility with her, despite our differing views and approaches to serious matters. Our interactions can be frustrating at times, but in the end, we always see eye to eye. I intend to keep it that way." I guess there's a lot to the Serafaes that I don't know or understand yet, so it's best I keep questions to myself since it's not my place.

"Humans once referred to you as the 'Flaming Demon', but after meeting you, I find that rather strange. If they had taken even a moment to get to know you, I think they'd easily realize that you are, in fact, one of the coolest beings to exist." Relief washes over her, and a smile forms on her face. She scoffs joyfully and lets out a deep breath.

"I think you see me differently because you are not like most humans. The moment they saw my red skin and black horns, they automatically looked into the eye of a 'demon'. I've had my fair share of demons, but we just call them Aerolights. I think the demons humans once spoke of are far different. I once heard a woman and her lover speak about demons and devils. They said these horrific monsters would murder innocent children as sacrifices and make their loved ones watch. Being compared to such a monster shattered whatever heart I have left for humans." Watching her head tilt down to the ground makes my heart hurt for her.

I scoot forward and reach for Phoenix's scaly hand while she continues to speak. She looks at me, confused, hesitating to reach out, but once she does, I hold it gently, observing her scaly skin. Her hand is very heavy and nearly twice times the size of mine.

I'd never looked this closely at her volcano skin before. Bright red and orange veins flowed under her black rocky scales, traveling down her arm and into her sharp, curved talons. Her body is warm to the touch and feels like hardened coal.

"You didn't think that of me when you first saw me…right?" Her eyes meet mine, filled with sorrow, as I glance up.

"Absolutely not. If anything, I was scared, but only because I thought you had died when you fell out of the sky in your beast form." Phoenix laughs lightly. "When I saw you flying from outside the barrier, I didn't know if you posed any danger and yet, I was still marveled by the sight before me. The first thing that came to mind was helping you." Phoenix's eyes widen in slight emotional shock. "The sight of you rising from the fire shattered my childhood illusions, replacing them with a reality I never thought could be possible. Dragons were once mere figments of my imagination, but now you stand before me, as real as me." I see nothing but a look of pure joy spread across her face. She releases a gentle sigh of relief and looks down, smiling happily.

"You're the only human to ever see me as I am." She looks up and the fire under her skin glows brighter, showcasing her joy.

"I give you my word that when I return home, I will do everything I can to bring peace and freedom to your home and unite our worlds. The Serafaes should not have to live in the shadows because of the ignorance of my people. We are to blame for your fear and anger." Phoenix's scaled brows scrunch together and she shakes her head slightly.

"Don't strain yourself, Vivalda. Everything will play out the way they must, but regardless, I appreciate you."

The thick burnt scales that cover most of Phoenix's body that covers most of her body sizzle and I can hear her fiery blood move under her skin. Her golden, wavy hair falls over her scales and bumpy skin without catching on fire, which makes me curious.

"How does your hair not catch on fire?" I blurt out the question without thinking, which makes me feel silly. Phoenix raises a brow while she untangles a thick strand of her hair.

"My fire only burns when I allow it to do so." She extends her closed fist, then opens it to reveal a sizzling ball of flames dancing above her palm. The fire is an abnormal, bright red, unlike the typical orange and yellow hues of a normal flame. As she moves her hand closer to me, I can feel the intense heat emitting from the fiery orb. Her gaze is soft and innocent while she admires her creation, while I look back and forth between the mesmerizing flames and her captivating expression.

"You feel the heat, correct?" She asks as the fire dances in her hand. I nod my head, trying to keep my distance from the flame but Phoenix slowly moves her hand closer.

"Touch it." My eyes widen and my gaze immediately meets her eyes. She must be crazy if she thinks I'm willing to touch a flame hot enough to set my entire body ablaze.

"I just told you I can feel the burning heat from here and now you want me to touch it?" I laugh awkwardly, unsure if she's being serious or not.

"And as I said, fire only burns if I allow it. If I wanted you to burn, I would have had you tossed in fire back on the fjord. Trust me." She says as she steadily moves closer. I stare down at the flame that's being held in her charcoal black hand and upon closer inspection, I see that her skin isn't being seared by it.

I eventually put my trust in Phoenix and I hold my shaky hand out over the flame. As I lower my hand down, my fingertips begin to touch the snapping blaze and to my surprise, instead of feeling scorching heat, I feel a cool breeze glide past my fingers. Phoenix gently moves my hand so my palm faces upwards and carefully slides the fire ball onto my hand. Although there is no weight to it, I can feel the gravitational push and pull of Phoenix's magic. Her magic force is strong and intense.

I let out a sigh of relief now that I know the flame will cause no harm. In no time, I get lost in the beauty of her fire before realizing my mouth is gaping open. The thick waving flames are visually pleasing to look at and the rich red tone of the fire is so pure, it leaves me speechless that I'm holding her fire.

A thought comes to mind and I decide I want to try something. I sit back, crossing my legs in front of me and I cup both hands under the fire as if I'm carrying a large, fragile egg.

I take a few deep breaths and call upon Vessoria. A cooling sensation quickly fills every vein in my body, making my skin tingle and the hairs on the back of my neck rise. For once, my mind is clear and I'm completely relaxed.

I look at my hands and see my veins are glowing blue with a subtle blue aura covering my arms. I look up at Phoenix whose eyes are fixated on my hands. The look in her eyes reminds me of a cat staring at a bird, waiting to pounce on it. She watches fascinatingly, waiting patiently to see what'll happen.

I pull away my left hand and watch as a blue electric flame seeps out from my palm. Both of our flames are so similar and yet different at the same time. My flames are thicker and heavier and each burning point flickers with positive crackling energy.

I slowly move both flames together and I stop when I hear Phoenix loudly gasp.

"I wouldn't. Our flames may dance, but they will never mix." The fear in her voice makes me feel bad, but there's a feeling in my gut that tells me to bring our magic together.

I look at Phoenix, assuring her I know what I'm doing. Once I bring the flames close together, red and blue sparks bounce from one hand to the next and once they completely touch, they bond into one burning flame. Phoenix's flames swirl up and around the blue flames like small magical spirals and they don't completely mix. I can easily see the separation of both magic sources. I panic slightly, worried both magic forces would cause a negative reaction but instead, we watch carefully as the blue and red blaze create a mesmerizing galaxy of fire.

I look around and watch the light from the flames rebound round the room, cascading beautiful colors on the wooden surfaces. The illuminating lights look like water reflections. Phoenix is just as fascinated as I am and I don't feel any discomfort.

"If we weren't floating over a giant body of water, I'd definitely be tempted to throw this at something to see what happens." I say lightly and Phoenix laughs.

"No human has ever been able to hold Serafae magic before. Typically if us spirits attempt to combine our powers in any way, it calls for inevitable doom. Your power compliments mine in a way I can't explain." The calmness in her voice sends chills down my spine and goosebumps rise over my skin.

"Every day, I find myself having more and more questions and less time for clarity." I say while continuing to look at the dancing flames that make my hands tingle.

"Maybe this journey holds all of the answers you seek." I nod and retract the blue fire slowly and the power is bound back to my core. The room grows dark but is quickly illuminated again by Phoenix sending tiny flames to the lanterns and candles that hang on the walls.

I feel cold air slowly leak through the wooden walls, causing me to shiver. I stand up slowly and the moment I get to my feet, my vision is fuzzy, and my head feels heavy and woozy. I stand still, making sure to keep my balance while staring at the floor and Phoenix catches my attention.

"Are you alright?" She asks worriedly as she stands up. I gently rub the sides of my temple and the blurriness fades away.

"Yes, I'm fine." I laugh it off and from the side of the room, we hear Calypso's boots quickly stomp down the stairs. She walks towards us, carrying in the clothing we bought on Darali.

"You should put this on now, we're on the outskirts of Yarrin." She hands me the clothes and I peer out a window to see it's pitch black outside.

"How are we almost there already?" I ask, confused because it feels like we left Darali just moments ago. Calypso stares at me, smiling strangely.

"I may or may not have ticked off flower brains up there." Her head tilts up and immediately, the ship rocks to the side and then goes back to normal. Phoenix rests her hand over her head, unamused.

"What did you do this time?" I ask and she pulls the tip of her hat forward and swings her arms back and forth and I put the warm clothing on over what I'm wearing.

"Listen, she was getting antsy and all I said was that if I could make the Nightwalker sail faster, I would. And then BOOM, she did the speedy boost thing again like she did back on the fjord. Did you both not feel the ship thrust forward? It nearly tossed me on my bum!" I laugh as I untie my hair and let it fall freely while running my fingers through it to untangle it as much as possible, then a loud thought bangs against my skull.

"Wait. What do you mean Silva was acting 'antsy'?" Calypso notices the serious shift in my tone and looks at me confused.

"Well, I mean, she was pacing back and forth and she was glowing so bright, I thought she was going to explode. At one point, I could have sworn I saw vines grow across her chest and her leaf ears started to glow too. I thought that was a bit weird. Her magic made the ship go so fast, I thought we were gonna tip over." I looked at Phoenix and we're both confused because neither of us felt the ship move abnormally.

"You found balance while discovering your abilities, so you weren't able to feel the boat shift. I, on the other hand, was too focused to notice." I lace up my black boots and slip on my gloves. Phoenix and Calypso remain silent, waiting for me to speak.

"Well then, let's go check on her and make sure she doesn't end up accidentally destroying the ship before we reach the island." Phoenix follows behind

Calypso and they begin to ascend up the stairs, but I hang back for just a moment. Phoenix looks back at me, wondering why I don't follow.

"Give me a moment. I have to fix my boots and I'll be right up. Go make sure Silva isn't going mad." She nods her head and continues up the stairs. Once I hear the wooden door close behind them, I immediately crash to the ground.

Something's wrong, but I can't figure it out. My heart beats so fast and hard, it almost feels like impending death is reaching for my soul. My skin feels like it's about to detach from my bones and I feel so much pain and numbness at the same time. I do my best to keep my thoughts silent to avoid catching Silva's attention and I hope the other two can keep her busy for a moment until I can get myself together.

While leaning over my hands and knees, I feel my chest tighten to the point where it hurts to breathe. I try to remain as calm and patient as possible and wait for it to go away on its own. All I can do is try to breathe through it because if I don't, I fear I'll lose control and grab the other's attention. I keep my eyes closed, focusing.

"I am okay. I am calm."

I whisper to myself, over and over again which helps me feel more grounded and connected. Eventually the painful tingling and numbing sensation goes away and everything goes back to normal. Finally being able to take a pain free deep breath is relieving. Even though the attack has gone away, I can't help but be stuck in my head, overthinking everything I'm doing. Something feels right, but everything else at the same time feels wrong.

For a moment, I keep my head held in my hand and allot myself a moment to recover and calm down the best I can. I slowly stand up and gain my balance before heading up the stairs and out the door. Once I turn the knob, the wooden door is forcefully swung open by a strong gust of wind, and I immediately see Phoenix and Calypso running to the nose of the ship. They both lean over the ledge, looking into the water. There's very few lanterns lit on the ship so all I can see are faint shadows. I rush out and look around but see no sign of Silva.

The air is freezing, and I can hear blocks of ice crashing into each other in the water. I quickly run over to Calypso and Pheonix to see what they're looking at and when I look down in the water, I see the water glowing green.

"What happened?!" The green sparkly magic in the water quickly travels over the ice chunks and darts away from the ship. My eyes follow Silva's green magic and when I look up, I see gigantic mountains of ice approaching us fast.

"Crap. Hold on!" Calypso runs to the back of the ship and quickly releases the anchor. I can feel the ship dragging and slowing down, making us avoid colliding with icebergs and large pieces of floating ice.

I keep my eyes on Silva as her magic particles dart up large pillars of ice and disappear behind a large mountain, causing the atmosphere to go completely dark. Phoenix stares blankly into the distance, her eyes glow yellow and the veins under her scales glow bright yellow. She looks angry.

"Why did she take off like that?" I ask, trying to spot her light, but all I see is large dark shadows from the icebergs and ice towers.

"She's rightfully paranoid and wants to scout out the terrain before we step foot upon the ice. The frozen water reeks of Aerolight remains." The ship comes to a harsh halt.

"This is as close as I can take you! If I take the Nightwalker any farther, I won't be able to get her out of the ice. And I'm sure beanstalk over there will be too busy to push her out of the bay." The look on her face is almost sorrowful, as if she doesn't wish to part ways. Calypso walks towards us with a lantern in her hand.

"Here, you may need this." I take the lantern from her and a part of me is sad that we're about to go our own ways. I'm unsure if I'll see her again which makes me sad. Phoenix climbs on top of the rail and I think that's her way of saying she's ready to go. I look back at Calypso and she gently nudges me with her fist.

"Don't worry princess, we'll for sure have to see each other again because I'll be dyin' to know how this next part of your journey goes. I'll be docked west for a while scouting the waters, so if you find yourself on that side of the kingdom, I'll be there." She smiles and tips her hat down.

"I wish you could come with us, but I'll make sure to tell you about everything when it's over. Thank you for everything, captain."

The softest and most genuine smile forms on her face. "'Calypso' will do just fine. Captain just sounds like an insult." Both of us share one last laugh before she takes a step back, puts her right hand over her chest and bows. Phoenix nods her head at Calypso and glares for a moment.

"If you tell anyone about us, you'll be the first human sacrifice." Phoenix teases and we all laugh in unison.

"Well lucky for you, there's no one to talk to once ya leave, so ya don't gotta worry about that." Calypso says quietly and it only makes my sadness weigh heavier.

"I'll see you later." I back up towards Phoenix and feel her large talons wrap under my arms and around my torso before spreading her gigantic black wings.

Calypso waves goodbye and before I can blink, I'm rapidly shot up into the freezing cold sky. The force from Phoenix's wings shakes the ship side to side. I keep the lantern held firmly in my hand. The atmosphere is so cold, I can barely keep my eyes open. Freezing snow slams into my face and my teeth begin to chatter. It's so dark and the only light I can see is the glow from Phoenix's skin and thankfully, her body heat helps me warm up a bit. Phoenix twists and turns gracefully, avoiding colliding with large mountains, pillars and hills of ice.

We finally land on solid ground and thankfully the small spikes on the bottom of my boots stop me from slipping on the frozen floor. The flame inside of the lantern has extinguished but once Phoenix notices, she takes her pointer finger and pokes her claw inside of the metal cage to cast a bright orange flame on the candle wick.

The flame burns so bright, I can look around and see our surroundings. There's nothing but ice everywhere and it's hard to tell where we're supposed to go because there's no paths laid out before us. Upon further inspection, I notice that not a single part of the island is made of stone or rock, it's all solid ice.

"Follow me and stay close. Silva's beacon hasn't gone off, so we shouldn't encounter any danger." Phoenix tucks her wings behind her and walks in front of me, stepping lightly with caution.

I follow her through caves and tunnels of freezing cold ice and the light from the lantern makes the ice turn a light green seaweed color. I'd assume all of this ice is built up from the sea and it grows bigger over time. I think it would have been easier if we had stayed in Darali a bit longer so the sun would be up.

We eventually reach a deep and narrow canyon that rests in the center of the island, and we see a faint glow coming from the distance and we see Silva standing in the middle of the ravine. She stands silently and her light glows very dim while her head hangs low, and she stares at the ground.

Once we reach her, I walk up to her cautiously. "Silva? Are you alright?" I inch closer to her, but Phoenix stays back. I hold the lantern up and I see her brows and lips quivering. I can't tell if she's angry or if she's affected by the cold.

Silva lifts her head and silently leads a massive wall of ice at the side of the canyon that curves over our heads like a frozen wave. She circles her hand towards the ground and throws them up, causing her magic to disperse all over the ice, illuminating the surrounding area.

The moment the ice is brightly lit, I drop the lantern on the ground, terrified at the sight before us.

Aerolight bodies are mixed in with the ice wall with the look of pain and fear permanently frozen on their faces. It looks like the once clear ice has been infected by poisonous magic. I turn around, looking at the other walls and pillars which are also tainted by spikes and swirls.

Phoenix stands behind us, raging with anger with her arms crossed in front of her and thick smoke blows out of her nostrils.

I carefully run to catch up with Silva as she walks along the wall of ice. "My suspicions were correct. They knew we were coming here and once they arrived, they unleashed their wrath on the island." Guilt immediately washes over me and my gut twists and turns. "The Aerolights are evolving rapidly in order to reach the destinations we're traveling to. I don't know how they know where we're going, but it doesn't matter right now. I have to find something."

She quickly wanders off, keeping her eyes on the glaciers and lighting up every cavity and cave she approaches nearby.

I begin to walk back over to Phoenix when we're suddenly startled by a loud cracking sound that echoes throughout the canyon. I look around, trying to figure out where the cracking is coming from and when I look over, Silva flies over and appears next to me. In front of us, a large crack begins to form, and we back up, staying out of its path. A block of ice begins to emerge from the ground, causing Phoenix to immediately fly into the air, keeping herself levitated and away from the ice.

I look closer and begin to notice ribbons of ice emerge from the ground, wrapping around the block, forming an odd shape. Upon first inspection, I thought the ice was splitting apart, but instead it's forming a body.

The ice that spews from the ground quickly morphs into a human-like body. The ground beneath us continues to crack and more shards of ice add to the figure being formed. In a short amount of time, a transparent face with long icy hair is crafted by the frozen water.

Once the body of a woman is casted from the ice, a bright blue light shines from her chest, nearly blinding Vivalda, causing her to shield her eyes in her sleeve. I keep my eyes fixated on the body, waiting patiently to see what'll happen.

The frozen woman's eyes form and glow and eventually, everybody part begins to move slowly. The ice forms a fully functional body and colors fade into the ice, revealing a woman with white and blue skin, blue lips, white hair. Her body is covered in thick ice and there's a frozen diamond carved into her chest that glows bright blue.

The woman's frozen strands of hair flow gently, causing a light clinking sound. She opens her white eyes and looks at each of us. Her face shows no emotion. I don't know if she knows who she is or what's going on. She turns her attention to the black tainted walls and her brows slowly furrow.

"It took you long enough. They almost capsized the entire island." Hearing her speak makes me let out a laugh of relief. Her voice is very quiet and soft and as she speaks, her ice crackles. Once Vivalda realizes we know each other, she walks closer, smiling with fascination.

"I deeply apologize. We had a tiny setback. But I'm glad you're safe." The icy woman looks around a bit more before looking up at Phoenix who continues to quietly hover in the sky. I watch as she slowly descends to the ground, standing far away, refusing to move closer.

"Do you say that because you were worried you'd lose an asset, or did you genuinely care?" She turns her attention to Vivalda before I can respond. "Is this the creature Vessoria chose?" She holds her hand out to Vivalda and the princess stomps forward, resting her fists on her hips.

"*Tsk*- 'creature'? I beg your pardon, miss...ice lady, who or whatever you are." Vivalda folds her arms, offended.

"Relax child, she bids no harm. This is Aerowen, the keeper of Yarrin and the only frost spirit to exist. Aerowen, this is Vivalda, princess of Vassuren. And yes, she is the one Vessoria chose." Vivalda's eyes widen, and she unfolds her arms, approaching Aerowen slowly.

"It's a pleasure to meet you."

"The honor is mine princess." Aerowen bows and gazes up at Phoenix once more. "I hate to cut the formalities, but there's important matters to discuss. Silva, how did the Aerolights know where you were headed? We once thought they couldn't survive the freeze, but the ones that attacked managed perfectly until I took care of them." Aerowen's voice is very firm, and her frozen brows remain arched downwards.

"You and I ask the same questions and unfortunately, I don't have answers. What happened when they arrived?" Aerowen walks between Vivalda and I and heads towards the wall that's full of Aerolight bodies. She places her hand on the wall and from her hand emerges bright blue magic that scatters across the mountain.

"They immediately attacked once as they reached the frozen sea. Some of them did everything they could to chase me down while the others tried to destroy the island and sink the ice caps. They raised hell unlike anything I've seen before. But due to their foolish actions, I destroyed them one by one, leaving their remains forever frozen in time. I don't know what exactly they were trying to do, but I didn't let them live long enough to figure it out." The dark magic intertwined within the ice crackles as it slowly melts away, leaving bright blue ice behind. Even though their bodies disappear, I can still sense the creatures' vile magic sifting away into the breeze.

"I never thought ice could be so scary." Vivalda says and Aerowen takes her hand off the wall and turns around to face her.

"My ice can do so much more than that, you'll see." She looks past Vivalda, eyeballing Phoenix who lands on a tall tower of ice.

"Well, let's waste no more time, shall we?" Aerowen says quietly and we return to the center of the ravine.

"Care to join us Phoenix?" The echo of my voice travels across the canyon to where Phoenix can hear me.

Her head pops up and I can see her arch her brows angrily. She flares out her wings and encapsulates herself with them like blankets as she holds a large flame in her hand, but her fire doesn't melt the ice.

"I'm fine where I am. This isn't my lesson to teach." I leave Phoenix to her solitude and turn my attention back to Vivalda and Aerowen.

"Silva has already helped me discover my powers and Phoenix has taught me about courage and strength. What lesson do you have to teach on the...ice." Aerowen gently taps her foot down on the ice and a light blue glowing light diffuses across the ground.

"I am going to test your balance. If you don't mind, I'd like for you to summon Vessoria." I can already tell the princess is uncomfortable and nervous but does her best to remain composed.

"Alright then. Surely standing on ice can't be that difficult." Her cocky remark makes both Aerowen and I scoff. Vivalda holds the pendant and quietly inhales. As she does, thunder rumbles quietly from above and Aerowen steps back, giving Vivalda space.

A blue light peeks from the dark night sky and a large lightning bolt descends down, striking over Vivalda. Following the impact from the lightning, the princess emerges through smoke, coated in her armor with the blue designs glowing brightly. She stands proudly with the sword in her hand, preparing herself for what's next.

As soon as she takes a step forward, her left foot slips out from under her, causing her to twirl on the ice, but she catches herself before she could completely fall over. Although her black boots are covered with armor, she no longer has the metal spikes to help tread the ice.

"You've been here only for a moment, and you already underestimate the ice." Aerowen remarks.

Realizing her mistake, Vivalda carefully puts her sword in the sheath that rests on her back and holds her arms out stiffly to keep her balance.

"Alright, I can already tell this will be the test I fail. So, let's get this over with." Aerowen and I walk several feet away from where the princess stands. Magic pours from the tips of Aerowen's fingertips while she walks, leaving a bright blue trail staining the ground on each side of where Vivalda stands.

The frightened look on Vivalda's face worries me more than usual.

Vivalda

Once Aerowen and Silva are far out of reach, Aerowen thrusts her hands forward and her magic creates two large barriers of spikes that form out of the ground, keeping me trapped in the center of an icy aisle. I'm instantly struck with fear, and my heart begins to race rapidly.

"Woah woah woah, you didn't mention anything about spikes of death! This is too much, don't you think?!" I shout loudly to Aerowen who's icy eyes stare into my soul. Silva analyzes each wall of deadly spikes but remains silent.

I stand as still as possible, watching as more large sharp spikes protrude from the ground, pointing to the center of the runway. The perilous frozen skewers rest roughly ten feet away from me on each side and I try to keep my feet still to avoid drifting off to the side and possibly being stabbed by Aerowen's ice. I look at Silva frantically while panicking on the inside, trying not to visibly show it.

"Here's your task princess. All you have to do is steadily make your way down the aisle, reach me where I stand, and the lesson will be complete." I see her blue lips curl into a smile. Silva's eyes widen in shock, and she looks at her in a scolding manner.

"While you travel down the pathway, your goal will be to dodge, deflect or redirect my attacks while keeping your balance to avoid colliding with the spears of ice. My foes tell me that impalement is pretty painful,

so hopefully you defend better than they attacked."
Bright blue magic constantly pours out of her fingertips.

I look at Silva with my eyes bulging out of my head. By the concerned look on her face, I know she can sense me on the verge of losing my mind.

"Can't you stop her?! This is nothing compared to the previous lessons I've learned!"

Silva bows her head slowly as if trying to tell me you can do it', or something else that's metaphorically wise but instead of saying anything, she stands silently next to Aerowen.

Silva's green glowing aura intensifies, causing the giant green leaves that rest in her hair to glow and perk up. I prepare myself to fight, despite the overwhelming terror I feel because I feel this trial will go terribly wrong.

Since I don't know what kind of attacks I'll experience, I decide to keep the sword in the back sheath to avoid being unbalanced. I'm decently familiar with Silva and Phoenix's abilities, but Aerowen's is completely unknown. Her frozen spears alone scare me enough, so I can only imagine what more she can do.

I slowly move my feet to get a proper feel for the slippery frozen ground below me. My boots have very little traction, and I'm bound to slip easily from the slightest movement. But I think as long as I take my time and keep my balance, I can avoid Aerowen's attacks and her deadly spikes at the same time.

As soon as I take a small step forward, Aerowen thrusts a thick stream of ice directly towards my chest. The Vessorian power kicks in, causing time to slow down, giving me time to shield myself. I cross my arms in front of me and once the ice hits my bracers, the ice cracks and breaks, causing sharp shards of ice to graze past me.

Due to the powerful force of her attack, I feel myself slowly sliding to the side. I throw my hand to the side and blast the ice with my blue magic which pushes me back towards the center of the aisle, leaving me where I started.

"This seems a bit impossible, wouldn't you agree?!" I yell at Aerowen and Silva as I slowly gain my balance.

I don't understand why Silva doesn't say anything or acknowledge me when it's easy to tell that I'm struggling.

"Take control of your path and use the slippery slope to your advantage." Silva's voice echoes in my head and I'm instantly taken by surprise. I know she can hear my thoughts, but I didn't know I'd be able to hear hers.

I look at her and she nods her head. I take her advice and prepare myself once more, ready to move forward. I feel the magic within me surging up and down from my head to the tip of my toes.

Aerowen raises her arms once more and I stand still, waiting patiently.

I take a small step forward and at the same time, Aerowen unleashes a powerful beam of magic. As I steadily slide towards her attack as it aims for my face.

Once it's close enough, I drop to my knees and lean backwards to slide under it. The icy beam rushes past me and crashes into a large sharp spike, breaking it in half as the walls slowly move closer to me.

Once I stop sliding, I slowly stand up and as soon as I'm faced forward, Aerowen already sends out another attack. She thrusts both hands forward, creating two beams of ice, but once they reach halfway down the aisle, her magic breaks apart into smaller pieces that zigzag and charge towards me like small sharp shards.

I instantly get dizzy from keeping my eyes on the ice, but I keep my eyes open, memorizing the movement and patterns of her attack. I quickly take out the sword and slash every particle that I can and any that I miss shoot past me and when I turn around, they loop around and charge at me. While my back is turned to the Serafaes, the ice particles that clash with the sword, causing bright blue bursts of energy to emit from the sword and the pressure helps push me backwards towards the end of the pathway.

When all of the shards have been destroyed a strange feeling creeps up my spine and the hairs on my neck stand. Before I can completely turn around to face the Serafaes, a large ray of white magic charges at me, but it's too late to react. The strong beam slams into my side and disperses into thousands of tiny snowflakes. The blow causes me to slip and fall on the ice and I instinctively jab the blade into the ice, hoping it'll stop me from siding towards the sharp spikes of ice.

I slowly come to a stop when I feel something slide under the shoulder armor and stab the side of my arm. Once I've stopped sliding and the sword remains firm in the ground, I look over and see a long pointy shard of ice has cut through my skin. I slowly move away, pulling myself off and away from the spike, leaving drops of blood trailing behind.

I use my non-injured hand to pull myself away and I pull the blade out of the ice once I stand up. Despite the freezing cold air, my arm is on fire and it's painful to move it. I can feel my hands beginning to shake and my nerves are shot. I didn't think I'd be put into a test that could be as fatal and terrifying as this one.

I slowly glide to the center of the aisle and when I look over, I see Phoenix swoop down in front of Aerowen with a bright fire lit between her horns. Without facing me, I can tell she's furious.

"Really?! You're allowing her to act like this, Silva? Last I thought, we don't train like this." Phoenix turns and growls at Silva who shows little to no reaction and Aerowen stares menacingly at Phoenix, not moving an inch. Seeing them stand before each other is honestly terrifying.

"Reconsider how you go about this, or I swear to the gods-" Phoenix's body begins to light on fire and strands of her golden hair begin to glow but it all fades away when I quickly interrupt her. The last thing I want is to witness an altercation between two Serafaes while I'm stuck in between two fatal spiky ice walls.

"No! Let her! I'm still standing." I can feel blood trickle down my arm, soaking the bodysuit under the metal armor.

"You may as well use everything you have, Aerowen! While you have the chance!" Phoenix hesitantly steps out of the way and Aerowen glares at me coldly with her brows raised. I can tell she's surprised that I'm willing to contest against her. She looks at Silva who, shockingly, shakes her head, disapproving.

"Well, if that's what the princess wishes, why not." Aerowen steps forward towards the aisle, moving away from the others. Phoenix looks like she's ready to raise hell with Aerowen and Silva is prepared to intervene.

I think I'm beginning to understand why Phoenix is so bitter and distant. As soon as we arrived, she was already disgusted to be here.

I feel a tight squeezing pain come from my arm and I look under the armor to see the large gash starting to close and heal by itself. My skin tightens, which inflicts more pain and once the process is done, it leaves a thick shiny scar behind.

I shift my gaze to Aerowen who stands uncomfortably still like a frozen terrifying statue. I don't know if she waits for me to attack or if she's planning something strategically. Just like nature, the cold is just as unpredictable.

I stand still on the icy slope, watching my frozen breath escape my mouth in a cloud of vapor. I hold the sword firmly in my right hand and I look at each side of the spiked barricade to map out where the largest spikes are so I can attempt to avoid sliding into those spaces and becoming a princess-kabob.

There are roughly three long and narrow spikes of ice on each side that make me nervous, but I try not to think too hard about it. If I do, I'll lose my focus and choke on my first step. I'm halfway down the aisle and I'm slowly getting closer to reaching Aerowen.

She raises both of her hands and waves them around in front of her. Her hands and arms move smoothly like running water and it's almost mesmerizing to watch. Her frozen fingertips flare outwards and ice dances down her arms, swirling around her hands and over her fingers. She bends her arms and pulls her elbows back with her palms turned inwards.

I charge a few steps forward and begin gliding smoothly across the ice. Aerowen pushes her hand forward, unleashing a turbulent tunnel of magic that causes the freezing wind to intensify and conjure a blizzard. Thick snow swirls around me as if I'm trapped inside of a narrow tunnel. I do my best to keep my eyes open and remain focused. More icy beams flow out of her palms, and they break up into small particles once more but now they're larger and much quicker. And with the blizzard raging around me, not only am I close to being thrown off balance, I have to keep an eye out for multiple bursts of magic. If one knocks me off balance, I'm in trouble. I use the forceful wind to my advantage and let it spin me around and I dodge and strike each attack, watching them dissipate into tiny flurries. Some of them I slash with the sword, while others, I strike with my opposite hand that burns with blue flames of energy.

I listen to some of the magical orbs zip past me and turn around to try to strike me in the back, but I quickly maneuver to destroy them before they can touch me.

I feel a force of magic pulling and tugging on the magic that surges in my core, indicating Aerowen has sent a second massive attack my way while my back is turned. I suddenly feel something solid hit the back of my heel and I look down to see a thick bump of ice protruding from the ground, stopping me from moving backwards.

When I look back, I see a massive ball of icy magic approaching me rapidly, but I notice it doesn't shift or break apart like the previous attacks. I immediately put the sword in the back sheathe I rest my right foot against the frozen bump and with all of my strength, I push off of it and glide toward the large ball of ice. I bend my knees and time slows down one more time, allowing me to quickly take out the sword and as I descend steadily to the ground, I slice her attack, causing it to explode and turn into a giant flurry of sleet. Once I land, I stab the sword into the ice so I don't move side to side from the blizzard that continues to rage on.

I look forward and see Aerowen using her magic to make the aisle grow tighter and more narrow. She angrily shrinks the size of the walkway, and the shards of ice quickly inch closer to me. I put the sword away and that's when the panic sets in.

If I slide off course, I'll be stabbed and crushed. The enclosing of the walls makes me feel claustrophobic and it's difficult to breathe and remain focused. My skin starts to itch and crawl and I'm ready to collapse but I'm determined to push through and use my fear to my advantage so I'll make it past this insane trial.

I keep my sight set on Aerowen while the deadly ice walls grow taller and closer. More large shards emerge from the ground, shooting out and towards the center of the walkway as I continue pressing forward. My eyes zip right and left, keeping an eye on the spikes. The panic begins to grow uncontrollable. I know I have to do something before it's too late. I feel an uncontrollable power surge up my back, down my arms and into my palms. Blue sizzling electricity crackling between my fingertips and I throw my arms out to the sides, unleashing all the power I have built up. I use the powerful force to push against the walls and I instantly feel Aerowen's magic fighting against me, refusing to let go.

The walls grow so close, two spikes begin to jab into my palms. More magic surges out of my hands and swirls around the frozen water like an invincible rope, allowing me to grip it firmly without slipping. I shift my hands over the ice daggers and grip them to the best of my abilities. I've never touched something so cold before in my life.

I inhale deeply. Aerowen's magic force is so strong, I fear it'll snap my arms in half. I scream as I do everything I can to push the walls back and the snapping of ice grows louder and louder until I finally feel the enclosing barricade begin to move back. I slowly lift my head up and see Silva pacing back and forth while Phoenix continues to fume with raging fire. Aerowen stares at me with an annoyed look on her face as she moves her hands closer together which makes the walls close in.

"This is enough!" Phoenix roars loudly and I can feel her fury rumble the ground as she stomps her foot on the ice, causing it to break under her which makes Aerowen turn around, drawing her attention away from me and the walls slowly move backwards.

I grip the frozen spike in my right hand tightly, causing it to snap in half. I catch the broken piece in my hand and quickly throw it at Aerowen like a dart to a board. The moment she turns back to look at me, she's startled by her own creation and shifts to the side, making the shard pass her and pierce a boulder that stands behind her.

With her taken by surprise, I take off on the ice, charging towards the end of the passageway as my feet slip back with every step. I keep my gaze firmly on Aerowen as she sharply pivots around and swirls her hands around in front of her, conjuring another enormous ball of icy magic and she throws it at me as if it's a last resort. I unsheathe the sword, gripping tightly with the tip of the blade pointed forward.

As I continue to run forward, I see blue flames arise from the surface of the blade. I run straight towards the large spear and drive the sword down the center, causing it to explode into thick clouds of vapor. I emerge through thick clouds and crash into Aerowen.

She stumbles back, falling on the ground and I slam onto the frozen ground, landing on one knee, driving the blade towards Aerowen's neck. She leans back as far as she can, in shock and breathing heavily, looking at the illuminating blade that's held against her. I make sure not to be too forceful because I don't cause harm, unlike what she did with her frozen wall of death. Aerowen looks at me and smiles.

Why is she smiling?

"There you go." Her pearly white teeth glimmer as snow falls from the sky. I keep the weapon still and I look at Silva who beams with satisfaction, wherefore Phoenix snarls angrily from across her.

"You could have killed me and yet you lay there smiling?!" My stress and fear has turned into boiling rage and agitation. Aerowen's tone and temperament has changed, and it makes me feel uneasy.

I'm not sure if it's because Aerowen has been beaten at her own game, therefore being submissive or if there's something completely different going on.

"The test is over; there's no need for more hostility." Aerowen says calmly. Despite my confusion, I pull back the blade. The blue fire dissipates, and the armor goes back to looking normal, no longer glowing.

Aerowen stands up, brushing the loose snow and ice off her frozen body.

Phoenix comes between Aerowen and I and without using even an ounce of fire and she pushes Aerowen back, slamming her into a wall of ice.

"What the hell is wrong with you?! You barely met the girl, and you already put her life on the line like that?!" I jolt back at the sound of Phoenix's strong roar. The rage in her eye makes me freeze and Aerowen looks at her, unphased.

"Oh, and don't tell me you didn't do the same. All I did was help her find her inner balance and now, she's unlocked even more of the Vessorian magic. Sometimes we learn a valuable lesson when being thrown into the hands of immediate danger!" Both Serafaes stare at each other silently and the tension between them is absolutely terrifying. Phoenix's hand curls into a tight fire enraged fist and when she lifts it up, I step between both of them, catching her hand in mine. Her flames crack against my stone skin and she glares at me. I instantly realize I've made yet another mistake and I let things go too far.

"Enough. This was my fault. I let it carry on too far." While yes, I'm glad Vivalda has unlocked more of her potential, I'm realizing I'm putting too much on Vivalda's shoulders at once. I look past Phoenix's shoulder and I see her standing still, silently panicking and I immediately feel even worse.

I release Phoenix's hand and walk over to Vivalda. I reach my hand out to her, but she backs away slowly, cowering before me which makes me feel even worse.

She shakes her head and holds her hands over her chest, trying to slow her racing heart.

"All of that just to unlock some glowing magic? No. That was too much." Tears begin to swell her eyes, and she walks away from us, glaring at Aerowen as she walks past her.

Phoenix looks at me, disappointed and follows Vivalda. Aerowen remains leaning against the thick wall of ice, and she appears to be disappointed in herself.

"I thought that was what we needed to do." Aerowen's voice is soft and gentle, and snow begins to flurry around her.

"It was. I thought she was more prepared. Now I realize I've pushed her too far, too fast."

Aerowen follows me down the canyon, going the opposite way from Vivalda and Phoenix and we chat a bit while the others have time to gather their thoughts.

Vivalda

Without saying a word, Phoenix walks next to me with her wing stretched behind me, warming me up from the bitter cold. We walk in silence for a few moments, following the lining of the canyon.

Typically, I'd feel awkward in such silence but with Phoenix by my side, I appreciate the silent company so I can try to wrap my head around what just happened. As we walk, I listen to the sound of the armor clanking against itself like a musical beat.

Everything has been moving so fast, and I feel like I have little to no time to adjust to anything.

"Keep your thoughts quiet while we speak. I know Silva can hear you and I don't want your privacy being spoiled." Phoenix releases a deep breath, and I do my best to keep my thoughts silent.

"I'm sorry for lashing out like that. I didn't like that little game they pulled. I knew there'd be a new lesson waiting for you, but I didn't know it'd go to that extent." I massage my hand, fiddling with my fingers and gently cracking my knuckles.

"It's not your fault. I appreciate that you did that." I look up at Phoenix and she smiles. A bright red fire is still ignited over her horns, but her heat doesn't melt the ice.

"I know I shouldn't speak for them but like I said about Silva, Aerowen means no harm. No matter how much her presence ticks me off, I know she was just doing what she was told. They push you to your limits because not only do they assume you can handle it, but they're also scared." I shift my attention to Phoenix and stop walking. Unbothered, Phoenix stops as well and looks at me.

"Why would they be scared?" My eyes bounce back and forth between her bright red eyes. I wouldn't take Silva or Aerowen as the type to be scared. Just moments ago, I held a blade to the throat of a magical ice spirit and never once did I stare into eyes of fear.

"They're scared they're wrong because if they are, we will fail. Silva thinks that by pushing you, you'll be ready to fight with us sooner. I don't know how she expects that to come to pass when the Serafae can barely work together on their own, WITHOUT the help of a human and Vessoria. They'll never admit to their fears, but their actions will show it." I look behind us to see Silva and Aerowen in this distance, walking the opposite way.

"What are they scared to be wrong about?" I ask quietly. Trying to avoid being heard by Silva's supersonic hearing abilities.

"They're scared you won't master your abilities in time and that without someone to wield Vessoria, they will be powerless, despite the great spirits they are. All we want is for the world to be safely at peace and this force is really getting to us. That all being said, I owe you an apology." She looks at me, eyes narrow and head tilted down. Her spiky ears flick backwards as if she's ashamed or saddened.

"For what? You've done nothing wrong." I say softly in hopes of easing whatever thoughts she may have.

"Back on Dragon's Fjord, I also pushed you a bit farther than I had liked. Granted, my test was also asked of by Silva and at the time, but I foolishly assumed you'd be capable of standing against a dragon. I guess that in a way, I was so excited that I'd forgotten how much more simple humans are compared to us. But now I understand that humans need a gentle push of encouragement versus a strong pull. When you slipped off the edge of the cliff, seeing the fear in your eyes shattered me in ways I didn't think was possible. That moment immediately changed the way I viewed you. I saw the way you feared me, and I've not stopped thinking about it since. That was when I realized Silva is going about this the wrong way. After everything she's gone through, I think it's her who needs the gentle push." I feel terrible knowing Phoenix has been so distraught.

"If it makes you feel better, it wasn't YOU I feared. It was the fall. But when you caught me, I knew I'd be in safe hands from then on. I've come to realize that when there's not a test to beat or a lesson to learn, Silva is very gentle. But when the tests arise, she's firm and tense. The Serafaes' fears are valid and now I understand much more than I did in the beginning. No matter what, it doesn't change the fact that I don't know what I'm doing or who I am anymore. Sure, my royal human life was complicated, but it was nowhere near as complicated as this. I miss that life. I feel so disconnected and I have a hard time pushing forward because there's triple the weight on my shoulders, and I have no choice but to carry it. All I want is to gain my father's and our people's love once again." Phoenix walks around and stands in front of me, stopping me from walking.

"I think we should start over. Granted, I'm not sure how much time we'll be allotted but it's worth a shot once we come around to it. We'll talk to the others together and we will all try to see eye to eye. No more heavy weight, no more deadly pressure and no more heavy pulls. It may be a tedious task, but I'm sure we can fix what was broken a long time ago. What do you say?" The soft gleam in Phoenix's eye is calming and reassuring.

"I think that would be great. But before we meet up with them, I have a question. You don't have to answer but what's with the grudge between you and Aerowen? Surely there's more to the tension than the catwalk of death." The fire over her horns flickers and sparks and she takes a deep and heavy breath.

"She and I have known each other for a very long time. I mustn't go into details right now but let's just say the fury of my fire and the bitter touch of her ice don't exactly mix. It's a situation I've put behind me, but I remain guarded around her. Despite our dispute, I can easily push it aside since we share a common goal and it's to find and destroy the Aerolight beacon." I refuse to dig deep into whatever past she speaks of. I'm sure if Aerowen travels with us, I'll eventually learn about this feud between them. The gears in my mind begin to twist and turn and for once, I'm starting to understand what I must do in order to return to the life I yearn for.

"I think I know what I need to do but first, I think it's about time to take off this armor."

While walking next to me, Aerowen glides her hand over a long wall of ice. I can tell by her silence that she's upset." Don't let it trouble you too much. You did as I ask and now, the bond between her and Vessoria is stronger than before and she's closer to becoming one of the most powerful allies we've ever known that'll help destroy the Aerolights. When the princess is ready and we are all calm, we will talk it over." I try to reassure her, but I can tell it doesn't help.

"What is the plan moving forward? Not even I know where the Aerolight beacon is. I tried sparing a few in hopes of getting information from them, but they're unable to communicate. I'm sure they were created like that for a reason." We continue walking through the glaciers of ice and Aerowen's magic casts over the ground, illuminating it brightly. I look up in the sky and see a large white owl fly over us. The sun is slowly starting to peek out, indicating our departure is coming up quickly.

"We will travel to Wildevale. Vivalda still has much to learn and I don't know how much time we have left. I don't know when-" I'm interrupted by a loud roar coming from behind us that causes the thick frozen walls to crack.

"SILVA!" Phoenix roars from behind us and we turn around to see her flying towards us. Upon looking closer, I see her holding Vivalda in her arms and I instantly know something's wrong.

Phoenix swoops down, landing heavily on the ground, keeping the princess in her arms, refusing to put her down. Vivalda is no longer wearing the armor and is back to wearing her black furry coat and her necklace dangles between Phoenix's sharp claws.

"What happened?!" I ask as I rush over to them, trying to get Phoenix to release Vivalda, but she refuses and keeps the princess close to her warm chest.

"I don't know. It's like what happened back on the ship. She took off the armor and immediately collapsed." I reach my hands out and glide them over Vivalda's body, trying to see what's causing her to continuously feel distress after wearing the armor.

"There has to be something you can see." Phoenix growls deeply, concerned and panicked. My magic flows around Vivalda, allowing me to see and feel the magic that swells her soul, mind and body. Her breathing pattern is normal, but she barely moves. It's almost like she's in a very deep sleep, unable to wake from it.

"Is she not a match for Vessoria after all?" Aerowen asks softly behind us. Phoenix glares at her and tries not to grow more agitated to avoid potentially burning Vivalda.

"If it wasn't a match, it would have killed her already or she'd be unable to summon the armor. This is something different. Silva, I know you see something, what is it?!" She roars loudly and runs out of patience. I try to focus but I'm left at a dead end, seeing nothing out of the normal.

"I don't know. Something's blocking my magic from seeing through whatever it is. She's alive, just unconscious. I don't know for how long and I don't know how to wake her if she doesn't on her own. We have to go now. Phoenix, take her to Wildevale and we'll meet you there. Fly low and as fast as possible. I'll cast a shield under you, so you won't be spotted. Once you're there, keep her warm, keep her safe and don't let anything happen to her." Phoenix glares sharply at me before spreading her large wings and taking off softly into the air, disappearing over the tall frozen mountains and into the thick fluffy clouds. I stay back with Aerowen to help her understand the situation.

"Almost every time the princess has called upon Vessoria, it causes her to grow weak and be on the brink of total exhaustion. I don't know why. Make no mistake, she is the chosen one, but something is stopping her from being able to remove the armor without repercussions if she keeps it on for too long, it drains her energy. There's no common ground and if this isn't solved soon, we're going to be in trouble."

PHOENIX

While soaring high in the sky, I pull Vivalda's fur hood over her head to shield her face from the freezing wind and I hold her gently against my chest so I can continue to feel her heart beating. I soar over tall boulders and rocks, and I see the main lands in the near distance. Thankfully, Yarrin isn't too far from Wildevale.

While soaring rapidly in the sky, my ears flick up when I hear a loud shriek echo all around me. It's a sound I'm far too familiar with and not a sound I wanted to hear any time soon.

Of course you show up now.

I look both ways and see two monstrous Aerolights approaching us at an alarming rate with their sharp teeth and talon bared. I look down into the water and all I see is my shadow but not theirs.

I have no way of using my magic and transformation abilities without risking Vivalda's safety. The only option I have is to dodge their attacks and use it against them. Hopefully my speed will be enough to get it to the forest safely.

They inch closer and closer, closing me in while screeching and growling loudly. The one on the right has hundreds of sharp teeth, red beaming eyes and fuming red magic that seeps from its smokey deranged body.

The one on the left is smaller and less powerful with red and black smoke trailing behind it like distorted fire.

I keep my balance while continuing to speed through the air. Due to the large size of my wings, I'm able to gain a lot of distance in a matter of moments. I keep my eyes focused on the forest in the distance, waiting to see a green beam of light to indicate Silva's arrival, but I don't see any sign of her, and it begins to concern me.

My instincts alert me that one of the Aerolights is preparing to attack and fear rattles through my scaly body because it'll be difficult to keep the princess safe and fight off my foes at the same time. No matter what, I hold on tightly to Vivalda and brace for the demon's attacks.

The beast on the right immediately darts towards me and I dive down, causing it to run into its partner.

The smaller one unleashes a blood curling roar, and I manage to gain distance away from them but when I look back, I see a raging ball of red dark magic heading for us. I dodge to the left, barely missing it by a hair and it explodes in midair. I cover Vivalda's head with my hand to shield her from the dark magic fumes.

I struggle to keep distance between us and the creatures as they continuously charge at us with their poisonous attacks. I do everything I can to dodge every single blast while staying on course for Wildevale.

Once we finally reach the edge of the forest, both beasts combine their magic together and send a massive flaming ball of dark magic at me, I block it with my wing, and it slams my body into multiple trees. Upon crashing into the forest, I manage to roll over, landing on my back. I cover Vivalda with my wings and protect her from the falling trees, branches and debris. My body creates a long-dragged crater in the dirt and I end up knocking over several large trees.

My wings and back pulsate with intense waves of pain but I refuse to let Vivalda go from my grip. I can still feel her heart beating steadily and her breathing pattern remain normal which is a relief due to how bad the crash landing was.

Once my vision comes into focus, I see the roaring creatures charging towards us but before they enter the border of trees, I thrust my hand out, searing them with an intense tunnel of fire that rushes out of my palm and claws. They let out loud, horrifying screams as they are burned alive. I release all the fire I have built up until the smaller one is destroyed. Its scream echoes in the wind as it disintegrates into black molten liquid, and it melts onto the ground.

My fire retracts and returns to me and the remaining Aerolight stands strong, quickly regenerating and healing from the flames. I breathe heavily, trying to catch my breath while feeling my chest tighten from using so much energy. Burning smoke melts out of my mouth and I look at my hand and watch as a layer of black burnt skin cracks and falls, revealing a new layer of red and orange scaly skin, meaning my energy level is slowly rising back up. I feel like I'm on the verge of passing out, but I remain awake for Vivalda's sake. In my left hand, I see her necklace dangling safely in my hand which makes me release a sigh of relief. I look back up to see the Aerolight slowly get up from the burnt ground as if it was never impacted by my fire.

I remain leaning back against a large tree with my wings curled around the princess, ready to defend us both. But as soon as I raise my hand I hear a large falcon screech over me. I watch it swoop down from over the treetops and attack the Aerolight, causing it to get flustered. And just in time, I see a large green beam of light attack it from behind, throwing its body into the ground. Once the beast is down, Silva emerges and rushes over to us.

"I'm so sorry we weren't here sooner. We were halted by decoys." She immediately notices the bright red burning blood trickling down my wing. She uses her magic to help heal it and the wound is slowly closed, leaving nothing but intense pain behind.

"Thank you. Two of them came out of nowhere." We both turn our attention to the Aerolight that creepily emerges from the dirt as it cracks its ghostly bones back into place.

"They're continuing to evolve. I'm not sure how much help I can be-" I try to speak but ultimately run out of energy to talk or fight.

"No, don't worry about it. Stay here with her and we'll take care of it. They're not immortal, so no matter what, they will be defeated." The caring tone in Silva's voice is helpful and reassuring. She smiles and nods before standing up and I see Aerowen appear from the edge of the forest.

She rushes at the Aerolight and attacks it with spikes of ice that she conjures from the dirt ground. Once a spike stabs the Aerolight, its body is turned into ice and once Aerowen closes her fist, the Aerolight's body cracks and breaks apart piece by piece. But after a moment, it regenerates once again, and it pulls its body together like a puzzle. When Silva realizes how much of a nasty opponent the beast is, she unleashes her fury on it, slashing it with her bright green magic, not giving it a chance to retaliate.

I rest my head against the tree I lean on, trying to regain my energy and hoping Vivalda will wake up soon.

Aerowen and I take turns attacking the monster. But no matter what we do, it continues to constantly revive itself as if it's not being touched. Aerowen and I step back for a moment to rethink our strategy before we run out of energy.

"What more can we do? Our magic is barely touching it. Since when are they this resilient?" Aerowen asks, catching her breath.

She stands over a pad of ice she formed under her feet and flares her fingers out towards the ground and a sharp spear grows from the ground. She holds onto the frozen weapon while keeping her eye on the Aerolight as it slowly reforms once again.

Once it's healed, it opens its large mouth to release a near unbearable scream. The red poisonous fire that spreads across its body forms sharp spikes that draw down its back like some kind of demonic serpent. It arches its back towards us and it shoots the spikes at us. Aerowen throws up her hand and forms a thick wall of ice in front of us, blocking us from the sharp spikes. I curve around the wall and unleash more of my power onto the vile beast. I keep both of my palms facing forward, releasing pure, powerful energy. The more I use, the more I feel the trees around me bend forward, lending me their energy without being drained.

I grow tall from the ground until I tower over the beast, ready to shove my hand into its body to find its life source. But as soon as I get close to grabbing it, a large falcon flies in front of me, catching me off guard and pounces on the Aerolight.

It stops me from attacking and I retreat back to stand next to Aerowen, watching carefully. Aerowen lifts the staff up and over her shoulder, aiming the sharp tip at the Aerolight. She throws it forward and the weapon stabs it in the eye, leaving an open window for the falcon to tear its body apart. As we remain on guard, we hear a ghostly voice emerge from the fight.

"I've had enough of you!" The voice is so clear and yet it sounds like it comes from far away.

"You heard that too, correct?" Aerowen asks quietly while the fight continues to unfold more seriously. The falcon gouges at the monster's eyes and tears open its smokey skin, making it poisonous blood drip onto the ground.

"I did." I respond and my leafy ears flicker to the sides.

The falcon takes off into the air and we step back, keeping a safe distance just in case. The majestic bird soars towards the treetops and turns to dive right onto the head of the Aerolight, causing a massive explosion that shakes the ground. A bright purple light pierces my eyes and I squint to see what emerges from the below.

Aerowen and I approach a wide crater that's left in the ground and a tall figure with long brown hair and gold curly horns slowly rises from black smoke. She snarls with her fists tightly clenched to her side while she stands over the Aerolight's body, gritting her sharp teeth angrily. Black smoke circles around her body in an unnatural way. Red ooze bubbles on the ground and the Aerolight's crushed body disappears with an eerie whisper.

The woman looks at us with beaming purple eyes. She breathes heavily and is visibly enraged. "You're telling me, you both couldn't handle that puny rat? Why am I not surprised?" She steps out of the crater with black smoke trailing behind her. She rolls her shoulders and stretches out her arms.

"We could have. But I wanted to give you an opportunity to relieve some of that built up anger. It looks like it benefited you. Didn't it...Zyla?" I say calmly and she turns to stare at me viciously.

She has four brown horns that glimmer and turn gold in the sunlight. Protruding from her head is two large curly ram horns and two thin ones that wave upwards. Half of one of her larger horns is broken, leaving a large hole. She wears a light gray wolf pelt across her chest and around her shoulders. Her skin is warm gold toned, she has a gold scar etched across her left eye and more bright yellow glowing marks that curve over her forehead with glowing spots that look like enchanted freckles.

She wears a black dress made of smoke that moves hauntingly with every step she takes. Her fingertips are black with sharp black talon-like nails that curve over towards her palms. Her long, pointy ears poke through her rich brown and red highlighted hair that shines vibrantly in the sunlight. Her black smoke seeps into the ground like poison, killing everything she walks over but I use my power to heal and bring it back to life while she circles around us.

"Thank you for your help. I appreciate it." I say and Zyla scoffs.

"I didn't do it for you. The last thing I need is for more of these things to reach the Lion's Eye and no one be there to take care of them. You think I'd wait for you to save the forest? Absolutely not. I don't have time for that." She continues to walk and notices Phoenix holding on to Vivalda while leaning against a tree.

"I say we drop this conversation and turn our attention to Phoenix and the girl." Aerowen advises wisely and we join Phoenix's side.

"You're traveling with a human?!" She shouts angrily and the ground rumbles from her energy.

"I don't have time for your fury Zyla." I say as I push my hand backwards in hopes she'll stay back and give us space to help the others.

PHOENIX

I sit forward and gently pull Vivalda away from
my chest, allowing cool air to brush over her since the
weather is warmer where we are. Aerowen and Silva rush
over to us and I see another figure disappear behind
them and reappear within the trees in front of me.

"Has she woken up yet?" Silva kneels beside me,
gently moving my wing over so she can see the princess
who remains asleep on my lap.

"No. Can't your magic wake her up? You've done
things like that before." Silva shakes her head.

"In past situations, I knew what I was dealing with.
But this is something completely unknown. If I use my
magic on her for the wrong purposes, I could
accidentally kill her." I feel my fiery heart start to
palpitate, and I grow more worried by the minute.
Aerowen keeps her distance, observing silently. She's
visibly shaken up, not from her cold touch, but from
fear. I try not to look at her for too long to avoid
awkwardly catching her attention.

The dark figure emerges behind her, peering over
Aerowen's shoulder, immediately locking eyes with me.

"Pathetic. This is exactly what happens when
magic chooses a human as its host." She says disgustedly,
crossing her arms and taunting us in a scolding manner.

"Stay out of this Zyla." I snarl through my fangs as
my internal fire rages and burns bright. Zyla holds up

her black stained hands up as if to surrender sarcastically.

"Alright fine, I guess you don't want me to share that your precious...thing there is poisoned by Sylphenic magic. But if I am such a bother, I will take my leave." My eyes widened and nearly burst from my skull. Zyla begins to disappear into a black wall of smoke, but Silva angrily sprouts glowing vines from the ground and uses them to grab Zyla's hands before she has the chance to completely vanish.

"What are you talking about Zyla? How do you know it's Sylphenic magic?" Silva lowers her tone, begging the enchantress for information.

Zyla looks down at the vine that wraps around her wrist, and she instantly kills it with her dark magic. Her brows lift and she walks back towards us.

"Oh...I thought you wanted me to stay out of it." She puckers her lips and fake pouts like an immature childling. Silva stands up, standing taller than Zyla and she looks into her eyes intimidatingly.

"Answer my question. How do you know it's caused by Sylphenic magic? How can you see it?" Silva stands impatiently, waiting for a response while Zyla stands with her arms crossed, staring directly into Silva's white eyes.

"Sylphenic is like my magic but worse...way worse and far more powerful. It's a force that allows the Aerolights to simply exist. The magic that creates them is both deadly and dangerous. I can only assume that from all the fighting, particles of their filthy magic have entered the girl's body, causing her to fall ill and be on the brink of death." Silva looks down, thinking to herself. I've never heard of dark magic settling inside a human body before. Typically, humans can't survive even being near such dark magic.

"Can you help her please? You know I wouldn't ask if it was something I could take care of myself." Silva begs and Zyla's face crinkles up with disgust.

"What makes you think I'd care to help a human?" She glares at Vivalda who lays in my arms before looking back at Silva whose patience is running thin.

"If you don't help her, we'll lose the chance of getting rid of the damn beasts for good. I thought you out of all Serafae would do anything to protect the ones you care about." Silva's words pinch a nerve and Zyla grows more angry. She steps closer to Silva and holds up her sharp talons.

"The last thing I need is for my own to be dragged into another living hell. Unless you want your trees pumped with poison, I'd keep her out of it." Zyla's threat doesn't affect Silva, and she takes a deep breath, trying to refrain from agitating her even more.

"Drop the pride for once. We'd do the same for you." I insert my thoughts, catching her off guard. "She is more than just some pathetic human you think she is. Help her wake up and she'll show you." I speak to her calmly and she growls with her mouth shut, holding back from exploding with rage. Her brows quiver and her internal anger causes the purple smoke at her feet to rise towards her hips.

"She has shown no ill will towards us or our kind. If anything, she's been nothing but fascinated by who and what we are." I heave through my words, wheezing in pain with every breath I take.

Zyla shakes her head, closes her eyes and takes a deep breath. Her dark magic falls to the ground, indicating she's more calm than she was a moment ago.

"Fine. But after this, she must learn to defend herself from the magic on her own because I won't be able to do this again." She lowers her angry tone and walks in front of me.

"Lay her down flat on the ground and keep your distance." I do as she says, and Silva helps me off the ground. She pulls me up with her incredible strength and we walk a few feet away from where Zyla sits next to Vivalda.

The princess's red and brown hair falls to the side and sprawls out onto the grass. It's difficult to look at her because she's so still to the point where she looks deceased. I keep my eye on Zyla, watching her every move, making sure she doesn't pull any tricks.

Zyla raises her hands over Vivalda's chest and keeps them still. The enchantress' veins begin to pop from her skin, and they glow dark purple. The veins start at her fingertips and grow all the way up to her face, looking like scattered lightning strikes.

Her hands begin to shake and black smoke seeps out of Vivalda's chest and is absorbed into Zyla's hands. The enchantress' magic causes black clouds to circle around in the sky and deep purple bolts of lightning descend from the sky. I can tell she's in pain, but she bites her tongue, refusing to show any signs of distraught.

The atmosphere grows dark, and Silva uses her power to make the trees grow taller and thicker, keeping us hidden. By the time the trees cover us, it's nearly pitch black, but she makes the plants around us illuminate and glow in different colors.

The veins on Zyla's body grow thicker and darker which is unsettling to look at. She closes her eyes and pulls her chin towards her chest, honing in on her power so she can suck out the poison from Vivalda's body. A loud boom echoes in the air, nearly blowing Zyla backwards. The clash between her magic and the Sylphenic magic causes a scary reaction. She lets out a long groan before quickly opening her eyes and looking at Vivalda. Her mouth gapes open and she looks terrified of something completely unknown. I look at Silva who panics silently.

Zyla curls her sharp nails towards her palms and with a heavy push, she flexes them upwards and when she does, more loud noises erupt around us. Zyla's voice blends in with the creepy sounds that circles us, and Silva's magic begins to flicker.

Something's wrong.

Zyla screams loudly, indicating she's in excruciating pain and discomfort. Suddenly, Vivalda's chest lifts up slightly from the ground and the rest of the Sylphenic magic leaves her body.

Zyla jolts back while she remains sitting and she pants heavily, out of breath. The purple veins that wrap around her body pulsate in and out and her violet eyes glow brightly. She's absorbed so much magic; it's made her look possessed. She slowly turns around and glares at Silva. Her hands shake and her eyes bulge out of her head. Black and purple smoke spirals around her and thunder continues to crack.

"What secrets are you hiding Silva?" Zyla groans as she pulls her hands to her chest, nearly digging her claws into her skin.

I slowly break away from Silva's grip, nearly falling over and I walk closer to Zyla. "What are you talking about?" I look down at Vivalda whose skin and hair looks more vibrant than before, indicating the Sylphenic magic is completely extracted.

"You, just as I very well know, this type of magic doesn't randomly feed on humans and Aerolights can't transmit their magic onto them. So how did Sylphenic magic end up in this human's body?!" Zyla stands up ferociously and stomps up to Silva, waiting for her to answer. Instead of reacting, Silva stands still, frozen with her fists clenched and her brows arched.

"Due to the circumstances, I have not had time to explain. I didn't think it'd get this far and I didn't mean to cause harm by staying quiet." Silva's stopped by the sound of Vivalda waking up. She groans and rolls over below Zyla's feet before slowly sitting up and rubbing her face. She yawns and looks at me confused.

"Oh, hi. Did I oversleep?" Once she looks up and sees Zyla standing over her, she goes completely silent. Zyla's purple lightning veins slowly disappear, and she looks down at the princess, repulsed. Vivalda lets out a shriek and scoots back in the grass closer to me.

"WOAH! Who are you?!" She looks at the enchantress, terrified.

Zyla sighs heavily. "Here we go. You just couldn't have waited for me to leave? Great. I'm Zyla and I don't care to know you. I saved your life, despite having zero interest in doing so…you're welcome." She says coldly and quickly before walking away with smoke following behind her like a shadow.

Vivalda

I follow the scary newcomer with my eyes as she walks away. My legs feel numb, and they pulse in heavy pain at the same time. Phoenix walks over and helps me up, keeping her arm around my waist. I lean over and see a large scar across her wing.

The more I look around, the more I get confused. My feet are planted on grass instead of ice and I quickly realize there's no way I'd fall asleep while traveling across a massive body of water.

"What's going on and where are we?" I look at Phoenix and see her dead-eyeing Silva silently, which draws my focus to her as well.

"You fell unconscious on Yarrin and I had Phoenix fly you to Wildevale, the southern forest." Silva speaks calmly but her body language is stiff and still.

"We were chased down by two Aerolights, Zyla helped get rid of them. How are you feeling?"

She slowly moves her arm out from under mine, allowing me to stand independently. Phoenix reaches her hand out with my mother's necklace dangling between her fingers. I take it and put it on, clasping it securely.

"I don't know at the moment. Is Zyla a Serafae? And what does she mean she saved my life?" I speak quietly because I can tell this new entity is annoyed by my presence. By the impudent sarcasm and terrifying look on her face, I can tell she doesn't want to be here.

"I am a keeper of what your kind calls 'dark magic'. Which means...if you tick me off, I could poison those pretty lungs of yours without laying a finger on you. But today, I decided to do the opposite. Despite us being dark magic users, the dark force that creates the Aerolights and the magic I bear is completely different." I don't know what's the cause of her harsh hostility, but I don't let it bother me since I've just met her.

"From what I've gathered, dear Silva here has kept you all in the dark about Sylphenic magic. I can't tell if she did that because you all were too stupid to catch on or if something else-" Zyla's purple eyes widen, and her sharp teeth poke out from behind her lips. Black smoke spirals around her and Silva walks closer to her, growing in height. Silva's emotions cause the wind to pick up harshly. I step back, worried the two Serafaes will get into a fight, but Phoenix rests her heavy hand on my shoulder, reassuring me everything is alright.

"Don't test me Zyla, or I swear I'll choke you with your own magic." Her echoing voice sends chills down my spine. My eyes widen and nearly pop out of my skull. I've never heard Silva say something so menacing before. I can tell she's fed up with Zyla and due to her temper, I start piecing something together.

"Hey! Obviously, you all don't get along very well and quite honestly, I don't understand why I happen to be the center of it! Since we're all in the dark about something, maybe a calm talk can help fix that. So, let's drop the spooky magic and try to get along for a moment." I shout at both of them sternly, their magic disappears at the same time and they slowly back away from each other.

Silva smiles at me and takes a deep breath before leading us deep into the forest where we find a wide concealed spot that's covered with large rocks and trees. I sit on a thick patch of grass, Phoenix sits on top of a tall flat rock, Aerowen and Silva sit across from me and Zyla stands, leaning against a tree away from us.

The plants around us breathe with Silva, beaming with a beautiful glow. No matter how much tension is in the air, her magic is always comforting and helps me relax when I'm tense.

"The magic that creates the Aerolights is called Sylphenic magic. It's the darkest force I've ever witnessed in my entire existence. Since your first encounter with the demons, you've been affected by their magic without realizing. I never thought it'd be possible for them to eject their own magic into a human body. When you collapsed on Calypso's ship, my magic could sense a dark presence, but I couldn't get rid of it. My magic is strong, but a fight between pure and dark energy can be a gruesome battle. If I had tried to heal it, I would have risked killing you. I didn't tell any of you because I didn't want to inflict more panic on you, and I wanted to wait until we traveled here to Wildevale so you could meet Zyla." I zone out, staring at the ground, absorbing everything she tells me, paying close attention. Everything she says so far makes sense.

"With the limited timer we were given, I couldn't rush to find Zyla because her whereabouts are often unknown and as you can tell, working with her can be a bit...tedious." Silva's cut off by Zyla scoffing in the distance.

"This is why I don't come out of the shadows. So, I don't have to help fix YOUR mistakes." Zyla growls before turning her back towards us. Silva pays no attention to her and continues to speak calmly.

"So, the Aerolights are growing stronger and are evolving in ways all of you have never seen and they always know where we're going. Why? Are they after something?" Silva shrugs her shoulders and Aerowen speaks softly.

"They follow and trick us on purpose because they know it's almost impossible for us to come together in order to destroy them. They know how to stir trouble to the point where we are thrown off balance from one another." She lowers her head, and I can tell she's referring to her trial and she regrets how she acted and handled it.

"Do we know where they're coming from?" I look up at Silva and she nods her head with her brows narrow.

"Not exactly. Over the past few days, I've felt a dark force pulling on my magic from the far northern region of Vassuren. I think that's where the Aerolight beacon is but since it's tugging on my magic, there's a chance it might be a trap." I feel a giant spark of hope suddenly hit me. Making me feel hopeful that the journey may be over and maybe I'll be able to return home sooner than I thought.

"And what if it's not a trap? What if we were to travel to that region and destroy the beacon where it stands?" The spirits look at me annoyed and slightly agitated. Silva's dark grey lips curl into a smile.

"I admire your determination. I know how much you want to go home, but we cannot run into this blind. I can't risk anything else going wrong. It may not look like it, but we've already come so far." Phoenix drops down from her rock and walks over to sit next to me.

"What she means by that is that the Serafaes haven't come together like this in a very long time. I'm sure you've noticed that by now. We have not gathered because we have foes to vanquish. We've gathered because you and Vessoria brought us together. And only until we fight as one, will we be able to destroy this dark force." Phoenix's tone is sincere and uplifting, especially after the talk we had back on Yarrin. I can't help but smile and feel some sort of relief. She tilts her head to the side as if waiting for me to speak.

"Well. If we plan to work together, the first thing that must change are those baffling tests of yours. I'd never turn down a fair challenge, but I don't want to look into the eyes of death as soon as I enter the playing field. If it's not too much to ask, I'd like to get to know you all better and not be threatened with razor sharp spikes of ice." I tilt my head to the side and look at Aerowen, smiling at her awkwardly and she chuckles, embarrassed.

"I'm sorry. That was completely out of my character. Can you forgive me, and may we start over?" Aerowen asks gently and the ice that lays across her chest and body glimmers in Silva's light. I can tell her words are genuine, so I nod my head and happily accept her apology. I have no reason to hold a grudge as long as that word is kept.

Phoenix gets up, walks over to Silva and whispers something in her leafy ear. I try to listen to what she says, but she's too quiet for me to hear but I can tell Aerowen and Zyla can hear perfectly because both of their attention is turned to them. Zyla's brows perk as if she's interested in something.

"Are we sure now's the time?" Silva asks out loud, looking at the others for approval. Aerowen and Phoenix nod their heads and Zyla smirks.

"If you think she's ready, we should get it over with now." Zyla slowly walks over to us. Silva and I lock eyes, and she smiles.

"There's still much to learn but she's ready for this." Silva perks up, sitting up tall and Phoenix stands behind her with a large smile on her face and her wings flared to her sides.

"If you say so, but if this goes wrong, it's on you Silva." Zyla remarks before sitting on a boulder behind the other three, refusing to get too close.

"Vivalda, what I'm about to tell you is crucially important and I need you to stay as focused as possible. This will not be a matter to quickly brush off. Do you understand?" Silva says as she waves her hands in the air, causing the trees to bend over us like a naturistic cave made of tree trunks and leaves. She thrusts her hands forward and creates a green illuminating fire in the center of where we sit. It doesn't burn like real fire, instead it simply illuminates the dark space we sit in.

I wait patiently to hear what she says. Phoenix returns to my side, and I feel my heart start to race due to intense curiosity.

"The souls of the Serafae were forged millennia ago by one who is unknown. We came to life in times when your world needed us most. You were called to fight with us because your heart is pure, and your mind is strong. Individually, our magic and power is not enough." My mouth nearly falls open due to how invested I am into the conversation.

"Upon coming to life, we were each given a jewel that we've kept hidden and guarded. And since the beginning of our lives, we've been missing a small piece. YOU are the missing piece." Silva reaches behind her head and plucks the purple flower from her hair. She holds the flower by the stem, and I watch as the flower transforms into a green glowing crystal shard that's half the size of her palm. It levitates over her hand, spinning slowly while sparkly particles drift off its surface.

I observe each of the other spirits as they retrieve a crystal shard from their bodies.

Phoenix picks off one of the black scales from her wing and it transforms into a red glowing crystal. Aerowen's frozen shard is in plain sight on her chest, embedded into her iced skin. She gently breaks it from the slivers of ice on her chest and it sheds itself, revealing a light blue gem. Lastly, Zyla pulls a purple jewel from the inside of her broken horn and walks over towards the other three to present it.

The four spirits bring the shards closer together. I can't help but stare at how beautifully they glow and sparkle in the dark.

"What are these for?" I look closer at each of the gems and notice that each of the Serafae's magic elements dance and swirl around them.

"Once these jewels join together as one, powerful magic will be born and can only be used by the one who wields Vessoria. Only until the host is strong enough to obtain the power of the elemental crystals, can it be used." Silva continues to explain while I remain fixated on the levitating jewels.

"So, not only do I need to continue working on working with Vessoria, but now I need to grow strong enough to use the crystal's power? Alright." I feel like vomiting now knowing I have more to learn.

"Maybe the odds will be with you, and you'll be able to harness it a lot sooner than you think, and it'll be easier on you. Try not to think about it too much. I know it'll be difficult, but we'll be there every step of the way. Even without the crystals, you're strong as you already are." The Serafaes move the crystals closer to each other which causes the stones to react strangely. They shake and rattle around as if they're giant magnets waiting to be pulled and pushed together. Once they're close enough, they all slide onto Silva's hand and with a swooshing *BOOM*, the shards merge together, forming a strangely shaped object that turns into a clear, iridescent stone.

Silva holds it steadily as it levitates over her hands. She slowly pushes her hands forward and with a gentle push from her magic, she guides the stone to me. I follow it with my eyes as it hovers in front of me, leaving me feeling unsure what I'm supposed to do. I look at Silva, confused and she nods her head, encouraging me to hold it.

I cup my hands together and hold them under the floating crystal and instantly it descends and lands in my hands. As soon as I feel the weight settle, I grasp it gently. I observe, being careful not to drop it. The crystal is cold to the touch, and I can feel its incredible power tugging on Vessoria.

As soon as Vivalda gently grips the crystal, bright blue magic bursts from within the stone, swirling around us. The magic that flows is pure and sacred.

Vivalda smiles and giggles, enthralled with the magic that continues to unravel around her. Once it disappears, she's left holding the clear crystal chunk, looking at it, confused.

"What now?" I can feel my magic surging powerfully throughout my body and I look at the others who are just as satisfied as I am.

"The crystal has accepted you. Now, when the time is right and once everything falls into place, you will be able to use the power of the stone." Vivalda continues to observe the rock with a wide smile on her face. I can feel her contentment and curiosity floating around like the gentle playful breeze.

Zyla backs away from the group, dusting grass off her smokey body. "Great. Now that's out of the way, and I no longer have to stash a pathetic rock in my horn. What do we do now? I'd like to finish this as soon as possible." Her constant unprovoked negative attitude and tone annoys me. But I don't let it bug me too much.

"Before we do anything. Vivalda, you will keep that crystal with you at all times, your and Vessoria will know when to use it, but for now, it'll remain bound to Vessoria. Do you understand?" We all watch as the crystal disappears from Vivalda's hands which makes her panic for a split moment, worrying she did something wrong.

"Uh oh, did I break it already?"

Vivalda flips her hands up and down, wondering where it went. "No, you didn't break it. It's safe." I laugh as Vivalda lets out a sigh of relief, resting her right hand on her chest.

"Thank goodness." The rest of the Serafaes laugh, except for Zyla who turns away from us.

"By the time we exterminate the Sylphenic magic, I suppose I'll just go home, right?" Her head falls low, and she twiddles her fingers in front of her, avoiding eye contact.

"If that is what you'll choose, yes." I reassure Vivalda and she looks up, smiling. I can feel her heartbeat race steadily, full of excitement and hope. She stands up and looks over at Zyla.

"Well, if we're going to be fighting against Sylphenic magic, I may as well spar with one who possesses similar magic. Right?" Vivalda taunts the dark enchantress and Zyla curls her hands into fists.

"Ah yes, what a marvelous plan, princess. Good luck finding that magical poser you speak of. I don't know what other dark spirits are out there who'd be willing to help a human." Zyla says under her breath but loud enough for us all to hear.

The rest of the Serafaes rise off the ground and I make the forest go back to normal. I look over and see Phoenix's fire raging subtly and she growls loudly, catching Zyla's attention.

The enchantress flexes her fingers outwards, nearly snapping them backwards as a puff of black smoke ejects from her palms. She turns around slowly, peering at everyone coldly.

"If you think for a split moment I will be some kind of training puppet for you, you're sorely mistaken. I don't feel like wasting my time." I give her a blank stare and Vivalda bravely walks up to her.

"Are you afraid I may beat you and your spooky magic? Sure, it saved me once, but I'm sure I could-" The princess teases and Zyla's gaze hardens while a gust of wind picks up from behind her, causing black fumes to sift from the ground. Her dark brown hair floats up with the wind, making her appear far more intimidating.

"I'd be careful princess. You're standing on foreign land in front of one who has vanquished more humans than any Serafae to ever exist. Don't think for a moment that just because you're royalty that I'll take it easy on you." She stares into Vivalda's eyes, and she doesn't break. Instead, the princess looks up at her, smiling.

Vivalda slowly reaches for her neck, she yanks it away and a strong force of windy magic pushes Zyla backwards, nearly knocking her off her feet. Vivalda walks forward, coated in armor. The blue designs glow and shine vibrantly and upon closely observing, I notice that her silver halo is a bit darker than before and there's three thick blue markings drawn from her eyes. Two marks draw down her cheeks and another stretches from the outer corners.

Vivalda grips her sword tightly in her right hand and Zyla observes the princess' armor and weapon. I've never seen her in such a state of shock before to the point where her intimidating mask nearly slips.

"Fine, if this is what you really want, so be it. But be warned...I won't hold back." Zyla turns and leads us into an open field.

Vivalda

Silva casts a temporary barrier over the open field so that no magic can be seen from above. Even though I'm not sure how good we'll be at keeping loud and colorful magic discreet. I assume Silva would let us know if any danger comes near, so I'm not too worried.

Zyla stands several feet in front of me, casting her dark magic and blackened smoke rises from the ground, releasing a ghostly sound that makes my skin crawl. Purple fumes ignite over her hands and she waves her fingers, ready to attack.

I hold Vessoria tightly in my hands and my reflection catches my attention. My eyes skim along the shiny dark silver metal and I pull the blade closer to my face when I notice three strange blue marks around my eyes and my lips are solid black. I've never seen these markings before.

What is this?

I look at Silva who stands to the side of the field with Aerowen and Phoenix. The smile on Silva's face shows so much satisfaction for reasons I don't know. I look back at the blade and I can't help but feel so incredible. The way I look and feel makes me feel incredibly strong. I turn back to face the menacing enchantress and put the sword in the back sheathe. I figure it's best to fight with magic versus the sword.

"Any moment now would be great, princess. I'd like to have you defeated by nightfall." Zyla gently pushes her black magic forward, filling the grassy arena with wispy smoke.

"It's Vivalda, not 'princess'. And what's with this hostility of yours? Why does my presence anger you so much?" Zyla pushes her hands forward, causing large waves of dark magic to charge at me. She lifts up the magic into the sky, making it form into a curved wall that slams over me from above.

I quickly raise my hands up and catch the heavy weight of her magic. Once her power collides with my hand, the black smoke is coated in blue electric energy. As I use all my upper body strength to push against her powerful fumes. Her power is so dark and suffocating that I almost feel overwhelmed and terrified to be in its presence. I knew what I was getting into when I challenged her, but her magic is far more powerful than I thought it'd be.

I peer over and look through the smoky wall and see Zyla walk through the wall, smiling menacingly, baring her four sharp canines. Using her magic gives her a toxic rush that satisfies her hunger for destruction and chaos. She's so strong that I feel the ground rumble below my feet. At any moment, I think the ground could split in half.

Then I have an idea.

I pull my arms down and slam her poisonous fumes into the ground, causing a large explosion and the land below our feet to crack and break apart. The blast distracts Zyla which makes her magic retract and disappear.

I back away and watch the cracks grow wider. I balance lightly on my toes to avoid falling into the deep craters. More loud cracking comes from behind and I turn around to see even more massive cracks forming, creating deep craters.

I'm left standing on a flat platform of land and when I look over the ledge, I'm instantly terrified of falling. Looking down into the cracks is like looking into a pitch black abyss that never ends. This has made the fight a bit more interesting and has given a decent challenge.

I look in the distance and see Silva slightly bent over in pain, agitated.

"I thought we agreed to NOT draw attention to ourselves! Was that necessary, Vivalda?!" Silva's voice echoes across the grassy plains.

"Sorry!" I shout back and I see a smirk form on her face.

I reach back for the sword and before I have it firmly in my grasp, I'm pushed backwards on the floor by a strong force that causes me to drop the sword and the armor is immediately retracted. Before I can completely roll off the edge of the platform, I instinctively dig my nails in the dirt ground and quickly pull myself back up onto the land.

I lean over on my knees with my heart thumping rapidly from fear. Zyla stomps up to me and picks the necklace up off the ground. I quickly realize that now, it's no longer gold and has turned silver.

Did her magic cause it to change?

I stand up slowly and with caution, keeping my eye on Zyla as she taunts me with the necklace, twirling it around and examining it.

"All that power is in this puny little thing? I'll never understand why magic clings to such pathetic life forms." Her bright violet eyes look at me angrily. My heart beats quickly, causing my chest to physically hurt. The menacing look in her eye shakes me to my core. I'm scared to speak because I'm worried she'll throw the necklace into the land craters if she gets mad enough.

I bow my head down and take a breath. When I do, time slows down and I look up to see Zyla standing frozen in time with an intimidating look of anger on her face. I look at the sword pendant that continues to swing back and forth in her hand.

I slowly stand up and I look at Zyla for a spare moment. There's something about her eyes that catch my attention. Her voice and appearance screams anguish, but her eyes whisper a soft pain, trying not to show itself.

"What are you hiding?" I ask out loud. My fear quickly washes away when I come to the conclusion that Zyla is not a threat. I look over at the silver necklace and think about grabbing it, but I choose not to. Time slowly speeds up and returns to normal and once Zyla sees me standing in front of her, she jolts back, confused.

"Where does that sadness of yours stem from?" I ask gently, trying to start a calm conversation. She looks at me disgustedly and her brows arch down.

She grits her teeth and her dark smoke begins to slowly gather at my feet. "Your kind once poisoned my home and now I'm forced to clean up your messes." She takes a step forward, trying to intimidate me, but I keep my feet planted firmly on the ground.

"We've just met. What do I have to do with your burdens when I've done nothing to you? Why am I to blame for the mistakes of others?" I continue to speak calmly and Zyla's eyes widen and her grip on the silver necklace loosens.

Zyla shakes her head and she talks quieter. "You have no idea what they did." Her magic intensifies and swirls around me rapidly and purple glowing veins scatter across her body. I look over at the others. Phoenix and Aerowen stand by, ready to attack and defend. But Silva holds out her hand, stopping them from moving forward and she listens patiently to our conversation.

"Then tell me. I've listened to a dragon, I can listen to you too." I look up as her smoke continues to reach over me like a terrifying hand of death. A purple light flickers within the black smoke, zipping around like a small lightning bolt. It looks so familiar and it finally hits me.

"This cold hearted rage of yours is nothing but a mask, isn't it? Just like the mask that casts over the Lion's Eye that scares humans enough to keep them out." Zyla's eyes widen in shock and the smoke above me begins to slowly pull away. "You helped Silva and I when we were caught by a couple of Aerolights in the Lion's Eye, didn't you?"

She glares over at Silva who has a proud smile on her face.

"So what if I did? I was bored. That's all there was to it." I can see her mask starting to fall but she does everything she can to keep it up.

"I don't think you're truly this cold hearted. You just want to be feared so you'll be left alone. Is that it?" My question catches her off guard. Her magic suddenly dissipates and her prominent veins seep back into her skin.

She looks at the silver necklace that remains dangling in her black stained hands and I can see tears glisten in her eyes. Her gaze quickly softens as if she's had a change of heart. She slowly walks up to me, shaking her head, refusing to answer my question.

"Your mind isn't completely connected to your magic, hence why your armor and weapon disappears when the sword is no longer in your possession. If you stay connected to that emotional bond, your magic will forever stay with you. When your mind is weak, so is Vessoria." Her tone changes drastically and she now speaks to me calmly while giving me helpful advice.

"Vessoria is not the sword itself, but the magic within it. Just because you lose the sword, doesn't mean you lose Vessoria." She hands the necklace to me, dropping it in my hand. I release a sigh of relief once the pendant is in my possession again.

"I guess that's the lesson I needed to learn from you, huh? Thank you." Zyla backs up and I can see a very faint smile form on her face.

"Let's continue." She says calmly in a deep voice and I nod, determined to have a good sparring fight.

I hold the silver chain in my hand and summon Vessoria. Once I transform back into the armor, Zyla observes, full of content. I can't decipher if the positive change in her demeanor is a good or a bad thing, but regardless, I'm ready to push forward. Zyla's advice has given me a boost of encouragement that I never thought

I'd hear from a dark enchantress with such terrifying magic. Maybe I'm right. Maybe there's more hidden in that stone heart of hers and one day, I'll know her story.

I briefly look over at the others and each of them smile proudly, especially Silva.

"Don't lose it again, I might not be so nice next time." Zyla says with a smirk on her face before standing in a battle ready position. She holds her left hand forward with her right arm pulled back. Her hands and eyes glow purple and her smoke surges around her.

I put the sword away and watch Zyla thrust her right hand forward, aligning with her left and she shoots out violet purple streams of powerful magic. I react quickly and follow her lead. I push out both of my hands and watch as both magic forces clash, causing the intertwining torrents to spark and rumble like two large powerful bolts of lightning smashing against each other.

The collision of both of our magic forces causes the ground beneath us to shift below me which gives me an idea.

As much as I want to cause as little destruction as possible, I'm also itching to cause a tiny bit of mayhem.

With one hand, I strike the platform that's next to her and I forcefully pull it back to slam it into the one Zyla stands on. She stumbles back and her magic shoots into the treetops, crashing loudly into Silva's shield.

Before I can take a step forward, something slams into my side, almost knocking me over. I look to the far side of the valley and see Silva's hands ignited with raging power. She looks annoyed but in a humorous way.

"Hey! What was that for?!" I shout at her and she laughs.

"I asked you both to keep this fight as clean as possible! Look at the mess I have to clean now!" Her voice echoes through the deep cracks in the ground.

"Oh, now you know how I feel!" Zyla retaliates and suddenly, the ground below me begins to move. Silva uses her powers to mend the cracks and put the ground back together like a giant puzzle. I tighten my core to keep balance as the ground moves rapidly, slamming into neighboring platforms. Once Silva binds the crack and the ground is back to normal, she stares at me once more with her arms crossed.

"Must you always intervene, Silva? Right when things were getting interesting." Zyla gracefully glides towards Silva while I remain standing in the center of the field.

Silva laughs. "Had I not stepped in, you both would have destroyed the entire forest for all I know. It is more than possible to fight fairly without causing such wreckage." Silva speaks to Zyla like a parent and Zyla doesn't argue back for once. While the Serafaes chat for a moment, I feel a stream of magic glide down my arm and a bright ball of energy forms in my hand.

Before Silva turns to face me, I gently throw the ball at Silva's shoulder and it doesn't make her move an inch. The other Serafaes look at me, holding in their laughter and Silva slowly turns her head to me, glaring at me intensely.

"Oops. It slipped," I say sarcastically while the others gather around.

Phoenix snorts loudly, causing a large puff of smoke to protrude from her nostrils but she quickly gains her composure when Silva glares at her.

"You think that's funny, don't you?" Silva tries to ask me in an intimidating manner, but I can tell she's also holding back laughter. From the side, Zyla quickly tilts her head at Silva, telling me to do it again.

"I mean...it made the dragon nearly choke on her own fire. So yes, I find myself to be hilarious." I twirl around like a child to form another ball to throw at her, but once I turn around, I see a large ball of green magic headed right for me.

Oh crap.

Before I can react, her magic smashes into me and it makes me flop backwards on my back like a limp fish. Thankfully the blast doesn't hurt and I lean up on my shoulders to scold Silva.

"That wasn't fair! I wasn't looking!" Everyone laughs besides Zyla. Hearing them laugh fills my heart with joy.

"Neither was I. I guess we're even." She smiles as I stand up and I feel nothing but an intense buzz of excitement flutter about in my body.

Phoenix walks out into the field. "Why don't you and I spar for a bit, Vivalda? I'd say our first round didn't count. And I promise this time, I won't scare you and make you tumble off another cliff."

I nod my head excitedly. "Why not? And I promise I won't freeze this time." Phoenix spreads her wings and flies up into the air, nearly knocking me off my feet from the strong wind current. She soars below the base of the tall tree trunks and she conjures a raging red fiery storm around us that doesn't burn or cause harm. Red flames and golden sparks fall to the ground as she conjures a red ball of fire in between both of her hands. From the ground, I can hear the ball crackle and snap over the sound of her fire roaring like a pride of lions.

I randomly think back to the time Phoenix and I shared on Calypso's ship when I carried her fire in my hands. Both magic forces joined but never mixed.

What if I could use her power against her?

Phoenix pushes her hands forward, creating a large spiraling tunnel barreling down at me. The weight of her wings helps push the blaze towards me and by the time the fuming tunnel is within arm's reach, I seize her power with my bare hands. The vortex of magic swells up in between my palms as I pull in her magic towards my chest. Her flames jump and bump around, ricocheting off my palms excitedly, trying to escape but I manage to gather the ball of flames like a fiery snowball. The ball snaps and crackles loudly but doesn't burn my skin. The scarlet red flare spins around in a circular motion while locked in my grasp and I watch blue magic seep out from my palms and fingertips and into the fiery globe, dancing with the red embers.

Once the both intertwining magic is under my control and is contained, I use all of my strength to throw the sizzling sphere into the sky, harmlessly striking Phoenix in the chest. Once her magic leaves my possession, a heavy weight is lifted from my core. The collision causes a loud explosion and beautiful red and blue sparks scatter across the sky and fall onto the ground. Phoenix lands heavily on the ground, nearly breaking it apart and she looks at me with her widened glowing eyes.

"Who taught you to do that?!" Silva shouts from the side, amused and surprised. Phoenix smiles proudly, knowing my answer.

"Phoenix and I had some bonding time back on the ship. Let's just say that was the first thing I wanted to try when I held our magic together the first time." I play with the blue mist that coats my hands and when I curl my fingers inwards, the magic disappears. Phoenix walks up to me with a red flame dancing between her horns, indicating she must be happy.

"You're doing very well. Slowing down has really helped you unlock the impossible." She rests her bumpy hand on my shoulder and her sharp claws clank against the metal pauldron. The other Serafaes join us in the center of the field.

"Why don't you and I have a go Silva? I think it'd be fun to spar against your sparkly wiggly woos." I say humorously, trying to persuade her.

"As much as I'd love to, I think you've used your powers long enough for the evening. I don't want you to overdo it and be tired in the morning." Silva's long wavy white hair and white dress flows gracefully in the air.

"Is that truly the case? Or are you afraid I'll knock you on your bum like I did Zyla?" I taunt the enchantress who stands behind the crowd. Silva giggles with her mouth closed.

"I swear I won't go easy next time." Zyla's voice hauntingly echoes in the air.

"Oh my goodness, my first grudge?"

"Oh yes, she won't let go of that. Try not to rub it in too deep. I don't want her going off the rails." Silva whispers after hearing my thoughts.

I pull the sword from its sheath and the transformation occurs quickly, leaving the silver necklace dangling from my hand.

"Do you know what those marks on my face were and why the necklace changed color?" I ask Silva while clasping the necklace around my neck.

"As we grow, the power and magic that resides within us grows as well. Vessoria has evolved to fit your physique. Aside from the fact that gold is not your color, your power and armor has officially bonded to you." I twiddle the silver sword pendant in my hand and I realize it matches my blue overcoat and its silver detailing.

"It may sound strange to make this comparison but there's a flower that grows in the Lion's Eye. It's called Eegladdite. When there's a storm of any kind, its petals wilt and fall. But once the storm is over, the petals regenerate and regrow, changing shapes and colors. A brand new flower bloomed after every storm. Maybe I'll show you a valley of them one day and you'll see what my storms can do. How about that?" Silva's gaze is soft and warm and I'm intrigued by these flowers she talks about. Hearing her talk about the Serafaes and their world leaves my imagination wandering wild as if I'm a child again. I think there's so much more out there I'm unaware of and I'm eager to learn more.

"I'd love that." Aerowen steps closer to me and I can feel her cold frost.

"How do you feel, Vivalda?" Aerowen asks softly. Her voice is mellow and delicate.

I can't find the words to use and instead, I find myself smiling.

"Since being away from home and everything happening the way it did, I felt alone and scared. But after getting to know all of you, I feel less...alone. Thank you all for helping me through this, I just hope it'll be enough in the end."

All of the spirits smile, including Zyla.

The sun begins to set and the sky turns pink and orange. After unraveling the trees, we forge into the forest to find a secured place to camp for the night. Vivalda and Phoenix wander to their own spot in the forest while remaining in the same proximity as the rest of us. Their voices echo slightly and we can hear them laughing. Phoenix lights a fire to keep Vivalda warm throughout the night and Zyla walks over to me.

"Thank you for helping her today. I didn't think you had it in you. I'm proud of you for that. You've come a long way." I look up and I see her brown lips curl into a small smile.

"Do you think she's ready?" She continues to observe the human and dragon as they enjoy each other's company, joking around and playing with their magic.

"I do. But it doesn't matter what I think. It's all up to her. I can mentor her for decades and in the end, it's up to her if she's ready to fight. No one can force her into this, all we can hope is she'll continue to stand with us." Zyla bends down to kneel next to me and her dark smoke drops down with her. Due to the atmosphere getting dark, the yellow markings on her face glow brightly.

"I can tell she clinged to you very quickly." There's a sad tone in her voice and when I look at her eyes, I can see them begin to fill with tears, but she keeps a straight face.

"She did and I'm grateful for that because now, we're closer than we have been in a long time." I cast a glowing green flame in front of us that illuminates the forest.

"We must get as much rest as possible. Our journey continues early in the morning." Zyla and Aerowen agree and go their own ways. I hear ice cracking loudly and watch Aerowen form an icy cave on the grassy ground. She rests inside of the cave and quickly falls asleep. Zyla finds a large tree to lay next to and her smokey magic covers her like a blanket.

Before taking my time to rest, I look up at the sky and all I see is the bright shining moon with not a single star in sight.

Vivalda

I sit with Phoenix while the others sleep. Well, except for Silva. Instead of sleeping, she sits tall and goes into some kind of meditative state.

I look over and see her sitting in front of her glowing green fire. She sits on her knees with her hands resting on her lap. Her eyes are closed and green sparkly dust drifts off her left ears. A green aura coats her body like a blanket and her magic pulsates to the rhythm of her heartbeat.

"What's on your mind, child?" Phoenix asks while she sits next to me with her large wing wrapping behind me. I can hear the lava under her skin move and bubble and her fire keeps me warm from the cold breeze. I look into the distance and see Zyla laying down by a large tree, surrounded by black smoke that's illuminated by Silva's fire.

"Do you know what happened between Zyla and humans?" Phoenix scrunches her brows and speaks quietly so the enchantress doesn't hear.

"I do. I was there when everything happened, but it's not my story to tell. All I can say is that she didn't ALWAYS hate humans. She doesn't have an easy past, so we try to be as patient with her as possible, even when we feel like slamming her thick skull into a tree." She laughs softly.

"I didn't think you two would share something in common when it comes to hatred for humans. Whatever they've done, I'm sorry." I look into the fire and hold my hands out to feel its warmth. The base of the fire is deep red and it fades into a vibrant orange and yellow color. The bottom of the flame doesn't burn the earth below it, keeping it safe.

"It's not your fault. She and I would rather stay hidden in our homes where humans can't reach us, but regardless of our pasts, I'm still lucky to have met you and that crazy pirate." I laugh at the thought of Calypso. I miss her humor and the silly things she'd do to mess with Phoenix and Silva.

"You two are proof that not all humans have bad intentions when it comes to the unknown. We just have no choice but to be cautious of all." I nod my head and agree. I don't blame them for having to keep their walls guarded due the past they've gone through. I think I'd be the same way if I was a Serafae.

"When my family saw Silva for the first time, they were so scared at first. But after taking the smallest moment to get to know her, they thought she was the most incredible thing they've ever seen. I've never seen their eyes light up before. My sister Riverlynn couldn't stop staring and she was all over Silva with endless questions. I miss her so much. I can't wait to go home." Phoenix slowly looks at me and her brows perk up.

I zone out and stare into the fire while thinking about everyone I miss back home. I miss the sound of my sister's voice and I miss when she'd braid my hair while sitting on the castle balcony. I miss Kyson's comforting company. And most of all, I miss my mother's presence more than anything. The look on Phoenix's face tells me she feels my sorrow.

"Once this is all over, you can return the power to its creator. Everyone will understand if that'll be what you choose to do. But for now, try not to think about it too much. You should try to rest. I heard Silva say she wants us to start traveling as soon as the sun comes up." Pheonix waves her hand over the fire in front of us and uses her power to widen the blaze.

"I really appreciate you Phoenix. You're easy to talk to. I've quickly discovered it's easier talking to a majestic beast versus a simple human. Thank you." Phoenix's eyes begin to water and despite her body heat, the liquid doesn't evaporate.

"Of course, it's the least I could do." She smiles and I rest on a soft, thick patch of grass while Phoenix remains sitting by my side and she waits patiently for me to fall asleep.

"Wake up."

A strange voice wakes me up and I quickly open my eyes. I jolt up from the ground, looking around, waiting for my eyes to adjust.

"Come with me."

A strange whisper floats around me, sending a terrifying chill down my spine. I look over and see Phoenix sleeping peacefully with her wing wrapped over her, covering her like a big scaly blanket. The sky is still pitch black, indicating I've only slept a short amount of time. The fire in front of us is still lit and the other spirits remain sleeping in the near distance. I slowly get up, making sure not to wake them and I try to listen for the voice to speak again.

"I'm right here."

I hold my blue overcoat closed as the bone chilling wind blows in my face, shaking the leaves and blowing them off the branches. The strange voice dances and flows between my ears and I realize it sounds very familiar. As I inch closer to the trees, the voice grows louder and I constantly look back at the others to make sure they don't wake up. I wouldn't want to disturb them.

A bright white speck of light catches my eye from deep within the forest and the small light bounces and floats in the air.

"Follow me."

I cautiously walk closer and the white glowing ball illuminates my path. For a moment, I hesitate to follow it but at the same time, I'm determined to figure out what the voice is and why it's calling for me. For all I know, it could be Zyla getting back at me for defeating her in our small duel.

"The truth is being hidden from you...Vivalda."

My ears perk up, my heart throbs in my chest and my eyes bulge from my skull. Now I know it has to be Zyla trying to be secretive behind Silva's back.

411

I follow the glowing orb vigilantly, making sure it stays in my line of sight. I jog lightly, dodging bushes, low tree branches and jumping over rocks as the light moves quickly in front of me.

"I know you're trying to be all stealthy Zyla, but I think this is far enough, wouldn't you agree?" I say quietly to avoid being heard by Silva's sensitive hearing.

The orb continues to move quickly and my legs begin to buckle under me due to exhaustion from running. I start to slow down and as I do; the glowing ball disappears and the atmosphere goes pitch black. Leaving me terrified since I don't know how far into the forest I've ran and when I turn around, I can't see either fires from our camping spot.

The only thing I can do that will help is summon the armor and hope the glow from metal will be enough. I gently grab the sword pendant and instead of pulling it from my neck, I unclasp it and hold it in my right hand. I can feel myself shaking due to my fear of the dark.

The sword pendant quietly transforms into the heavy weapon and the armor slowly forms to secure my body. The blue glow from my armor isn't enough to see in the dark so I ignite the sword on fire, revealing a bright blue electric flame that pours down the blade. Once I'm ready, I search for the glowing orb and listen for the voice, hoping it'll speak again.

I use the sword as a torch and hold it up to inspect where I was led. I take a step forward and feel the ground crunch below my feet. I look down and see the terrain is colorless and burnt to a crisp. I hold the sword up, look around and realize the trees around me are lifeless and burnt but if I look back in the far distance, the grass is lively and normal. The sight makes my skin crawl and my heart race.

"I've seen this before." I say to myself quietly and instantly feel sick to my stomach.

It looks just like the dead land I saw before going to Palavon before it mysteriously disappeared. I'm confused why I'm seeing this circle of death once more.

I recall back when I first met Zyla, her power kills whatever she touched, but...why would she bring me out here away from the others? Was she following me the entire time before this journey started?

"Why did you bring me out here?" I ask as I circle around the burnt circle, stretching my arm out, trying to find the orb. I hear a deep menacing chuckle echo from beyond the dead trees.

"The Serafaes weren't kidding when they said Vessoria bestowed itself on a random human. I'm surprised." A female voice taunts me from outside the burnt patch.

I instantly realize this is not Zyla's voice because we already established what she says.

"Who are you? And how do you know my name?" My voice shakes and a part of me wants to race back to the others or scream for them to let them know where I am. But the suffocating fear is too much to beat around.

I can hear light footsteps strolling along the charred ground but the rebounding echo throws me off and I can't tell exactly where the noise and voice comes from.

The voice continues to chuckle and it sends chills down my spine. "I knew your name before you were born. You could have known me but time was a thief...and a killer." I freeze where I stand. I try to take a step forward, but it feels like my feet are bound to the ground by an invisible force. No matter what, I keep the sword held tightly in my hand.

"What are you talking about?" I watch as a tall, dark and terrifying figure emerges from the shadows. Her eyes are pitch black and they glisten like glass from the light of the sword. I lift the fiery blade higher and see the outline of four black horns that sprout from her head. Two thin horns rest closer to the center of her head and spiral upwards while two massive horns curve out from the sides of her head.

She has long black hair that swirls and loops over and around the horns messily, like many small curtains that drape over metal rods. Her sharp ears poke through the rest of her hair that remains resting over her chest and they twitch slowly back and forth.

Her skin is pale white and she has black patches that cover her chest in an unusual decorative manner. The rest of her body is coated in pitch black magic that shifts and turns in such an eerie way, it's unsettling. Her lips are also black and her eyelids have smokey black and smudges on them. She's terrifying to look at and I don't know what to do.

She notices I'm staring at her because she ominously tilts her head to the side glaring at me with the most horrifying eyes I've ever seen. Looking into them feels like I could fall through a never-ending void.

"Who are you?" I say sternly, keeping a firm gaze on her.

The magic that cascades throughout her body is the most terrifying thing I've ever felt. It's far more terrifying than Zyla's. I'm sure that in the snap of a finger, this new entity could pulverize me in the blink of an eye.

The sensation I feel is overwhelming and suffocating. I can feel my heart racing rapidly to the point where I'm on the brink of fainting but I remain standing, trying not to physically show the crippling fear that tears me apart on the inside.

"Your beloved friendly giant didn't tell you about little ol' me?" She covers her mouth sarcastically and when she moves her hand down, she bares her sharp teeth that glisten in the light.

Her hands and arms are white with her fingertips being black like Zyla's and her black nails are incredibly sharp. She slowly walks towards me with dark magic surrounding her.

"Why am I not surprised? I always knew she'd keep secrets from the daughter of the almighty Aladora, next in line to the throne." She taunts sarcastically. "Well...I assume that's changed after you betrayed your people and whatever's left of your precious little family." Hearing my mother's name fills me with immediate rage. She has no right to talk about my family or my friends. I impulsively swing my sword across her chest but she disappears into a cloud of smoke and drifts away from me. I hear her cackle quiet to herself and I turn around to see her standing in front of a large dead tree, tisking while waving her pointer finger side to side.

"Now, now, that's no way for royalty to treat their people. I'm just here to have a simple conversation." She continues to taunt me even more and I begin to grow impatient and irritated.

"Cut the crap. I'm in no mood for mind games. Tell me who you are or I'll call for MY people and it'll be five against one." My threat doesn't faze the dark figure while she continues to snarl and laugh while walking around me.

"Granted, I've changed drastically since the last time I saw you, but I at least thought you'd know something about me. The beanstalk really did a number on that precious little mind of yours...didn't she?" I try to wrap my head around what she's saying but I'm confused. "Pathetic. If it weren't for her magic, you wouldn't have to question who I am. But allow me to reintroduce myself...sister. It's been what? Give or take five thousand moons?" A scary grin forms on her face and my heart drops to my stomach.

The blue flame extinguishes and the only light left is a bright red light illuminating from the woman's body. The intense shock I feel causes me to nearly drop the sword but I quickly remember what Zyla said about keeping it in hand and mind.

"I don't have the patience to be toyed around. I don't have a second sister and I never did. What do you mean Silva did a number on my mind?" I say slowly, trying to breathe steadily through my words, staring at the ground, disconnecting myself from time itself.

"Mmm, I won't be the one to explain that. Mother nature can explain herself. I'd prefer to have a little fun. I only found you because you have something I want." I look up with tears swelling in my eyes and my lips quivering. "I know the...spirits gave you something. If you give it to me, I'll give you all the answers you seek. And unlike your...friends, I won't lie. What do you say?" I stare at her for a brief moment before reluctantly shaking my head. I assume she's referring to the crystals the Serafaes gave me. I have to do my best to play smart to avoid getting into more trouble than I already am.

"Whatever you seek, I don't have. I have no reason to trust you and I think it'd be best if you leave." I stare at her coldly, standing my ground with the sword raised.

"Oh...don't try to play the role of some hero. I know you have the crystal; I can feel it." The woman laughs loudly and her echo rebounds around and through the trees, making many of them disintegrate without being touched.

"I'd leave before my friends get here. You wouldn't stand a chance against them." My intimidation tactic only humors the woman even more.

"And they will fail to save you just as you failed to save your own mother." She scowls before rapidly approaching me, standing just a couple of feet away. A red beam of light glows in her black eyes.

"You have no idea what you're talking about. You know nothing about my mother and I." My face tenses up as I speak to her and my rage summons Vessoria's magic and I can feel it surging through my veins. I'm so close to jabbing the sword through her chest but knowing the odds, she'd vanish and teleport again.

"Silva, where are you?"

I try calling for her in hopes she can hear me from how far away I am. The woman scoffs while leaning over me. "I'm sure that castle servant of yours knew so much more about your mother than you." Once again, my heart sinks to my stomach and I feel like vomiting profusely.

She can't possibly know anything about my family.

"What's her name again? Lyla?" She smirks and runs her sharp nails over her cheek in a snide manner.

"What do you know about her?" I ask while slowly lifting the sword up and out to the side.

"Eh, more than you. I always thought it was a terrible name for a god hiding amongst mortals."

A GOD?!

My eyes widen and I feel my heart skip a beat. I shake my head vigorously, not falling for whatever manipulation tactic she's trying on me. "Silva isn't a god." The woman waves her long nails as if she's ready to claw out my heart. This is nothing but a game to her and I'm tired of playing.

"Oh please. You've seen the immense strength of her power and you've never noticed her gray skin cracking when she's angry?"

Despite not being able to think clearly, I know exactly what she's talking about. I remember seeing the skin round Silva's eyes cracking when she was upset.

"Maybe I've spoiled too much. I'm sorry you had to find out like this." She looks at me and smiles maliciously while twiddling her fingers. Her twisted humor angers me and a switch in my heart flips.

Blue magic surges powerfully through my body and into the sword and while releasing a loud, painful scream, I charge at the woman and aim for her throat with the blade. Instead of colliding into her body, I dive right through her, tumbling to the ground behind her.

Why can't I attack her?

My heart beats out of my chest and I begin to hyperventilate. "Oh...I forgot to mention...you can't touch me because I'm simply not here. But if I was, I'd tear the crystal from your soul and end you right where you stand."

My mind races with even more confusion than before. "Silva's not a god. You're not my sister. You speak nothing but lies. What do you want with the stone?" I slowly stand up, keeping the sword firm in my grip.

"Telling people the blood curling truth is what I live for." She waves her hands towards me as deep red magic bleeds from her skin. I shield my eyes as the red smoke coats my body. Upon opening my eyes, I see we're now standing roughly ten feet from where Silva, Zyla and Aerowen sleep. They haven't moved an inch and they're left unbothered.

She teleported us.

"You've given these 'friends' all of your trust, only for them to be slowly breaking it behind your back without you knowing. Who knew a god would hide behind a wilting face? It's disgraceful." The woman circles around Silva, walking over the green fire that remains lit. Something about her simply walking tells me something is off. When she walks over the fire, the flames don't move.

"These pathetic riddles of yours are starting to really piss me off." I keep my eyes on the woman as she slowly circles around the Serafaes, tauntingly observing each of them. She walks over to Silva and stands behind her.

"I'm going to show you what you missed that night." The dark figure raises black smoke from the ground and makes it circle around me like a tunnel. When the black vortex drops, I see I'm back inside the castle walls.

I'm home? But how?

I look around and don't see the scary woman anywhere. I start running down the hall when I hear my own voice shout loudly from behind me.

"Lyla! Where are you?" I frantically turn around and see a past version of myself running down the hall. I try to speak but no noise leaves my throat. I watch as the past me runs directly through my current body as if I'm a ghost. I wrap my hands around my body and slowly begin to cry, terrified of what I'm witnessing.

Her magic has physically taken me back to a time I can't bear to relive. This is all too real.

The woman suddenly appears in front of me, watching the other me run down the hall. "Well...where is she?" She asks in a serious and dark tone.

"I know where she was." I begin to sob and panic. The vile entity shakes her head before using her magic to teleport us into another area of the castle. We're now placed in a narrow hallway I'm not familiar with and I see Lyla running away.

Lyla?

"Where are you?!" I hear my other voice echo from far away.

Lyla stares at me sorrowfully, but I know it's not the current ME she's looking at. It looks like she wants to find me, but instead she runs to the end of the hall and out a door that leads to the garden.

"Where did she go?" I begin to walk towards the door but the view in front of me grows foggy.

"I'll show you." The entity's voice echoes around me and she teleports us again. Now, we're in a forest. It's pitch black outside and I can barely see anything. I take the sword out and ignite it in blue electric light once more.

When I look around, I see nothing but trees surrounding me. As I walk forward, I quickly realize I'm standing in an open field and I immediately recognize I'm in Alsfield. Once I know where I am, I know where Silva's stone statue is and I run to find her.

"Silva!" I shout as I run towards her. Once I'm close, I hear the sound of footsteps rapidly approaching from the opposite side of the forest.

I stop dead in my tracks at the sight of Lyla running full speed towards the statue. She walks around to the front of Silva, the look of worry and panic melts across her face and she breathes heavily as if trying to make a critical decision.

"What are you doing?" I croak softly as I begin to cry.

Lyla looks back at the castle before placing her hand on Silva's. I step closer and watch as magic transcends out of each of their hands.

White magic particles pours out of Silva's stone hand and circles around them both. Lyla's physical body begins to turn translucent like a ghost.

Her body is merging with Silva's.

Lyla's body is absorbed into the statue and before I know it, Silva breathes heavily and comes to life.

I cover my mouth with my hand and scream as loud as I can.

"No!" Silva shifts her attention to the distance, her green leafy ears twitch rapidly and once she hears something, she runs off and disappears behind a green flash of light.

The entity's voice echoes hauntingly around me like a ghost.

"Your mother suffered a great deal of pain that night and Lyla- I mean...Silva did nothing to help her." I tuck my chin down while tensing every muscle in my body, trying to shake away and block out her voice while holding the sword shakily in front of me. My rage begins to bottle up to the point where I'm ready to blow. "I mean...think about it! What could have possibly stopped a mighty god from saving one simple human?" I feel the dark force standing behind me. I grit my teeth and rapidly turn around, swinging the blade around and pointing it at her. Her visionary magic drops and we're back in the forest where the Serafaes sleep.

"ENOUGH! You're lying!" I try to catch my breath and stop myself from crying. "You're just telling me things to make me mad!" I keep the blade pointed at her chest and her eyes glow red like a demon.

"If Silva was there, she would have done ANYTHING to protect her!" I stand my ground and the figure cracks a smile.

"And she didn't." My heart skips a beat and my arms feel weak. "My magic is so dark, it cannot lie. Only light magic has the ability to lie in order to 'protect' the innocent. It's a terrible philosophy if you ask me." She rolls her eyes. I want to take her life where she stands but I know there's nothing I can do.

I peer behind her and look at Silva who remains unbothered. Not even her ears flicker or twitch. "You are no sister of mine. My mother would have told us." I say firmly and the woman scoffs.

"Humans are so stupid. No mother would ever tell the world she birthed a demon." Hearing her call herself a 'demon' chills me to my core. If she's truly my sister, surely she wasn't naturally born like this.

"I am Melantha, first born of Aladora. No one in all of Vassuren knows I ever existed because she commanded that overgrown lima bean to wipe the memory of every human in the land. And she did so because she wanted to keep you all 'safe'. I guess that didn't last very long." I can feel time running out and all I want is for the Serafaes to wake up and help get rid of Melantha. If I can't touch her, surely the others can do something.

"What do you want with the crystal?" I ask sternly while carefully circling around Melantha to stand in between her and Silva.

"It was stolen from me many years ago. I simply want it back so I can feel whole again." I look around at the others, making sure they remain safe from any surprise attacks Melantha may have up her sleeve.

"Silva, if you could wake up now, I'd greatly appreciate it." I put my hand on her shoulder and my hand glides right though her body as if I'm a ghost. I begin to panic because it feels like I'm trapped in some kind of cage where I'm not real.

Melantha laughs. "You can't do anything because you never woke up." She waves her hand over towards the direction where the fire burns in front of Phoenix and that's when I see myself still sleeping next to her.

Seeing myself sleep while spiritually awake makes me feel sick. The internal panic sets in more and more and I realize how powerful Melantha truly is while not seeing the full extent of her magic.

"What if you don't obtain the jewel you desire so terribly?" My voice shakes and it's hard to speak properly. I keep my gaze on Melantha and watch as she walks over to Zyla who remains sleeping next to a tree, curled over on her side, resting her head on her arm. She looks peaceful when she sleeps.

Melantha bends down next to the enchantress and holds out her long sharp claw, inching closely to Zyla's chest. Her dagger-like nail grows and thick black ink begins to bleed down her finger.

"What are you doing?!" I rush forward, stopping her from moving closer and Melantha looks at me with beaming red eyes and the black veins around her eyes begin to spread down and across her face.

"Even though I am in the Sylphenic realm, make no mistake, I can take real life from here. I've done it before and it's why you're all here. If you object to giving me the jewel, I'll pierce your little friend here in the chest and I'll poison her with more Sylphenic magic than her body can handle. One more drop and she's as good as dead." The smallest part of her nail penetrates Zyla's skin, causing the enchantress to squirm and twitch around and I see thin black veins begin to spread on her chest like a gruesome sickness.

"NO! STOP! I'll give it to you!" She quickly moves her hand away as a drop of Sylphenic magic falls to the ground, burning it to a crisp. Zyla stops wincing and twitching around and I release a sigh of relief and then I remember something.

The Sylphenic Realm?

I begin to piece information together and I don't think there's any way I could be wrong. If Melantha speaks the "truth", then I know exactly what she is. I look down at the sword while Melantha begins to walk away from me. The blade glows blue and its power begins to pulsate rapidly and the designs on the armor glow even brighter.

I can feel Vessoria surging through my soul. Surely, if I'm not physically here, I shouldn't be able to feel the magic course through me. Maybe Vessoria is guiding me when there's nothing else to be guided by.

Before Melantha can walk away, out of arm's reach, I take the sword and glide the blade against her side, cutting her slightly.

She turns around and hisses at me while staring threateningly. The bright red glow in her eye catches my attention again and it looks like her sharp teeth grow longer. "How did you-" Before she can finish her question, I step closer to her, keeping my eyes locked on hers.

"Don't threaten my people...again." Melantha smiles, baring more rows of sharp teeth. The black veins around her eyes move under her skin like small worms.

"You're the Aerolight beacon...aren't you?" I ask quietly, trying to hide my blood curling fear. Melantha's smile disappears, she freezes up and grows more angry. My words irritate her so much that more poisonous black veins swell around her eyes and her horns turn sharply inwards, stretching out towards me. She pulls back from me and the blade and walks away, refusing to answer my question.

"Due to the...properties of the crystal, you'll have to bring it to me at Helsen's Peak. It's the furthest island, north of the main lands, across Rempengough's Tide and through the Echoing Rift. If I don't see you in two moons, all of your people will suffer more than they do now." She continues to walk towards the forest as black and red trails of smoke follow behind her and grow upwards, creating a giant wall.

She turns around and holds her arms up as dark red magic sparks in her hands.

"Maybe you'll have a chance to redeem yourself. I'd hate for you to be the cause of another death." She continues to taunt me, but I don't let it get to me.

"Oh, and just so you know. The dead land you stepped on is there in real time. But...it's not me who caused it." She smiles menacingly. "Oh, and on that note...ask your stone hearted friend where she was the night your mother died." She completely disappears behind the wall of smoke and I can still hear her voice echo around me.

"It's time to wake up." Two loud claps echo in the air and before I know it, I open my eyes and I'm back laying in front of the fire. I rapidly sit up and despite the freezing cold breeze, my dress is covered in sweat and I pant heavily as if I just went for a very long and tedious run. It feels like my heart can't keep up with me and my body feels nonfunctional.

I sit up, wiping my face with a dry section of my dress, trying to calm down and I accidentally wake up Phoenix. She uncovers herself from her wing and she leans over close to me, gently placing a hand on my back while making the fire turn red so no heat emits from it.

"What's wrong?" She asks softly, trying to help calm me down but I can't think straight or clearly so my words don't make much sense when I try to speak.

"I'm fine. I just had a um- bad dream. That's all." I look past the fire and into the pitch-black forest. I can feel myself begin to cry and I feel the ground rumble slightly. I look over and see Silva teleport herself over to where Phoenix and I are and she looks at me worriedly.

"Hey. What's going on? Was it the armor again?" Silva asks calmly, observing me, making sure I'm not physically hurt or distraught. After having that nightmare, it's hard to look at Silva without more tears filling my eyes.

"Whatever's going on, I promise I'm here-" Before she can finish her sentence, I instinctively lunge into her arms and hug her tightly.

I can tell I've startled her because it takes her a minute to wrap her arms around me.

Vivalda holds me tightly and begins to cry, which confuses me because I don't know what's wrong. I try to listen to her thoughts, but everything is silent. I don't know what has caused her to feel so distraught. I look at Phoenix and she shrugs her shoulders, indicating she's just as confused.

I take a deep breath and gently put my arms around Vivalda to hold her while she continues to cry in my chest. Without saying a word, I continue to take multiple deep breaths and I can feel Vivalda trying to calm down so she can do the same. I can feel her hands and legs shaking while she tries to relax.

"Release." I say calmly while taking a deep breath and she breathes with me, but that breath is suddenly cut short.

There's an immediate disturbance in the atmosphere and Vivalda slowly pulls away from me. I look down and see her eyes are bright blue. The sad look in her eye worries me and makes me begin to panic.

"What's going on? Please talk to us." I try to persuade her but she stands up, nearly stumbling backwards, holding her shaky arms around her stomach.

"I'm sorry. I'm just a bit overwhelmed. I had a bad dream and I can't let it go." She talks while walking around the red fire.

"If you need to talk about it, we're happy to listen." Phoenix adds while standing up, keeping her wings held out to the side.

"I don't umm- I don't think it's worth talking about. I promise it's fine. I think." Vivalda stares at the fire, confused and distraught.

"Silva!" Aerowen shouts from behind us, catching everyone's attention. All we can see is Aerowen's body glowing bright blue and she leans over the base of the tree Zyla lays next to.

Vivalda's eyes widen, and she immediately runs over to Aerowen and Zyla and we follow close behind.

Once we stand next to the others, we see Zyla curled in a ball on her side, holding her hands to her chest. Zyla's dark magic lifts from the ground, but it doesn't hurt us. Vivalda falls on her knees right next to Zyla and moves the enchantress' hands to the side to see what's bothering her.

I kneel next to them and we all gasp when we see a small black hole in her chest with black veins growing out of it.

"It wasn't a dream."

I slowly turn my head when I hear Vivalda's thought.

"Someone explain to me right now how Sylphenic magic got into my body before I rain hell on each of you!" Zyla groans and chokes on her words while trying to speak. I step forward and place my hands over her chest. Before I can use my magic, Zyla grabs one of them and almost sinks her claws into my firm skin.

"I don't know how, but she was here." Zyla looks at me, her eyes sunken and black. She's fighting off the Sylphenic magic with her own. Phoenix and the others are highly worried, but they don't know what to do in order to help.

"Vivalda, it's crucial you answer me right now. What did you see in your 'dream'?" My magic begins to freely pour over Zyla's body and begins to help her heal.

Vivalda swallows heavily and looks at the others, shaking.

"I- uh, I don't know. I didn't mean for this to happen." At this point, I'm starting to get overwhelmed. Zyla sits up off the grass and pushes my hand away.

"I'm so sorry, I didn't mean for this to happen. I didn't-" Vivalda begins to speak but Zyla quickly silences her.

"Shut it. All I must do is absorb the dark matter. It'll take a while, but I'll be fine." Once Zyla is on her feet, she leans against the tree, and I turn to Vivalda.

"This...I saw this. There was a terrifying woman, she had black claws, and she poisoned Zyla while telling me things that were impossible, and I didn't-" She looks up and turns her attention to the forest. The moon is still at its peak and the forest is pitch black. Without saying another word, Vivalda dashes off into the dark forest.

"Where are you going?!" I shout at her but she doesn't look back. I quickly follow here while the others stay back to help Zyla.

I continue to chase Vivalda into the forest, lighting up the trees and plants, so she can see where she's going.

"Vivalda, stop!" Vivalda ignores and keeps going. After a long time of running, Vivalda suddenly stops in front of me, and I nearly run into her.

I look around and notice the glowing stops roughly five feet in front of her. I look down and see a massive circle of dead trees and plants that have no ability to light because there's no life left in the circle to absorb my magic.

I stand frozen in place, speechless.

Vivalda

The sight of the dead land reminds me of the dead circle I saw back on Palavon, but it's very different at the same time. The dead land back on the Palavon road looked like it was poisoned. But the land here looks like the life of the plants were sucked out of it completely, not being able to be revived.

Everything I saw in that nightmare is unraveling as the moments pass and it's overwhelming me to the max.

"A dark entity in my nightmare spoke of you." I stand still, staring at the ground, refusing to turn to look at her. Silva steps up next to me, but I try to casually inch away.

"I'm sure it was just a bad dream, everything is-" She holds her hand out and I turn away.

"She brought me here and she spoke of something called the Sylphenic realm and when I asked if she was the Aerolight beacon, she poisoned Zyla and threatened that if I don't give her the crystal, she'd do something far worse." Tears begin to swell in my eyes and my blood begins to slowly boil at the same time.

"Vivalda, I-" Silva tries to stop me as I walk out into the dead part of the forest, analyzing the lifeless trees, bushes and grass.

"The worst of it is, that's not what's bothering me. Thank the gods Zyla is okay, but-" I look over at Silva and I can tell she refuses to step onto the dead part of the land.

"Yes, it's a relief she'll be alright." She says and I slowly turn to face her and look her in the eye.

"You're not the god I thank." I can feel Vessoria flowing through my veins, reacting to my anger that begins to boil.

"If you listen to whatever that voice told you, it'll ruin everything that we've worked for." She holds her hands up, still refusing to step forward towards me.

"If she was here Silva, Vivalda already knows. There's no point in hiding." Zyla grunts while being held up by Phoenix and Aerowen walks next to them. Silva sighs heavily while shaking her head. I take a step closer to Silva, keeping my guard up and she keeps her head lowered.

"Were you ever going to tell me? Surely a god knows better than to lie to those who look to them for guidance." Silva finally looks up at me and she looks distraught.

"Yes, I was going to tell you, but I prolonged it because I was scared. It's not everyday a god feels fear, but when we do...most of the time, something terrible comes from it." I can't tell if she says what she does because it's a mistake or it's nothing but an excuse. I begin to choke on my words and my lips begin to quiver from me trying to not cry.

"I don't know where to start. I knew Lyla my entire life and I now find out she was never...real."

"I know I've caused you pain by keeping all of this from you, but I had no choice. Your mother begged me to keep a promise that I'd explain everything once the Sylphenic magic is gone." I begin to pace back and forth, trying to bite my tongue and refrain from losing my temper.

"That doesn't make any sense. My mother would never keep such secrets from me!" Out of the corner of my eye, Zyla steps forward into the circle with her hands held over her chest where she was poisoned.

"She speaks the truth. Your mother thought wholeheartedly she could keep you out of the situation. But now, it's only caught up to you and has become far more serious than any of us could have thought. Silva and your mother were only trying to protect you." I slowly approach the enchantress while feeling more overwhelmed and growing impatient.

"You have no right to speak on matters that don't involve you. You didn't know my mother." Zyla's eyes widen and begin to glow, along with the markings on her face.

Zyla closes her eyes and golden tears slide down her face. Her hands curl into fists as if she's holding something back and refusing to speak. Silva steps up behind me and speaks gently.

"Zyla and I have known Aladora personally since she was around your age." I rub my eyes and cover my face with my hand, desperately wishing that this was just another never-ending nightmare.

"Everything...was a lie. Lyla, my older sister, my mother, that night. Everything was all hidden from me!" My cries and screams reverberate through the forest as I sob into my hands. With my eyes closed, I feel a hand rest on my shoulder.

"Vivalda..." Instinctively, I grab the sword pendant and immediately transform into the armor. I raise the blade up and over my head before slamming it down on Silva.

She effortlessly catches the blade between her hands and stares at me coldly.

I look at the blade that's held between my hands and I can feel my stone heart begin to crumble. I push Vivalda back across the floor, causing her feet to dig into the dirt. Seeing her threaten me with her weapon causes a fire to rage in my soul but I try to keep myself composed because I know where her rage stems from and she has a right to take her anger out on me. I look down and realize I've stepped into the dead circle of land which causes me to feel sick and my magic doesn't touch it.

The Serafaes quickly join my side, hoping to deescalate the situation but I hold my hand back and they back away.

"Vivalda, I understand your pain. You have no idea the pain we also had to bear and witness-" Before I can say another word, Vivalda slowly approaches me, with her blade pointed at me.

"You DON'T understand my pain! If anything, you've only added to it!" Before Vivalda has the chance to charge at me, I make vines grow out of the ground where the land isn't dead and they stretch out to wrap around Vivalda's legs, stopping her from moving forward.

"Why didn't you tell me in the beginning?!" The princess struggles to get out of my grasp while she continues to lash out.

"I made a promise to your mother. That's why." I continue to speak calmly, trying to help her make sense of everything. There's so much to explain and so much for her to understand.

While struggling against my vines, Vivalda looks up with her eyes glowing blue and her brows arched down. She pants heavily and raises her sword. The dark silver blade ignites and is coated in electric blue flames.

"Since when does a god bow to a queen?!" She twists around and slashes the vines with the blade, cutting them apart and making them dive back underground. My hands throb in pain but I don't pay attention to it.

I remain standing still as Vivalda slowly approaches me, dragging the tip of the sword on the wilted ground.

"Your mother wasn't my queen. She was my friend and my family. Same with you and Riverlynn. Family always came before magic-" I try to ease Vivalda's thoughts but she cuts me off.

"Oh that's rich coming from you! If my mother had this god forsaken power instead of me, it could have saved her!" She runs up, swinging the blade at me once more and I catch it with one hand.

I pull the blade down and look at Vivalda as she tries to pull the weapon out of my grip.

"Magic can't save everyone, Vivalda." Immediate rage fills her eyes and I watch as the vibrant blue marking grows down her eyes, almost like permanent tears and they glow brightly.

"I find that hard to believe." She says in a deep voice and she fixes the grip on her hilt. "What could have possibly stopped a GOD from saving one simple

HUMAN?! If you loved her so much, why didn't you do anything!" Vivalda uses incredible strength to pull the blade out of my grip, grazing the surface of my stone skin. I feel my skin under my eyes begin to slowly crack.

"Don't test me Vivalda." I feel the ground begin to shake and my magic surges powerfully throughout my body. The look on the angered princess' face tells me she's looking forward to a fight.

Aerowen steps up to me and rests her freezing cold hand on my shoulder. "Silva, don't. She doesn't understand." Aerowen's soft tone helps me relax. My fists slowly unclench and I speak calmly.

"I can feel your anger, Vivalda. But this isn't how we should handle it. Once you are ready, we will have a proper conversation." I gently lift Aerowen's hand off my shoulder and turn to walk away with the Serafaes.

"Vivalda, don't!" Phoenix roars loudly and before I can turn around, I'm struck in the back by Vivalda's blazing blue magic. My skin shatters like thick glass and the crack pieces itself back together and heals from the impact. The forest that surrounds the dead piece of land turns into colorful flashing utopia and the Serafaes quickly gather around me.

"Don't engage with her. You know how it'll end." Zyla says calmly as we continue to slowly walk away but I can still feel Vivalda's magic surging around us invisibly.

"You spoke truly about one thing. My mother's death wasn't my fault...it was yours!" Vivalda shouts from behind us and I immediately stop and slowly turn around to face her.

"I wouldn't do that...princess." I say harshly through my teeth, trying to refrain myself from getting more angry.

"Or what? You're going to turn your back on me like you did my mother?" Vivalda says coldly as she stands in a battle-ready position, with her sword held at her waist. The stone around my eyes begins to crack down towards my cheeks and my power ignites in my palms.

"Let this be your final lesson."

PHOENIX

Vivalda pulls her hand back and unleashes a heavy wave of electric magic that aims for Silva. The glowing beam crackles and roars as it soars and before it can touch her, I take off into the air and swoop down in front of Silva to block the blue blaze with my fire. I instantly vanquish Vivalda's attack and hold out my hand to absorb all of the flames back into my veins. I cautiously walk to her, keeping my hands held to my side and Silva stays behind, keeping her gaze on the princess.

"Viv, I know this is difficult but please don't do this. The past can't be rewritten but you can forge a new future and we can do it together." I rest my hands gently on her shoulders and she looks up at me with a stone-cold gaze. "This is a fight you don't want to pick and it's not one I want to witness." I try my best to persuade Vivalda to back down but I know deep down, she won't yield.

I suddenly notice there's a strange aura to her that I've never seen or felt since meeting her and it worries me terribly. I watch as the marks down her eyes shift from blue to pitch black and the same thing happens to her eyes. I slowly move my hand away from her and prepare to retreat, terrified of what I'm seeing.

"She brought this upon herself when she decided to keep the truth about the past from me." She says coldly as I try keeping her attention away from Silva who remains behind me and her fury continues to shake the ground.

"I know, I know and I'm sorry I also partook in that. But I need you to listen to me. This is what Melantha wants, she wants to see us be torn apart." I speak calmly in an attempt to snap her out of this terrifying mood she's in.

Vivalda shakes her head slowly, keeping her eyes on mine with her brows sharply curved downwards. My attention is drawn to her jawline as black liquid suddenly drips down her neck like poisoned blood. Once I realize what's happening, I quickly throw both of my hands back on her shoulders and gently shake her back and forth, trying to snap her out of it.

"Vivalda, you have to snap out of this! This isn't you!" I roar loudly, hoping she'll listen to me. "Don't make the same mistake-" Before I could say another word, something slams heavily into my back, causing me to collide into Vivalda and we both crash onto the ground.

What have I done?

Vivalda

I quickly recuperate from the blow and get up, ready to rage hell. Aerowen and Zyla rush to Phoenix's aid and Zyla's dark magic fills the air, killing every plant it touches outside of the dead ring of land. I look at Silva and the look of terror crosses her face. Her own magic hurt her friend. I put the sword away and charge at Silva but before I can get far, I can feel Aerowen's ice approaching behind me. I use the skills I learned from her back on Yarrin and once the ice covers the ground behind me, I keep my balance and run perfectly without slipping.

"Vivalda!" Aerowen yells for me but I ignore her.

Vessoria's magic ignites in my hands and Silva's powers ignite around her, prepared for a clash.

Once I'm in close proximity, I notice the stone around Silva's eyes cracking like how I saw back on Darali. The angrier she gets, the more her skin cracks.

"Let's see what else you're hiding."

Silva hears my thoughts loud and clear and I can feel the force of her magic raging from halfway across the field.

She quickly throws her hands down and up, causing a giant wall of green magic to tower over me like a massive wave that's ready to capsize a ship. I quickly come to a stop and glide over the dirt ground, waiting for the wall to cave over me. The magic wall sounds like

442

rushing water that echoes from deep within a hollow cave.

The sparkling magic curves over my body and crashes right on top of me. I throw my hands up and catch the end of the curving wave. Her magic weighs down on me, trying to crush me under it like a heavy blanket and she begins to push my body into the ground, causing a crater in the dead circle of land. I strain to keep myself up because I'm worried she'll cause my legs to snap at any given moment.

I feel Vessoria's electric power flow through my veins and into my fingertips. With a loud scream, I watch dark blue sparking magic swells over Silva's green wall and I feel my soul grab complete control of her power. I can feel Vessoria wrap itself around the wall and squeeze it tightly, slowly suffocating it and sucking the life out of it.

I see through a small crack in the magical wall and see Silva standing on the opposite side of the wall. She keeps her arms held forward as powerful streams of power flow out of her hands, feeding more power into her attack. Once I look around, I realize, she's completely surrounding me under a circular dome that closes in on me rapidly.

She's trying to contain me and Vessoria at the same time so I can't use any of my powers. Thankfully, she doesn't notice me looking at her, but I can see so much determination behind her eyes as she continues to try to trap me in her blanket of death.

I continue to push up against the heavy dome and suddenly, I feel a strange wave of sadness swell in my heart. I feel my heartbeat slow down and thump heavily against my ribs and it becomes difficult to breathe.

Time slows down and everything around me turns black and white. All I can hear is my heart thumping heavily in my chest.

"What am I doing?" I slowly pant while I turn around and see Phoenix, Zyla and Aerowen standing far in the distance. Each of them look angry and distraught. When I turn back to look at Silva, a faint whisper echoes in my ear.

"Your mother would still be here if it wasn't for her."

The dark eerie voice instantly snaps me out of it and my eyes shoot back up to Silva. The rage becomes unbearable and when I look up at my hands, I watch black veins begin to bulge under my skin.

I keep my palm faced up towards the cover and watch as the dark blue magic quickly turns pitch black, suffocating the green magic like a parasite. I curl my hand into a fist, pull my arm back and I use all of my strength to punch the dome, causing it to shatter over me like thick glass.

Once the wall disintegrates, I pull out the sword and dig my foot into the ground in order to lunge at Silva with the sword held out to the side.

By the time I reach her, she has little to no time to react and all she can do is block the blade by crossing her arms in front of her. Once the metal and stone clash, it causes a huge explosion of black and green light to emit from my strike. Thunder crashes loudly above us and it begins to rain heavily.

The atmosphere is brightly lit by a dangerously dark green light and once I try to pull away from her, I realize the blade is stuck, penetrating Silva's skin. Her grey skin breaks apart and dark green blood drips onto the ground. She lowers her arms, taking the blade with her and once her arms uncover her face, I see yellow glowing eyes staring at me angrily. The stone skin across her eyes, hands and arms has broken and fallen off, revealing bright green skin. And glowing green leafy vines grow up her chest and over her collar bones.

Heavy wind picks up and her long white hair flows dramatically with the current.

"Look at yourself! This is what happens when you go too far! This is what I have warned you about!" Her voice changes tone, it's stronger and more firm. I look down and see the blade is veiled by black fumes and flames.

The silver blade darkens and my reflection catches my attention. My face and neck is covered by dark markings. Even my eyes are pitch black.

Silva pulls her arms down to her side and the blade detaches from her skin. But before she can move an inch, I quickly thrust my hands forward and strike her with as much power as I can. My large beam strikes Silva in the chest and she tries to grab my raging steam of magic with her hands, attempting to endure the blast. I can see her lips moving as if she's talking, but I can't hear her over the sound of Vessoria's black electric energy roaring loudly in my ears.

I lean all of my weight in and push Silva onto her knees, leaving me standing taller over her.

A sudden bright light emits from her hand and before I know it, she throws me back, striking me with intense power I haven't seen before. I manage to keep the sword in hand while tumbling on the ground. I quickly get back on my feet and feel my heart racing. I look over at Silva and realize her true form must be hidden under the stone mask and the power that comes with it is far more stronger. The skin over her arms and eyes are the only parts of her that have shattered and broken apart. Her arms continue to bleed heavily, but she remains unphased by it.

I look over and see the others in complete and utter shock. Zyla restrains Phoenix, keeping her away from the fight and the dragon does everything she can to break free. Aerowen, shocked and saddened, keeps her distance, trembling with her hands covering her face.

I want to go to them, but before I can take a step, the ground below rumbles violently, nearly making me fall over and Silva pushes me back with her magic. The sword falls out of my hand and stabs the petrified ground, but to my surprise, it doesn't disappear and the armor remains intact.

Once Vivalda is out of the proximity of the dead circle, I make two strong tree branches reach out and wrap around her arms, pulling them each to the side. She tries to pull away from the glowing branches, but they're too strong for her.

I slowly approach the princess and look at the sword that remains stabbed deeply into the ground. I'm shocked to see Vessoria still bonded to Vivalda after watching her emotions get the best of her.

My arms pulsate in pain and I look down at the gashes beginning to slowly close and heal as my blood continues to drip onto the ground.

"Your mother would have never wanted to see you like this." I say calmly as Vivalda continues to try to break out of my grip.

"You can speak for the living...but never for the dead!" She shouts and I can physically feel her use all of the strength Vessoria allows her, pulling strongly on the branches. I try to resist her but in the blink of an eye, she yanks her arms down, breaking both branches. The feeling of her magic breaking mine apart causes a strong wave of pain to overcome me.

I bend over, holding my throbbing chest and when I look up, I see Vivalda using her magic to turn one of the branches into a thick and powerful rope that glows dark blue and black. Seeing her enchant the branch and turn it into something it's not, is unsettling. The look in her pitch-black eyes terrifies me. Not because I'm worried her power exceeds mine, but because this is not who she is. Despite feeling the intense raging anger that she's feeling on the inside, she looks emotionless on the outside.

"Vivalda, this has to stop!" The princess wraps one end of the glowing rope around her right hand, gripping it tightly. I look over at the others, worried for their safety and before I can do anything, Vivalda whips the magical lasso out and it wraps tightly around my arms and torso.

Vivalda pulls the rope down and I have no choice but to submit and not retaliate. If I do, this tussle won't end and I won't be able to get through to her.

The Serafaes begin to run charge over, but Vivalda snaps her head around and a vibrant blue fire circles around the edge of the dead patch of land, leaving us in the center. The Serafaes don't try to break through and instead, they continue to observe.

I look up at Vivalda, hoping she'll listen to me.

"Don't make the same mistake I did. If you don't get your emotions under control, it'll destroy you before you have a chance to face your sister. And I know that's what you plan to do, so please, let me help you."

Vivalda pants heavily, trying to keep herself from breaking down. "Since I was a child, I trusted Lyla...I trusted YOU." Her voice is deep and raspy, she doesn't sound like herself. Her lips quiver as she's on the verge of crying.

"I know you did...that's why I left that night."

Vivalda

I keep the rope held tightly in my hand and I look at Silva, confused.

"What are you talking about?" I ask quietly while continuing to feel the electric fire buzz in my hands. Silva takes a deep breath and she looks absolutely defeated, not because she's exhausted, but because she doesn't want to speak.

"Aladora begged me to stay in the castle that night because she knew you'd leave to find her." I loosen my grip on the rope slightly and take a small step back, even more confused. I do my best to keep my thoughts collected so I can take everything one step at a time.

"If you respected my mother so much, why did you leave?" Silva keeps her gaze on the ground and her shoulders tense up.

"Because I thought I could bring her home." Silva says quietly and I feel my heart shatter over and over again.

"Exactly...and you didn't." I growl loudly while leaning forward and pulling back on the rope. Silva squints her eyes and her magic surges like a heavy heartbeat.

"No! I didn't save her because I COULDN'T!" She looks up at me and her eyes are full of dark green tears that begin to slowly slide down her face. "What are you not understanding?!" I feel a sudden pinch in my heart and instead of seeing Silva, all I can see is Lyla and instantaneous sorrow washes over me.

I shake away the pathetic sadness. "How could a god not-" Before I can get another word out, Silva yanks back on the rope and her magic flows out and into the rope. The rope slowly turns green and I can feel her magic wash over me. "Gods can't fix everything, Vivalda!" Before I know it, everything goes black and Silva's voice echoes and drowns out.

My eyes are open but everywhere I look is black. All I hear is wind howling through rustling treetops and a storm raging heavily.

"I didn't want to show you this. But if you can't hear my truth, I'll make you see it instead." Silva's voice returns and continues to echo loudly as if she's right behind me.

I see a green light flicker in front of me and it slowly gets bigger and bigger as if it's getting closer to me.

The green anomaly lights up the surrounding area and I quickly realize I'm standing in the middle of a forest in the middle of the night. The green light zips away and I quickly follow it without a second thought.

I reach out, trying to grab it, but it continues to bolt away. From all around me, I begin to hear terrifying whispers coming beyond the trees, slowly growing louder and louder. I come to a sliding stop and stand still, staring at the ground, listening carefully.

My heart races rapidly while I listen to the thunder crashing loudly overhead. I stand frozen, not knowing what to do or what to think. I don't know what kind of spell Silva has cast upon me, but I'm not in the mood for it.

Before I can call out for her, I'm taken back by the sound of several loud grotesque creatures running up

450

behind me, growling and snarling viciously. I quickly turn around and as soon as I do, a large pack of Aerolight canines charge at me. Instinctively, I scream while crouching down, covering my ears. Once I peek up, I realize they're not charging at ME. I look down the path they follow and realize they're chasing down Silva.

Without a second thought, I race towards her, running faster than the entire pack, closing in on her green light. As soon as I approach her light, she suddenly transforms, running as fast as she can, paying the canines no attention.

"Where are you going?!" I try calling out for her, but I'm ignored.

I look back at the Aerolights and see nothing but blood lust behind their eyes and black poison dripping from their salivating mouths.

Silva turns her head to the side frantically as if something else catches her attention.

"Vivalda." She says in a worried manner before looking back to see how close the monsters are.

I watch Silva prepare to fight the monsters, with her powers ignited in her hands. She comes to a stop and fights them off and after a while, she tries to run, but she's pulled back by more Aerolights that claw at her and pull her back with their teeth. While fighting them off and tearing out their hearts, another strange voice begins to float with the stormy wind.

"Stay out of this!" The voice shouts loudly and Silva's leafy ears turn to the side, listening carefully over the sound of her hands tearing apart the Aerolight bodies. With a loud and angry growl, Silva splits one of the monster's bodies in half and continues running

through the forest with more beasts tailing behind her, swiping their sharp claws at her every chance they have.

"Don't do this." The other voice says weakly, causing Silva to be so distraught to the point where the stone skin under her eyes begins to crack and her eyes slowly turn yellow. She fights through her pain while extreme anger overcomes her like the storm she's causing to intensify.

"Let me find you!" Silva yells with the crashing thunder mirroring her turmoil, roaring with her.

I continue to silently run by her side and I finally piece it together.

She's looking for my mother.

My anger has overwhelmed me so much to the point where I didn't connect the dots until just now.

The beasts continue to snarl and roar loudly as they inch closer and closer to Silva and she does what she can to keep them off of her. I try listening for the voice again but before I know it, thunder crashes so hard that it causes the ground to shake. I suddenly realize I'm running alone and once I turn around, Silva is standing still, frozen in anger with her hand curled into fists.

I slowly approach her, wondering why she's stopped moving and from behind her, I see the massive pack of demon dogs running like bats out of hell, charging at her, ready to tear her apart.

"Silva, move! What's wrong with you?!" I shout and before I know it, she crashes to her knees and the dogs maul over her to the point where she's left buried under the canines that bite and claw at her body.

I'm left standing frozen in my tracks. There's nothing I can do. This is nothing but a memory. One that can't be changed.

A bright white light begins to emit from under the demon dogs and I can hear Silva screaming in agony, suffocated under the beasts.

Silva screams loudly and at the same time, a violent explosion occurs and the Aerolights disintegrate instantly. Along with a large ring of land.

My heart races faster and faster and a wave of shock washes over me alongside the rain. Once her light dims, I see Silva sitting in the middle of a large dead patch of land. Every plant and animal in the surrounding area is dead. Silva's face is stained by green tears and there's deep glowing green cracks covering her body.

She pants heavily with her fingers dug into the dirt. She continues to sob and once she looks at what her magic has done, she cries even harder.

She is her own weakness. She's destroyed a part of herself.

The anger that once consumed me begins to fade away, leaving behind a deep sorrow that overcomes my entire being. My heart, once ablaze with fury, now aches with a dull pain. Every beat of my heart inflicts more physical pain.

She tries to use her magic to heal the dreaded land, but it doesn't regrow or heal.

Seeing that painful look on her face is a sight I will never forget. Silva looks up, her eyes full of fury and rage.

453

"Guide her to me." The voice says weakly and Silva squints her eyes tightly, causing more green tears to leak down her cheeks. She holds up her shaky hand and a white orb of magic grows over her palms. She throws it up into the air and I watch as it soars into the air and curves behind us as if aimed for something specific.

A subtle *boom* echoes from the distance and random images begin to pop into my mind as if a message is being shared with me. I see visions of the mysterious tree that appears in front of me while I traveled down the road towards Palavon.

The tree opened the path to my mother. You purposely lead me to her.

Silva gets up, her skin is torn and dark green gashes spread across her body, slowly healing. She begins to take off, running very slowly but she quickly comes to a stop.

"Go home, Silva." The voice continues to speak weakly, causing her to cry and pant heavily.

"You are my home!" She cries loudly before taking off into the forest.

This voice...is my mother's thoughts. I'm hearing what Silva hears in her mind.

Silva disappears into the trees and I'm left standing in the middle of the dead circle of land that Silva created out of pure anger and sadness. And I suddenly feel everything she did and still does.

More sounds begin to circle around me, but I remain standing still. When I look over to the side, more visions of memories begin to circle around me. I hear a horse neighing loudly and its hooves running through wet mud. A vision becomes clear and I see a white horse being chased by terrifying monsters of all shapes.

The muddy horse transforms into a brown falcon and it uses its wings to attack as many as it can, striking and skilling a few.

"Zyla! Find her!" Silva shouts in Zyla's mind and without hesitating, Zyla unleashes a huge attack, stunning and killing many beasts, giving her a chance to run away.

The falcon screeches and dives deeper into the forest. The memory fades and a new one plays before me. This time, I hear my own screams echoing around me and I watch as I'm being chased by more of Melantha's pawns.

I tumble down a very tall hill and once I reach the bottom, my body is slammed into a large tree. Right before the Aerolights can dive down and reach me, a blinding light emits out of thin air, blinding the beasts, causing them to screech. Once the light fades, I see my mother standing in front of me. Her scarlet red dress is torn and her skin is beat. My eyes close and my mother is relieved to have found me. She carefully scoops me up in her arms.

"We're over here! Hurry!" Her voice and the memory fade away and I close my eyes, shaking my head in disbelief of what I'm seeing. I want Silva to stop this sorcery. It brings me too much pain knowing what I know now. But before I can beg for the magic to be stopped. I hear the horse neigh in a disturbing manner as if it's in pain.

When I look up with tears in my eyes, I see Zyla buck my mother and I off her back as one of the Aerolights stabs the side of her stomach with its razor-sharp claws. I cover my mouth with my hands while releasing a loud gasp.

Zyla leaves my mother and I before darting out of sight, making the Aerolights follow behind her, keeping them away from us.

Once out of sight, Zyla transforms into her normal self with her stomach dripping with sparkly golden blood that slowly turns black from the Aerolight's poison. She nearly falls over, but Silva appears out of thin air to catch her and keep her on her feet.

The Aerolights approach them rapidly and right before they can attack, they suddenly stop dead in their tracks and the strangest thing happens...they fade away and seep into the ground as if being recalled by something.

"I'll see you again. I promise." My mothers voice echoes, the memory fades away and everything turns pitch black.

When I open my eyes, I'm brought back to Silva sitting in front of me with my lasso still wrapped around her tightly. Her magic returns to her and I realize my face is wet from tears I've shed while looking at the memories Silva showed me. She looks at me with a mix of anger and sadness in her eyes.

"Now, do you see?" She asks quietly and I look over at the others. Once my gaze lands on Zyla, she looks down and the markings and scar on her body are glowing gold.

"You were there?" I ask shakily as I try to hold back my cries. And without saying a single word, Zyla nods her head slowly, keeping her eyes on the dead land below her.

My eyes look at the ground and slowly move over to glance at the magical rope that remains wrapped around my hands.

"This is the same place where it happened?" I ask Silva and she also nods her head.

"I know I've kept great truths from you but my love for you, Riverlynn and Aladora was never false." I look down and watch her fists slowly uncurl and she breathes heavily with her green tears stained on her face. "We did everything we could." I slowly release the rope and it disappears. I look at my hands and see my veins are blackened and look infected. I can imagine the monster I must look like. This isn't me. I take a slow step back but Silva remains on the ground.

"Earlier, you wondered what the marks around your eyes are. They represent the pain you've kept hidden deep down. They were never visible in the beginning because you refused to allow anyone to see that pain. But as we came together, you've slowly realized that we all share the same pain and you've shared that pain with us." Silva says and I shake my head, wanting nothing more to do with her or the Serafaes.

I have no voice.
I have no strength.
I'm exhausted.
I'm done.

"You've opened my eyes to the things I didn't know...but none of this should have been kept from me. You and my mother should have been honest since the beginning." I say weakly. My voice is hoarse and my body begins to ache. Silva shakes her head, looking down at the ground.

"Lyla was like a second mother to me. I never had the chance to truly tell her, but I'm sure, deep down, she knew. Now, she's just somebody I used to know." Despite my efforts to suppress the heartbreak I feel, tears continue to leak from my eyes.

Silva gets up and steps forward, holding her hand out as I begin to walk away.

"Don't. I need to be left alone." Before I turn to walk away, Phoenix catches my eye. Her sorrow and heartbreak are reflected in the dimness of her fire's flames. I want to run into her arms, but after this, I don't think I'll ever feel the same.

I let Vivalda run off into the forest so she can attempt to calm down and the Serafaes gather by my side. Each of them, concerned, angry and worried. I lower my size down to be at the same level as the others and I wipe my hands over my cheeks, smearing away my dark green tears. I feel the gashes on my arms close and heal and the glowing vines on my chest shrink down and disappear.

The forest glow darkens and the flame between Phoenix's horns is all that remains lit. I slowly fall to my knees and stare at the ground. I rest my hand down and feel the leaves and dead grass crumble under me. No matter how hard I try to heal it, it no longer regrows.

"I'm sorry. I'm so...so sorry. I didn't mean for it to go this way." I say out loud and feel more tears slowly slide down my face, bleeding into the parts of my face that remain solidified in stone.

Phoenix lays her hand over my shoulder and I turn to look up at her. "It's not your fault. We knew this would happen. I think I speak for each of us when I say that we are not mad at you. We didn't know Melantha could walk beyond the Sylphenic realm." She speaks softly, trying to hold back her own sadness.

"It's obvious that she is evolving and she's learned new tricks that we are unaware of. So, knowing that, what do we do?" Zyla steps closer while still covering her chest with her hands. I look up at her, making sure she's alright and she quickly notices what I'm looking at. She shakes her head. "Don't worry about it, I'm fine." She says quietly with a slight growl in her voice.

I trust her but I still feel terrible that Melantha was able to cause harm without her presence being known to me.

"I should have known she was here. I couldn't hear her. I couldn't see her-" I stop mid-sentence when a small thought comes to mind. "Melantha knew I couldn't see, hear or sense her presence. This was all done on purpose for her own entertainment." I slowly stand up and a terrifying chill creeps down my spine, making my ears flick back. I peer deeply into the forest while the others wait for me to continue.

"I think a trick is being played on us right now as we speak." Aerowen's frost slowly grows colder and Phoenix's blaze burns brighter.

"What makes you say that?" Aerowen asks softly. I shake my head, trying to get my thoughts together.

"I'm not sure yet but until I figure it out, we need to stay together. As long as I can feel Vivalda's presence, we'll be okay."

"Are you sure I shouldn't go to her? I'm sure I can help." Phoenix asks with a deep, harmless growl. It's easy to tell she's worried about Vivalda and I know how much she yearns to be by her side.

"As I've watched her grow, she's never been one to be forced into socialization. When she's ready, she'll come to us. We can't force our comfort upon her." Phoenix's head hangs low and she takes a deep breath. "I know how much you care for her. I still care for her like she's my own. Just give it some time." I lead the Serafaes out of the dark patch of land and I light up the same area of the forest we were previously in. I sit down in the grass, the others surround me with her elements surrounding them and I listen to Vivalda's thoughts that float around and I speak to her silently in my mind.

"I know you're tired."
"I know you're angry."

"But I'm not going anywhere."

Vivalda

I continue to trudge through the thick mud and dirt as it continues to rain and the sky begins to lighten up but remains covered by dark clouds. The rain drops *clink* against the armor and it sounds like a song made from nature itself.

I want to scream and cry until there's no voice left in me, but I keep it bottled, not making a single sound. I feel so weak, I don't know how much farther I can go. I have no idea what I'm doing or what I should do. I quickly remember that Silva can probably still hear my thoughts and feel my presence, so to avoid her potentially bothering me further, I close my eyes and conceal my aura and thoughts. In order to keep Silva thinking I'm near them in the forest; I disconnect from some of the magic that bottles inside of me and let it flow around freely so my trail stays behind.

Hopefully that'll keep her off my back.

I think to myself and stand silently, listening to the forest to see if Silva responds in any way and thankfully, the forest remains as it is.

I find a large boulder deep in the forest and when I reach it, I slam my back against it and lean back, trying to get my thoughts together as they race rapidly in my mind.

So much was taken from me. My mother, my guardian, my sister, my kingdom and my friend. I feel like I've lost my entire life in the blink of an eye. I was just beginning to heal from my mother's death and now that giant wound has been unbound.

I rest my head in my hands, doing everything I can to stop myself from crying but the voices, images and the thoughts become too much to contain.

My heart hammers against my ribs like a monster trying to break out of a cage. This amount of heartbreak should kill me, yet I remain breathing at a time when I'd rather drop dead. This is the most pain my heart has endured in my lifetime. I never thought grief and betrayal could be so physically painful.

The noise in my head becomes too much to the point where I begin to scream and at the same time, I twist around and punch the large boulder, shattering it into many small pieces. At the same time, loud thunder crashes in the sky, masking my scream and the sound of the boulder obliterating.

I step back and catch my breath. My hand throbs for a moment, but the pain quickly subsides. Once I feel some tension leave my body, I pull the sword out and look at my reflection in the blade. Melantha's voice rings in my head while I continue to stare at my reflection in the sword. A part of me says to finish this fight on my own, but the other says to run back to Silva and the Serafaes.

If I give Melantha the crystal, the madness stops.

But...how do I know I can trust her after what she's done?

Maybe the threats are to show how serious she is.

After a long moment of thinking intensely to myself, I make the choice to venture off to Helsen's Peak. Thankfully, I remember how Melantha said to get there.

Before putting the sword away, I take one last look at my reflection in the dark glistening blade. I'm completely unrecognizable.

Now I understand what Silva meant by the armor and its power relies on my emotions. When my emotions get out of hand, it turns me into a...monster. I quickly put the blade away so I don't get more irritated than I already am.

I look around to see where I am. I don't know how far I've distanced myself from the others but thankfully, I see no evidence of a trail being left behind me due to the heavy rain, but I'm not sure if that's a good or bad thing.

I gather what remaining strength I have and I wander even deeper into the forest in hopes of finding my way to the sea.

My eyes jerk open as if something has woken me from a dream and a sudden fear creeps up my back. Phoenix stops pacing in front of me and rushes over to me.

"What's wrong?" She asks anxiously while kneeling down in front of me. I take a moment to catch my breath until I'm completely calm.

"Nothing. I'm sorry. I can't hear Vivalda's thoughts anymore but I can still sense her aura. She's not too far." Phoenix releases a sigh of relief and her shoulders fall, relaxed.

"It's been a while, should we go to her now?" She asks and I have a hard time answering.

If we go to her and she's still enraged as she was, we may run into the same altercation all over again and I can't guarantee the world will stay in one piece if that happens.

Seeing the desperateness in Phoenix's eyes ultimately makes me cave in.

"Alright, we will go and check on her, but if she wants nothing to do with us, we will leave her be. Understood?" Phoenix smiles and nods her head before helping me up and I lead them to the area where I sense Vivalda's aura is hiding.

We come across a wide muddy path and I can sense Vivalda and her magic, but I can't see her anywhere. The Serafaes spread out and look around for Vivalda and after several long moments, they return back to where I stand.

"Are you sure you can sense her magic?" Aerowen asks as her frosty magic crackles under her feet while she walks. I turn my head and glare at her, slightly offended.

"Don't test my judgment please. Yes, I know she's here. She has to be." I walk around a wide parameter, looking for the princess.

"Vivalda!" I shout at the same time the thunder roars and I begin to panic. "Vivalda, where are you?!" I shout as loud as I can.

"Silva!" Phoenix roars from behind me and I see her kneeling down by something in the ground. Once I approach her, I see a large boulder has been blown to bits in an unnatural way.

My hands begin to shake and I feel sudden dread and fear. I can feel Vivalda's presence, but I can't see or hear her and seeing a massive boulder blown to bits overwhelms me.

"You don't think Aerolight could have found her...right?" Aerowen asks, worried.

I don't know what to think or say. I'm trying to wrap my head around it all, but nothing brings me any sense of peace or reassurance.

Without responding, I take a step back, cross my arms in front of me before throwing them down, unleashing a huge wave of green magic that emits from my life force and it washes over the forest, making everything go dark.

The veins of tree trunks are left glowing and when we all look around, we see thin blue strands of magic flowing around us slowly and freely.

"What is that?" Zyla asks as she reaches up to touch it and it looks like she touches the body of a ghost.

I lift my hand, beckoning the blue magic to gather to my palms. We all watch as the blue strings bind together and wave around everyone to gather into a single glowing ball in my hand.

Once all of the magic is gathered, the green glow from my own magic slowly fades away and I observe the blue wisp, immediately knowing where it came from.

"It's Vessoria..." The Serafaes look up in complete shock and disbelief.

"What do you mean- how is that possible?!" Phoenix steps forward, growling loudly.

"Maybe the Aerolights were here and we didn't-" Aerowen steps in, speaking very softly and observing the magic that levitates in my hand.

"NO!" I shout, startling her and I quickly gather my composure. The last thing I want is to take anymore anger or frustration out on them and make matters worse. "I would have known. We have to split up and look for her. She has to be around here somewhere." I speak calmly despite the blood curling fear I feel for Vivalda's safety. I step forward and the ground rumbles below me.

"Phoenix, take the sky, fly as far north as you can. Zyla, check the western side of the forest. And Aerowen, check the castle trail. There's a chance she may have run home." Before I can continue, Phoenix takes off into the sky, soaring high over the land and my magic follows her, creating an invisible barrier under her so she won't be seen.

Her determination to find her friend burns bright.

"If any of you find anything or if you're caught up by Aerolights, send out a signal and we will gather." Aerowen's body turns into a small bright blue glowing wisp and she immediately zips into the forest, flying towards the nearest human road.

I look over at Zyla and her magic begins to swell around her like a tunneling blanket.

"Silva, hold on. What happened to staying together?" Zyla asks and I can hear the unsureness in her tone and see the worry in her violet eyes.

"Well, that was before one of us went missing. GO!" Zyla nods her head and black smoke covers her entire body. Once the smoke drops, a large golden-brown falcon soars into the sky, screeching loudly.

I look over and watch the blue magic in my hand slowly fade away, not leaving a trail of its existence behind.

I'll find you.

PHOENIX

I keep my eyes peered on the forest ground as I soar against the intense rain and see no signs of Vivalda, Aerolights or Melantha.

"Did Melantha really go beyond the veil while we slept?" I think to myself, waiting for a response from Silva if she can hear me.

"Yes and if she was able to physically threaten Zyla's life force without being physically present...I don't want to know what other trick she's learned since being banished from the kingdom. Have you seen any signs of Vivalda?" Silva's voice echoes in my head, bouncing between my ears. Her voice is so pure and loud that she nearly drowns out the storm.

"No. But I will continue to go north until I reach the edge of the Lion's Eye and once I can no longer fly, I'll scout on foot."

Silva goes silent and I continue to focus on the search for the princess. Silva's mind can only be heard by others if she opens the conscious pathway that allows many bodies to hear the same thoughts. I know she's very focused on finding the princess, not just because she wants to end the Melantha's reign of terror, but also because she wants to end the darkness that consumes Vivalda. She wishes to fix what's broken between them.

I continue to fly rapidly in the sky as thunder rumbles and I move swiftly to avoid the strong lighting strikes. The last thing I'd want is for fire to clash with electricity.

All I wish is to be by Vivalda's side.

Vivalda

I throw my body into a large tree, nearly knocking it over and I try to catch my breath from the constant running. I can feel the power of the armor weighing me down but I refuse to take it off just in case anything happens and if I collapse again, I don't know if I'll be found.

I take a long and deep breath to listen to the forest around me. After hearing nothing but heavy rainfall and thunder rumbling, I hear strong waves crashing in the distance and the smell of salt collides with the earthy rain.

I gain my balance and follow the sound of the water until I eventually find an opening in the forest that leads directly to a beach. There, I am met with roaring waves and light gray skies.

Once I step out of the forest, I hear something *clanking* loudly from the far side of the beach and I nearly cry out of relief to see the Nightwalker docked on the shore, beginning to depart.

I look closely and I can see Calypso walking around on the top deck, throwing things around frantically. I immediately take off and run as fast as I can towards her ship while screaming her name.

"Calypso!" My voice immediately catches her attention, causing her to stumble and fall down backwards. She quickly gets back up and runs to the side of the boat and shouts.

"Vivalda? What the heck are ya doing out here?!" She holds on to her hat as the strong winds blow. I look at the base of the boat to see she's slowly moving away from the beach. I look around for a way to get to the ship without having to go into the water.

In the distance, I see multiple tall boulders popping out of the water.

I run as fast as I can towards the rock and use all the strength I can to leap onto the boulders, jumping on them one by one and once I get to the last rock, I push myself off as hard as I can and reach out for a rope that hangs off the side of the ship, safely secured. Once I manage to grab it, I slowly pull myself up. Calypso rushes over and helps pull me over the ledge of the ship and we both fall over.

I lay flat on my back, trying to catch my breath and I can feel every part of my body pulsing painfully. Running all day has taken so much power and energy out of me.

"What the hell, mate? You're crazy, ya know that!" She says excitedly while quickly getting up and helping me stand. She has a huge smile on her face but that joy slowly dissipates by the time she looks at my face and the armor. I know she can tell something is wrong.

"What happened to ya? It looks like you've been through...a lot." She says softly. I try my best to crack a slight smile.

"Yeah...you could say that I guess. I need your help with something and I'll explain on the way." Calypso lifts one brow. Confused but intrigued.

Zyla

Due to the strong winds, it becomes more strenuous to fly and despite my keen sense of smell, I can't pick up Vivalda's scent anywhere. It's almost like she has completely vanished.

The scent of saltwater clogs my nostrils and makes me want to vomit. But I feel my instincts pushing me towards the sea to scout the terrain. As much as I don't want to go near the sea, it wouldn't hurt to cover all of my bases before returning to Silva.

From a far distance, I can see the water line pop over the edge of the forest. I pull my wings in to give me a speed boost as the wind pushes against me.

"Silva, can't you take control of this storm? It's a bit difficult to fly through!" I say in my mind and I can hear Silva speak back with an irritated tone in her voice.

"I can't control the storms, I can only add to them, you know this"

Once the forest is behind me, I fly lower in order to analyze the beach and in the sand I see a ton of footprints scattered across the beach that begin to fill with water and wash away.

"Zyla, have you found anything?" Silva's voice echoes and she speaks frantically to the point where it's almost hard to understand her.

"I'm not sure, I found footprints in the sand on the northwest shore but they trail towards the water. I'm going to search the beach."

Silva goes silent for a moment but I know she's still honing in on my thoughts.

"I need you to search the sea for a large ship that's controlled by a single pirate and keep me updated with what you see."

I push forward and look out into the distance, using my keen sight. I quickly spot a tiny speck floating on the water in the far distance and upon further inspection, I quickly realize it's a ship.

After a long time of flying, I eventually catch up to the ship and land on a loose ladder that hangs off the side of the vessel.

I won't be seen where I've perched, but I remain vigilant in case I do get spotted.

After a moment of silence, I hear a human voice I don't recognize, which must be the pirate Silva spoke about and eventually, Vivalda's voice echoes from the top of the ship while she and the other woman talk.

I release a sigh of relief knowing I've found her when I was worried we wouldn't.

Vivalda

We remain standing at the ship's helm as I wrap up telling Calypso what happened in Wildevale. She stares at me with her mouth gaping open.

"Woah. Alright, that's too much even for my mind to wrap around. Where do I start?" Calypso thinks to herself for a moment and I chuckle nervously.

"Yer tellin' me, ya have a sister ya didn't know existed 'cause green bean wiped the kingdom's memory. Spooky sister is out to get ya and spooky sister controls the big demon things? Ya, no, I get it but don't. Why would the magic bozos keep all that from ya?" I nod my head while looking out into the distance, watching the lightning crash gently over the water.

"I mean...if it makes ya feel any better, the new armor matches ya at least!" She nudges my shoulder with her arm in a playful manner, trying to get me in a better mood. Even in dark times, there's never a dull moment with the captain's sarcasm and I appreciate it after all the strife I've recently had to deal with.

"That's a lot for even me to digest and I'm not the one who went through it. I can't imagine what you must feel. I'm so sorry this has happened." Calypso says sentimentally, dropping the sarcasm. "What exactly do you need my help with?" She asks curiously as she navigates us through intense waters and waves.

I look up and raindrops fall into my eyes and the wind grows colder.

"The demon 'sister' of mine told me to meet her at Helsen's Peak, through Rempengough's Tide and past the Echoing Rift in the north." I see Calypso's gaze drop to the ground and she grips the wheel so tight, I'm scared she'll break it. "No no no no, I- I swore I'd never try to sail that tide ever again. Rempengough's Tide never EVER rests." She shakes her head and sudden irritation crosses her face, feeding into her tone.

"What do you mean? Why-" Before I can let out another word Calypso looks at me angrily.

"Listen. I may be one of the best sailors out there, but no one and I repeat, NO ONE will ever be able to sail through that tide. It's a beast to navigate, let alone get past." The look on her face confuses me and I feel like there's something she's not telling me, but I don't bother trying to figure out what.

"Well, from what I know, there's never been a previous sailor who has ever sailed with a 'magical bozo', so maybe we'll have a better chance." Calypso closes her eyes, takes a deep breath and shakes her head.

"Unless you're too scared, then I completely understand." I tease her and she quickly turns to glare at me.

"Excuse me? Wanna run that by me one more time?" The glare in her eyes makes me laugh. I clear my throat and fan my hand towards her.

"Oh nothing. But in all seriousness." I take a deep breath and compose myself in order to speak about the serious manners at hand. "If I don't get to the peak and give Melantha what she wants, more innocent people will die." Calypso zones out into the sea, trying to make a decision. She scoffs and groans loudly while throwing her head back.

"I swear to the gods, if we don't make it through that passageway, I'm killin' ya...twice." I can't help but let out a little laugh. I look out into the distance and see nothing but endless miles of water. I figure getting to Rempengough's Tide will take a long time and it's time I don't have to spare.

A thought comes to mind and I walk over to the back ledge of the ship.

"What are ya doin'?" Calypso looks over to see what I'm doing.

While standing at the edge, I stand tall and I pull my arms back. "Just giving us a little push!" I immediately feel the power charge up and flow through my veins like an opening barricade. "You may want to hold on tight!" I push forward and black magic releases from my hands and hits the surface hard as if it's solid matter and the force causes the ship to move forward rapidly.

Calypso nearly loses grip on the wheel but quickly gains her balance.

Zyla

The ship takes off with the help of Vivalda's powers and I tightly grip onto the ladder with my sharp talons, being blown around by the strong current.

"Silva! Can you hear me?" My thoughts scream for her as I keep my balance as the ship pushes forward.

"Yes, I'm here!" Silva shouts frantically in my mind. I figure she must still be running quickly through the forest.

"I found Vivalda. She's with a pirate and they're sailing to Helsen's Peak as we speak!"

"Thank goodness she's alright. I need you to stay with her. The rest of us will gather in the Lion's Eye." I can hear other voices chime in due to Silva using her magic to merge other voices into the same mind waves.

"I'm going to push north. I'm almost to the edge of the Lion's Eye and Rempengough's Tide isn't too far from there. If I'm lucky, I may be able to reach Helsen before them." Phoenix's voice is full of determination and her voice slowly drifts out of the wavelength.

"Alright, in that case, Aerowen and I will meet with you all very soon. I'm going to do what I can to buy us some time. Maybe I can get them to head for shore. Everyone, tread the sky and sea safely." Before Silva goes completely silent, I hear the thunder grow more intense and it begins to rain even harder.

I look around and spot an open window at the back of the ship and I steadily fly inside, landing in a very large room that's full of maps, drawings and journals.

I wait patiently in the Lion's Eye, walking back and forth and behind me, I hear a soft twinkling sound. When I turn around, I see Aerowen's white ball of magic hit the ground and turn into a small sheet of ice. I watch as she quickly grows from the ground and her ice cracks while her body is formed.

"What is your plan?" She asks urgently and I take a moment to gather my thoughts before giving her my for sure answer. I speak out loud while opening the mind waves so that Zyla and Phoenix can hear me.

"Everyone, listen to me carefully. I'm going to raise the storm in hopes it'll encourage Vivalda and the pirate to dock on land." Aerowen's eyes widen and I immediately know she doesn't agree with the plan.

"Are you insane?! You know how stubborn that pirate is. Knowing the odds, she'll want to sail straight through it! You'll kill them both before they reach the peak!" Phoenix's voice roars in my mind.

"No I won't. I've learned my lesson twice now. No matter what, they can NOT reach Helsen before us."

Vivalda

After pushing the ship forward for a long period of time, I finally pull away from the heavy stream of magic and lean over my knees, panting heavily, trying to catch my breath.

"Are ya alright?" Calypso shouts for me while keeping control of the wheel.

"Yes, I'm fine." I slowly walk over to join her while doing my best to keep my balance as the vessel bumps up and down and teeters side to side. Calypso keeps her focus on the horizon while carefully guiding us over every large wave.

I look up in the sky and large water droplets hit my eyes and face while thunder continues to rumble loudly.

"This storm is only gonna to get worse! I think it'll be best if we dock until it passes! Don't get me wrong, I've sailed through storms before but there's somethin' strange about this one!" Calypso shouts over the roaring winds and crashing tides.

The atmosphere rumbles loudly and I see a strange light peek out from behind a thick black storm cloud. The sky growls louder and a raging lightning bolt descends down, barely missing the ship and striking the ocean. At the same time, I hear Calypso yelp and the blast causes the vessel to sway heavily to the side and I nearly fall over.

"Aye, that'll do it! I'm docking the ship!" Calypso begins to turn the wheel to the right.

"No wait! The storm is getting worse on purpose!" I shout over the strong winds and Calypso looks at me like I'm crazy.

"Well, I reckon that's how storms work, don't ya think?" She continues to turn the ship as more intense waves slam into the side of the ship.

"That's not what I mean! Turn it back and keep going!" Calypso does the opposite and turns the wheel all the way to the right.

"Princess, I'm not riskin' my ship being blown up because you want to test a storm!" Another lightning bolt strikes the sea, but this time, far away from us.

"It's not the storm I want to test!" Calypso looks at me with her icy grey eyes wide opened and one of her brows arched.

"What's that supposed to mean?!" Her voice is high pitched and she squeals fearfully.

"I'm going to test a god!" I say while holding on to a wooden post, trying to keep myself from falling over.

"WHAT?! Are you crazy?!" She shouts frantically while laughing awkwardly.

"Why not? She said she'd show me what her storms can truly do." We continue to sail through the storm, hoping to avoid being struck down by a raging lightning bolt.

And as each moment passes, the storm grows stronger.

"Please tell me you know what you're doing. How do you know you won't accidentally strike the ship down? And what if this makes everything worse?" Aerowen looks at me unassured of my actions while I sit on my knees as green smoke floats around me and the grass under me glows brightly. I keep my eyes closed, wave my hands slowly in front of me, raising the sea storm, making it more angry.

"Yes, I do know what I'm doing. I don't need to be physically present to know what I'm casting and since Zyla's aura is on board, I know their location. If the storm scares them enough, they'll dock until it's over." As I turn my hands upwards with my fingers curled inwards, I can feel electric energy collide with my magic. I feel and control every thunder strike that's added to the storm. And I feel every flash of light and every wave that rocks the ship.

"I just need Vivalda to open her mind so I can speak to her. I know what she's trying to do and she won't be able to do it alone." I can visualize the ship, Calypso and Zyla, but I can't see or feel Vivalda.

"Only until Vivalda lets me speak to her will I end this storm."

Vivalda

Calypso and I struggle to keep our balance as the ship rocks and bumps harshly against heavy waves.

"I thought green bean could only control plants and stuff! How is she makin' the storm expeditiously worse?!" Calypso shouts as she tries keeping the wheel steady.

"Like I said, we don't question magic. She's trying to get us to turn around, which means there's something she's keeping me from!" We try to keep the silly chitter chat to a minimum so we can focus on getting to Helsen and getting away from the storm.

There's a beaming light that shines directly above us as the sky rumbles and cracks. An electrical current charges up directly above the ship. I react quickly and run down the steps to stand under the beaming light and as soon as the lightning begins to descend, I feel intense power surge throughout my body. I throw my hands up and as soon as the electric current crashes into my hand, thunder crashes loudly around us.

I keep myself steady and balanced while holding the burning electricity in my hand. Black magic collides with yellow current and it makes my skin tingle. The pure energy continues to crackle in my grasp until I throw out both of my arms, making the bolt crash loudly and I watch as it dissolves into fiery sparks.

"She did not just aim for my ship!" Calypso says angrily, steadying the helm.

After seeing how close she was to striking the vessel, I growl loudly and finally break to allow Silva to hear my thoughts. I speak out loud and think at the same time so Calypso can hear me speak to the tyrant who's causing problems.

"What the hell do you think you're doing?!" I shout loudly as the storm around us continues to rage and the red pieces of my hair blow in front of my face and stick to my cheeks from the rain.

"Oh, thank goodness! Please don't shut me out and listen to what I have to say!" Silva pleads and the storm quickly quiets down.

The rain lightens up and the rumbling stops. The sky is still dark and Calypso continues to fight against the current but it's easier now that there's no lightning bolts to be wary of.

"You just threatened the safety of the ship just to talk to me in your mind! What makes you think I want to hear from you?! I only opened up so you'd stop!"

"There was no other way I was going to get your attention. Now, listen to me, please! You CAN NOT fight Melantha on your own. If you think the Aerolights are a menace to fight, you have no idea what you're getting into by facing Melantha, especially alone." I'm already fed up talking to her and I start to get irritated.

"You're just saying that because Melantha will tell me whatever truth you're trying to keep me from." I snap back.

"No! Since the day you were born, I took on some sort of responsibility to care and look out for you! I don't know what I'd do if I lost you too!" I feel my heart thump against my ribs and I stand silently, feeling myself get emotional. I remain silent to hear what Silva has to say.

"I heard your thoughts when we went to the Lion's Eye for the first time. You felt a familiar connection to me and it's because you felt Lyla's presence. You felt her comfort but through the eyes of another being. Despite my previous actions and appearance changing, I'm still that same person you knew. Never was my love faked and that same love existed BEFORE Vessoria needed to choose a host." For a split moment, I think about Lyla and I realize that Silva is right. Even though I know now who she truly is, I can't deny her love for me. My mind is at a crossroads. Before I can respond, Calypso shouts behind me.

"Vivalda! We're approaching the gorge!" I run to the front of the ship and I see two long mountains with a path in between them, indicating we're approaching Helsen's Peak. My heart begins to race once I realize how closer we are to the destination and I suddenly feel nothing but fear.

"Calypso! Turn us-" Before I can finish my sentence, the ship suddenly jolts to the side and the sky grows dark. Both of us shout at the same time as we're flung backwards.

"Calypso! Get us out of here!" I look back and see her pulling one of the wooden handles that sticks out of the wheel, trying to make it turn.

"I'm trying to! She won't budge!" Calypso shouts as she tries to turn the wheel, leaning all of her strength on the wheel.

The boat begins to turn to its side and it feels like something is pulling the ship forward. I quickly rush to the front of the ship and when I look down, I see the water begin to move in a strange circular motion, making the nose of the ship tilt downwards.

"What the hell kind of storm is this?!" Calypso shouts and I can feel the ship beginning to rock.

The swirling path of water gets wider and wider until it's double the size of the ship. My heart sinks and my knees grow weak once I've come to the realization.

"It's a whirlpool!"

"What the hell is she doin'? I thought you both were making up!" Calypso screams from behind me.

"I told you; she can't be trusted! Can you steer us away from it?" I look back to see Calypso struggling to steer the ship away from the whirlpool as it begins to pull us down and into the canyon that's divided by two huge mountains.

"Well, uhh- I don't typically ask this, but can you give me a hand?!" I rush up the stairs and join her side to help turn the wheel away from the massive whirlpool, but the ship doesn't budge an inch.

"Can't you use your magic wiggly woo hands to get us away from it? If we let it pull us in, it'll swallow the ship and if we make it though, we might crash into the walls!" I keep both of my hands on the wheel, resisting against it.

I look at the whirlpool that grows wider, the current becomes stronger and I quickly see we're getting dangerously close to the left side of the canyon.

"I can't do this! I've already tried getting through this once when there was no whirlpool! I can't!" The fear in Calypso's voice is heartbreaking.

I use Vessoria to make time slow down so only Calypso and I can move and talk and I speak to her quickly before time runs out.

"You are the most badass captain in all of Vassuren. If there's anyone who can fight the sea, it's you and you're not alone. I know what you've lost and I promise you're not about to lose more because I'm here to fight with you." Calypso looks around at the grey atmosphere that moves very slowly.

"Look at me." I say softly and she stares at me with her eyes wide open. A single tear slides down both of her cheeks and her black stain lips quiver. She keeps looking over at the terrifying whirlpool that tugs on the ship.

"I'm right here, I'm not going anywhere and we will make it through this as long as you trust me. You've gotten this far, don't give up now." Calypso looks out into the canyon. Her lips curl into a determined smile and her brows arch down.

"Aye. I follow ya lead." We both nod and time slowly returns back to normal. I run down the stairs while shouting directions at Calypso while running to the right side of the ship.

"Keep her steady and turn towards the edge of the vortex the best you can!" I immediately feel the ship turn left and we begin to ride on the rim of the whirlpool.

"I don't know how long I'll be able to hold it!" Calypso leans her entire body onto the wheel, trying to hold it in place, fighting against the strong tide.

"You own the sea! Now wrangle her in!" I look over ledge as the ship tilts to the right, allowing me to get a wider view of the perilous raging vortex that roars loudly, echoing down the canyon.

I grab onto a rope and use it to lift myself up onto the ledge. I tremble badly to the point where I nearly slip off but I remain holding the rope firmly. I lean over the ship and see the lower wooden platform that's getting splashed by water.

When I look back, I see we're inching closer to the other side of the canyon and close to colliding with the mountain. Indicating, it's now or never.

"Calypso, let go, NOW!" I scream, hoping she can hear me.

"WHAT?! YOU WANT US TO PLUMMET IN THE PIT WE'RE TRYING TO AVOID!" Her voice is faint but I can clearly hear her and her trembling fear as speaks quickly.

"Just trust me!" I shout as loud as I can and I grip the rope with both hands and jump down onto the lower platform, landing on it heavily and slamming my back into the body of the ship.

After gaining my balance, the ship immediately shifts and is seized by the wrathful sea. Salty water splashes into my face and the breeze slams against me harshly. I tie the rope around my waist just in case I end up falling over.

I push my feet against the wooden wall and blast the whirlpool with as much power as possible. My goal is to push against the whirlpool so that it will slingshot us out the way we came in.

The entire ship rattles and shakes abnormally as the ocean continues to roar. I hear a strange noise coming from the bottom of the ship, but all I see is raging waters.

"WHAT NOW?! WE CAN'T KEEP RIDING THE EDGE OR ELSE THE SHIP WILL START TO TAKE SERIOUS DAMAGE!" I can feel the ship turning outwards which means Calypso is doing what she can to turn us out of the hole since we're close to the canyon entrance.

I continue to do everything I can to push us up and out of the whirlpool but I've used too much magic to the point where my hands throb in pain. I've never used this much magic in such a short amount of time and it's taking a toll on me. I'm worried I'll run out of stamina and send us into the pool of death. Suddenly, the wooden floor that holds me up begins to crack. Time's running out.

"HOLD ON A LITTLE BIT LONGER!" I shout over the angry sea as Calypso continues to turn the wheel against the current, waiting patiently.

The vessel is slowly brought deeper into the swirling pit and water starts to flood over my feet. I use all my core strength to push against the sea but I begin to worry when I notice my hands are visibly shaking. I fear I'll lose grip on the tide. I can feel the power draining from me quickly but I refuse to give up until we've made it out safe.

With one last strong push, I blast the sea and it sends us shooting out of the whirlpool and we slowly sail away from the whirlpool.

The nose of the ship slams down and I fall to my knees, choking on air and water. I pull myself up with the rope and I fall over the ledge, trying to catch my breath while feeling my body pulse and throb in significant pain.

"You did it!" I shout at Calypso as I stare up at the sky, watching it clear up as the rain and thunder begins to disappear. Indicating we shouldn't be in any further danger.

"I can't believe that damn celery god tried to kill us! If I see her again, I swear, I'll...uhhh- I'll figure it out later." Calypso says humorously as Calypso falls over and sits against the wheel's post.

Our relaxation is interrupted by a loud *BOOM* that escapes from the depth of the sea.

"What was that?!" Calypso shouts and I slowly stand up, feeling my arms and legs shaking so much to the point where the armor rattles.

I look around, trying to figure out what caused the noise. I look in front of the ship and see the water begins to bubble as if it's being boiled.

I squint my eyes to make sure what I'm seeing is real and suddenly, a massive mountain bursts out of the water, pushing the ship backwards.

"What the hell?!" Calypso instantly jumps to her feet and turns the wheel all the right to steer us away from the mountain and we're left with no choice but to steer back towards the whirlpool.

"Silva! I did what you wanted! Please stop this!" I scream for her, hoping she'll respond.

At this point, Silva has completely gone completely mad and I don't have time to try to communicate with her any longer. I could try to break down the mountain, but that would put us at even more risk.

"Calypso! Steer directly into the eye of the whirlpool!" I yell at the captain while she fights against the current one more. I can see the exhaustion in her face and her hand shake violently from using all of her strength to fight the sea.

"Oh great! You wanna kill us too?! I guess you're crazier than I thought!" She shouts back as I run back up the stairs and stand at the back of the ship, facing the mountain, ready to push against it like I did with the whirlpool.

"There's no other choice! We're blocked in!" I respond and Calypso releases the wheel, letting the sea devour us.

"If my ship gets destroyed from this, I swear I'll kill you!" She screams and shrieks while hanging onto the wheel while we move forward rapidly.

I turn to face the mountain and thrust my hands out and hit the mountain with whatever power I have left. The pain I feel is excruciating and unbearable, but I'd rather risk my health than Calypso and her ship.

The force that's pushed against the mountain causes us to zoom forward rapidly. Calypso hangs on for dear life and I keep my balance, nearly digging my feet into the floor. I look back for a split second to see the water start to swallow the ship as it begins to flood the top deck.

I throw all of my body weight forward and use all my strength to push the ship through the center of the vortex.

I can feel my body beginning to crash so I lower my head and close my eyes, focusing on my strength and keeping myself standing.

"What is this?!" Calypso shouts and when I open my eyes, I see the ship covered by a bright blue aura. Vessoria has coated itself around the Nightwalker like a shield. I can feel the magic stretching around and protecting it.

I look back and watch as we intensely hit the eye of the whirlpool and bump over to the other side which causes the entire front half of the vessel to go airborne for a split moment. By the time the ship slams over the water, it pulls itself up and away from the whirlpool.

I release the magic and collapse once more, panting hard, trying to catch my breath. Thankfully, the current is no longer pulling us in and Calypso finally takes full control of the ship once again and we steadily sail down the canyon. I watch Calypso fall to the ground, landing dramatically on her back.

"Good thing Silva finally laid off, but I swear, if we get pulled into another one, I'm gonna lose my marbles. As if I have any left at this point." Calypso pants loudly. While she tries to recuperate, I get up, approach the wheel and steer us perfectly straight down the gorge.

"Get your hand off that wheel or I swear I'll cut it off." Out of the corner of my eye, she holds up her pointer finger towards the sky while she remains laying on the floor.

"Good luck with that captain, your dagger isn't in your scabbard. I'd let you borrow Vessoria, but I fear it'll kill you." I respond and Calypso's arm goes limp and crashes to the ground.

"Ya, I know. It's underdeck because I was sharpening it. Ya know what? I'm too tired to care. Just don't make us crash." Her sound of defeat makes me laugh under my breath and look down to see her cover her face with her hat.

"Damn, last time I approached this canyon- " She pauses. "Never mind, I won't get into it." She sounds silly with her voice being muffled under her hat.

"Well, now you must tell me because I'm interested in what you were going to say." I say weakly and Calypso lets out a long groan.

"Nope, that's a twisted tale for another day, mate. I've already told ya the gist. I'm more interested in knowin' where this gorge leads." She stands up and wobbles as she puts her hat back on.

"I'm goin' to see what damage was caused by that death pool." She walks downstairs and walks to the door that leads to the bottom deck. Before walking into the room, she turns and glares at me.

"You be one lucky bastard 'cause no one besides me has EVER steered my ship. Don't do anything stupid." She points at me as she walks through the doorway and disappears.

I hear a loud heartbeat thump in my ears and my vision becomes blurry and hazy. I've used too much power and have kept the armor on for too long.

I can't take any chances.
I can't remove the armor.

Calypso finally returns with the dagger in her hand and she looks like she's just seen a ghost.

"Are you alright?" I ask her and she shakes her head while flipping the dagger up and smoothly sliding it into her belt

"Aye, ya, it just looks uhhhh- messy down there. Nothing I can't fix." She walks awkwardly away from the door and I turn my attention forward, waiting to see a change in the terrain, hoping it'll lead us somewhere.

Calypso joins my side and politely takes the wheel. "What about ya? Ya alright?" I slowly sit down, feeling my muscles and bones throb. I take a deep breath and speak slowly.

"No. I don't understand what just happened. I can't believe Silva would do that. All I know is I need to find Helsen and get this over with." Calypso fluffs out her hair and runs her fingers through it, undoing the wet knots.

"So...all ya just gotta do is give her somethin' so she'll stop sending out screaming spooky dogs?" I nod my head and cough up some water, spitting it out on the wooden floor.

"Yes. Watching her almost end Zyla's life from some kind of ghostly realm was enough for me to make up my mind. You have no idea how terrifying it was to witness. I've lost too much already and as long as it's in my control...I'll do whatever I can to avoid more casualties, no matter how much I'm betrayed by those I trusted." We continue to sail and the sun begins to set behind us, cascading shadows over the mountains that we travel between. We twist and turn down the canyon until we're met by a dead end.

"Oh, how nice. A god almost kills us with spinnin' water, just to come across a dead end? That's just...stupid." Calypso says as she slams her hand over her face. I analyze the terrain. There's a wide circle of water that is bordered by mountains and it looks like one big end and nothing looks out of the ordinary. Something feels strange.

"I highly doubt we got pulled into a gorge, just to be met by a dead end. Keep us steered to the left side of the mountain." Calypso does what I ask and I walk to the right side of the ship to look around. Behind us, I hear a falcon screech as the water crashes against the mountain. Once I look at the water for a brief moment, I realize the water is moving outwards in a circle as if there's something in the center of the canyon.

"The water is moving weirdly." I say while continuing to stare at the rippling waves.

"Aye, well, the water did just try to eat us, so I won't be surprised if there are weirder things out here." She says sarcastically and I can tell how exhausted she is.

I hold up my hand and it ignites in black electric fire that flickers slowly, indicating I've used too much power. Instinctively, I pull my right arm back and gently push forward, releasing a black ball of fire from my palm.

"Woah mate, relax! I don't think there's anything smackable around here!" Calypso yells sarcastically behind me.

The ball soars far out into the distance and suddenly crashes into something solid in the middle of the canyon. Once the beam flies multiple feet away, it crashes into something solid, causing black fumes to spread in midair as if it slams against an invisible wall. The impact causes a loud warbling echo to emerge through the air and travel loudly down the canyon, ricocheting off the sides of the mountains.

"Oh crap, is that one of those force shield thingys Silva makes?" The captain slips and almost steers us into the mountain. I look at the space I attacked and I don't see any iridescent shimmer that Silva's barrier usually has.

"I think this one is different than the others." I have Calypso steer us that way, being careful not to crash into the invisible barrier. I look around the gorge and spot a small opening to the far side of the gorge.

"There's an opening down there that should be big enough for you to get out of. When I jump off, leave immediately because once I break through the seal, I'll disappear and I don't think I'll be able to see you. Do NOT stick around, no matter what you see or hear. Understood?" Calypso gazes at the exit and turns back to look at me, I can tell she's worried and unsure.

"I don't mean to doubt your judgment but...you know what you're doing right?" The captain asks cautiously.

I look at her, nod my head and smile. "I'll be fine. Hopefully after this, we'll meet once again and I'll repay you for your help." I say as I climb on top of the ship's railing while holding onto a wooden pole.

"Fate brought you to me twice now. I'm sure we'll see each other sooner than we think." She tips her hat down and smiles. "As long as you don't get ya self killed." She adds sarcastically while hiding her fear behind a sweet, fake laugh.

I turn to face the water and I take a deep breath before pushing off the ship, diving into the water. The height from the ship makes my stomach jump up to my chest. And once my body is submerged in the water, I immediately kick and swim as hard as I can to avoid being swept under the ship. Swimming with the armor tests my strength even more and with the little energy and stamina I have left, I'm not sure how much harder I can push forward.

I hold out my arm until I reach the invisible shield and once I bump into it, I try to push through it but it doesn't budge like the other ones.

Bobbing up and down in the water makes it difficult to breathe and if I stop kicking my feet, I'm sure I'll drown due to the density of the armor and the heaviness of the sword.

My hands ignite once again and I grip the shield like I'm about to tear it open. Once I dig my fingers into the shield and get a good grip on it, I'm immediately pulled into it like a powerful magnet.

I'll pull the shield apart until the opening is large enough to swim through and I move as quickly as possible to avoid being snapped in half by how strong it is.

I push through the barrier and start swimming. Upon looking back, I immediately realize I can't see through the shield. I don't see Calypso's ship and instead, I see the mountains that stretch around the water.

Once I twist myself around, I see dark red skies, black clouds and bleeding waters that run as red as blood. I look up and see bright glowing sparks of fire fall from the sky, sizzling and disintegrating into small puffs of smoke before touching my body or the water. There's a tall mountain that has black smoke coming out of the peak like a volcano. I look around and find a black stone pathway that leads into the mountain.

I quickly swim to the stone bridge and struggle to pull myself onto the surface. I lay on the ground for a split moment before getting to my feet. I can hear fire crackling and thunder rumbling above me. Eerie whispers float around in the air like ghosts and the mountain reeks of absolute death. This land is full of nothing but dark and evil energy that's so strong, I feel like it's already starting to suffocate me.

I stare down the stone pathway, hesitating to walk forward and I see two black doors covered with black poisoned vines that move like worms. I have no choice but to enter the mountain and search for Melantha.

The inside of the mountain is just as eerie and terrifying as the outside. A bad feeling immediately crawls up my spine and shakes me to my core.

Black and red smoke fills the enormous dark room and distant, inaudible whispers shoot past my ears. The entire mountain is hollow and there's a very small hole at the top where the smoke seeps out. I pull out the sword and continue to walk cautiously to the center of the mountain. I slowly turn around in a circle, making sure there's nothing around me.

The stone walls are coated with more black and red vines that secrete poisonous black magic. My footsteps echo and bounce around the walls and I hear a terrifying voice speak in my right ear, causing me to twist to the side.

"About time. I was beginning to think you weren't adequate to make the journey." I jolt around and see Melantha sitting on a throne made of black and red smoke and vines. I keep the tip of the blade pointed towards her ready to stab her through the heart.

"Ah, judging your new appearance, you've really pushed your limits. Soon you'll become a spitting image of me. Then we'll finally share something in common." The way she teases so menacingly angers me and I'm left standing frozen in place.

"I heard a rather unusual disturbance in the gorge. Was it you out there causing all that ruckus?" She stands up and while slowly walking towards me, her horns move in such a demented way that makes me sick. The tip of the two larger horns begin to point forward as if ready to strike. She runs her black long nails over her face while staring at me menacingly.

"Someone was trying to stop me from finding you, but that's of no importance." I respond under my breath, not interested in striking a conversation. Melantha smiles and her sharp teeth spoke out from behind her teeth.

"Then I assume you're here to give me what's mine." She begins to walk around me in a circle and I turn steadily with her to keep an eye on her.

"Let's get this over with so I never have to lay my eyes on you ever again." My chest begins to tighten and I'm on the verge of collapsing but stay standing tall, ready in case a simple talk escalates. "Thankfully for you, I'm in no mood to play silly little mind games...unlike your friends." Despite my disappointment in the Serafaes and Silva, her words still strike a nerve.

"Show it to me." She growls demandingly while holding her hand out, waving her scrawny finger towards her. I hesitate to call upon the crystal and a part of me screams for me to run.

"What do you plan to do with it?" I ask Melantha and she crosses her arms dramatically before walking back to her throne as her magic trails behind her.

"Oh, nothing much. Like I said, the stone was mine before those weak Serafaes stole it from me because they deemed I wasn't worthy of keeping it. I've had the crystal since I was practically born and I simply want it back so I can feel like myself again." She holds both hands over her chest and lowers her head. "I wouldn't suppose you know what it's like to have a huge piece of you missing and it hurts so much that it eats you from the inside out?" At first she sounds sarcastic but then she sounds sorrowful. I carefully walk towards her, keeping the blade pointed at her.

500

Melantha grows impatient and she walks to the center of the room.

"I don't think you realize what's at stake, princess. Let me show you." I watch as she lifts her arms up, casting thick clouds of smoke to grow from the ground. As the smoke suffocates me and makes me cough, I can hear the distant voices of men, women and children screaming.

I look closely at the dark and terrifying pillars and see strange visions start to fill inside the smoke like terrifying twisted mirrors. I look closer and watch in terror as I see Palavon being attacked and trampled by large groups of monstrous Aerolights.

Buildings are burning.

People are dying.

The village is destroyed.

I twist and turn around, watching each horrifying vision play before my eyes in each mirror of dark magic.

The voices of my people fill the air and I instantly begin to panic.

"NO! Stop them! They've done nothing wrong!" I feel helpless because there's nothing I can do to stop them. I shake my head and rub my eyes. "No. This isn't real. You're just trying to anger me so I'll give you the stupid rock!" Melantha laughs and emerges from behind the thin wall of black and red smoke.

"Oh please. Not even I'm bored enough to fake something like this. It's all happening right now as we speak. And only until you give the crystal to me, will I call the Aerolights back." Melantha faces me with her black brows arched, her lips curled and her hand reached out to me.

The screams of my people continue to fill my ears and my heart begins to race uncontrollably. My hands begin to tingle and my knees tremble under me.

Melantha tilts her head to the side and looks over at another pillar of magic that's next to me. "What if I just..." Melantha walks over the wall and waves her hand over the smoke to reveal a different vision.

My eyes widen in horror when I see a young boy being chased by one of the monsters. The boy screams while running for his life down a secluded dirt road. The beast roars and charges at him baring hundreds of razor-sharp teeth and massive talon claws. The boy continues to run until the monster spits out a gooey substance that lands in front of the boy and once he steps in it, his feet glue to the ground, making it impossible to move. He tries to break away from the gooey poisonous sap, but he can't.

"No...stop this!" I scream while Melantha smiles while continuing to watch the boy struggle.

"Only until you hand over the crystal will I rid your precious kingdom of this terror. Surely you don't want to see these beasts kill another innocent life." Tears flood down my cheeks as I watch the Aerolight lean over the terrified boy. The look in his eyes is something I never thought I'd ever witness.

"Call them off! NOW!" I scream as loud as I can and I feel power surge through my body, being influenced by the rage that begins to boil.

The Aerolight leans back while opening its massive mouth and before I can watch further, I run up and push Melantha away the vision wall, slamming her back into the wall.

"Here, take it!" I scream so loud that her magic begins to flicker and disappear. I release the power of the crystal and feel it form in my left hand. Once it's fully formed, I toss it at Melantha and she instantly catches it. She begins to pant hysterically, happy to have the stone in her possession. She looks at me before turning around and waving her hand over the vision.

I turn back to look at the vision and see the Aerolight mysteriously disappears and its gooey trap under the boy's legs seeps into the ground. The boy scuffs backwards and cries loudly before getting up and running away to safety. All of the other visions begin to disappear and I no longer hear the voices of the helpless ringing in my ears.

I look over and see Melantha caressing the stone with her hand.

"See? That wasn't so hard, was it? Maybe...just maybe. Had you acted sooner, there would have been less casualties. Let that be your lesson for next time." Melantha walks past me and I nearly fall to the ground from the overwhelming stress and guilt I feel.

I hear Melantha sigh in a satisfied manner and when I turn around, I see her filling the crystal with her sinister magic, making the clear crystal turn pitch black.

A heavy wind picks up and swirls around the mountain. I tighten my grip on the sword and Melantha's magic intensifies and swirls around her. Black and red smoke and vines grow around her body. It looks like she's trying to absorb the crystal.

I look over and see the door to the cave swing open and use this opportunity to slowly make my way towards it while she's distracted. Before I can get halfway there, Melantha lets out a horrifying demonic scream that hurts my ears.

I twist around and see Melantha bent over, holding the crystal low below her stomach. The crystal's power flickers in her hand and Melantha looks up with black tears running down her face and red veins protruding around her eyes. She looks at me with her eyes glowing dark red, her hair falls over her face and her horns curl up.

"Why is there a piece missing?!" She screams and before I have a chance to question what's going on, three clouds of smoke seep out of the ground and a strange growl emerges from below the mountain. The clouds of smoke quickly form the body of Aerolight canines that snarl loudly, bearing terrifyingly sharp teeth and claws. Black saliva drips from their mouths and they arch the front half of their bodies down, ready to attack.

After realizing how screwed I am, I put the sword away and hold up my hands. I'm in no position to fight three large canines and Melantha at once. I don't think I have enough strength to fight just one of the monsters alone.

"I gave you what the Serafaes gave me! I swear, I didn't know there was a part missing!" Melantha waves her hand down and up, using her incredible force to push me back against the wall.

After having the wind knocked out of me, her smoke suffocates me even more, making it difficult to breathe.

I try to push away from her, but she slams her left hand into my chest, causing the breastplate to dent and cave in, making it even more difficult to breathe. She keeps me held against the wall, with her black eyes fixated on me while the vile canines gather around her, snarling and barking loudly.

A bright red light catches my eye and when I look down, I see a red ball of magic spawn in her other hand. Its magic whirls and buzzes with toxic fumes that the armor can't block out and I can feel the broiling heat of her powers. Her hands shake violently and I'm too scared to speak or move.

"I swear I didn't know, they never told me something was missing-" There's so much physical pressure on my chest that I feel myself beginning to pass out and my vision begins to blur. Melantha observes me for a moment, turning her head to the side as if she's an animal ready to tear her prey apart. Her arched brows lift up and her lips curl into a smile.

Melantha, unexpectedly, lowers her hand and the raging ball of corrupted magic and it slowly dissipates.

"Mmm, I guess I have no choice but to believe you after what they've done." Her voice is low and raspy and has a monotonous echo.

She pulls away from me and I collapse to my knees, coughing violently, trying to breathe.

Melantha walks away from me and I glide slowly against the wall, heading for the door. Melantha stops and holds her hand up which makes the Aerolight dogs roar loudly.

"I said I'd spare your people. I never said the same for you." My feet freeze in place and her dogs walk towards me while crouching, ready to pounce at her command. My knees buckle under me and my back tenses up. I'm so scared, not a single word leaves my mouth.

"You swore!" My voice croaks and my throat itches painfully.

"Here's the thing, princess." She slowly turns around with the black crystal floating in her hand. "How can I cross my heart when I didn't have it until now?" She smiles and my own heart shatters in my chest when I realize what I've done. She holds the crystal to her chest and her skin absorbs the stone in the most grotesque manner and once the crystal enters her body, a deep red aura covers her body.

"I also didn't say I'd spare the Serafaes." My attention turns to the dogs that get dangerously close to me and I watch their bodies split into multiple pieces that morph into even more bodies. It horrifies me to see one small canine turn into eight large and terrifying monsters. The newly formed beasts stand before me with disfigured bodies and razor-sharp teeth and they stare at me with pitch black eyes that resemble Melantha's.

I grab the sword and slash it in front of the monsters, hoping it'll scare them off, but it doesn't. They keep slowly moving forward and Melantha watches, entertained by her creation. The Aerolights begin to bark and howl so loudly while backing me up against the wall. My heart races because I know I'm in no position to fight and it won't help my case if I kill just one of them. Five Aerolight dogs lean down and lunge forwards simultaneously and all I can do is close my eyes tightly and scream as loud as I can.

"SILVA!" Right before the canines can reach me, something large slams into the mountain and huge chunks of rocks fall, leaving a bigger hole in the mountain.

Melantha jolts around and turns her attention to the gaping hole in the mountain and the dogs run back and circle around her as if they're trying to protect her.

I shield my eyes from the dust and debris that falls. The entire mountain rumbles and shakes and I hear a loud roar come from outside. My skin goes cold and my heart races quickly when I see Phoenix dive into the mountain in her dragon form. When she lands heavily on the ground, she lifts her hand and smacks Melantha and her canines across the cave, keeping them away from me. She roars threateningly while keeping her blazing gold eyes on Melantha and her hellhounds.

She stands in front of me, shielding me from Melantha and her parasites. Burning hot fire and lava flows under her scales and smoke protrudes from her nose.

"Thank goodness I reached you in time." I hear Phoenix's voice echo in my mind and I look up at her, confused and exhausted.

"Don't let her know you can hear me." She turns to look at me and I nod my head.

"Zyla is here too and the others will be here shortly, just hold on and stay close to me." She speaks in a deep voice and pants heavily before turning her gaze back to Melantha as she and her dogs get up and look at Phoenix in awe. The dogs crowd around her and I look around, trying to figure out where Zyla is when all I see is nothing but darkness.

"Aww. The beast comes to save the beauty. How cliché." She snaps her fingers and two large walls of smoke grow next to her and transform into bigger hideous creatures.

Phoenix bends forward, ready to attack and in the blink of an eye, Melantha sends the Aerolights to charge at us. I begin to panic because Phoenix doesn't move and instead, she watches them steadily.

I watch the dogs that follow behind the two larger beasts and one of them looks different from the others. It's bigger and looks like an actual wolf instead of a demonic dog.

I watch as the black smoke coated wolf charges out in front of the others and turns around, instantly striking them down and killing them one by one. The wolf takes them by such surprise that the others don't have time to react and are immediately slaughtered and their hearts are destroyed.

Melantha looks absolutely disgusted as she glares at the wolf that remind standing in the center of the floor.

"What the hell is this?!" She screams loudly and a bright white light catches my attention and I look up to see two beams of light dive into the cave and they gather in front of the smoky wolf.

Once the two light sources touch the ground, Silva and Aerowen grow with their elements and the black smoke that surrounds the wolf drops, revealing Zyla under the mask. Melantha growls, annoyed at the sight of Silva and the Serafaes.

"How nice of the mighty calvary to finally show up. I was really hoping the Aerolights would keep you busy just a tad bit longer." Silva's hands curl into magic ignited fists and an icy spear grows out of Aerowen's hand. Zyla walks around them to face Melantha with her magic trailing behind her.

"Was that the same mindset you had when they tried to sink the ship in the gorge?" Zyla asks in a deep voice. I move out from behind Phoenix's wing and look around, confused by what she's talking about.

"Wait. She's the one who-" Before I can continue, Silva steps closer towards Melantha, growing in height, standing taller than the others.

"Yes. She tried to make you think the whirlpool and the mountain spurting out of the water was me so you'd turn on me, which is exactly what I was trying to warn you about. She wanted to turn a human on a god so there was no truth to believe." Silva says, annoyed as she turns her head slightly, looking at me out of the corner of her glowing yellow eyes. By the tone in her voice and the way she stands, I can tell she is exhausted.

"She sent the damn beasts out to sink the ship once you started putting up a fight. Thankfully, she didn't know I was there and they didn't have a chance." The more Zyla continues to explain, the more foolish I feel after causing all the trouble I did.

"It took us longer to get here because we were busy defending the village from her Aerolights until she called them off." Aerowen adds and her frost flurries around here and the ground under her feet is frozen.

I instantly think back to the visions Melantha showed and the terror painted across the young boy's face remains burned in my mind.

"Imagine that. With one hand, I was distracting you two and with the other, I was trying to drown a ship while exhausting the princess' powers! Who knew it'd all play out so well?" Melantha smiles and chuckles mischievously. She's a lot smarter than I thought and I start to feel sick once I realize I fell for a trap and I lead the others right into it.

"Was that always your plan? To send your pawns out to find and kill your sister? Like you did the same to your mother?!" Silva shouts angrily and my own nerves spike once I hear of my mother.

Melantha taunts us with her magic as it flows freely around her and she runs her black sharp claws over her chest where the crystal is now barred.

"Who knew one who knows so much could know so little at the same time?" Melantha walks up to Silva and the Serafaes stand still, prepared to fight and Silva stands her ground while looking down at Melantha with her powers ignited in her hand.

"I have a secret to tell you." Melantha uses her black magic to carry her up to Silva's ear and she whispers quietly but loud enough for everyone to hear. "I don't need the Aerolight to take care of something so simple." In the blink of an eye. Silva pushes her hand forward, striking Melantha in the chest with her magic and slamming her into the wall, causing the mountain to rumble. The Serafaes' magic all ignite powerfully at the same time and each of their elements fill the atmosphere.

"Ooh, did I strike a nerve?" Melantha lifts herself off the ground, laughing and wobbling around. Silva stands angrily with her shoulders tense and her fists curled. Aerowen pushes her hands forward and freezes Melantha's wrists to the wall while growing a giant sharp spike from the ground that points towards Melantha's chest.

Melantha looks down at the spike and continues to laugh, unbothered by both Silva and Aerowen's magic.

Silva stomps forward and her magic intensifies around her even more.

"You killed her?!" Silva shouts so loudly, the volcanic cave shakes. Tears instantly stream down my face, and I rush forward, but before I can get far, Phoenix pulls me back with her tail and holds me gently.

"NO!" I scream loudly while Melantha looks over at me deviously with a black smile on her face.

"Welllll, whether by my hand or the Aerolight's, it was going to be me regardless." Melantha shakes her head dementedly, purposely irritating Silva. I begin to hyperventilate and break down hysterically, wanting nothing more than to destroy Melantha.

"PHOENIX, LET ME GO!" I finally break from Pheonix's grip, but when I do, Melantha laughs and black smoke swells around everyone, blocking them from my view.

Her menacing laugh echoes around me like a haunting melody waiting to sleep me to death.

"Silva! Pheonix?!" I shout, trying to find them, but all I see is thick black smoke and once it drops, I'm left standing in a very dark forest. Everything is silent. Nothing in this atmosphere moves.

Am I outside of Helsen?

I ask myself while looking around, trying to figure out what happened.

"Does it not feel familiar?" I hear Melantha's voice speaking out loud as if she was able to hear my thoughts. "This is the night your world came crashing down." I try moving around, but my body hurts too much to take a step forward.

"No, it isn't. This is just another one of your tricks!" I shout with tears sliding down my cheeks and my cry getting stuck in the back of my throat. Melantha laughs menacingly, sending shivers down my spine.

"My magic is dark but make no mistake...it never lies." Her voice disappears and out of the corner of my eye, I see a subtle red explosion occur in the distance. I look around and see no signs of Melantha and I'm left with no choice but to find what caused that light and explosion.

Running makes my entire body feel like it's on fire and on the verge of breaking apart.

Once I'm closer to the red light, it begins to zip off into the forest and I do what I can to keep up with it.

While running in the forest I can hear the whispers and shrieks of Melantha's Aerolights running through the forest all around me. I assume we're after the same light.

I run up to a steep grassy hill that's covered by trees and large boulders and below, I see a figure run out into the flat field, looking at something that's chasing them.

I swiftly descend the mountain, skillfully maneuvering around trees and rocks, and making every effort to maintain my balance.

The armor begins to weigh me down but taking it off poses a bigger risk that I'm not willing to take right now.

Once I reach the bottom of the hill, I run out into the field and realize the red light has vanished and the Aerolights continue to howl and roar in the forest around me, separating and going in different directions.

They're looking for me.

I instantly realize where I am in the moment of time, and I look around to see any signs of movement or activity. And before I can make another move, something runs behind me and I hear metal clashing with magic. A powerful gust of wind pushes me forward and when I turn around, the red light stands before me.

But it's not a light...

It's a woman.

I run as fast as I can to keep up with Aladora who's trying everything she can to reach her daughter at this moment of time. After realizing she's being closely pursued by Melantha and her monsters, she stops in the middle of the field and turns around with Vessoria in hand and her red and gold armor ignited.

She holds her sword in front of her and Melantha appears out of the ground behind a gust of smoke.

"What is it you'll gain from destroying the kingdom?" Aladora says firmly while painting and standing strong, ready to fight.

"Freedom." Melantha responds while keeping her distance with her sharp black horns moving around slowly like snakes. "There'll be no one to trap me on a god forsaken island." The demon says with her brows furrowed and her pitch-black eyes holding nothing but tunnels of darkness.

"You really think that's possible after a *god* was the one who trapped you there in the first place?" Aladora asks while taking a few steps back. She constantly looks back, listening for Vivalda who has just left the castle walls.

"Let me tell you a little secret." Melantha steps closer and Aladora pulls her sword back, ready to use it. "Once my heart is returned, I'll open the Sylphenic Realm and devour every inch of the land. And the 'god' you speak of will have no way healing what remains permanently dead." A menacing smile forms on the demon's face and her sharp teeth protrude from behind her black lips.

Aladora and I turn our attention to the distance when we hear one of the Aerolight canines howling loudly.

"Looks like one of my pets has found one of your precious daughters." Melantha says with a smirk on her face.

"My daughters have nothing to do with this! Please! I know Kalvara is still in there! Please set her free and we can make amends. No more barriers. No more isolation." Aladora pleads with Melantha, hoping she'll budge and the demon stares at her with a smirk on her face.

I observe Melantha's figure and realize it's glitchy, indicating she's standing between reality and the Sylphenic realm. With every movement, her body shutters and moves abnormally. She's here and not at the same time.

She can touch reality, but it can't touch her since her body is back on Helsen.

I can't help but watch in utter silence since I know the events unraveling before me are nothing but painful memories and I'm determined to see what happens.

I begin to hear too many sounds at the same time. I can hear me running through the forest, Vivalda running on her horse through the rain, the Aerolights growling and Aladora's thoughts racing.

"I need to find Vivalda."

"I can't take on Melantha by myself, but I have no choice."

I close my eyes tightly. Hearing her and seeing her as if she's truly here shatters what remains of my heart. I want to do everything I can to break this memory, but it's impossible.

"If only you didn't abandon poor Kalvara the way you did...you'd wouldn't be in this predicament." Melantha says in a deep voice while raising both of her hands up, making a thick wall of black smoke grow from the ground.

The smoke turns into several Aerolights that charge at Aladora and she attacks them one by one, slashing and stabbing them with her sword.

"I didn't abandon her! You put it in her head!" Aladora shouts while fighting, tearing the beasts apart.

I walk around the fight and stand closely next to her. Any Aerolight that gets in my way brushes through my body as if I'm a ghost. "You weakened her! You made her feel worthless so she'd be easier to possess!"

With her left hand, she strikes one of the beasts in the chest with her powers. With the sword in her right, she slices another monster across the chest, killing it instantly.

Seeing the satisfied look on Melantha's face makes my anger rise. I can feel my magic boiling under my skin like an active volcano on the verge of erupting.

Melantha catches my attention and I notice her begin to slowly retreat from the fight with nothing but a sinister smile on her face. I watch her wave her fingers towards the ground and she grows one more Aerolight from the ground and it stands tall over her, covering her from Aladora's view.

When Aladora turns around, she aims for the last remaining beast that stands in front of Melantha. The queen takes her sword with both hands, lifting the blade up over her right shoulder and she swings it across the monster's body. As soon as she attacks, I see Melantha's form beginning to shift and change in a demented way. When the Aerolight dies and disappears, a cloud of smoke grows and falls in front of Aladora, revealing her eldest daughter, Kalvara standing before her.

Melantha dropped the possession.

Aladora and I gasp simultaneously at the sight of the princess looking like herself. Her physical appearance is black, but she looks beaten and terribly exhausted. The bags under her eyes are black, her skin is pale and skinny and malnourished due to Melantha's corruption.

Kalvara's straight long hair is thin and greasy and strands stick to the side of her face and fall over her shoulders. All that covers her body is a torn black dress she wore the last time I saw her as herself, hundreds of moons ago.

This poor child...she's been through so much...and we can't see it.

When Kalvara looks up, she can barely stay standing when she looks at her mother. Both of their knees buckle and Aladora instantly drops her sword with the blade stabbing the ground. She and her daughter run up to each other and embrace each other with a hug.

Aladora and Kalvara cry in each other's arms and fall to their knees.

"Oh, my baby. I'm so sorry. I'm doing everything I can to save you." Aladora sobs as I walk closer to them, still keeping my distance, cautiously looking around to see if any other Aerolights will appear.

I never thought I'd see such a sight, it's haunting beautiful and yet at the same time, something feels wrong.

"I know..." Kalvara says weakly with her head in Aladora's chest. "But in the end..." She takes a deep breath and I see a dark red light forming from her hand that rest between them. My eyes widen in horror and I step closer, thinking for a moment that I could stop the memory.

"ALADORA, IT'S A TRICK!" I begin to lunge forward when a sudden pain strikes me in the stomach and holds me back from reaching Aladora.

"You were never enough." Kalvara says and at the same time, Melantha's voice fades in, wiping Kalvara away and possessing her body once again, showing her true form.

When I look down, I see Melantha slowly returning to her demonic form and in her hand is a black shard of dark magic that's impaling Aladora in the stomach, through her armor.

As Kalvara fades away, I can hear her scream in horror at what she's done. Although, it wasn't HER...Melantha made her do it against her will in order to trick the queen.

Melantha leans closer to Aladora and they both lock eyes. Aladora is too hurt to move and seeing her in such pain again shatters my soul and tears begin to swell in my eyes.

I should have been here. I could have helped her.

And I couldn't. I CAN'T!

"I expected more from the 'mighty Aladora.'" Melantha says while observing the pain she has caused, watching the Sylphenic magic spread through Aladora's body like a virus. I don't have the heart to look at my friend who's in unimaginable pain.

"I've done my part. Now the next of the mighty will rise. And she will destroy you." Aladora says weakly, choking on air and blood that begins to rise from her stomach.

"Mmm, I doubt it. Look how that's played out so far." Melantha suddenly turns her attention to me, looking at me dead in the eye.

This is a memory...how is she looking at me?!

The pain in my stomach that synchronizes with Aladora's intensifies and I can't help but let out a scream. Before I close my eyes, I see Melantha smile and chuckle.

I close my eyes tightly while enduring this pain and once I open them again, I'm back to the current state of things and I'm taken out of the horrid memory.

When I look down to see what causes me such pain, I see Melantha holding a large sharp piece of Aerowen's ice that's been infected with her dark magic, stabbing me all the way through my stomach.

"SILVA!" Vivalda screams violently.

I look at the monster in the eye, trying to keep myself together as I can feel my magic raging inside me like an uncontrollable storm. I can't help but let out a slight laugh. I take my right hand and rest it on the spike of ice.

"You really thought you could trick a god?" I ask and Melantha laughs in my face.

"No." She says slowly while taking a deep breath while continuing to push the spike through my body.

"It wasn't you I was trying to trick."

PHOENIX

I continue to hold Vivalda back while she sobs loudly over my tail. I can feel her tears sliding down and dripping onto my scales. Melantha and the others continue to face off with each other, having a quiet conversation when something makes my ears perk up. A strange sensation fills the air and I feel an odd magnetic force tugging me to the side.

I scan the cave and once I reach the wall to the far left that's right in front of Vivalda, I notice the stone is moving unnaturally. It isn't crumbling, but instead it moves like thick liquid.

Melantha laughs maniacally and a terrifying demonic voice intertwines with hers, making her sound like a creature from Hell.

Before anyone else can react, my attention rapidly turns to the wall as a massive hideous monster protrudes from the rock.

Its body rapidly disconnects from the mountain and it pulls away as if it's glued to the stone. I roar loudly and pull Vivalda closer to me, taking her by surprise and causing her to shriek.

From the corner of my eye, I see Silva break away the ice and immediately attack Melantha, with Zyla and Aerowen joining forces to keep her back.

I lunge in front of Vivalda, keeping her held back from the fight I prepare to take on with the giant. Once I have the monster in my beastly grasp, I release Vivalda from my grip once she's at a safer distance and the Aerolight throws its body at me.

As soon as our forces collide, we're surrounded and coated by blazing flames that spin around us like a tornado. The Aerolight lunges forward and digs its teeth into my skin, penetrating the solid layer of scales. It slashes me with its razor-sharp claws and roars loudly.

I retaliate by sinking my claws and teeth into its body and dragging my hand down, tearing apart its body. The large brute opens its mouth widely and before it has a chance to attack, I spit a raging torch of fire into its gaping mouth, burning it from the inside out, killing it instantly. Its body disintegrates and its remains get swept up by the swirling vortex of fire.

I catch my breath as the fire continues to rage around me and I see the Serafaes backing up to protect Vivalda who is overwhelmed and disoriented. Silva's body begins to heal and due to the Sylphenic magic, her magic isn't as strong as usual.

More Aerolights spawn in behind Melantha like parasites.

Before joining the others, I look down at my hands and realize I'm no longer in my beast form. Fires spark in my palms and I swipe my hand over the fiery tunnel and push them forward, striking Melantha and her pawns with raging tunnels of fire. Once Melantha sets her sight on the fire, she jumps back behind the Aerolights and they shield her from the flames.

"If you want to fight nasty, don't have your pathetic pawns do it for you." I growl at Melantha who's angered to see her puppets melting around her.

I walk over to join the others and Vivalda moves closely to me.

"Oh darling." She chuckles. "They're not pathetic if they get the job done." Silva looks at me and her eyes widen. I can tell behind her glowing yellow eyes that she's absolutely horrified.

I take both of my hands and slam them down into the stone floor, causing it to rumble and crack. Craters are formed in the ground and large boulders grow, encapsulating Melantha. I pull my elbows back and as when I thrust them forward, I create another fire raging tornado that spins around Melantha, keeping her trapped. Despite blistering heat from the flames, she manages to summon the rest of the Aerolights that remain hovering outside the mountain and they dive into the cave like a flock of bats.

"Zyla!" Silva shouts and the enchantress rushes forward to combine her dark magic with my fire. Her purple magic intertwines with my flames, acting as a magnet that sucks the Aerolights into the tornado of fire. Their bodies spin and swirl around rapidly, burning their bodies to a crisp. The death of her pawns causes Melantha to fall to her knees and scream in agony.

"We need to go now! It'll hold her off!" I shout at the others before turning to face Vivalda who is in tears, frozen in fear.

Without saying a word, I bend down and scoop Vivalda in my arms before taking off into the sky. Zyla transforms into a falcon while Silva and Aerowen shift into bright glowing wisps. The sound of Aerolights screaming and dying echoes behind us and slowly drowns.

When we exit the mountain, Silva opens the barrier so we can all get out of it and once we've all made it through, Silva closes it and strengthens it. Together, we take off quickly and make our way to the Lion's Eye.

While flying, my attention then turns to Vivalda who coughs violently and I look down to see her wiping blood from the corner of her lips.

"She's used too much power, Silva." I say in my mind and Silva quickly responds.

"I know, we'll take care of it as soon as we reach the forest. Fly steadily." I nod my head and proceed to check on Vivalda.

"I'd ask if you're okay, but I know you'd say yes despite looking so terrible." I say lightly. I can tell Vivalda is going through so much emotionally and physically.

"I've made a mess of everything." She cries and covers her face with her hands.

"Don't think like that right now. There's nothing you've broken that can't be fixed." She coughs some more, I can feel her body drop heavily in my arms due to extreme exhaustion. I hear Zyla's wings flapping heavily and I look to the side to see her flying irregularly. Her golden eyes are heavy and she begins to slow down.

I get her attention and gesture to my back. She looks over and willingly flies over me and lands on my back. I feel her body shaking terribly. Everyone is exhausted from using so much power. By the time the edge of the forest is in sight, Zyla flies off my back and dives into the trees.

"Hopefully this landing won't be as rough as last time." I say and Vivalda tucks her head into my chest.

Due to my large wingspan, I hover over the treetops and find a clear opening under the leaves and branches. I tuck in my wings and slowly descend to the ground and I manage to land on my feet, making the trees quiver and shake.

Once we're safe on solid ground, I gently put Vivalda down. Her legs shake and she has a hard time standing. Her eyes are still pitch black and the white areas of her eyes are now bloodshot, which makes me worry even more. But thankfully, the black tears that ran down her neck have disappeared and the black marks around her eyes are slowly fading away.

Silva and Aerowen quickly land in the forest and Zyla remains perched on a large tree branch before transforming back to her natural form and slouching back against the trunk of the tree, catching her breath.

Aerowen and Silva immediately transform into their normal selves once their glowing orbs touch the grass. Aerowen looks less blue and more gray and Silva's light glows dim and almost colorless.

"Zyla, are you alright?" Silva asks her as she looks at the tree Zyla lays in, hidden within the shadows.

"Yes. I'd prefer to be left alone please." Her voice is muffled and she sounds exhausted.

We give her space and turn our attention to Vivalda who stares at each of us, one by one. She tries to speak but all that comes from her is instant tears. Before we know it, she immediately begins to fall on her knees, but before she touches the ground, Silva rushes to her and catches her in her arms.

Vivalda's body falls limp in my arms and she cries in my chest with her hands cupped over her face. I keep my arms wrapped around her and let her take out her anger and sadness.

"I can't get it out of my head." Vivalda sobs into my body and the rest of us cry with her after witnessing the memory Melantha showed us.

"I'm so sorry, Silva. I should have listened. I never wanted-" She weeps quietly, running out of breath.

I slowly sink into the ground while holding Vivalda in my arms and I feel the blades of grass wrap around the bottom half of my body.

I take a deep breath. "Release." I say softly while breathing out slowly. The princess wraps her arms around me tightly, nearly digging her nails into my stone skin. I allow her to do what she must in order to let go of her bottled pain.

I take a deep breath and when I do, the forest lights up and its heart beats with me. I look up and Aerowen and Phoenix's bodies also illuminate, adding a beautiful ambiance to the atmosphere. A playful breeze comes in and sweeps under everyone and the plants bend towards me as if hugging me and hugging everyone.

"Nothing will hurt you. I'm here." Once Vivalda realizes she's safe and there's nothing stopping her from screaming, she lets out the most heartbreaking, yet relieving cry I've ever heard.

As she screams and sobs loudly, I feel green tears slowly gliding down my face. Vivalda continues to cry in my chest and I continue to speak to her, even if she can't hear me.

"In some way...we all tried to reach the same goal. We tried to reach each other beyond the unknown." I try to hold my cries back but the sound of everyone's sorrow shatters me.

"You and I are more similar than you think, Vivalda. We both reacted out of anger and learned a valuable lesson from it."

Vivalda pulls away from me and I keep my hands rested on her shoulders. She looks at me with puffy red cheeks and sunken eyes.

"Even a god needs to release her pain." I proceed to hold her tightly and our sorrow intertwines as one. I feel two arms wrap around Vivalda and I and when I look over, I see Zyla leaning in, hugging us both.

Vivalda looks up and is shocked to see her. The enchantress pulls both of our heads close to her and we all lean against each other.

"This doesn't change my hatred for humans. It just changes my heart for a few." She says while golden tears stream down her face.

I feel something cold touch my hand and Aerowen joins us, holding both mine and Vivalda's hand.

Aerowen's ice glows brightly and the frozen strands in her hair glisten and twinkle in the light. Vivalda continues to cry softly and I can feel her heart beginning to feel content. Phoenix also joins us and she sits right behind Vivalda, resting her hand on the princess's shoulder.

Two tears slide down my face and fall onto the grass and when the soil absorbs them, a beautiful bundle of glowing flowers sprout from the grass. One beautiful bud blooms and faces each of us and it beams with the rhythm of my heartbeat. I feel myself beginning to smile.

"We're going to get through this together." I softly and we all sit up to face each other. Everyone has tears in their eyes and love beaming in their hearts. I reach out and hold Vivalda's face in my hands while wiping away her tears and as I do, her black marks and the designs on her armor begin to turn blue again.

"Whatever you need in order to heal, we'll be here, okay? No more secrets." Phoenix says behind her and Vivalda nods her head, smiling.

"This pain and loss what we share now. We can grow and overcome together." Zyla says softly, reassuring everyone. It's obvious that everyone is shaken by the memory we all shared. But I can't imagine how much heavier that burden is for Vivalda to carry.

"I promise I'll never do something foolish like that ever again." Vivalda looks up and around and once she locks eyes with Zyla her smile widens.

"I knew there was more to that stone cold heart of yours." Vivalda teases the enchantress as she scoffs. Zyla takes a deep breath, contemplating on speaking.

"Well, since we're all here being sappy together." She rolls her eyes and pauses, observing the others before continuing. "You and Aladora are the only humans I've ever found love for." Vivalda's eyes widen and her mouth gapes open slightly. "You remind me a lot of my daughter. When I looked at you and your mother, all I ever saw was me and my own." A few more tears begin to stream down Zyla's face, but she quickly wipes them away before they can drip onto the white and grey fur pelt that rests across her chest.

"Aww I never thought a Serafae as strong and spooky as you could have such a gentle heart." Vivalda rests her hands over her heart and continues to tease the enchantress.

"Now, you're pushing it." Zyla growls playfully with one brow raised and a smile crosses her face. We all share a laugh together.

"In all seriousness. I didn't know you had a daughter. Will you ever tell me about her?" Vivalda asks gently and Zyla looks at her with heavy eyes and a gentle smile.

"If you get us through the battle ahead, I don't see why not." I look around and see everyone smile. I look down at Vivalda's armor and see that it's gone back to normal.

"Before we decide what we need to do, there's something crucial we need to handle. I need to remove the armor." Vivalda looks at me, absolutely terrified. "It'll be okay. No matter what happens, we'll be here to ensure you stay with us." Everyone stands up and the Serafaes circle around Vivalda, giving her space.

I can sense her paranoia and I hear the thoughts that tell her she'll pass out like last time.

"We'll be here to catch you if you fall." I reassure her as she takes deep and steady breaths.

Zyla's hands ignite in purple and black smoke, indicating she's ready to retrieve whatever Sylphenic magic may be residing in Vivalda's body. Vivalda takes out the sword and holds it with one hand. She takes a deep breath and as she exhales, a gust of wind and smoke circle up and around her. When the smoke disappears, Vivalda remains standing in her long blue overcoat with the silver necklace in her hand. Her eyes widen and she looks at me, confused as to why nothing has happened and I look at the others who are just as confused.

"Please tell me we're all just as equally confused. Why didn't anything weird happen?" Vivalda asks sarcastically.

"Don't jinx it, you could drop dead at any moment." Zyla says in a serious tone but Vivalda thinks she's joking.

Zyla steps forward and waves her hands over Vivalda, allowing her magic to flow gently around her body. Once it's done and Zyla's magic returns to her, a wave of surprise washes over her.

"There's not a single drop of Sylphenic magic in your body." Zyla closes her hands and crosses them in front of her, trying to understand how it's possible.

"I'm not taking any chances, try it again." Vivalda urges the enchantress while wiggling around anxiously and Zyla looks at the princess expressionlessly.

"No." She says in the flat tone which offends Vivalda.

Phoenix laughs quietly behind her and Vivalda snaps her head around to scold her.

"I trust Zyla and her magic. Sylphenic magic isn't prone to hiding itself unless another force is covering it." I ponder to myself for a split moment before coming to a strange realization.

"I think in the process of you doing all the fighting that you have and after using your power to its extent, you may have dissolved her magic all by yourself without realizing." Vivalda's eyes shoot up at me and she instantly panics.

"So, you're saying I'm going to be evil like her?!" She squawks and her silly concern makes the rest of us laugh which helps ease the tension.

"No, by dissolving magic, you simply break it apart and make it disappear. She pushed the boundaries of your power so you have room to absorb her magic, thinking it'd kill you." She looks at me even more confused and I try to simplify my words so it's easier to understand. "It's similar to when you get sick and your body's reaction is to fight off...the infection-" I pause and my mind begins to wander through several thoughts. The other look at me, confused, waiting for me to say something.

"What are you thinking?" Aerowen asks.

"There's some things you should know about Melantha and her past." Vivalda looks at me and her interest is immediately piqued. I lead them to a large tree that's in the middle of a small field and we gather around to rest while I speak to Vivalda.

Phoenix sits next to Vivalda while she leans against the tree and the rest of us circle round.

"It won't take Melantha long to break through the barrier. So, to make a very long story short, as you were able to tell by the memory, Melantha hasn't always been...Melantha. She was born as Kalvara." Vivalda's brows scrunch and she looks down, saddened.

"Is that who that girl was?" She asks and I nod my head.

"Once Kalvara knew Aladora was pregnant with you, she was ecstatic to be a big sister. And the moment you came into the world, you became hers and she loved you and River so much." The princess looks at me as if she doesn't believe that statement and I don't blame her. I wouldn't believe it either if I were in her position.

"One day, she was consumed by dark Sylphenic magic that latched onto unwanted negative thoughts and emotions. By that bond being forged, the Sylphenic magic slowly took over. As time went on, your mother and I couldn't keep her magic hidden from other humans. People started to act out in fear, worried that the kingdom was doomed and that Kalvara was a bad omen sent to punish humans for all they've done wrong in the past. On one of the last days where Kalvara was still in control, she ran away in order to try to protect you all, and your mother did everything she could every day to find her and bring her home." The thoughts in Vivalda's mind begin to click.

"So, I'd assume that the kingdom of Astry doesn't exist? My mother was just leaving to find Kalvara?" She asks curiously and I nod my head.

"Yes. Unfortunately, the Sylphenic magic grew to be too strong and eventually, Melantha took complete control of Kalvara, using her body and nothing but a host. She turned your sister into the monster that a voice in her head told her she was. With that monster being Melantha." Vivalda looks down, distraught by the information I share.

"I heard her scream after Melantha took over her body again...she wasn't in control." Vivalda adds and I can feel my chest continuing to throb, even after it's been healed.

"I had no choice but to trap her on Helsen. That's where your mother would go every day when she left the castle in hopes to bring Kalvara back home, but nothing worked. Your mother and Melantha would get into altercations and fights before Aladora would make it out of the barrier. During Melantha's days of isolation, her magic only grew more and more powerful to the point where she found a way to use the Sylphenic realm to roam the land without being physically present." I can tell Vivalda is trying to make sense of everything I tell her and she's piecing everything together very slowly.

"The Sylphenic realm is nothing but death and darkness. Nothing lives, except for the dead. If she has her heart, she can permanently break a hole between reality and her dark reality. Since she has part of it, her powers stronger but it doesn't allow her to keep the Sylphenic Realm open. On the day you fell asleep, both your mother and I sensed Melantha creating the Aerolights. She spent a long time perfecting that dark trick and once she was ready, she unleashed the monsters into the kingdom. Which was the same day your mother died." Vivalda looks at me with her eyes wide open.

"Do you think it's possible to separate Melantha from Kalvara?" Vivalda asks and all of the Serafaes turn their attention to her.

"Yes. That's why Vessoria chose you. Even if you can't reach Kalvara, you can still destroy Melantha." Vivalda looks down at the necklace in her hand and she clasps it around her neck.

"I know there's still much more to explain and I'm sorry that-" Before I can continue Vivalda gently holds out her hand.

"No. No more apologies. I think some things are to be left in the past untouched. I know everything I need to in order to finish this. What's important is how we handle the situation at hand." I smile and agree with what she says, as do the others.

"Melantha will break out of that barrier soon and when she does, she'll raise hell like no other. Will she be after the last remaining piece of her heart?" Aerowen asks.

"The missing piece will allow her to release the full potential of her magic and open the bridge between both Vassuren and the Sylphenic Realm. With or without the final piece, she'll be hellbent on destroying the kingdom regardless." Zyla's voice is deep and serious and she ponders to herself, thinking about what we should do next.

"How long do we have until she breaks through the barrier?" Vivalda asks while leaning against Phoenix's wing that covers her like a blanket.

"Maybe a day or two. I will sense the barrier shake once Melantha begins to break through and once the barrier falls, we will be her first target. I can almost guarantee she'll keep the Aerolights by her side so she can grow an army." I continue to explain and Vivalda's head perks up.

"Why would she need an army if she can keep creating them?" The princess asks, slightly confused.

"She can only create new monsters if she's focused. Without focus, she can't spawn them out of thin air, but she can keep them hidden, making it look like she's creating them in current time. If we keep her distracted in a fight, it takes her longer to conjure them."

Vivalda nods her head, and a cold breeze brushes over us.

"Let's try not to worry about it tonight and let's get some rest while we can."

Vivalda

I continue to sit with Phoenix for a moment while the others find a spot to rest.

"Thank you for saving me, again." I look up at her and she smiles.

"Don't thank me. I think you humans have a saying 'it's what friends do for each other'." I nod my head happily and I can feel Phoenix's heat emitting from her body, warming me up from the cold night. I look around and see the others getting ready to rest.

Phoenix yawns loudly and growls quietly when she exhales.

"Wow, you must be really tired, huh?" I joke with her and watch a gentle smile form on her face, barely revealing the tips of her fangs.

Phoenix rests her hands on her chest and stretches out her left wing before resting it back over her body.

"Well do forgive me, *your highness*. But after all that flying and saving your bum twice in one day, yes, I'm quite exhausted." She teases back and laughs before sitting comfortably against the tree. Phoenix looks at me for a brief moment and I watch her eyes graze past mine as if something catches her attention behind me.

"What are you looking at me like that for?" She asks while tilting her head to the side. I look over to my right and see Silva blatantly staring at Phoenix, not saying a single word. "Someone read her mind, because I can't." Phoenix jokes and laughs.

Silva's awkward silence confuses me and I can tell Zyla and Aerowen are just as equally confused because they exchange a concerning look between each other. Silva gets up, glides over to us and kneels in front of Phoenix.

"What's wrong?" The motherly tone in Silva's voice instantly causes the others and I to worry. Zyla and Aerowen quickly rush over to us and I feel my face go cold and numb.

"Goodness, what's the calvary panicking for? I know all but one of you has seen a sleepy dragon before." Phoenix tries to make us laugh but we remain silent. I look back and forth between her and Silva, waiting for an explanation as to what's going on.

"You both are scaring me. What's going on?" My voice trembles and my teeth begin to chatter.

Silva gently waves her hands over Phoenix and uses her powers to carefully move her left wing away and to the side, revealing Phoenix's scaly arm wrapped around her stomach.

"Move your arm." Silva says seriously and Phoenix stares at her awkwardly with her brows arched, trying to keep her pride attached. But she ultimately obeys and does what the god asks.

She hesitantly moves her arm away and I instantly gasp and cover my mouth when I see a pit of dark magic eating her thick scaly skin away, causing her skin to crack and decay.

Aerowen's frost grows colder and Zyla's hands turn completely black and her eyes widen in horror. Silva remains composed and speaks softly.

"When did this happen?" Phoenix looks down at her wounded area and covers it with her arms once more.

"The memory was nothing but a distraction. While we remained frozen in time, diving into the memory, she made a damn Aerolights grow out of the wall. She knew striking you with Sylphenic magic wouldn't do anything. It was a distraction to get to me." Her head lowers and she breathes heavily, struggling to speak. I instantly begin to cry once more and I lean in closer to her, making sure not to cause any more harm.

"You- you guys can do something right?" I frantically turn to Silva and I see Zyla storm off and screams at the same time a loud crash of thunder crashes in the sky.

"WHY DOES THIS KEEP HAPPENING?!" She screams loudly as the thunder dances with her cry. She tensely curls her fingers and her magic flows freely, not harming anything.

"No no no. It doesn't even look that bad, I'm sure you'll be fine. Right..." I look at Silva for reassurance but her gaze is frozen on Phoenix.

"Silva, please!" I try to lean over Phoenix and use my own power to try to see if I can help, but she uses her wing and opposite arm to keep me sat next to her. I feel her arm curl around my waist and she looks at me, shaking her head with a smile on her face.

"Please, we have to try something!" I scream and Silva pulls away, shaking her head while crying.

I try to break away from Phoenix's grip but I'm too weak and I'm scared I'll hurt her more.

"Vivalda-" Phoenix tries to get my attention but I continue to cry and scream frantically.

"Zyla took away the Sylphenic magic when I- and everything was- you're going to be-" My words get jumbled around and I begin to panic.

"VIV, LISTEN!" Phoenix roars loudly, grabbing my attention. I can't look at her without breaking apart. I feel so helpless and weak. All I want to do is help her, but there's nothing I can do.

"I need you to look at me." Phoenix tugs on me gently and uses her other hand to gently turn my face to her.

Once I have the courage to look her in the eye, more tears flood my eyes to the point where her face and body turns into a watery blur and when my tears fall onto her skin, they don't sizzle or evaporate away.

I can feel rain drops beginning to fall from the sky, slowly mixing in with my tears.

"I would have intervened, no matter what kind of Aerolight variant stood in my way. Had I not, you wouldn't be here. You're too valuable to me. Even if healing was possible in this situation, I'd deny it because I've done my part." The golden glow in her red eyes slowly fades away and my heart breaks even more.

"No, I can't lose you too! Please, we have to try!" I turn my face to shout. "ZYLA!" I scream for the enchantress who stands out in the rain, refusing to look back and Aerowen covers her face with her hands, standing still.

"Goodness, you are so stubborn." She smiles and tries to laugh, but she's losing energy by the second.

"Phoenix...please." My voice cracks and I can barely speak without my cries interrupting me.

"If there's one thing I need you to remember is that none of this has been your fault." My eyes widen and she looks at me reassuringly. I fall over her and lay my head on her chest, wrapping my arms around her.

I feel her arms wrap around me, with one of her hands rested on the back of my head, holding me close. She then takes her wings and rests them over me.

I feel the warmth in her chest begin to fade.

Silva continues to let the thunderstorm rage on quietly. I can hear her pain scream with the crashes of thunder. Phoenix takes a painful deep breath and it makes me cry even harder. It's heart-wrenching to witness her suffering, especially when there's nothing I can do to help.

"I never thought a beast could be so lucky to have a friend like you. Thank you for not running away from me." She says quietly with a smile and the color in her scales, eyes and skin begin to fade, turning grey.

"Please don't go. I didn't mean for this to happen!" I cry in Phoenix's chest.

"But I did..." She whispers, using what strength she has left to keep me held close to her and both of us refuse to let go.

From behind my tears, I watch Aerowen walk over and kneel down next to Phoenix on the opposite side of where I sit, curled in her arms. Aerowen's tears turn into fragile icicles that fall to the ground and shatter.

A soft smile forms on Phoenix's face. She winces in pain and her breathing becomes slow and shallow. We lock eyes one last time and Phoenix smiles before leaning her head to the side and slowly closing her eyes.

Her wings droop down and fall limp and her grip around me loosens.

When the last drop of color on her body fades away, she takes her final breath.

My best friend is gone.

TO BE CONTINUED

Made in the USA
Columbia, SC
21 March 2025

55472746R00300